Talking 'Bout My Generation

The Amazing Journey of Pete Townshend's Woodstock Special

ECKHARTZ
PRESS

A Novel by
William J. Wagner

Copyright © 2022 William J. Wagner

Published in the United States by
Eckhartz Press
Chicago, Illinois

All rights reserved.

No part of this book may be used or reproduced in any manner whatsoever without written permission except in the case of brief quotations embodied in critical articles and reviews.

ISBN: 979-8-9861972-3-4

Aldo — the Man,

Never let go of hope!

[signature]

To Cassie, Cole, and Olivia

PROLOGUE

Pete Townshend and his guitar had issues. That much was clear.

Sure, there were good times. Even in dysfunctional relationships, there always are. For Pete—for this gangly, lonely kid who sprang from the rubble of post-World War II London—the guitar was a tool for prying himself open and spilling out his pent-up feelings before they made him burst.

He learned how to play as a teenager, and it was a win-win undertaking: sandbagged inside his bedroom with nothing better to do, he (1) had plenty of time to practice and (2) got away from his grandmother, with whom he'd been sent to live because his parents, professional musicians, were always on the road. Grandma wasn't exactly the doting type. She was, in fact, batshit crazy, amusing herself by drinking copious amounts of brandy while rambling on about her do-nothing grandson. Pete would poke his oversized nose out of his room to yell, "Bugger off." Then he'd turn up the amplifier.

When he was old enough to move out of that hellhole, he had developed a fast-paced style that emphasized strumming rather than picking. He formed a band with three other lost souls from his working-class Shepherd's Bush neighborhood—Roger Daltrey on vocals, John Entwistle on bass, and Keith Moon on drums—and eventually they settled on a name: The Who. As the fledgling group was trying to make the shift from covers to originals in 1964, the other three asked Pete if he'd take a stab at writing a song. To his surprise, he penned a UK hit, "I Can't Explain," and chart-toppers like "Anyway, Anyhow, Anywhere," "My Generation," and "Substitute" followed in short order.

Pete's music had a smoldering dynamic: toe-tapping melodies pitted against blistering distortion, moments of uniformity that broke down into anarchy. These wild mood swings reflected the confusion and upheaval of Pete's formative years, and with The Who gaining an international following as the decade progressed, his generation obviously related.

Things were changing fast—not only for Pete and his band but also in the world at large, especially across the pond in America. By 1969 a hippie counterculture had taken center stage, and rock and roll had become politicized, an agent of idealistic change, of a revolution. If the forward-thinking kids were running the show instead of their establishment-shackled parents, there'd be no Vietnam War, no racism, no oppressed women, no nukes, no pollution, no homeless people—you name it. Peace, love, and understanding would rule the day.

With flower power in full bloom that year, The Who released *Tommy*, a "rock opera" about a deaf, dumb, and blind pinball player who becomes a messiah. Truth be told, Pete himself wasn't exactly sure what *Tommy* meant, but it mattered not. The hippies glommed on to just about anything that had a trippy and spiritual bent, and *Tommy* fit right in.

Or did it? The instrument that had given so much to Pete over the years—that he had used most recently to compose *Tommy*, the soundtrack of '69—was also a receptacle for his rage. When The Who played live, there was cathartic music…and then unspeakable carnage. Maybe he was still pissed at his parents for sending him to live with his loon of a grandmother or just pissed at the world; maybe something as simple as a popped string or a sloppily played song would set him off. Whatever the reason, Pete took out his frustrations on his poor, defenseless guitar.

The end rarely came immediately: he'd start by spinning the guitar like a top or by heaving it into the air and sneering as it bounced off the stage with a high-voltage wail. But the end always came eventually: he'd hold the guitar by its neck, raise it like an ax, and crash it against the stage until its body had been reduced to splinters and the noise had turned to silence. It was hardly an act of peace, love, and understanding, and the pattern didn't change. Regardless of the models he played—a Rickenbacker in the mid-1960s, a Fender Stratocaster in subsequent years—they were never long for this world.

And so it was with the Gibson SG Special, Pete's model of choice during the *Tommy* era. The Special was the ultimate in rock and roll cool, with a cherry-red mahogany body that had twin cutaways resembling animal horns and a black wraparound pick guard. Its sound—loud and proud—matched its look. But for all its bluster, the Special was no match for Pete Townshend, as he contemptuously proved night after night.

On August 16, 1969, the inside of Pete's gig bag was a particularly perilous place for a Special to be—the future did not seem promising. The blokes from Shepherd's Bush had veered way off the beaten path, onto Max Yasgur's six-hundred-acre dairy farm near the town of Bethel in upstate New York to play a three-day event called the Woodstock Music and Art Fair. This was the last place Pete wanted to be, but he had agreed to perform after being hounded by the festival's organizers. Envisioned as a quaint gathering of hippies in the country, Woodstock had mushroomed into a free-for-all that was hundreds of thousands strong.

Pete's ill humor was exacerbated by conditions that were far worse than he'd imagined. Heavy rain had turned Yasgur's farm into a foul pile of mud, and the problems extended to the stage, where standing water had caused members of the Grateful Dead to be shocked by their equipment during their set. As if the prospect of electrocution wasn't enough of an impediment, the extreme humidity made it difficult, if not impossible, for the musicians to keep their instruments in tune.

Due to the rain and the mounting technical problems, The Who's start time kept being pushed back. Pete, Roger, John, and Keith had hours to kill in the backstage "dressing room" (some wooden planks in a tent) and little in the way of sustenance beyond cups of fruit juice that were being passed around. They were unaware that some of the drinks were spiked with LSD, and John wound up drinking a fully loaded cup. The normally quiet and withdrawn bassist didn't exhibit any dramatic changes in behavior after the acid took hold—except for a crooked, slightly vacant smile that wasn't unlike the one worn by the deaf, dumb, and blind protagonist from *Tommy*—but would he be able to play something resembling a note? No one knew.

Roger just wanted to get it over with and move on to the next gig; his blond mane flowing down his back, he paced the planks as if he were in a cage. Keith made the best of the situation, dipping liberally into one of the bottles of Courvoisier he'd had the foresight to tuck into his gear.

And Pete? He sulked in a corner. *Some revolution. A field six feet deep in mud and laced with LSD. Fuck the lot of them.*

Sometime before 5 a.m., after seven hours of delays, Pete finally unsheathed his Special, and he and his bandmates stepped onstage, where they encountered half a million wet but hopeful faces. Though it hardly seemed possible, Pete's mood worsened from there. The four members of The Who had done so many gigs together that they could practically play by rote, but this night was different. Between the humidity, the ungodly hour, the LSD, the Courvoisier, and the haywire sound system, they felt like they were in a racecar whose brakes were shot. They eyed each other in panic at every turn, narrowly averting disaster.

And after *Tommy*'s "Pinball Wizard," the unthinkable occurred: someone stormed the stage, *Pete's stage*. The trespasser was Abbie Hoffman, the big-haired political activist and cofounder of the rabble-rousing Youth International Party. Hoffman loved a scene, and Woodstock was the mother of all scenes. As Pete futilely tried to tune his guitar, Hoffman grabbed a microphone and shifted the focus from the deaf, dumb, and blind kid to the jailed poet/activist John Sinclair.

"I think this is a pile of shit," Hoffman hollered, his nasally, whiny tone undercutting his revolutionary message. "While John Sinclair rots in prison—"

"Fuck off," Pete interrupted.

"Eh—"

"Fuck *off*. Fuck off my fucking stage."

Pete followed by doing what he did best: he swung his guitar, in this instance connecting with a human target, Hoffman, who tumbled off the stage and disappeared into the night. Ever the showman, Pete underscored the moment with a couple staccato bursts of sound from his Special and then, as if to mock this entire festival of slop, some hippie slang: "I can *dig* it."

The Who skidded through the remainder of its set, and the hippies, mostly oblivious to the band's sonic travails, swayed blissfully. During the closing notes of the finale, "Naked Eye," the sun started coming up. It was the moment of truth. Pete held his guitar high above his head for all to see before jerking it down to hip level, whereupon he gyrated and jumped maniacally. Falling to his knees, he clutched the Special's downward-pointed body with his right hand and secured the base of the neck with his left for leverage.

Bam…Bam…Bam…Bam!…BAM!

The Special's collisions with the stage caused it to squeal at an ear-piercing pitch, but it remained intact, at least for the time being. After resting the guitar against Keith's bass drum and walking toward the side of the stage, Pete turned around abruptly to finish the job. Given the events of the night, a gruesome fate assuredly awaited the Special. The obliteration would be primeval.

But just when the end seemed nigh, something strange happened. This Special wasn't transformed into a pile of mahogany sawdust. This one lived.

While trotting back to his guitar, Pete paused ever so briefly. He looked out beyond the crowd—past the ancient woodland, past the miles of fertile farmland, all the way to the horizon—and saw shafts of morning light piercing the storm clouds. Glorious sunshine encircled the expanse like the columns of a celestial coliseum, framing everything as one.

Fucking fantastic. After all the bad vibes I put out tonight, I don't deserve a sight like this. Incredible.

A new day had dawned. In a moment of serenity—a moment of peace, love, and understanding—Pete gathered the Special, cradling it in his arms before walking to the edge of the stage and holding it out like a religious offering. He then gently tossed it into the mass of hippie humanity.

CHAPTER 1

Jumbo Bauer pointed his thumb upward and waited for a ride. Jumbo wasn't his real name. Edgar was. But Jumbo fit much better. He'd had that nickname since the fifth grade, when he led some classmates into the boys' bathroom and showed them his "creation"—Edgar's phrasing—floating in the toilet.

"Ew, that's jumbo," one of the classmates said, referring, of course, to its enormity.

The classmates gradually transferred the word "jumbo" from the turd to the boy, and it stuck. Ten years later, he had grown into his nickname. He was indeed jumbo, standing 6'5" and weighing 260 pounds.

Anyway, Jumbo was getting tired of standing in the hot summer sun on New York State Route 17 East. Plenty of cars were motoring by, but none would stop. It had seemed so quick and easy when, a week earlier, he had spread out a map of New York and connected the dots. The starting point? His hometown of Corning, a remote glassmaking burg surrounded by the primordial Finger Lakes, which were over six hundred feet deep in some places. And the endpoint? Bethel, about 155 miles east, the site of the Woodstock Music and Art Fair.

Jumbo had done the math: if he averaged fifty-five miles per hour, he'd arrive there in roughly two hours. His calculations wouldn't amount to anything, however, until a car picked him up—Bethel would remain but a dot on a map.

To be clear, Jumbo was no hippie. The closest he had come to identifying with a counterculture was when he was hunched over the greasy strip of Formica at Sullivan's Diner in Corning. He didn't listen to music, art wasn't his thing, and he hadn't given any thought to peace, love, and understanding.

Jumbo had other reasons for making this pilgrimage. He had seen an ad for the festival in Corning's newspaper, *The Leader*, and had gotten to thinking: *It'll be open season.* Jumbo liked to smoke the occasional joint, and he really liked women. He figured any place that had lots of both was worth checking out. And since he didn't have a full-time job to tie him down—just his mom yelling at him down in the basement to look for one—he clipped the ad, thumbtacked it to his bedroom wall, and waited.

For the first time in a while, Jumbo had places to go, people to see. In the haze of Woodstock, amid the pot smoke and the LSD hallucinations and the hypnotic hum of the music, there was even a possibility that he'd blend in. Who'd know the difference? With a back-to-nature hippie look he had adopted purely coincidentally—bushy hair, faded blue jeans, and a tattered pocket tee—Jumbo would bear at least a superficial resemblance to the natives.

But again, Woodstock was still a long way off. There wasn't a hippie haze hanging over the outskirts of Corning, only a sharp late-morning sun that didn't seem to be casting Jumbo in a favorable light. A Chevy Nova zoomed past him. Then a Buick Skylark. Then a big black Caddy. Then a Plymouth Valiant. And so on.

Patience wasn't among Jumbo's virtues. After a few dozen cars had come and gone, he started kicking up clouds of dust on the side of the road. By about car number fifty, he was gesturing wildly with his hands, as if he was engaged in a bitter argument with someone who was standing next to him.

Of course, no one was standing next to Jumbo. From a hundred yards away, a motorist might have mistaken him for an ax murderer sans the ax; from fifty yards, maybe just a crazy homeless person; and from twenty-five yards, maybe a country bumpkin, which wouldn't have been completely off the mark. Regardless, Jumbo's chances of being picked up were growing slimmer by the minute.

Enter the anthropologist, a wisp of a man with a goatee and a head of thin brown hair parted straight down the middle. His day had started in nearby Ithaca, where he taught at Ithaca College, an oasis of higher education by the shores of the Finger Lakes. He was bound for a conference at the Gray Horn Retreat near Middletown, New York. In roughly twenty-four hours, he'd be delivering a lecture, "Lost Cultures: Tales of Industrial Carnage," to a room filled with dozens of his esteemed colleagues. It promised to be a big moment for him.

The anthropologist first noticed Jumbo from about two hundred yards out; he was but a speck against the verdant Allegheny foothills. At one hundred yards, the anthropologist wasn't spooked by the seemingly threatening gesticulations that were coming into focus. He had once spent several months in the Amazon studying the Yanomami, a fearsome tribe that lived in a state of perpetual warfare—this was nothing. At fifty yards, he still didn't feel any trepidation, perhaps only a pang or two of pity. And at twenty-five yards, as Jumbo scratched an itch on his sweaty crotch, the anthropologist's intellectual curiosity was piqued: he noted a certain simian quality in the hitchhiker that prompted him to stop.

"This looks interesting," the anthropologist said to himself. He reached over and pushed open the passenger-side door of his little VW Bug, and Jumbo squeezed in.

Amiable as always, the anthropologist said, "Hello there, traveler."

"Hey."

"Where are you headed?"

"Bethel. About 150 miles away."

"Right, right, I know exactly where that is. It's where that little music-and-arts festival is taking place. Are you going?"

"Yeah."

"I read about it in the *New York Times*. It seems like good summer fun."

"Yeah."

"I'm Nathan Diller, *Dr.* Nathan Diller." The anthropologist always emphasized the doctor part when introducing himself. "What's your name?"

"Jumbo."

"Hmmm. Interesting name." The anthropologist's voice rose steadily in order to lend a quality of grandeur to his pronouncement: "Good fortune has smiled upon you, Jumbo. I'm driving right by Bethel."

"You'll drop me there?"

"I certainly will."

Jumbo nodded.

The Timex on Jumbo's wrist read 11:35, which meant, according to his figuring, they'd hit Bethel by around 1:30. That would give him plenty of time to get the lay of the land before Woodstock officially started the following day.

Time was something of a factor for the anthropologist too. He'd taken a slight detour to Corning to buy a half-ounce of pot from a former student, Yonder, who had been affectionately christened as such by some friends because he lived somewhere off in his own world. Though Yonder hadn't amounted to much in the classroom, he'd found his calling as an entrepreneur, setting up shop in Corning as a prolific pot dealer. Yonder's wares would no doubt be appreciated by the anthropologist's conference cronies while they sat in a hotel room and talked deep into the night about cannibals and apes and maybe even Jumbo.

The anthropologist pressed the accelerator; one by one, the red oak and maple trees fringing Route 17 faded into the distance. By Elmira, a slightly larger and grittier version of Corning, the anthropologist had deduced that Jumbo wasn't a conversationalist. But he kept talking anyway: "Tell me what you do."

"Do?"

"Yes, where do you work?"

"A strip joint. McHale's."

"McHale's? Right, right, I've seen McHale's." Corning was a small town, and McHale's was right around the corner from Yonder's apartment/pot emporium. "What exactly are your duties there?"

"Working the door a few nights a week."

"A bouncer, eh? Rugged work. It sounds exciting."

"Not really," said Jumbo, staring straight out the windshield as the trees rushed by. "It sucks."

It was an eighty-degree day, yet the anthropologist was clad snuggly, if not ridiculously, in a turtleneck. His clothing choice hung over the cramped quarters of the Bug with academic lordliness, along with a trace of damp odor. Had he been wearing a blazer with elbow patches, his ensemble would have been complete. Jumbo rolled his window halfway down, and refreshing air whooshed through the Bug.

Seventy-five miles into the journey, just beyond Binghamton, they reached a mountainous region. The road began to rise and wind, and the oaks and maples became interspersed with pines. Outposts of civilization appeared here and there—a weatherworn cabin pitched awkwardly on an escarpment, a turn-off to a gravel road that presumably led somewhere—but otherwise the anthropologist and Jumbo were all alone.

The anthropologist drank in the leafy beauty of the valley below. "Extraordinary weather we've had this summer. Do you enjoy the outdoors?"

"Yeah," Jumbo answered, still staring straight ahead. "I hunt. Deer."

"Deer, eh?" With the slightest hint of moral superiority in his voice, he added, "I've never hunted."

"Didn't think so."

After a while, Jumbo noticed that the road had finished rising and was now dipping, and traffic was picking up. The hands on his Timex read 1:17. "We should be almost there," he said.

The anthropologist glanced at his own watch. "Actually, not for another hour. It's another fifty miles to Bethel."

No way, Jumbo thought—he had done the math. His mind creaked through the calculations again. Then: "Fuck."

"Is something wrong?"

Jumbo turned toward the anthropologist, maybe for the first time since Elmira, and glared. "Just keep driving. Okay?"

"No worries, my friend. We're making outstanding time."

Nevertheless, the anthropologist decided to do less talking and more driving, postulating that patience wasn't among Jumbo's virtues. He pressed the accelerator ever harder, and the Bug's H4 engine responded with a trusty buzz. That and the whoosh of the air were the only sounds that broke up the ensuing silence.

All the while, though, the anthropologist's mind remained vigorously active: *The term "upstate New York" is something of a misnomer. It vaguely lumps everything together that isn't in New York City. "Up" implies "north." Yet I'm driving straight east through the state of New York right now, not due north. Funny.* The anthropologist let forth a chuckle that went unnoticed by Jumbo, whose eyes were focused straight ahead again.

If Jumbo hadn't been aboard, the anthropologist would have continued on Route 17 until reaching his conference. Even though he'd now have to detour onto Route 17B East, a backcountry road that led to Bethel, it was only a bit out of the way. Besides, picking up Jumbo had been better than driving alone, if only marginally.

The traffic had grown thick, but the anthropologist was reassured by the buzzing engine and whooshing air. Jumbo, meanwhile, was enlivened by a girl in a red tie-dyed shirt who leaned out the backseat window of a Dodge Dart, gave him a peace sign, and shouted, "See you there!"

The Bug veered onto Route 17B. "Only about ten more miles," the anthropologist said, "which means in fifteen minutes at the most, we'll be…"

Before the anthropologist could put the finishing touches on his impromptu math lesson, he was forced to downshift into neutral and press hard on the brake. The serene countryside surrounding Bethel (population: 3,900) had been transformed into a rush-hour metropolis. There was neither a buzz nor a whoosh, only inertia as a line of bulky, gas-loving cars—Detroit's finest—stretched as far as the eye could see.

The anthropologist's foreign-made Bug idled incongruously in this pileup of star-spangled steel. Its diminutive H4 engine was all but drowned out by the full-throated stuttering of a '66 Pontiac Bonneville that was inches ahead. A college-aged traveler with tousled hair sat Indian-style atop the Bonneville's considerable trunk and plucked his guitar; a girl sang along next to him, her baby blue eyes shimmering in anticipation of the days to come.

"My God," said the anthropologist, stroking his goatee thoughtfully. "The *Times* estimated there would be fifty thousand people at this festival. There are fifty thousand people *right here*."

Jumbo's eyes darted to and fro. *People everywhere.* On the roadside, a hippie who was dressed like him in faded jeans and a tattered pocket tee held up a sign. The word NIRVANA was scribbled on the cardboard along with a squiggly arrow pointing, Jumbo figured, toward the festival. Though he wasn't sure what the word meant, he knew this much: it had to be good. He opened his door, stepped into the throng, and inhaled the exhaust-filled air.

"Where are you going?" the anthropologist inquired.

"Later."

Jumbo shut the door and followed the arrow.

CHAPTER 2

The vibe surrounding the Chicago Cubs was surprisingly positive, and University of Illinois classmates Jimmy Fitzgerald and Dave Weiss were among those soaking it up under the late-summer sun at Wrigley Field.

This '69 edition of the team was in first place, a comfortable six and a half games ahead of the hated New York Mets. Soon enough the season would end as every other Cubs season did: badly. August's Boys of Summer—Banks, Santo, Jenkins, Williams, and the rest—would become September's Boys of Bummer. But Jimmy and Dave didn't know this, of course. They didn't know that a month from now, in a pivotal series against the Mets, a black cat would run onto the field at Shea Stadium, hexing the Cubs and sending them into a death spiral. They didn't know that the Cubs would fail to win a World Series for the sixty-first consecutive time since 1908. They might have had their suspicions, but they didn't *know*.

Nope, these Cubs were going places. And as it turned out, so were Jimmy and Dave.

"You know what?" Jimmy said as the Cubs were wrapping up a 4-3 victory over the San Diego Padres. "I've been thinking about it for a couple days, and I have a mind-blowing idea."

"And just what is this one?" Dave asked.

"Let's go to Woodstock."

"Woodstock?"

"The rock festival."

"I know—I've read all about it. But where on earth did that come from?" Motioning toward the diamond, Dave said, "We're at a ballgame. The Cubs are on a monumental roll."

"That's great and all—no doubt about it—but this…" Jimmy produced a folded piece of newspaper from his pocket and straightened it, pointing at a drawing of a dove on the neck of a guitar that was accompanied by the words "3 Days of Peace & Music." He tapped the ad with his index finger. "*This* is where it's at."

Jimmy and Dave had been friends since being placed on the same floor of Allen Hall three years earlier as freshmen at Illinois. They didn't have much in common, really—just baseball. Jimmy was big and burly; Dave was average-sized with a confoundedly boyish face. Jimmy gallivanted around the bars on Green Street when he should have been studying; Dave enjoyed reading Vonnegut. Jimmy grew up in a ranch amid the wide-open cornfields of central Illinois; Dave grew up in a ranch amid other ranches in the northern suburbs of Chicago. Jimmy was the youngest of six kids; Dave was an only child.

But now and then, their mutual love of America's pastime brought them together, most memorably at Wrigley Field. The wind coming off Lake Michigan. The "L" trains creaking north and south beyond Wrigley's bleachers. The smattering of unemployed men sitting in lawn chairs atop the apartment buildings that hovered over the ballpark. The ivy-covered outfield wall and the hand-operated scoreboard in center. The half-filled grandstands, which made it easy to sneak up from the cheap seats to the $3.50 boxes next to the field. The lazy gait of the games, of the Cubs' endless struggle to turn themselves into something special. For Dave, anyway, it was all so comfortable and reassuring. Woodstock was bold new ground.

"I don't know," Dave said. "I just—"

"What's the matter, Weiss, are you afraid you might have fun? I'm telling you, it couldn't be more perfect."

"Maybe, but—"

"But what?"

"I've got a lot going on."

"Like what?"

Jimmy cut through the layers of Dave's reflexive excuses until reaching the heart of the matter: there was no good reason for him not to go. Classes at U of I? They wouldn't start until after Woodstock. Dave's summer internship as an agate clerk in the sports department of the *Daily Herald*, a newspaper in Chicago's northwest suburbs? It would end in a couple days, just in time for them to make the trek to upstate

New York. The Cubs? They were about to head west on a road trip, so he wouldn't miss any baseball at Wrigley in this season of such surprisingly great expectations.

And last but certainly not least: "My car's on its last leg, Weiss—sometimes it won't even start. I barely made it up here for the ballgame. If we take your car, I'll pay for all the gas. Your only cost will be your food—it's a can't-miss deal for you. Can you think of a better way to end the summer? It'll be three days of some of the best music you've ever heard. The Grateful Dead. Jefferson Airplane. Joe Cocker. The Who. Creedence Clearwater Revival. Mr. Jimi Hendrix. For once in your life, you owe it to yourself to do something spontaneous. How 'bout it?"

Dave had to admit it sounded tempting, though he was apprehensive about taking his '68 Ford Galaxie, a highland-green sedan that was the product of every job he had held since age twelve (with a bit of financial assistance from his trusting parents). With its 390-cubic-inch engine and stylish hideaway headlamps, the Galaxie was his only indulgence, and he didn't want anything to happen to it.

Nevertheless, the inevitable occurred in due time: Dave agreed to Jimmy's plan. He wished the record to show, however, that he had nagging reservations extending beyond his car, specifically:

- What if no one came? What if they hauled across the country to Woodstock only to find two prostitutes from Jersey, a waif from Vermont, a gun-toting lunatic from Philly, and acres of empty farmland?
- What if the weather didn't cooperate? What if it rained the whole time? What if it was miserably hot? What if it was unseasonably cold?
- What if the mood became sour? What if the weight of a youth movement that had been building throughout the decade proved to be too much, and the whole thing collapsed upon itself in a field in Bethel, New York? What if—*what if*—it turned out to be a fraud?

"Who knows what we'll find there?" Dave said from the Galaxie's passenger seat as Jimmy took the first shift behind the wheel on their journey.

"Holy crap, Weiss, that's the whole point. You think too much. Your theories are making me nuts, and we've only been on the road two hours. By the time it's your turn to drive, I'll be about ready to throw myself out the window."

"Yeah, yeah, yeah. Just keep your eyes on the road. You I can live without, but the car I like."

Jimmy rolled his eyes and laughed. "Fortunately for you, this thing is built like a brick shithouse."

Jimmy took a hand off the wheel to push an eight-track tape, *Living the Blues* by Canned Heat, into the player. Pretty soon he was singing along to "Going Up the Country" while banging the steering wheel like it was a drum kit. He paused to look at Dave, who responded with an arched eyebrow.

"What? I still have a hand on the wheel and an eye on the road. That's all I need. Relax, brother." His attention drifting back to the music, Jimmy said, "These guys'll be at Woodstock." Then he started singing again.

Somewhere on the interminably flat and straight East-West Toll Road in northern Indiana, the Galaxie began craving fuel. They pulled into a Stuckey's, where Jimmy stretched his legs and dutifully hovered over the car while a white-clad attendant satiated it with a tankful of gas. The fumes escaping liberally from the nozzle were visible in the late-afternoon sunlight. They created a gauzy lens through which Jimmy viewed a man at an adjacent pump who was wearing purple bellbottoms and the type of round, wire-rimmed glasses that had been made cool by John Lennon. As the man talked to his friend, Jimmy heard something that sounded like "sock" or "shock." Or maybe "stock."

Jimmy took an educated guess: "Hey...are you guys heading to Woodstock?"

"You got it," the man answered. "You?"

"On our way."

"Far out. We heard so many people are showing up, they're making it a free concert."

"Seriously?"

"I don't know, man, that's just what we heard."

"Awesome," Jimmy said, flashing a broad smile.

When they got back on the road, it was Dave's turn to drive. After about fifteen miles, Jimmy leaned toward Dave and studied the speedometer: the needle stood firm at fifty-five. Dave stole a look at Jimmy, who answered with a slow shake of the head.

"What?" Dave asked.

"Could you go any slower? At this rate, we'll get there right as the thing is ending."

"Hey, I'm going the speed limit."

"Of course you are, and that's the problem. What's the point of having a car like this if you don't air it out?"

Jimmy and Dave drove past the steel mills of Cleveland in northeastern Ohio, the rich farmland of Amish country in western Pennsylvania, and the abandoned coal mines near Scranton in northeastern Pennsylvania. They drove and drove and drove—straight up the country, nearly 800 miles in all, stopping only for gas and side-of-the-road catnaps—until they could drive no more. Not because they didn't have the will, but because they didn't have a way. Directly ahead on Route 17B West, fewer than ten miles from the entrance to the festival, traffic was at a near-standstill.

"You know how you were worried no one would show?" Jimmy asked.

"Yeah."

"Cross that off your list."

Dave tried to go with the flow, or trickle, but Jimmy couldn't stand to be held back. "I wonder if there's a shortcut," he said, tapping the steering wheel with his index fingers.

Dave unfolded his map and studied it. "I don't see anything."

No sooner did those words come out of Dave's mouth than Jimmy pulled off the road and parked in front of a nondescript diner. "Maybe someone here can help us."

"I highly doubt it."

Jimmy gave the diner a shot anyway, and Dave followed.

"Excuse me," Jimmy said to one of the locals. The man, seated with his friends, glanced up from his breakfast. He had horn-rimmed glasses, a silvery crew cut, and a face made leathery by Pall Malls and the farming sun. Displaying the most charming smile in his repertoire, Jimmy continued, "You wouldn't happen to know if there's a shortcut to the festival? Traffic's really backed up out there."

The old codger had nothing against the thousands of kids who were descending upon his homeland. They looked kind of funny and talked kind of funny, but generally, they had been polite. His eyes circled the table in search of unspoken approval from his friends. A moment later, he said, "Sit down."

He unfolded a napkin so that he could scrawl out a map on it. "You're right here. You'll drive through this cornfield like so for about three miles, then you'll hit a dirt road. Follow the road for a mile, then take a right into this field. Go straight for about another mile. You'll see it."

They returned to the Galaxie with newfound hope…and, in Dave's case, a tinge of apprehension.

"It's your car," Jimmy conceded. "You game?"

Dave thought about it, thought back to the summer jobs he had held: mowing lawns, washing dishes at Wing Ho Chop Suey, painting houses, typing agate at the *Daily Herald*. He thought for a second about his trusting parents. Then he looked at the ever-growing line of cars. "Okay, let's give it a try."

"You want to drive?"

Dave seriously doubted he was up to the challenge. Grinning uncomfortably, he said, "Go ahead—you're the central Illinois hayseed. I'm pretty sure you have a knack for driving through cornfields."

Actually, Jimmy had never driven through a cornfield—not in mid-August anyway, when the stalks reached five feet high. But what he lacked in know-how he made up for with commitment. "Adios, amigos," he yelled out to the procession on Route 17B before circling to the back of the diner and, with a flick of the steering wheel, guiding the Galaxie into the cornstalks.

"Bumpy," Dave said, clutching his armrest.

"Awesome," Jimmy said, pressing the accelerator.

As the Galaxie picked up speed, corncobs began bouncing off the car. Occasionally an entire stalk plastered the windshield, momentarily obstructing their view of the endless rows of incoming stalks.

"Jesus, I said drive the car, not total it," Dave blurted. "This corn situation is crazy."

"We're in a cornfield, Weiss. Cornfields have corn."

"Great insight, but—"

"I've got this under control. Stop worrying."

They plowed through the field for what seemed to Dave like a near-eternity, though it was really closer to ten minutes. Holding the napkin with his free hand, Dave tried to decipher the old codger's directions.

"I don't know what the hell," he said. "Where are we?"

"You tell me," Jimmy answered, swerving left, right, and left again in an attempt to avoid the corncob barrage.

Before hope could turn to despair—or for Dave, acute anxiety—a dirt road appeared.

"Thank God," Dave said. "That was like Dresden in '45."

"As if you were even there."

"If I had been, that's exactly what it would have been like."

Jimmy started to turn right onto the road.

"Left, left," Dave said. "The napkin says left."

Jimmy corrected his course, and for the next few minutes the route, while still bumpy, was free of flying corncobs.

Dave's mind began to relax. "I wonder if the Cubs will win today," he said.

"Who knows?"

"They're playing the Giants. Tough team." Looking down the road, Dave snapped back to the here and now. "See that wooden post?"

"Yeah."

"The napkin says to turn right there."

"I'm on it."

With another flick of the steering wheel, they were under attack again: *Bang, bang, boom*—corncob, corncob, cornstalk. *Boom, boom, bang, bang, bang, bang, bang*—cornstalk, cornstalk, corncob, corncob, corncob, corncob, corncob. *Boom, bang, bang*—cornstalk, corncob, corncob.

The onslaught ended with these words from Jimmy: "Holy shit."

And these from Dave: "Holy shit."

Up ahead in a vast, sloping meadow was the epicenter of this whole happening: the stage. Or more precisely, the back of the stage. It was slapdash in every way—in fact, it wasn't even finished yet, as evidenced by the sound of power tools, the smell of sawdust, and the sight of long-haired carpenters scurrying around—but it certainly was impressive. A series of speaker towers rose from the meadow like gigantic totem poles. In twenty-four hours, the opening act, Sweetwater, would walk onto the stage, and music would start blaring from those towers.

Jimmy found an empty patch of grass in the haphazardly formed rows of Detroit's finest. "We made it, Weiss," he said proudly. "What'd I tell you? *Stop worrying.* Things always work out in the end."

Dave wasn't so sure, but to his surprise the Galaxie was none the worse for wear aside from a coating of dust and the remnants of a cornstalk wedged in the grill. All things considered, he'd take it. After grabbing blankets and knapsacks from the trunk, Jimmy and Dave walked with a happy herd of people to a collapsed section of a chain-link fence encircling the festival grounds.

"Guess that guy in Indiana was right," Jimmy said. "It is a free concert."

One by one, two by two, three by three, the pilgrims streamed through the opening. Most were young, like the earnest sophomore from Middlebury College who was carrying antiwar pamphlets that he planned to distribute. Some were old, like the drifter with stringy gray hair who exclaimed "Righteous!" as he stepped over the crumpled fence. Most had traveled great distances, like the sculptor from Santa Fe whose father had recently died of cancer. Some hadn't, like the curious shop girl from a county over who had badgered her big brother into taking her. But young or old, near or far, there was at least one common denominator: everyone was searching for *something*.

Then there was Dave, who wasn't really searching for anything. Beyond Jimmy's can-do prodding, he questioned why he was even here. Dave bought into much of the counterculture movement—the ideal of equal rights, the protests against the brutal incoherence of Vietnam and the creepy leadership of Tricky Dick Nixon, the empowering qualities of rock and roll—but his self-consciousness put him at odds with its communal aspect. This vague, gooey notion of free love made him uncomfortable.

Dave followed Jimmy through the opening and into the meadow, where the masses were assembling. Since the real estate near the stage had already filled up, the best spot they could secure was a good hundred yards back.

"Bingo," Jimmy said as they spread their blankets. "At least there's a clear view of the stage."

"Home for the next three days, huh?"

"Home base. Now let's go explore."

"Think someone will take our spot?" Dave asked.

"It's Woodstock. Who cares? We'll find another spot if we have to."

"But the blankets—"

"Forget the blankets. They'll be fine. Let's go."

Their explorations wound to a playground next to a series of large canvas canopy tents that housed art exhibits. Dave surveyed the playground in astonishment. *How nonsensically considerate*, he thought. From the looks of it, Woodstock had massive shortages of toilets, showers, and other essentials, yet the organizers had decided it would be neat to erect a playground for all the children. Problem was, there weren't any children in sight, just those of the flower variety.

The scene reminded Dave of Halloween back home on Elm Street in Glenview. By the swings, someone was dressed as G.I. Joe, save for his shoulder-length hair and the peace-symbol patches sewn onto his fatigues. By the slide, a woman in bright orange from head to toe was a bowl of sherbet. And by the jungle gym, a woman in only a bra and panties was a stripper, though Dave noted that he never saw that particular costume on staid Elm Street.

The sweet scent of pot smoke lingered by the teeter-totter, where a woman and two men had set up a residence. With her leather headband and braided jet-black hair, the woman could have passed for Sacagawea. The two men were her Lewis and Clark. Instead of shirts, they both wore brown-fringe suede jackets that were scuffed and faded from the rigors of living on the trail. All they lacked, Dave thought, were hats made from beaver pelts.

Sacagawea was preparing her version of a frontier meal: marshmallow-and-Wonder Bread sandwiches. Meanwhile, Lewis and Clark were passing a joint back and forth to each other, and sometimes to Sacagawea.

Noticing that Dave was staring at him, Lewis pulled the joint out from between his lips and pointed to it. "Want some?" he asked.

Jimmy quickly intervened: "Yeah, man. Smells awesome."

"It is," Lewis said with the gusto of a true adventurer. "Acapulco gold. It's…far out."

Yes, this was like Halloween, and the people here even shared their candy. Jimmy took a hit—*pfffffffffft*—and passed the joint to Dave. Unlike many of his classmates at the University of Illinois, Dave rarely smoked pot. It compounded his self-consciousness, making him quiet and withdrawn. But this was Woodstock after all, so he took the joint from Jimmy's outstretched hand: *pfffffffffft*.

After the joint had circled several more times, Jimmy, Lewis, and Clark became engrossed in a conversation about the possibility of time travel. Dave stared into space.

"Want a sandwich?" Sacagawea asked Dave.

"What?"

She waved the food in front of Dave's bloodshot eyes. "A sandwich. Want one?"

"Um…sure. I guess I am a little hungry."

Dave bit into Sacagawea's exotic concoction with trepidation, but his senses burst to life as he chewed it. "Wow, it has a fluffy feel," he said. "This is sensational."

Grinning triumphantly, Sacagawea said, "I know, isn't it? Want another?"

"Yes, please."

Dave ate the sandwiches almost as fast as Sacagawea could make them. Between bites, he noticed the bowl of orange sherbet going down the slide. She looked tasty, too. Eventually, however, Dave was beset by sharp stomach pains, due to all those sandwiches and the start of an anxiety attack from the Acapulco gold.

"Another sandwich?" the ever-accommodating Sacagawea suggested.

"No, I couldn't possibly." But he stuffed one into his mouth anyway.

"Another hit?" asked Lewis, who had taken a break from his conversation with Jimmy and Clark to roll a new joint.

"No, I couldn't possibly." But he grabbed the doobie anyway: *pfffffffffft*.

Minutes later, Dave was down for the count, lying on his back and watching clouds gather in the sky that looked like the marshmallow-and-Wonder Bread sandwiches he hadn't been able to stop eating. He heard Jimmy in the background: "The next thing I'd do with my time machine is check out the dinosaurs." And a chortling Clark: "What a trip that would be." Dave's stomach pains intensified.

"You look kind of green," Sacagawea noted. "What's the matter? Maybe another sandwich will help."

"God no," Dave groaned. Sacagawea seemed a little hurt, but he no longer had the strength to be cordial. Limply placing the back of his hand on his forehead, he said, "Go on without me. Leave me here."

"Go where?" inquired a perplexed Sacagawea. "We're not going anywhere. We're camped out on this playground, having a blast."

"Oh…that's right."

Indeed, this girl wasn't really fueling a cross-country trek to the Pacific Ocean with an endless supply of sandwiches—she was simply here for the party.

"Just the same," Dave continued, "I need some space."

Sacagawea backed away reluctantly, turning to the heady talk of time travel. Dave continued to watch the marshmallow-and-Wonder Bread sandwiches coat a sky of blue, but his view was suddenly obstructed by Jimmy, who had returned from the dinosaurs and was standing over him.

"You okay, Weiss? You okay?"

CHAPTER 3

Jumbo had left Corning with only twenty dollars in his pocket, but he hadn't been worried, figuring he could live off the land. Five miles into his hike to the festival, as he traversed yet another cornfield, he was doing exactly that. Whenever he became hungry, he snapped an ear of corn off a stalk, peeled away the husk, and gnawed on the kernels. Jumbo liked raw corn. Provided it was fresh, it was crunchier and more flavorful than cooked corn.

Jumbo's pace was hindered only by his right knee, which he had torn up playing football. He had been an unstoppable offensive tackle for Corning East High School—football had been his saving grace. By his senior year coaches from Syracuse and Pitt started showing up at Corning East's games to watch him play, and recruiting letters from schools in exotic locales as far away as Nebraska were appearing in the mail.

As usual, all eyes were on him when Corning East hosted Elmira Free Academy late in that senior season. Then on a halfback draw, a play he had run hundreds of times, a defensive end rolled into the back of his leg, and his knee buckled. That was that—his future, his dream, was shredded right there. He couldn't even go fight in 'Nam, having been 4-F'd because of his bum knee. Now he was reduced to working the door at McHale's for chump change.

But for the time being anyway, Jumbo was free from those disappointments. He passed clusters of hippies in the cornfields that seemed joyfully unsure of where they were going. Jumbo likened them to the so-called sportsmen he would see back in Steuben County on opening day of deer-hunting season, which was always a big party. With drunken, once-a-year hunters filling the woods, chaos was a given. One opening day, Jumbo's Uncle Tucker took an inadvertent twelve-gauge blast right to the ass; it was months before he could sit without wincing.

Of course, the people here weren't wielding shotguns. Though equally clueless, they posed no threat. Trekking through the backyard of a farmhouse that was cut into a cornfield, Jumbo came upon a cloud of pot smoke rising from a hippie cluster. It smelled inviting. The centerpiece of the group, a stick figure who was all hair with his afro and full beard, held an apple that he and his friends had cored into a pipe.

Jumbo minced no words as he fixed his eyes on the apple: "Got any of that to sell?"

Afro Man was more of a consumer than a peddler, and he wasn't sure what to say to this brusque behemoth, so he settled for the first thing that entered his woozy mind: "Groovy reefer."

Jumbo pulled two wadded-up fives from his pocket. "How much will that get me?"

Afro Man looked over at his friend, a doughy sort who was leaning against a red wooden shed. Like Afro Man, Doughy Man was merely a recreationalist when it came to pot, but he took a shot at answering the question: "A dime bag? Can you dig that?"

"Let me try some first," Jumbo said.

"No sweat," Afro Man responded.

Jumbo took a hit from the apple, and Afro Man tensed up, hoping it would meet with the giant's approval. After exhaling an enormous plume of smoke, Jumbo handed the apple back to Afro Man, who tentatively asked, "Groovy?"

"Uh-huh."

Afro Man's bony fingers tiptoed over to the giant's hand and cautiously procured the bills. Moments later, Doughy Man produced a baggy that was filled an inch high with pot. No one noticed the distrustful yet fascinated pairs of eyes that were peering through the slats of the shuttered windows inside the farmhouse.

"Enjoy," said Doughy Man.

"Later."

So ended Jumbo's lone interaction with humans since his hours in the Bug listening to the yammering of the anthropologist. By nightfall, after passing countless other clusters of wayward souls, Jumbo was hunkered down in the woods just outside the festival grounds. The powerful shot of adrenaline he had experienced upon seeing the hippie with the NIRVANA sign had worn off, and his knee was throbbing something awful.

Jumbo decided he'd come far enough for one day. He sat against a maple and took a jackknife and an ear of corn out of his back pocket. Borrowing from Afro Man's playbook, he cored the corncob into a pipe. All the while, he listened to the howls of partygoers in the distance. Jumbo filled his corncob pipe with Mother Nature—it was indeed *groovy*—and smoked it until he fell into a deep sleep.

The dawn's light exposed the clouds that had moved in. It was August 15, the much-anticipated first day of the festival, but the hundreds of thousands of people who had come to this place would have to show some peace, love, and understanding and hang on a bit longer. As morning turned to afternoon and afternoon lumbered toward evening, there was still no music blaring from the totem poles by the stage. Sweetwater, Woodstock's opening act, was MIA, stuck somewhere out on Route 17B.

That left Richie Havens, the singer-songwriter with the soulful voice and the social conscience. Sitting on a backstage plank, Richie fretted about his backing band, most of which was, like Sweetwater, marooned on 17B. He was accosted mid-fret by one of the principal organizers of Woodstock, Michael Lang. Part hippie, part entrepreneur, the curly-haired and full-lipped Lang had spent months booking bands, securing the land, hiring workers, and building the infrastructure on the sprawling site. Now everything was unraveling.

"Richie, you're on," said Lang, his eyes a conflagration of both panic and purpose.

"But my band," Richie protested. "I never play without my band."

"You are today. Look, you're all we've got. The natives are restless."

Petrified but compliant, Richie reached for his acoustic guitar and set out to save the day. He played everything he knew, as well as some stuff he didn't, for two long hours. Every time he looked to the side of the stage, Lang shook his head. Only when Sweetwater was located and choppered in did a sweat-drenched Richie return to the backstage planks, the day having been saved.

Jumbo was still deep in the woods. Although he had heard a sudden cheer from the meadow and then Richie's nonstop strumming, Jumbo was occupied with his own scene. Late that morning, a hippie cluster had stumbled upon him. Conversation had ensued—actually, the hippies had done most of the talking, about running out of gas and abandoning their car on the side of the road—followed by something bordering on ball-team camaraderie.

Since they didn't seem to be in a hurry to leave, and Jumbo didn't much mind their company, he decided to make a bonfire for their entertainment. He led them to a small clearing he had found earlier, instructed them to help him gather firewood, and arranged their findings into the shape of a tepee. Jumbo's mastery was such that it took only one strike of a match to ignite a brilliant blaze.

The hippies dipped into their duffel bag and pulled out two bottles of Wild Turkey; Jumbo dipped into his pocket and pulled out his pot. With the music playing faintly in the background—from Richie to Sweetwater to Bert Sommer to Tim Hardin—the Wild Turkey and the corncob pipe were passed around the fire. And when night fell and the upstate air turned slightly chilly, everyone was kept warm by Jumbo's flickering blanket.

By ten o'clock the flames were moving to the mystical strains of Ravi Shankar's sitar. Then without as much as a thunderclap to warn them, the sky opened. Jumbo's fire hissed valiantly, but it couldn't withstand the drenching, and soon there was only smoke.

"What a drag, man," said one of Jumbo's guests, who had introduced himself as Frank but began referring to himself as Aero sometime after the first bottle of Wild Turkey had been emptied and ceremoniously heaved into the fire. ("Sounds like *arrow*," he had informed a befuddled Jumbo, "but it's spelled a-e-r-o.")

Aero stumbled onward, into the darkness. The rest of the cluster followed, but not Jumbo, who found a dry place beneath the thick canopy of an oak tree and smoked his corncob pipe until he drifted off into another quiet slumber.

Time no longer seemed to matter to Jumbo. He had started this journey with such a head of steam out on Route 17, but now he wasn't in a hurry to get anywhere. He felt strangely at peace, the result of his dime bag's mellowing qualities and the pleasant distractions provided by the woods. Nevertheless, Jumbo knew he had to venture forth as the second day of Woodstock unfolded. There was a party in the meadow—he could hear it jingling—and that was precisely why he had come to this festival in the first place. Without further delay, he walked out of the wilderness, over a collapsed section of chain-link fence, and into the meadow's temporary city.

Due to intermittent downpours, it had been touch and go in the meadow all day long. Whenever the rain started, the music stopped while Lang and his cohorts scrambled to protect the stage and the sound system with tarps. The meadow dwellers improvised during these delays, entertaining themselves by turning the muddy field into a mammoth Slip 'n Slide. Now it was evening, and the schedule of events was shot.

Jumbo stood at the edge of the meadow as the Grateful Dead bravely played on despite occasional zaps from their instruments and a lack of stage lighting. He was energized by all the people whirling around—his knee didn't hurt in the least. It was at the field's edge that Jumbo encountered someone in a rain poncho who, with the practiced conviction of a carnival barker, chanted "Acid…Acid" to everyone who passed him. Jumbo had never taken LSD, but the time seemed right to start.

He pulled a five and five ones from his pocket, the last of his money. "What'll this buy?"

"Five doses."

Jumbo exchanged the cash for five squares of paper. Together, they were no larger than his thumbnail. "That's all there is?" he asked.

"That's all you *need*…and then some."

Unlike the boobs in the cornfield who had sold him the pot, the acid vendor seemed like a pro, so Jumbo took him at his word. He stashed the squares in his pocket and nodded goodbye.

Heading deeper into the meadow, Jumbo was captivated by the array of women who were moving to the music. Tall and short, skinny and round, stacked and flat, voluptuous and delicate—they made up a delightful smorgasbord. It was like McHale's times ten thousand, except these girls weren't dancing for dollar bills. They were genuinely enjoying themselves.

Jumbo was deceptively light on his size-fourteen feet—it was one of the qualities that had made him such an unstoppable offensive tackle. On this evening his feet took control of his brain, and he instinctively infused rhythm into his gait, mud splattering his jeans as he bopped through the tightly spaced collection of people.

He fixated on a woman whose butt fit perfectly into a pair of Levis. The enticing bundle rocked back and forth to Creedence Clearwater Revival's "Proud Mary," and Jumbo couldn't help himself: he pinched it. Spinning around and standing on her tiptoes to get up in his face, she said, "Keep your hands to yourself, asshole." Jumbo shrugged and continued through the meadow.

Midnight had come and gone, but the hippies refused to wear down. Jumbo was a gamer, too—he matched them soggy step for soggy step. Along the way, he came across another irresistible rear end, this one covered only by a bikini bottom. Jumbo's primal urges got the better of him again, but this girl didn't seem to mind being pinched as much as the first one had. She smiled at him furtively before turning to her friends again and continuing to dance to Janis Joplin's "Raise Your Hand."

Around the time The Who came onstage, Jumbo was in need of a boost. Though he still felt wide-awake, his knee was starting to throb. So he did what most people in the meadow would have under the circumstances: he self-medicated, eating two hits of acid. Fifteen minutes passed; he felt no effects from the LSD. Jumbo flicked the other three paper squares into his mouth. Fifteen more minutes passed; still nothing.

And then: *Kaboom!* The totem poles beside the stage seemed to explode as Pete Townshend excoriated Abbie Hoffman: "Fuck *off*. Fuck off my fucking stage."

It was game on—Jumbo's brain was ablaze. The music started again, and he watched The Who's crazy guitarist leap all over the stage, leaving hallucinatory trails behind him. The stage lights, which had been working like a dream since the Grateful Dead's ill-fated set, were equally mesmerizing. Sending out a swirl of colors, they beckoned him. Jumbo heeded the call and began muscling his way toward the stage. The closer he got, the denser the crowd became, but Jumbo was unstoppable.

"Watch it, man," an overmatched hipster squeaked when Jumbo pushed him aside.

"Hey," another hipster feebly objected when Jumbo rumbled past him.

By the finale, "Naked Eye," he had reached the front row. Pete smashed his instrument against the stage—*Bam…Bam…Bam…Bam!… BAM!*—and a shot of adrenaline rushed through Jumbo. He felt an even more powerful surge when Pete walked to the edge of the stage and tossed the Special into the crowd.

Everyone has a role to play, and this was Jumbo's: he homed in on the guitar like it was a fumbled football in the state championship game, watched it fall into the arms of a poet from San Francisco. With a glimmer in his eyes, the poet held it for a split second before 260 pounds of Jumbo came crashing down on him. The poet offered no words to describe the moment, only shrieks of pain. And as he crumpled onto the wet turf, Jumbo tore the instrument from his hands.

Jumbo stood and raised the Special high above his head for all to behold. Veins bulging from the sides of his neck, he celebrated his epic triumph with a guttural "Yeah!"

CHAPTER 4

Crouched uncomfortably on a backstage plank, Pete Townshend was having second thoughts about parting with his Special. It wasn't as if he couldn't afford another—he was now rich beyond reason, a millionaire thanks to the success of *Tommy*. And it wasn't as if he hadn't heartlessly destroyed untold other guitars, leaving them in pieces onstage. This one, however, seemed different.

After his epiphanous moment of peace, love, and understanding just minutes earlier, Pete felt edgy again. Edgier than ever, in fact. He took a swig from Keith's seemingly bottomless reserve of Courvoisier—no luck. He wiped sweat off his face with a grimy towel—no luck. He closed his eyes and breathed deeply, rhythmically—no luck. He picked up an acoustic guitar and strummed it—no luck. He called a backstage hanger-on a "wanker"—no luck.

Pete was at a total loss, so he turned to Clive Lerwick, who was standing a few paces away with his arms folded. Clive was the ultimate accessory for rock and roll kings: a heavy. After ascending to the realm of royalty with the release of *Tommy*, The Who had hired him on guitarist Eric Clapton's recommendation.

"I want that guitar back," Pete instructed Clive. "There was a bit of a scrum. Then I saw a git who looked like Tarzan hold it up. Can you find it?"

"I'll see what I can do, mate," Clive answered in a baritone drawl.

Clive's long, frizzy hair was always tied back into a ponytail to keep it from getting in his way when he worked. After all, his was a physical job. It fell on Clive to sort out the women who literally threw themselves at Roger and Keith, and to nudge one of those birds Pete's way so that the gawky guitarist wouldn't feel jilted. It fell on Clive to dispose of the evidence from Keith's benders before hotel management caught wind of the mayhem, a task that generally involved carrying away busted-up TVs and furniture that had been thrown from the window. Basically, it fell on Clive to do whatever he was asked.

This latest assignment would require the same physicality, plus some sleuthing. Clive was every bit as large as Jumbo but not as fleet afoot. Whereas Jumbo was all muscle, Clive had an outsized belly that lent itself to a lumbering pace. Nevertheless, Clive knew how to make the most of his resources: he used his stomach like a road grader as he moved into the meadow, clearing away the hippies who were in his path.

Periodically, he stopped to ask one, "You seen a bloke with a guitar? Big, like Tarzan?"

The response was often a blank or baffled stare, a shake of the head, or the passing of a joint his way. Clive's search for the Special was progressing slowly, but at least he was getting a good buzz out of it.

After an hour or so, he finally sniffed out a promising lead: a fragile sort with a scraped right cheek who was sitting in the slop while his friends cared for him. It was the poet. Staring up at Clive, he couldn't believe his bad luck: fate had loosed yet another colossal, barbaric figure upon him. The poet had come here to find inspiration in the togetherness, in his generation's coming of age. This was most unexpected.

"You seen a bloke with a guitar? Big, like Tarzan?" Clive asked.

The poet still had no words to offer, only an outstretched arm and an index finger pointed toward the swollen heart of the meadow. Clive's eyes traced a line into the crowd, where every damn person looked the same.

Back by the planks, Pete gulped more of Keith's Courvoisier. For reasons he was unable to articulate, he needed the blasted Special. It was a tangible reminder that something innocent and wonderful had occurred that morning beyond the woodland and farmland. It seemed one (the magic) couldn't continue to exist without the other (the guitar). If Pete could just get his Special back, perhaps he'd be able to recreate the moment in his mind and loop it indefinitely.

His thoughts were interrupted by the jarring sound of engine-driven rotors. It was a Bell Huey landing in a clearing behind the stage—ironically, the same type of transport helicopter that was being used in Vietnam, the very war the hippies here were protesting.

"It's the last chopper out till this afternoon," a worker, one of the soldiers in Lang's peace corps, yelled above the racket. "If you miss it, you'll be stuck here. Peace is hell, boys."

Roger, Keith, and John quickly headed for the Huey; Pete straggled behind them before stopping altogether. *Come on, Clive. Where are you?*

"What are you waiting for?" Roger hollered from the door of the Huey. "Get your arse over here."

Pete looked toward the meadow, then the helicopter. *Fuck me.* His head down and his hair blowing in the whirlwind created by the rotors, he reluctantly joined his bandmates.

"Let's get the Christ out of here," Roger said, buckling in.

"What about Clive?" offered John, who was able to cobble together some sentences now that his acid trip was ebbing.

"Piss on Clive," Keith said. "He'll find us. He always does."

As the Huey ascended, Pete gazed upon the hippies-turned-dots in the meadow. *Fucking madness.* The moment of peace, love, and understanding was slipping further away. And after the meadow had disappeared from view, it seemed gone altogether.

Clive was still down there searching, but it was of no use. The Special was untraceable, now being dragged through the mud by its new keeper. Having shed his shirt and shoes, Jumbo was communicating only in grunts. His brain remained ablaze, and the Special, which he was using as an ornamental walking stick, heightened his sense of importance. The sea of people parted as Jumbo rambled through—maybe out of fear of him, maybe as a reverential gesture toward the instrument, or maybe a little of both.

CHAPTER 5

"All right, friends, you have seen the heavy groups," Grace Slick, the bawdy singer for Jefferson Airplane, called out to the crowd. "Now you will see morning-maniac music. Believe me, yeah. It's a new dawn. Good morning, people!"

Dave awoke with a start. He rose unsteadily to his knees. He chipped dried mud off the side of his face.

The Airplane's guitarist, Jorma Kaukonen, blasted out the intro to "Volunteers," an anthem about the hippie revolution, followed by alarm-clock vocals from Slick and Marty Balin. Dave could almost relate. Each time Spencer Dryden struck his drum kit, Dave experienced his own revolution: his throbbing head yearned to gain independence from his body and find somewhere *quiet*. Day three of Woodstock had begun. Dave only hoped it would turn out better than day two.

His attempt to ascend to his feet was courageous yet fruitless, so he settled for putting on his sunglasses, which acted as a shield from the pupil-piercing light. Turning his head gingerly from one side to the other, he located Jimmy by their blankets chatting up a few people whom Dave suspected he was supposed to recognize but didn't. Jimmy—inexplicably bright-eyed, like he'd slept eight hours on a featherbed—bebopped over to his fallen friend.

"Finally awake, huh?" Jimmy said over the din of the music.

"Awake enough to feel the pain."

"Yeah, you were in rough shape, but don't worry, I smoothed everything over. The worst thing is, you missed it."

Dave wasn't ready to broach the "smoothed everything over" part. "Missed what?" he asked.

"The Who, brother."

There was a long, uncertain pause before Dave said more to himself than to Jimmy, "Crap, that's right. The Who."

It seemed like weeks since they had been by the teeter-totter with Sacagawea, Lewis, and Clark. After Dave's high from the Acapulco gold had finally worn off—a process fraught with generally directed panic and ending with a sizeable bowel movement—he made something of a comeback. He and Jimmy bid adieu to the frontier trio and continued their own roaming. All the while, Dave was more of a spectator than a participant, taking great care to keep his wits about him.

Until The Who, the one band Dave had really wanted to see at Woodstock. Sometimes Dave felt a lot like the deaf, dumb, and blind kid: an outsider who lacked the means to break through and fit in. But it wasn't simply the music from *Tommy* that appealed to Dave. Songs such as "Substitute," "I'm a Boy," and "Happy Jack" captured his own sense of awkwardness, the type that led to, say, his pot-tinged misadventures by the teeter-totter.

Dave and The Who were kindred spirits, which was why he was downright jubilant when the band came onstage and Pete Townshend unleashed the opening chords of "Heaven and Hell." Although The Who appeared small and remote from Dave and Jimmy's distant vantage point by their blankets, the totem poles were discharging a larger-than-life sound. By "Amazing Journey," Dave was playing along with Pete on air guitar, stopping only to drink from jugs of red wine that were being passed around.

Suffice it to say, Dave wound up doing more drinking than playing. This may not have turned out to be an issue if, in the previous several hours, he had eaten something more substantial than granola, a new kind of back-to-nature food that had been provided by Lang's peace corps. As it was, the wimpy oats and nuts in his stomach were overwhelmed by the waterfall of wine, and midway through "Sparks," Dave reached his tipping point: the electrified meadow, the dark sky, and everything in between began to spin. He desperately needed fresh air, something he wasn't going to find here among the huddled hippies.

"Sssscuse me," Dave said as he staggered down the row in search of an open space.

Jimmy watched Dave zig into several people. "What now?" he said to himself under his breath. He watched Dave zag into several other people. "Weiss, where the hell are you going?" he yelled.

Talking 'Bout My Generation

Dave heard nothing, not even the music. He kept pushing forward. "Sssscuse me."

Out of focus though it was, Dave saw an opening. *Fresh air. A few more feet.* But he didn't make it to that happy place. Instead, a reddish mixture of wine, nuts, and oats shot out of his mouth, landing on a horrified assortment of innocent bystanders.

"Oh God," gasped one.

"What the hell?" gasped another.

"Fucking gross," gasped a third.

"You asshole," gasped a fourth.

So much for peace, love, and understanding.

Dave staggered on. Finally, he reached the pocket of empty space, and it was welcome relief: he passed out facedown in the mud, no further damage done.

Jimmy, meanwhile, attended to the horrified bystanders, though he tried not to breathe through his nose so that he wouldn't take in the pungent odor. He had nothing useful to give them—no soap and water, no towels, no Lysol—only a snippet of sympathy: "Sorry. I'm so sorry." As quickly as tact would allow, he got out of Dodge and went to Dave.

"You okay, Weiss?" he said, tapping Dave's shoulder with his mud-caked foot. "You okay?"

Dave responded with a groan and a snort.

Satisfied that Dave was still breathing and merely needed to sleep it off, Jimmy focused on the remainder of The Who's set. He saw Pete smash his Special against the stage at the end of "Naked Eye"—*Bam...Bam...Bam!...BAM!*—and waited excitedly for the grand guitar-smashing finale. It didn't unfold as he expected: Pete, shrunken in the great expanse, froze onstage at the same moment a hush of "Ooooos" and "Aaaaahs" rose from the crowd. The person next to Jimmy turned around, as did the person next to him and the person next to her and the person next to him. All the way down the line, heads were turning.

After watching Pete cast his guitar into the audience, Jimmy turned, too, absorbing the otherworldly beams of light that were breaking through the clouds. So taken was he by this sight that he instinctively reached for his neighbor's hand and spoke words that were imprinted on his brain from a childhood spent attending Mass with his family: "Peace be with you." The neighbor, similarly entranced, replied, "Peace be with you," and the two men hugged.

Jimmy explained it all as best he could to a still-on-his-knees Dave. "It was weird," he said. "It was like…like…I don't know, it was like light coming into a church through stained glass."

"I can't believe I missed it. Figures. It's just my luck."

Jimmy offered his hand to Dave. "Here, grab ahold." Dave wobbled as he rose, but he didn't go back down. "Let's get cleaned up. You look like shit."

"I feel like shit. I'm never drinking red wine again. Where'd that swill come from anyway? The bottom of a sewer?"

"I'm not sure, but like I said, you sort of look like you've been living in one. Let's go."

"Where? It's not like this place has any usable showers. You won't find—"

"I heard about some ponds. C'mon."

There were, in fact, three ponds, all of which were beyond the official festival boundary. Once the showering situation had become untenable, people began migrating to these ponds—much to the chagrin of the neighboring farmers who owned them—so that they could wash off the sludge and splash around a bit. Jimmy and Dave slogged through the mud toward Filippini Pond, which was really more of a small lake and was a few hundred yards past a mess tent Lang had set up for his overworked peace corps.

"Why does it seem like we've been walking uphill the whole way?" Dave asked.

"We've been going downhill the whole way, Weiss. Just keep on truckin'. It should be at the bottom of the slope."

When they arrived at Filippini Pond, it was Edenic in its splendor. A quick look out at the water revealed that clothing was optional.

"Fuck yeah!" Jimmy roared. "The Sea of Love." He put down his knapsack, tore off his duds, and belly-flopped off a dirt ledge into the water. Wading out toward a group of women who were in varying states of undress, he said, "What are you waiting for, Weiss?"

"Give me a few minutes. I need to rest."

"Make it quick. You don't want to miss this, too, do you?"

Though Dave was quite a distance from Spencer Dryden's drums, the echo from each thwack nevertheless ping-ponged around the inside of his cranium. Exhausted, aching, and hungry, he sat near the water's edge with his head hung low. *Just as I suspected. Woodstock is a total bust.*

Bust, as it happened, was an apt word. Dave's head rose almost magnetically, and he spied a woman emerging from under the water only yards away. After her head broke the rippling plane, her neck, breasts, and midriff slowly followed. She smiled at him from the waist-deep pool. For a blurry second, Dave glimpsed her bare chest; just as quickly, his eyes shifted awkwardly toward the ground. She couldn't help but notice.

"Oh, a gentleman," she said with a giggle that was cheerfully high-pitched and reminded Dave of the clinking of champagne glasses.

He blushed, to which she responded by walking out of the water and straight toward him.

"Don't look," she teased, giggling once more.

This time Dave savored the sight, every inch of it. Then he blushed again.

Dave thought of Ursula Andress, the well-endowed Bond girl who famously stepped out of the surf in *Dr. No*. If this hippie girl had appeared from an ocean instead of a pond…if she had been blond-haired instead of brown-haired…if she had been blue-eyed instead of brown-eyed…if she had been fair-skinned instead of olive-skinned…if, finally and not incidentally, she had been wearing a swimsuit instead of nothing at all, she would have looked *exactly* like Ursula Andress in *Dr. No*. As it was, the hippie girl looked better.

She was now standing so close to Dave that droplets of water were falling from her body onto his shoes. He drew in her dewy scent, felt the breeziness of her breath on his skin. Taking his hand, she tugged him toward the Sea of Love.

"You might want to get rid of your clothes," she said. "Trust me, it's much easier to swim without them."

Dave suddenly resisted her tugging.

The smooth skin on her forehead crinkling with concern, she said, "Is there a problem?"

"Oh no. Everything's fine."

"Then come on."

The truth was, Dave did have a problem: an erection. It was as if he was fourteen again, when he had been a puppet to his hormones and would pop one in the most inopportune places, like at the front of the classroom while giving a report.

She started pulling again, which forced Dave into an act of desperation: he imagined Boog Powell, the squat slugger for the Baltimore Orioles, standing at home plate clad in nothing but a pink teddy. It worked almost instantly: the blood rushed out of Dave's penis. With feigned nonchalance, he doffed his clothes and walked into the Sea of Love.

Remarkably, Dave's head hurt less than it had before, and he wasn't as tired or hungry. The hippie girl swam farther out; Dave swam farther out, too. Together, they treaded water.

"I'm Leyna Vallas, by the way."

"I'm Dave Weiss."

"Dave Weiss. I like it—simple, to the point, nothing too ornate. Really great to meet you."

Splashing him playfully, she giggled some more. She seemed kind of pushy, and Dave had no idea what to make of her. But rather than obsess about the mystery that was this nymph from the surf, he simply splashed her back. And he smiled. Not a forced smile or a grimacing smile or a self-conscious smile or a polite smile or a coy smile. Dave let loose with a pure and joyful smile.

"Who are you here with?" asked Leyna, bobbing in the deep water, the occasional nipple coming into view.

Dave gestured toward the group of women in varying states of undress. "My friend Jimmy from back home. He's in there somewhere."

"Where's back home?"

"Chicago."

"What are the odds of that? We're almost neighbors."

"Oh yeah?"

"I'm just a few hours up the road at the University of Wisconsin in Madison, the home of crazy keg parties and semi-regular Vietnam protests."

Leyna swam back toward the shore; Dave swam back toward the shore, too. Together, they stood in the waist-deep water. Dave thought it best to imagine Boog Powell again, but in the process he lost track of what Leyna was telling him.

"...go...Mayor Daley...Chicago...Democratic Convention... go...like...six...know...wonderful...Muddy Waters...I wish...maybe someday," he heard her say. He tuned back in at the perfect instant: "When are you headed home?"

"Tomorrow morning. What about you?"

"I'm not quite sure. I came with some friends from UW, but we got separated last night during Janis Joplin. They went one way, I went another."

Dave contemplated the utter horror of such a predicament.

"Oh well," she said. "I guess I'll see them back at school." She took his hand again. "Want to walk around, see what's out there?"

"Sure," he answered, glancing at the sky. "Looks like the sun is here to stay for a change."

This, Dave surmised, was free love. Maybe it wasn't so bad after all.

Once they were ashore, he put on a clean T-shirt and pair of jeans from his knapsack. Leyna's apparel—what little there was, Dave noted—was under a nearby tree: a flower-print sundress that she slipped on over yellow panties (but no bra), toe-loop sandals, and a leather satchel with a red bandana tied decoratively to the strap.

She caught Dave eyeing her curiously and giggled again. "What? I like to travel light. Ready?"

"Yep. Let me just find out what's up with Jimmy."

Pinpointing Jimmy proved difficult, as he was still surrounded—swallowed up, really—by the group of women in varying states of undress. "Jimmy, you ready yet?" Dave yelled in his general direction.

Hearing him proved easier, thanks to his booming voice: "I'm staying here."

"You're not ready yet?"

"I'm staying here. Go ahead. I'll catch up with you later."

"I can wait."

"No need to. I'm fine. By the looks of it, you're fine, too. Enjoy. Go on."

"We'll see you later then. Back by the blankets. How 'bout around eight o'clock?"

"Okay, brother."

Dave never saw Jimmy again.

CHAPTER 6

A lot of lives changed at Woodstock—some by design, others not so much. An exhibit in the latter category: the anthropologist.

His first error in judgment had been picking up Jumbo, which had caused him to veer off his course to the conference and onto Route 17B. After that, there was no turning back…or going forward. He was stuck.

The anthropologist didn't initially grasp the permanence of his pickle. An optimist at heart, he thought the cars would start moving again. When they didn't, he passed the time by trying just a smidgen of Yonder's pot, which he'd stashed under his seat along with an onyx pipe that was fashioned into a miniature replica of one of the mysterious *moai* statues on Easter Island.

This further clouded the anthropologist's judgment. From his vantage point in his Bug, the passersby, many of whom were stoned themselves, seemed loosely unified in a sacred quest: reaching the festival. He was reminded of the ancient Kogi of Colombia, who spent their days chewing coca leaves to help them ascend to a higher spiritual plane they called *alúna*. Once again, the anthropologist's intellectual curiosity got the better of him.

"Looks interesting," he said.

The anthropologist came to terms with an absolute truth: he wasn't going to get to his conference, not before his big speaking engagement anyway. Luckily, he was a resilient man. After transferring his pot to his pocket, he wedged his Bug on the side of the road between an AMC Rambler and the '66 Pontiac Bonneville whose trunk had so easily accommodated the guitarist and his blue-eyed girl. Then he joined the quest.

Not fifty steps into it, he made his first friend: Cocked Hat, Delaware's very own Gil Hughes. Gil was an accounting major who was supposed to meet some buddies near a campground at the intersection of Perry and West Shore roads, wherever that was. He had a duffel bag strapped to his back and a bucket of day-old fried chicken in his hands. The chicken caught the anthropologist's eye.

"Looks scrumptious," he said.

"I figured I'd need plenty of food," Gil responded.

The anthropologist hadn't eaten since Corning, so he bartered two pipefuls of Yonder's wares for three pieces of chicken. "Mmmmm, delightful," the anthropologist said as he chewed on a rubbery leg.

He and Gil started walking. One thing led to another, and they gathered up Brooklyn, New York's very own Dino Moretti, who seemed oddly placed in these parts. Dino was an electrician who had come to Woodstock with his girlfriend Carla. She had thought it would be fun to escape to the country for a long weekend and see her favorite band, Sha Na Na, made up of fifties-style greasers who seemed equally misplaced here. Dino wasn't interested in either the country or Sha Na Na, but Carla had promised him a "reward" for taking her, so he had kept his mouth shut and gone along with her harebrained idea. They had become separated, however, when she had traipsed into a cornfield in search of a Porta-Potty.

"You's two know where you're going?" Dino asked.

"Follow us," answered the anthropologist.

The anthropologist, Gil, and Dino started walking. One thing led to another, and they initiated Ashland, Missouri's very own Scooter Kerwin into their fledgling tribe. Scooter was a twenty-eight-year-old aspiring singer whose credits didn't extend beyond performing for himself in his bedroom at his parents' house. He had journeyed to Woodstock to learn by listening to the masters sing. Since he didn't have any friends, he was thrilled about the sudden prospect of companionship.

"You fellas mind if I tag along?" Scooter asked.

"The more the merrier," the anthropologist said. "I'm Nathan Diller—*Dr.* Nathan Diller. These good gents are Gil and Dino."

The anthropologist, Gil, Dino, and Scooter started walking. They wandered and wandered without ever really going anywhere, but their quest was fruitful nonetheless. By the time Richie Havens started playing the next day, their tribe was ten strong; by dusk the day after that, it numbered twenty.

Tired and squishy, the tribe of twenty decided to rest for a bit in a large clearing next to some woods, the very woods Jumbo had called home before leaving just hours earlier for his date with destiny in the meadow. The tribesmen passed around a canteen of water someone had generously given them during their travels. Unbeknownst to them, it was spiked with LSD.

As the acid kicked in, it was as if the anthropologist's head was on a swivel. Looking side to side, side to side, he took immense satisfaction in his rustic new surroundings. For too long, he had been cooped up in a classroom, and it was liberating to be back in the field.

While prepping the grounds for the festival, Lang's peace corps, armed with bulldozers and other pieces of heavy machinery, had dumped several large piles of excess soil where the tribesmen were now gathered. The anthropologist climbed atop one of these mud heaps and presided over the clearing like a high priest. His senses seemed heightened as he sat there: he sniffed the fresh fragrance exuded by the pines; he felt the rich wetness of Mother Earth on his rear end; and he heard the beating of drums emanating from the giant totem poles in the meadow.

Little Scooter joined the anthropologist on the mud heap. "Nothing is quite right," Scooter said fretfully. "Things are out of focus, and there's a buzzing in my ears. What's happening?"

The anthropologist thought long and hard about hippie customs before arriving at an answer: "You're tripping, my son, as we all seem to be. LSD. I'm not exactly sure how it happened, but I suspect it was the water we drank from the canteen. Just go with the flow, so to speak."

Scooter felt much better now that he knew it was just the drugs and he hadn't gone insane. "A million thanks for the diagnosis," he said.

Henceforth, the anthropologist was known to one and all as Dr. Trip. Make that *Dr.* Trip.

Klamath Falls, Oregon's very own Benjamin Foote took his turn on the heap. "*Dr.* Trip, do you see the same colors I do?"

The anthropologist looked around. "I think so. Rejoice in them, my son."

Dino mounted the heap. "Yo, *Dr.* Trip, I gotta piss."

The anthropologist pondered Dino's predicament. "There are trees everywhere. Find one, my child."

The anthropologist reveled in his exalted status. He stood up mightily and tore the sleeves off his turtleneck, proclaiming, "I'm no longer burdened by the shackles of modern civilization. I am free." But as many great leaders through the centuries had learned, power could be fleeting. The anthropologist lost his footing on the slippery slope, and he rolled to the bottom, muck covering what was left of his attire.

Laughing uproariously, Charlottesville, Virginia's very own Boyd Kutz yelled, "Look at *Dr.* Trip, y'all! He fell!"

The tribesmen howled like jackals as the anthropologist picked himself up—and just like that, all hell broke loose. Bangor, Maine's very own Wayne Murphy worked himself into a lather snapping branches off the trees. Scooter Kerwin sang the worst rendition ever of "Purple Haze." Gil Hughes crawled through the brush looking for berries to eat. And Dino Moretti pissed on Boyd Kutz.

"My people, settle down," implored the anthropologist. "We come in peace."

No one was listening.

At some point, a tour bus parked near the mud heaps piqued the tribesmen's interest. It belonged to a group of Brazilian tourists who had landed at LaGuardia Airport a week earlier for a sightseeing trip in New York City. Upon hearing about Woodstock, however, they had altered their plans, chartering the bus and heading into the heart of North American hippiedom.

While the Brazilians were off in the meadow, the driver was supposed to watch over the bus, but he had abandoned his post to follow the trail of a girl who had given him a come-hither look. It was a relatively harmless infraction. And if he had been bright enough to take the ignition key with him, nothing would have come of it.

Raising his fist in the air, Dino led the charge toward the bus. "C'mon, you's schmeboygahs. Let's break the devil's dishes."

The others followed Dino, except the anthropologist, who pleaded from the rear, "People…my people…"

Dino claimed the driver's seat, and his minions hooted and hollered with excitement as they piled in. After taking the bus for a few harrowing loops in the clearing, Dino turned onto a narrow dirt road that led into the woods.

"And away we go," he called out.

The anthropologist ran after the bus until realizing the chase was futile. Alone on the road, he gasped, "Where are you going?"

The bus rolled noisily along, clipping tree branches as it went. After about a mile, the road dead-ended at a swamp, and Wheat Ridge, Colorado's very own Dennis Yankin looked out the window and sighed. "What now?"

Shifting into neutral, Dino raised his fist again. "We sink it. We sink the son of a bitch. Everyone out. Help me push."

They piled out of the bus and positioned themselves around the rear bumper.

"Push," exhorted Dino. "Push."

Straining to move the giant block of steel, they let out a ghastly assortment of noises.

"Keep pushing, you's schmeboygahs," commanded Dino.

The bus inched forward until its front wheels disappeared beneath the gurgling water. Though this wasn't an all-out sinking, it was good enough for the tribesmen, who erupted into cheers. The bus settled into the sediment, a sacrifice to…to…*whatever*.

Elsewhere that same night in the vicinity of the anthropologist's Bug, other vehicular mischief was occurring. It came courtesy of the Pirate, who had been on a daylong joyriding binge. He was known by this name to his friends and associates because of his gift for hotwiring cars. Mostly he did it for money, but times like this were for fun. He was the luckiest kind of man: one who loved his work.

His journey had started outside Manny's Tap in his hometown of Newark, New Jersey, where a '66 Cutlass with a black racing stripe down the middle struck his fancy. In Warwick, New York, the Pirate was taken by a Chevy station wagon in front of a five and dime, so taken that he took it. *Roomy and comfortable, like a house*, he thought. *A nice change of pace.* By Poughkeepsie, New York, he was in the mood for something sporty; a ragtop Mustang in an A&P parking lot fit the bill.

The traffic began to increase on the outskirts of Poughkeepsie, and the Pirate couldn't account for it. As a matter of habit, he followed the taillights. They led him to the countryside around Bethel, where a blockade of parked and/or abandoned cars ground everything to a halt. Ditching the Mustang, he hoofed it through the damp, dark night.

"Peace," said a hippie who was passing him from the other direction.

"What *is* this?" asked the Pirate.

"You're kidding, right?"

"No." The Pirate hadn't been reading the papers.

"It's Woodstock, man."

Hoofing it wasn't the Pirate's style. He was itching to commandeer a car, so he stopped at a VW Bug—coincidentally, the anthropologist's VW Bug.

Haven't driven one of these for a while. And what do you know? The owner was nice enough to leave it unlocked.

Ignoring the musty smell inside, the Pirate brought the car to life with some deft twists of the wires beneath the dashboard. That was the easy part. His navigational options were limited to the very edge of a gravel shoulder, which he rode until it was rendered impassable by several cars that were parked even more arbitrarily than the others. A shrug of his shoulders later, he turned hard to the right and vanished without a trace into a cornfield, the car's wheels spinning furiously as they tried to grip the slippery earth. The Pirate traveled a ways into the cornstalks before a particularly troublesome mud slick abruptly ended his latest joyride. Undaunted, he left the Bug in the sludge and hoofed it back to the road to select a sturdier vehicle.

A couple miles away the anthropologist had been reduced to a tribe of one. The last vestiges of *Dr.* Trip were a headache and the creeping realization that he had screwed up massively. His only desire now was to make it back to Route 17B, where his Bug would be parked like a rock of stability in a world gone mad.

It seems like I've been walking forever. What have I done? And where am I? Fate, oh cruel fate.

The anthropologist was indeed operating without a clue. Mired in the corn, he had no idea whether he was heading east, west, north, or south. He couldn't even use the stars as a guide since a ceiling of clouds obscured them. But maybe fate wasn't so cruel after all: clueless as the anthropologist was, he happened to be bound straight for where he had left his Bug.

His pace quickened when he spotted the car-packed strip of asphalt that was Route 17B, and it shifted into a gleeful gallop when he saw the words THIS IS OUR MOMENT in fluorescent paint on a telephone pole he had first observed while sitting in the Bug waiting for traffic to start moving. By the time he stepped from the field onto the road, his faith in the cosmic flow of things had been all but restored.

The anthropologist recognized the little white guidepost with the missing reflector…and the patch of cornflowers next to the rusted-out Buick Electra…and the Bonneville with the ample trunk and the AMC Rambler. As for the empty space between the Bonneville and Rambler? He thought about this odd configuration, though not for long.

"My…car."

The anthropologist clenched his fists so tightly that his knuckles turned white and the hairs on his sleeveless, dirty arms nearly stood at attention. Although he abhorred the coarseness of profanity, a "fuck" slipped from his mouth, sparking a blitzkrieg of f-bombs: "fuck, fuck, fuck, fuck, fuck…"

His verbal assault on the universe continued until the golden hue of the morning's coming light distracted him: "…fuck…fff…uck…ff…u…ckkk…fffff…ff…f…"

Finally, there was nothing—the anthropologist was speechless. All that mattered was the sunshine cutting through the clouds. The rays steadied him as they touched his skin, delivered a sense of equanimity. This, he instantly knew, was *alúna*.

The anthropologist spread open his arms to welcome in the light. Never mind that his car was gone and he had no way home. For one spellbinding moment, everything seemed okay.

CHAPTER 7

Pete Townshend first saw Jimi Hendrix play in 1966 at Blaises, a club in the basement of London's Imperial Hotel. By the end of the set, Pete was several shades paler. He clutched his friend's forearm and said, "That was bloody horrifying. I'll never be able to play like that. I should just quit right now."

It seemed fitting that Jimi had the high honor of being Woodstock's closing act. It seemed equally fitting that no one knew exactly when he'd be Woodstock's closing act. His performance was originally slated for around midnight on August 17, but the accumulated delays meant he'd be idle until sometime the next morning. By the backstage planks, in an uncharacteristically deferential move, Lang offered him the chance to play earlier.

"It's starting to empty out," Lang said. "You sure you don't want to go on while people are still around?"

"No, no, man, I'm cool," Jimi said in a voice so soft that Lang had to lean in to hear the words. Jimi's light-blue tasseled shirt, the epitome of hippie chic, flowed easily from his lithe brown body. "All I'm gonna do is just go on and do what I feel."

When Jimi finally took his turn beside the totems at about nine o'clock the next morning, only forty thousand people were still in the meadow. The departed had left behind clumps of trash and mud-coated camping gear, and the air had a stale smell not unlike that of a bar the morning after a wild Saturday night. Lang's peace corps would have their work cut out for them returning the meadow to its natural state.

Jimi was feeling it, especially during his version of the national anthem. He had played "The Star-Spangled Banner" dozens of times, but never with this ferocity. The song came apart as familiar patriotic notes were overridden by noises that fit more within the range of war machines than a musical instrument: air-raid sirens seemed to wail, and fighter jets seemed to roar through carpet-bombing runs. Greater Bethel became an auditory reflection of the blown-out jungle nine thousand miles away in Vietnam.

It was enough to stop Dave and Leyna in their tracks on their way out of the meadow. As they stood and listened, Leyna looked around at the remaining hippies, who were haggard from their days up the country. Some had also stopped to listen; others trudged onward.

"Have you noticed that Jimi Hendrix is, like, the only black person at Woodstock?" Leyna asked.

"I've been thinking the exact same thing," Dave said.

"Weird," said Leyna.

"Not really. I mean, think about it. How could blacks have crashed this jamboree for middle-class white kids from the suburbs? Most of them are stuck in Vietnam. They're dodging bullets while everyone else with the ways and means to dodge the war seems to have wound up here. So much for equality."

"No, it's weird that we were thinking the same thing."

"Oh."

"At any rate, you're right. So much for equality."

Dave and Leyna had spent the previous night back by the blankets. Although the sky above them had been clear—perfect for stargazing—there had been more on Dave's mind than the heavens, specifically the whereabouts of Jimmy:

- What if he was at the bottom of Filippini Pond?
- What if he had been abducted by Mexican pot dealers?
- What if he was chained to a post in an angry farmer's basement?

Wisely, Dave kept those theories to himself, only saying, "Still no sign of Jimmy."

"From how you've described him to me, I'm sure he's fine, probably more than fine," Leyna reassured. "He sounds like a pretty self-sufficient guy. Really, I wouldn't worry. This is Woodstock, not Vietnam."

"What about you? You never did tell me how you're getting home."

"That's because I don't know yet."

"You're not concerned?"

"Why should I be? Look at all the people here. Some are sure to be headed west, right?"

"Well, we're heading west, and we've got plenty of room."

"That's sweet of you."

Dave grinned sheepishly. "It only makes sense. We live in the same neck of the woods…almost anyway."

"All true, and I think I'll take you up on it. If you could get me as far as Chicago, that would be fabulous. But in the meantime, let's listen to the music. It's the last night of Woodstock."

As they sat there, it became a chilly night at that. Reasoning that Leyna's sundress was no protection against the dropping temperature, Dave wrapped Jimmy's unused blanket around her; she, in turn, wrapped some of it around him and scrunched up against his body so that he'd also be warm.

Well after midnight, David Crosby, Stephen Stills, and Graham Nash—otherwise known as Crosby, Stills & Nash—provided more togetherness with their intricately fused voices. Their songs wafted through the meadow like lullabies. Sometime between "Helplessly Hoping" and "Marrakesh Express," Leyna nodded off, her head resting on Dave's shoulder. Her breathing was soft and steady, and it occurred to Dave that this was the most relaxed he'd been since departing for Woodstock. Soon he was asleep, too.

Now, hours after awakening with the sun, Dave and Leyna were listening to Jimi Hendrix—and there was nothing relaxing about what he was doing. Paralyzing was more like it. They didn't start walking again until the final blast had sounded and an eerie silence had enveloped the meadow.

"Hey, dumb question," Dave said as they followed a bald-earth path that had been pounded out by thousands of feet. "At the pond, why did you swim over to talk to me anyway?"

"I'm not sure. You looked ragged and lonely, I guess, like you really needed a friend. And now with all the mud washed off and some color back in your face, you're kind of cute. Warm eyes and a warm smile, nice thick hair—kind of like a Teddy bear. You're funny, too."

"Cool," he said, blushing per usual.

Dave recognized the collapsed section of fence where he and Jimmy had entered the meadow.

"The car should be just up ahead. Maybe Jimmy's there."

Smiling, Leyna shook her head. "You're true blue, aren't you, Dave?"

"What do you mean?"

"You know. True blue, as in loyal."

"It just seems kind of strange, that's all, leaving without him. I mean, we came together."

"Yes, but look who you're leaving with."

"Good point. Forget Jimmy."

They laughed, but the lightheartedness passed as Dave's thoughts detoured toward his Galaxie. He was pretty sure the car would be trashed in some unspeakable way. *Will it even be there?* To his unending surprise, it was. What's more, it looked okay…except for one detail: a hulking figure wearing only ripped jeans was leaning against the hood.

Call it divine intervention or fate or maybe just dumb luck. The hulking figure was Jumbo, and he was holding a guitar—and not simply any guitar.

Leyna elbowed Dave giddily. "I'm sure that's Pete Townshend's guitar. It must be."

"You think?"

"Who else's would it be? Look at it. It's red with carved-out cutaways. That's exactly what he was playing. Remember when he threw it into the crowd? It was magical, wasn't it?"

Not wanting to explain why he had missed the magic, Dave took a pass on answering her question directly and went with something more open-ended: "Um, I think you're right."

"It's beautiful."

"God yes," Dave said, this time without a scintilla of ambiguity in his voice. "What a prize."

Not for Jumbo. In fact, now that his brain was no longer ablaze and his knee was throbbing again, he wondered why he'd spent thirty hours roaming around the meadow with it. He had no shirt, no shoes, no food, no money—nothing. This worthless guitar was all he had to show for himself.

Actually, that wasn't entirely true. Standing next to Jumbo was a girl who had followed him around during his victory tour with Pete's guitar. She sort of looked like Mama Cass Elliot, all two hundred pounds of her, from the band the Mamas & the Papas. But alas, this girl was no singer—she was a film student at Boston University. Mama had offered to give Jumbo a lift on her way back to school. She wasn't exactly what Jumbo had envisioned when he had spread out his map of New York a week and a half earlier, but beggars couldn't be choosers. He needed a ride, and she had a car.

Mama had started trailing Jumbo because she had been attracted to the guitar. Eventually, though, she became attracted to him. There's no accounting for taste. Mama was smart enough—a straight-A student, in fact—but this wasn't about smarts. A certain primal quality in Jumbo got her hot. During Jumbo's walkabout, her body sizzled every time he waved the Special and grunted. She made it her business to start talking to him—a decidedly one-sided yet strangely satisfying proposition—and now here they were, back by her roomy Ford Country Sedan, which happened to be parked right next to Dave's Galaxie.

"That guitar," Leyna said to Jumbo. "Is it Pete Townshend's?"

Jumbo shrugged.

"The one he tossed from the stage?" she added.

"The one and only, honey," Mama interjected in a coarse Beantown accent.

"Amazing," Dave said.

If it had been a humongous plate of food—a rib eye with all the trimmings, maybe—Jumbo would have been amazed. As it was, he felt unmoved.

"You want it?" Jumbo asked Dave.

"You sure you shouldn't think twice about that?" Mama said.

Jumbo wasn't big on thinking twice. Sometimes he wasn't even big on thinking once. Luckily, this was a no-brainer.

"Thirty bucks," Jumbo said.

"You're serious, right?" Dave asked.

"Thirty bucks and it's yours."

Dave reached into his pocket and pulled out three tens before

Jumbo could change his mind. Peace, love, and understanding had passed him by the first time—he had been facedown in the mud during the transcendental sunrise at the end of The Who's set—but this was something better. This *was* the moment, preserved for all time. He could see it. He could touch it. Why, he could even play it if he ever learned how.

Dave handed over the bills, and Jumbo passed the guitar to him like it was a baton in a relay race. Jumbo felt a surprising twinge of regret as he let the Special go. It had, after all, brought him an element of status among the hippies. On the other hand, the thirty bucks would more than cover the cost of his entire trip—Jumbo knew that much.

As a matter of courtesy, Dave said, "My name's Dave."

"Jumbo."

As an additional matter of courtesy, Dave shook Jumbo's hand, which proved to be a mistake. The strength of his grip brought a grimace to Dave's face. "I really, er, appreciate, er, this."

"Later."

Jumbo scratched his itchy armpit, causing Mama's flesh to burn. And minutes later, they were inching away in her Country Sedan.

"I can't believe you have Pete Townshend's guitar," Leyna said, beaming.

"Neither can I," Dave said, beaming in equal measure.

"What are the chances? A million-to-one? And we owe it all to Jimbo or Jocko or Jerko or whatever his name was."

"Jumbo."

"That's right…*Jumbo*. He wasn't a particularly talkative guy, was he?"

"No, but he's as strong as an ox. I have the aching hand to prove it."

They shared a laugh at Jumbo's expense, though only a brief one.

"Well, Jimmy doesn't seem to be anywhere around here," Dave said. "Think we should wait a bit longer?"

"It seems pretty obvious to me that he's not coming. If he wanted to be here, he'd be here. I don't know how else to put it. But he's a big boy. He'll be okay—you'll see. I'm sure of it."

How can she be so sure? Dave thought. *She's never even met Jimmy.*

How can she possibly know? Not that these questions mattered. For reasons that transcended logic—reasons that had more to do with his whirling hormones—he trusted her judgment. He simply nodded and said, "Yeah, you're right. Jimmy knows how to take care of himself."

Using a rag from the trunk, Dave wiped the Special clean. The mahogany body was nicked around the edges from Pete's banging and Jumbo's dragging, but otherwise his prize seemed immaculate. Dave carefully loaded it into the backseat as Leyna slipped into the front.

"In the immortal words of Simon and Garfunkel," he said, "we're homeward-bound."

What an unforeseen turn this trip had taken. Not only had Dave gotten the girl, but he was also leaving with Pete Townshend's Woodstock Special.

CHAPTER 8

Yes, Bethlehem was somewhere out on the horizon—not the steel town in Pennsylvania, the Promised Land—but arriving there would take awhile. Among the casualties of Woodstock was the napkin bearing the directions through the cornfields. Sometime during The Who's set, between Dave's first swig of wine and his drunken nosedive into unconsciousness, it had come out of his pocket and had been claimed by the quagmire.

Dave knew he'd never make it through the corn maze without those scribbles. *Why did I bring that stupid napkin along with me in the first place? Why didn't I just leave it in the car?* He made no mention of the shortcut to Leyna, not wanting to give her any crazy ideas.

Although there was less congestion on the way out of Woodstock than there had been going in, traffic wasn't exactly moving at an *Easy Rider*-style clip. Dave and Leyna had been in the car for over an hour and had only just made it past the festival exit and onto Route 17B. As the afternoon sun beat down on the Galaxie, they could feel themselves sticking to the black vinyl seats. A/C had been extra beyond Dave's financial means, and they were really missing it now.

"I wonder what's going on in the world," Leyna said, and she turned on the radio, spinning the dial until she found something other than static.

…ended. By some estimates, half a million people came to Max Yasgur's dairy farm to watch the thirty-two musical performances. The overflow crowd forced state officials to close a portion of the New York Thruway for the first time ever, but no major incidents of unrest were reported over the festival's three days. Despite what they say will be heavy financial losses, organizers are calling Woodstock an overwhelming victory for the hippie youth movement.

"We know, we know, Mr. Newsguy," Leyna said. "We were there, and it was wonderful."

She spun the dial again.

...total disaster. In addition to the heavy rainstorms, the festival was marred by a malfunctioning sound system, shortages of food and water, and dangerous drugs.

Pointing her nose upward indignantly, Leyna said of this newscaster, "What a square. I wonder what's going on in the world *besides* Woodstock. Anything?"

She gave the dial another hearty spin.

...with all those other cars. And if that doesn't get you up off your lethargy and into a Pontiac showroom, look at it this way: Maybe you don't need a new Pontiac right now, but your ego does.

"Guess not," she said, switching off the radio. "Seems like we've really been off the grid."

"Doesn't it, though? It's been one big blur."

"A happy blur."

"It is now."

Dave took his eyes off the road to smile at Leyna, who leaned over and planted a juicy kiss on his forehead. She eagerly awaited the inevitable blush, and when it arrived, she placed her hand on his flushed cheek, giggled, and said, "Always the gentleman. It's charming." To her delight, this caused the shade of red to deepen.

Noticing a hunched-over traveler standing on the other side of the road, Leyna said, "Aw, look at the poor man."

The poor man had splotches of mud all over his body. The poor man appeared not to know that a piece of shrubbery was matted to his thin brown hair. The poor man was wearing a turtleneck whose sleeves were torn off. The poor man was none other than the anthropologist. His right thumb was in a hitchhiking pose, but he seemed unsure of where he was and where he wanted to go.

"Sorry, dude, we're going the other way," Leyna yelled out the window.

The anthropologist stared at her vacantly as the Galaxie plodded by him.

"Talk about human carnage," Dave said.

"Right. I mean, you looked pretty bad when I met you, but nothing like him."

"Um…thanks?"

"No, really. That man's a mess. He looks like he's been through the wringer."

Smirking, Dave couldn't resist: "He looks like…he looks like he bathed in pig shit."

Neither could Leyna: "And what's up with that idiotic turtleneck?"

They snickered until a wave of guilt washed over them.

"Poor man," Leyna said, fighting to replace her playful smile with an expression that better reflected the gravity of his plight.

Dave followed suit by straightening his body into a more dignified pose. "Yes, such a shame. Such a crying shame."

Maybe it was because they were tired and loopy from their stay in hippiedom, but they couldn't contain themselves: they just lost it, laughing so hard that tears rolled down their cheeks. When they emptied onto Route 55, however, the traffic outlook suddenly changed from "slow and slower" to "clear and cruisin'," and their attention was directed elsewhere. Leyna stuck her hand out the window to feel the rushing air; soon her head was out there, too.

"Open road," she cheered, her long brown hair blowing every which way. "It feels so wonderful."

The Galaxie settled into a groove, humming across the Pennsylvania border on County Road 11, through the backwoods on Route 434, into Scranton on Interstate 84, and out of it on Interstate 81. These were the same roads Dave had traveled just days earlier, yet everything seemed different. Dave looked into the rearview mirror and saw the Special sitting upright in the backseat like a passenger, its body moving almost imperceptibly in response to the vibrations of the car's machinery. He looked to the right and saw Leyna daydreaming, her bare feet pressed against the front of the dashboard and her sundress casually hiked to her upper thighs as she tried to beat the heat. He looked straight ahead and saw the tree-lined horizon in the distance, its lush promise spread out before him.

Dave thought of Jimmy: *What road is he traveling right now? Is it this one? Or is he headed in another direction?*

His ruminations were cut short by a glance at the fuel gauge that indicated the Galaxie needed to be fed. At the next exit, they turned off the interstate and bounced along a marginally paved country road until spotting a Standard station near the blink-and-you'll-miss-it town of Sugar Notch.

"I'm going inside to get a newspaper," Leyna said after they pulled in. "I'll be back in a sec."

Sitting in the car, Dave watched an attendant squeegee the insect-splattered windshield. His graying hair was greased back, save for a stray string hanging over his forehead that swung like a pendulum as he wiped the glass. When the man finished his work, he eased around to Dave's open window.

"Lotta dirt on your car," he said. "Where you coming from?"

"Woodstock, in upstate New York."

The attendant spit a stream of tobacco juice onto the pavement and said, "You one of them hippies?"

"No, not really."

"Heard there was LSD up there. Lots of it, too."

"I guess there was. I'm not really sure, though. I, ah, didn't do any."

"Lucky for you. You know it's a commie plot, right?"

"What is?"

"LSD."

"Uh…"

"Yep. The Russians are using it to take over our country. Russian spies have spread it around to our kids."

Dave glanced at his wrist like he was checking the time, even though he wasn't wearing his watch; it was a nervous habit. Next he looked out the window to see if Leyna was coming, but there was no sign of her.

"And it's working, too," the attendant continued, spitting more tobacco juice. "They think if they can ruin our kids' minds with that LSD, they can wipe us out. They're rotting our country from the inside out. Cheaper than building A-bombs, I reckon. You seen anyone suspicious up there?"

"Not that I can recall, no."

Leyna appeared at last, sweeping across the pavement like a willow in a gentle breeze.

"Hi," she said upon getting into the car, all smiles.

"Hi," Dave answered, and he turned to the attendant. "How much do I owe you?"

"Let's see. You got eighteen gallons. That'll be five dollars and sixty cents."

Dave handed him six dollars. "Keep the change."

"Thanks." The attendant stared squarely into Dave's eyes and added, "You be real careful now."

"Will do." With uncharacteristic haste, Dave hauled out of the parking lot, leaving behind a cloud of dust. "You were in there awhile," he said to Leyna.

"Sorry about that. I was having a nice chat with the woman at the register."

"About what?"

"Daffodils."

"Daffodils?"

"Haven't you noticed all the daffodils around here?"

"Frankly, no. I don't remember seeing a single daffodil anywhere. I've been busy fending off the local lunatics, like that attendant at the gas station. He's nuts. He thinks LSD is a Soviet conspiracy."

"Seriously? That's hilarious."

"Sure it is, right up until he puts me in a shallow grave next to your daffodils."

Leyna giggled.

"Glad you're amused."

"Anyway," she said, "I bought a copy of the venerable Harrisburg *Patriot-News*." She spread it across the top of the spacious dashboard. "Wow, a huge hurricane hit the Mississippi Gulf Coast yesterday. Hurricane Camille."

"What kind of damage?"

"It doesn't say. Looks like it made shore late last night." Leyna flipped the page. "More horrible fighting in Vietnam."

"No surprise there."

"Apparently, there's an ugly battle going on somewhere called the Que Son Valley."

"Where's that?"

"The article says it's about thirty miles south of Da Nang."

"Wherever that is."

"I know, right? It all seems so far away and pointless."

"Not to change the subject from death and destruction, but do you mind seeing how the Cubs are doing?"

Leyna opened the sports section, nosing around until she located the box scores. "Cubs…let's see…Cubs…Cubs…there they are. They played two games yesterday against the San Francisco Giants. They won one… and lost the other."

"They're still in first place, right?" Dave knew it was mathematically impossible for them not to be (he had been gone only four days after all), but since these were the Cubs, he figured he'd better check.

"Um…yes. They're ahead of the New York Mets. At least I think that's what all this gibberish means."

"See, finally some good news."

"What's your fascination with sports anyway?"

"I wouldn't say I'm fascinated with them. It's just that sports are one of the few things in life that make complete sense. You can look at those box scores and see exactly who won and who didn't. They're simple, without ambiguity."

"Clarity, huh?"

"That's a good way of putting it. Maybe we can go to a baseball game together someday. You'd have fun."

"I'll try anything once, even a baseball game. It's a date."

They eventually merged onto Interstate 80, a road that would take them all the way to the Pacific Ocean if they were so inclined. The Special continued to oscillate in the backseat as Leyna read Vonnegut's new bestseller, the antiwar novel *Slaughterhouse-Five*, which she had brought forth from her satchel. A girl after his own heart!

By Ohio a crescent-shaped moon had settled over the Galaxie, and

Leyna asked, "Want me to take a turn driving? You've been at it all day. You look like you could use a rest."

"Actually, I was thinking that maybe we should stop for the night."

Leyna examined the landscape to her left and right—farms and woods everywhere. "It doesn't look like there's anything around here."

"Not true. I'll show you a little trick I learned."

After double checking that the coast was clear, Dave made a sharp turn off the road and spun the Galaxie into the heartland.

"Why are we going into a cornfield?" Leyna asked, laughing hysterically.

"To find a place to camp."

"*Here?*"

"Why not?"

Leyna thought about it for all of two seconds. "Sure. Why not?"

Since Dave was driving about half as fast as Jimmy had during their off-road foray at Woodstock, the corncob onslaught was minimal, but the bumps were still such that the Special bounced erratically. They reached a strip of unfarmed earth that wasn't much wider than the Galaxie, and Dave stopped abruptly.

"How's this?" he asked.

"Perfect. Much better than a Holiday Inn."

Dave switched off the rumbling engine and the headlights, and nature expertly filled the void with a convivial chorus of crickets and a glow from the moon that provided all the brightness he needed to locate a couple spare blankets in the trunk. After he spread them behind the Galaxie, they sat down.

"This works," he said.

"It smells so fresh out here, so fertile. You know what this occasion calls for?"

"What?"

Leyna dove into her satchel, and it wasn't long before she came up with a joint and a pack of matches. Waving the doobie like she was Groucho Marx with a cigar, she giggled and fired it up. She tried to pass it to Dave after taking a few hits, but he said, "Uh, no thanks. Pot spaces me out too much."

"Really? It relaxes me."

"I had a bad experience with it at Woodstock."

"Well, the last thing we want is for you to freak out. It's too nice a night for that." She stubbed out the joint, dropping what was left of it back into her satchel.

Dave couldn't take his eyes off Leyna as she gazed at the moon. His inspired jaunt through this cornfield notwithstanding, it struck him that she was everything he wasn't: cheerful, outgoing, carefree, optimistic, confident. Kind of like Jimmy, only way more attractive.

With his heart pounding so powerfully he could almost hear it, Dave slid his arm around her slender shoulder. She turned and kissed him; her mouth tasted sweet from the marijuana. He grew hard instantly, but this time he didn't have to conjure disturbing images of Boog Powell—he could let himself go. Dave started to remove her clothes, an undertaking that should have been straightforward since she was wearing only a sundress and panties. Somehow, though, he botched it, tangling the dress around her head. She experienced no such mishaps undoing his jeans.

Struggling to catch his breath, Dave said, "I don't have any rubbers."

"That's okay. I'm on the pill."

Problem solved—or was it? Dave desired nothing more than to explore the inviting contours of her naked body, but he couldn't keep his mouth shut. The confession spilled out:

"I've, uh, only done it once. Mary Jo Womack. Last summer on the sixteenth green at Pine Ridge Golf Club after a friend's party. It lasted about forty seconds, if that. I don't think that even counts."

Leyna started to giggle, but she caught herself. "It all counts."

"Only technically."

By a certain point Dave had simply wanted to get losing his virginity over with so that he could move on to life's next awkward rite of passage, and Mary Jo Womack, unwieldy though she was, happened to be available. Some promising flirtations followed the Womack incident—bookish Gwen Turpin from his modern lit class; boisterous Crystal Sogg from the Circle K near his dorm; and buxom Janie Jefferson from the ad department at the *Daily Herald*—but Dave just wasn't a closer.

Fortunately, Leyna was. "Welcome to the age of Aquarius," she whispered into his ear.

With a wink and a smile, Leyna wrapped her arms around him and didn't let go. Not during the first time they had sex, the second, or the third. By then Dave was moving easily—gloriously, even—inside her. He knew this because the small of her back arched spasmodically when she climaxed, accompanied by exultations that were louder and a good octave higher than they had been initially. Dave's chest heaved against hers as he let loose with his own exultations, and the two of them created a chorus that drowned out those convivial crickets.

Once the orgasmic ruckus had faded into tranquility, Dave rolled off Leyna and onto his back. The moon, suspended over the horizon, looked to him to be a shade more brilliant than before. As sappy as that seemed, he swore it was true.

"Mary Jo Womack has nothing on you."

Leyna grinned and stroked his chest. "Don't you forget it."

How could he? Aside from the itching of fresh mosquito bites on his bare butt, Dave's body tingled all over.

CHAPTER 9

Benjamin Drake sped down Fox Lake Road in his brand-new Cadillac Eldorado, straight past his home, which sat picturesquely behind a grove of hickory trees.

Located near the hamlet of Angola in the northeastern corner of Indiana, Benjamin's home was lovely indeed, a five-bedroom colonial built from the sturdiest pine and painted white. Green shutters provided traditional accents, and a front porch outfitted with rockers stretched around both sides of the residence. Inside were a wife, two kids (a boy and a girl, of course), and a black-and-white cat named Tuxedo.

Benjamin had every intention of returning there, but first he needed to work up the courage to tell his wife about a secret of his that had been uncovered. So he drove on to the cool waters of Fox Lake before turning around and zooming past his house again and toward Angola. Back and forth, back and forth—it was a circuit he had been running continuously on this August afternoon. *One of these times, I'll stop*, he kept thinking.

Not three hours earlier, Benjamin had been a man of standing in the community, an executive vice president of First Federal Savings Bank of Angola. It was the only place he had worked in his adult life, thanks to his father, Vernon Drake, who had joined First Federal as a loan officer during the dark days of 1934 and had quickly made a name for himself with practices that were prudent yet profitable. The bank survived the Great Depression, and Vernon eventually became president. When Benjamin, his only son, graduated from Wabash College in 1954 with a degree in economics, Vernon pulled him into banking. Fifteen years later, Benjamin was firmly entrenched. He didn't know any other way.

Benjamin certainly looked like a banker, with short-cropped hair that was parted neatly on the right side. The length of his locks never changed, not even slightly. In his profession, consistency counted. So did the serious nature of achievement, which was why he favored black three-piece suits made of virgin wool.

He also acted the part, figuring into the requisite extracurricular organizations around town. On Sunday mornings, he dutifully tended to the collection baskets at First Congregational Church, for which he volunteered as treasurer. On Saturdays in the spring and summer, he could be found hitting fungoes to the Little Leaguers at Commons Park. And on Fourth of July, there he was in the parade with the Lions Club, looping around the seventy-foot-high Civil War monument in Public Square and then striding through the crowded downtown.

Benjamin's world seemed like a model of order, right up until the phone rang on that August day while he was settling behind the large wooden desk in his office following lunch.

"Benjamin Drake," he said in a tightly wound tone that revealed little to no emotion.

"Benjamin, it's Pastor Timmons."

"Yes, Pastor."

"I'll, ah, get right to it. There's a problem with the church's finances."

Benjamin's heart skipped a beat, but his voice stood firm: "And what would that be?"

"Funds were withdrawn—fraudulently so—from the church's gift account. Upwards of five thousand dollars have gone missing."

"Any idea how it happened?"

"I do. I've traced the withdrawals directly to you." Pastor Timmons heard a faint sigh on the other end of the line. With grim resignation, he bellowed, "I waited to contact you until I was absolutely sure. I've thought a lot about it—prayed about it—and I have no choice but to alert the authorities."

"There must be a misunderstanding. I can assure—"

"I don't think so, Benjamin. There also seems to be a problem with the collections: more missing money. That was traced to you, too."

Although Benjamin was caught dead to rights, his tone remained flat and detached when, following a pause, he said, "I see. May I at least talk to my wife before this goes any further?"

"Fair enough. We'll address the matter tomorrow."

Pastor Timmons was in the forgiveness business after all—he could do that much for Benjamin.

Benjamin hung up the phone and stared into space. *I'm finished. Once Pastor Timmons decides on something, he doesn't waver. And he's clearly decided on this.*

The irony of this whole fiasco was that Benjamin didn't need the money—he hadn't spent a dime of it. On a whim one Sunday in the summer of '68, he had skimmed some cash from the collections. This act of deceit had been so easy and so invigoratingly out of character that he kept repeating it. Benjamin's secret was the one part of his life that belonged to him and him alone. It filled him up. Eventually, however, he felt hollowed-out again, so he raised the stakes and began pilfering money from accounts he had set up for the church at First Federal.

He had always planned to return those funds, but it was too late now. All he could do was delay the inevitable by running back and forth on Fox Lake Road. He drove past Pug Miller's farm on his left and Jeremy Crandell's on his right. Angola was only a couple miles away, but he didn't want to go there. Instead he followed his circuit, arcing through a bend in the road, spinning his Cadillac around at a STOP sign at the intersection of U.S. Route 27, and heading back toward Fox Lake.

What am I going to say to Anne? Eleven years of marriage. She'll be crushed.

The beauty of Fox Lake Road was its lack of traffic. Such serenity was good for the soul. It was one reason Benjamin chose to live out here rather than in Angola proper, and now more than ever, he was glad to have the road to himself.

Maybe I'll say, "Anne, we need to talk about something. There's money missing from the church, and Pastor Timmons mistakenly thinks I took it." No, no, no—that's all wrong. Too abrupt, not to mention it's a lie. Enough of the lies.

Benjamin reached his house. Once again, he didn't stop.

Maybe, "Anne, some things have happened. It's a long story, and I'm not even sure I can explain it. I just want you to know that I love you." No. Closer, but not quite right.

At the end of the circuit—Fox Lake—Benjamin turned abruptly into a gravel parking lot by the water's edge. Emil Ryan, who was loading his fishing gear into his pickup, saw him and waved; Benjamin waved back. Then Benjamin was gone, off toward Angola again.

Not surprisingly, Emil was a First Federal customer. Nearly 50 percent of Pleasant Township had deposits in First Federal, from small fries like Emil to big companies like Indico Tool & Die. It seemed as if the entire region revolved around Benjamin's bank.

All these people trust me. They look up to me. What will they think when they find out about this?

Benjamin's house came and went.

Marla. Jeffrey. They look up to me, too. What will they think? Will they even understand? Some father I am. How will they be able to show their faces at school? Kids can be so mean.

The Cadillac flew past the Miller and Crandell farms.

I can't believe I got caught. Never in a million years did I think I'd get caught. This isn't how things were supposed to turn out. Carelessness…I became careless. What if Dad were alive to see it? Thank God he isn't. The name he spent his life building is about to become dirt. A banker stealing money from a church. Jesus. The Herald will have a field day with this one. Maybe I can talk Pastor Timmons out of telling the police. No, that will never work—he won't budge. Still, I have to try. What if I go to jail? Holy Christ. Jail. Could this be any worse?

Benjamin Drake was thinking deeply about these problems—more deeply than at any point in his circuitous journey home—which was why he spaced out the STOP sign at the intersection of U.S. Route 27 and slammed into a highland-green Ford Galaxie.

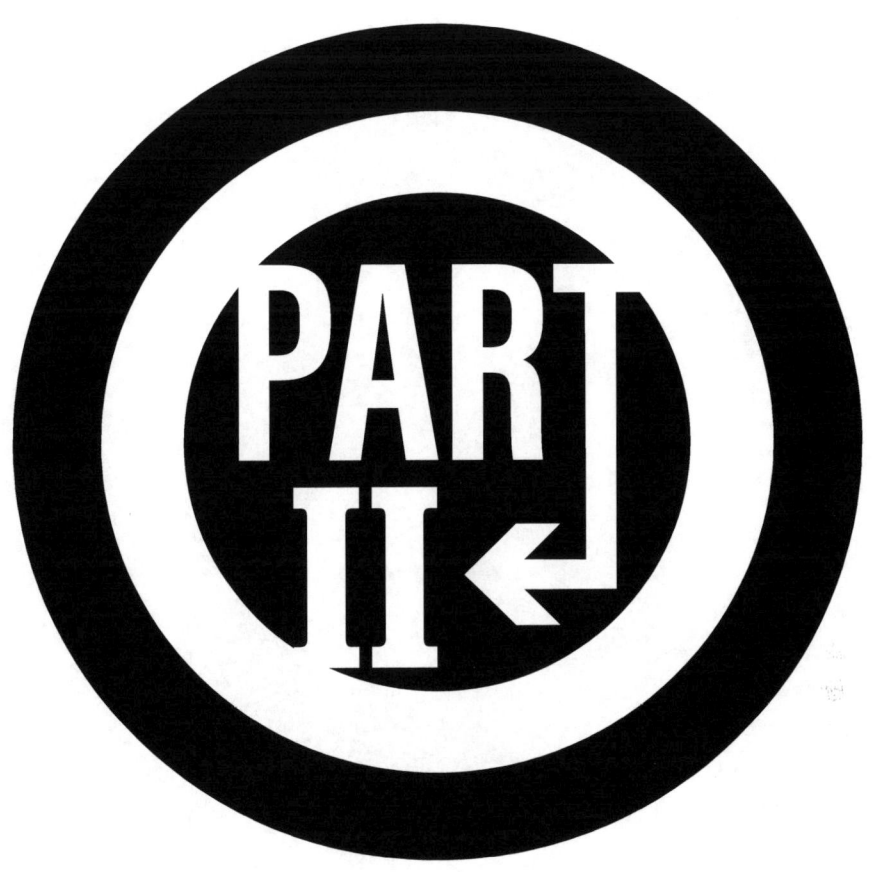

CHAPTER 10

Centuries ago the Roman poet Virgil wrote, "Love conquers all." It was an alluringly compact observation that had been repeated in one manner or another by luminaries through the ages.

But was it true? Could love really conquer all? For starters, could it conquer fear?

Being one who habitually mulled over life's mysteries, Dave had given some thought to the matter over the years. He had decided there were two types of people in this world: those who'd instinctively rush into harm's way to save the day and those who'd freeze up. Which was Dave? He couldn't be sure. Until the moment of truth actually arrived, no one could be.

It wasn't as if he had built up much of a track record. The closest he had ever come to heroism was freeing the family cat Bea after she had gotten locked in the neighbor's garage.

Sitting in a waiting room at Cameron Memorial Community Hospital and looking back on it—the car crash, not the plight of Bea—Dave still lacked answers. He wanted lucidity, certainty, but all his mind could evoke were fragments. Fragments of steel. Fragments of flesh. Fragments of sound. Fragments of speech. Fragments of time. Fragments of motion. Fragments of stench. Fragments of color. Fragments of pain. Fragments of adrenaline. Fragments of thought. Fragments of emotion.

When the Galaxie was struck, there was a mighty jolt. And a sound, like a bomb exploding. Everything turned black after Dave's head was thrust against the steering wheel, or maybe the dashboard. His eyes opened after however long. Confusion reigned. He saw sparks whenever he blinked.

There was Leyna, limp against the passenger-side door. A trickle of blood was running down her temple. Her eyes were closed.

"Leyna, you okay?"

There was only stillness when Dave nudged her repeatedly. Then panic.

"Leyna! Leyna!"

There was a sigh of relief after he placed his fingers on her chest. They moved up and down, though irregularly.

Thank God.

"Wake up, Leyna."

There was a smell. Gasoline.

"Leyna! We need to get out of this car. Now!"

There was a plan: Dave reached across Leyna to open her door. It was punched in. It wouldn't budge.

Fuck.

There was smoke. Lots of smoke. Something was burning. The Galaxie.

Holy fuck!

There was another plan: Dave's door. It was punched in, too. And jammed, too.

Think. Think. Think.

There was more panic. The backseat of the car was smoldering. Black smoke. The noxious smell of burning vinyl.

Trapped. Oh God. No.

There was a glimmer of hope, a moment of clearness: he realized the window on his door was blown out. An opening.

The only way.

There was resolve. Dave pulled Leyna across the seat, right next to him. More black smoke. Blistering heat. He gasped for breath.

Hurry. Fuck. Hurry.

There was a show of strength as Dave climbed out the window. He fell to the ground with a thump. He sucked in the fresh air.

"I'll get you."

There was a burst of energy. Dave reached into the black smoke and grabbed Leyna by her armpits. He began to pull her headfirst through the blown-out window. He strained. He coughed. Her inert body wouldn't cooperate.

"C'mon, Leyna."

There was a shredding noise, Leyna's sundress being torn by stubborn little pieces of glass that rose from the bottom of the window opening like crooked teeth. More pulling. More straining. More coughing. More shredding.

"Sorry…sorry…sorry…sorry."

There was salvation. Sweet salvation. Leyna's feet cleared the window. He carried her as far he could from the Galaxie and laid her down.

"Leyna, stay with me."

There was vomit—vomit everywhere—after he noticed her femur sticking out of her right thigh. Open wounds always made him queasy.

Oh Jesus.

There were Dave's crimson-colored hands after he wiped his face with them.

What the fuck? What happened to my face?

There was more vomit. Then a BOOM! And a ball of fire. Dave shielded Leyna with his body. Black smoke and the reek of burning chemicals filled the air, and the Galaxie disappeared into the flames. Dave cradled Leyna. He could feel her breathing.

"Still here. You're still here."

Yet as Dave sat in that waiting room at Cameron Memorial Community Hospital, he questioned whether love had conquered *all*. Things weren't that simple. Leyna was still here, true, but this seemed more random than destined. It could just as easily have gone the other way:

- What if he had remained unconscious in the Galaxie?
- What if the driver-side window hadn't been blown out?
- What if the car had exploded ten seconds earlier?
- So much about the crash had been beyond Dave's control, so much had been dictated by chance:
- What if they had stopped at the next exit instead of Angola to gas up and go to the bathroom?
- What if the gas-station attendant hadn't bragged so convincingly about the scenic spots in the lake-dotted region?
- What if he and Leyna hadn't been tempted to explore before returning to the tollway?

- What if he had driven one mile per hour faster that day?
- What if he had driven one mile per hour slower?
- What if he had been looking right instead of straight ahead while crossing the intersection of Fox Lake Road and U.S. 27?

The X factor had been Benjamin Drake, and nothing could have saved him. His Eldorado's 472-cubic-inch engine ripped through the dashboard and split him in two. No one ever found out why Benjamin had spaced out that STOP sign—it remained a mystery. Out of respect for the dead, Pastor Timmons didn't go public with Benjamin's secret.

Hundreds turned out for Benjamin's funeral. Standing with the gathered on the steps outside the First Congregational Church, his tie askew, Pug Miller said, "He was always a straight shooter."

"One of Angola's finest," chimed in Todd Lockerhoef, the owner of Lockerhoef TV & Electric.

"He made his family proud," added Delilah Taylor, who headed up the Angola Historical Society. "Especially his father."

Inside, Pastor Timmons delivered the eulogy as Anne, Jeffrey, and Marla, dressed in black, sat tearfully in the first row. "God's will is impossible to explain," Pastor Timmons intoned. "Many of you knew Benjamin as a pillar of our community, but God saw something else. God had a different plan for Benjamin."

Benjamin Drake didn't make it, but the Special did. The Special lived. Dave learned this improbably good news when Sgt. Strohm, one of the several police officers he had gotten to know in the two days since the accident, whisked it into the hospital waiting room. Its arrival distracted Dave from his ruminations, his gnawing questions.

"Bill Davis found this today in his field," Strohm said as he gave Dave the guitar. "It was just lying there. Figured it had to belong to you."

"It does. Thank you so much."

"It must have gotten thrown from your car. I bet it flew seventy-five feet."

Dave pulled the Special close and examined it. Except for a hairline fracture along the top of the neck, the guitar appeared intact. *Amazing.*

"How's your girl?" asked Strohm. "She holding up okay?"

"She's in surgery again. Something to do with the pins they put in her leg. I'm keeping my fingers crossed."

"She's come a long way since we brought her in here. Things'll work out."

Holding the Special tightly, Dave said, "Yeah, the doctors basically said the same thing, provided she doesn't get an infection or anything."

Even with the guardedly optimistic prognosis, Leyna's broken femur would need awhile to mend, maybe as long as six months. Dave was comparatively lucky. He had needed twenty-two stitches to close the cuts on his face—a procedure that nearly brought forth additional vomit—but other than that and a lot of general soreness, he was okay.

Dave decided a visit from the Special would do Leyna good. The day after her surgery, when she had regained her wits following an anesthesia-induced haze, he brought it by her room. "Look what I've got," he said.

Leyna was pale, bruised, and drawn, a far cry from the vision of vitality that had bubbled to the surface of Filippini Pond. When Dave held up the guitar, however, a wave of rosy color temporarily washed over her face. "Wow," she said in a glorified whisper.

"Can you believe it? Apparently, it was flung into a cornfield. It's almost in good enough shape to play. Too bad we don't know how."

Leyna forced a giggle that was too raspy to be mistaken for clinking glasses. "That's a bit of a problem, eh?"

Resting the Special on Leyna's bed, Dave said, "We'll just have to look at it. It's definitely a sight for sore eyes."

"Sore being the operative word."

Dave's tone turned more serious: "Speaking of which, my parents are coming here to pick me up. I obviously need a ride home since my car is no more."

"Right. Your poor car."

"Tell me about it," he said with a wistful shake of his head. "Anyway, it's you I'm thinking about. No one's talked to anyone from your family yet."

"I've been a little preoccupied," she responded, and she gestured toward her surgically repaired leg, which was in traction.

"I know, and unfortunately it looks like you'll be out of commission for a while. You'll definitely miss the beginning of school. We can give you a lift to your parents' house, but it occurred to me that I don't know where that is."

For the first time ever, Dave saw anger in Leyna's eyes. "'Home' is Racine, Wisconsin, and I'm not going back there."

"I know you want to get back to school, but like I said, it'll be a little while before you can crutch around campus."

Now Dave saw tears in her eyes—another first. "I'll stay here for all I care. I'm just not going back *there*."

"I guess I'm not following you. I—"

"I'll spell it out for you then, if I must." Leyna's head rose defiantly from the pillow, and her voice rose, too. "I haven't seen my father since I was five. I barely remember him. My mother? She's a neglectful drunk. I haven't seen her in three years. When I got a scholarship to UW and left home, I vowed I'd never go back there. And I haven't."

"Leyna, I'm sorry."

"Don't be." She collapsed back onto the pillow, and her voice grew faint again. "I'm a broken-home cliché, I know. Damaged goods."

"You're anything but damaged goods. You rock."

Leyna reached over the guitar to squeeze Dave's hand, and, yes, he blushed. He felt a little dizzy, too, like the room was moving without him. It wasn't surprising he was so discombobulated. He was really living now—this precarious game of chance was speeding forward at a rate that was becoming difficult to follow. In the past week, he had:

- Freaked out on weed.
- Blacked out on wine.
- Met the coolest girl ever.
- Lost his friend.
- Wound up with Pete Townshend's guitar.
- Left Woodstock with the coolest girl ever.
- Had sex in a cornfield with the coolest girl ever.
- Fallen in love with the coolest girl ever in record time.
- Saved the coolest girl ever (and himself) from certain death.

- Vomited repeatedly.
- Watched his Galaxie—the product of every job he had held since age twelve (with a bit of financial assistance from his trusting parents)—go up like a Roman candle.
- Seen the remains of a fellow man—a banker named Benjamin Drake, he had later learned—be hauled away in a body bag.
- Been reunited with the Special, which had survived the wrath of Townshend, the tyrannical grip of a lug named Jumbo, and the horrors of a car crash.

Now something else was about to happen. With this question, he was about to add another bullet point to his rapidly growing list: "Do you, um, want to come back to my parents' house with me…recuperate there?"

CHAPTER 11

Wearing a button-down flannel shirt, athletic shorts, and no shoes or socks, Dave scurried out the front door of his parents' Glenview ranch and into the autumn chill to retrieve the mail. Twenty steps to the mailbox at the curb, twenty steps back to the warmth of the house. It was an uneventful routine.

This time, however, Dave noticed the colorful corner of a postcard poking out of the stack of bills and solicitations, and he pulled it free. The front featured a row of bikini-clad women tanning on the beach with the words CALIFORNIA DREAMIN' set against a perfect blue sky. The back was even more intriguing:

Weiss,

Heard about your car accident through the grapevine. Big bummer, but I'm glad you pulled through. I'm out in California, around Santa Cruz. Came with a couple girls I met at Woodstock. Learning to surf. Working at a restaurant. Having the time of my life. Take care, brother.

Jimmy

P.S. Can you believe the Cubs blew it again? How the hell did that happen? Guess we'll have to wait till next year...

Dave shook his head with a mixture of relief, envy, and irritation. *What grapevine? And isn't that just like Jimmy? No return address so I can write him back. No nothing. Only some tits and ass and good cheer.* At any rate, one of life's mysteries finally had been solved. As Leyna had predicted, Jimmy had landed on his feet.

Not that there had been much time to think about Jimmy, or anything else from his old life at the University of Illinois, over the previous couple months. Hunkered down in Glenview while Leyna healed, Dave had enrolled in a political science class at Oakton Community College and was working at the *Daily Herald*. Out of the kindness of his heart, the *Herald*'s managing editor, Ben Cross, had given Dave a part-time job on the copy desk: five nights a week, 6 p.m. to midnight, five bucks an hour. "Just don't shit yourself and make me look bad," Cross had told an eternally grateful Dave.

It was a step up in both pay and hours from his internship over the summer, and Dave hadn't yet crapped his pants. Presumably this day would unfold the same way: his poli-sci class would convene in a couple hours followed by a shift of compiling box scores from the local high school games under the mad rush of deadline. Postcard in hand, Dave walked down the hall to his bedroom to start getting ready.

His room was as he'd left it upon first departing for U of I a few years earlier, with childhood relics crowding the walls such as a clipping of the very first article he wrote for his high school newspaper, ribbons from track meets, a *Rubber Soul*-era Beatles poster, and a picture of JFK torn from the pages of *Life*. There was, however, a key addition: the Special, which he had carefully hung soon after coming home. Dave had then purchased a red lava lamp and placed it on a dresser directly beneath the Special. When the other lights in the room were off, the lava lamp lent a complementary glow to the guitar that Dave thought was cool.

He thumbtacked Jimmy's postcard next to the Special and padded to the bathroom to shower and shave. Running a razor across his face, he paused as he always did to look at his scars from the car wreck: one was above his left eyebrow, the other was on his right cheek. He still hadn't grown accustomed to them.

They made him think of the nineteenth-century German and Austrian dueling societies he had read about in a history class at U of I. These ritualistic groups were comprised of university students who sought to prove their worth by letting loose in fencing matches. Since their sabres weren't blunt-tipped, things could get messy—in fact, that was the object. The facial gashes the combatants suffered, otherwise known as "bragging scars," were viewed with the utmost reverence, as signs of hard-earned worldliness. Dave had thought these people had been nuts upon first reading about them, but now he could almost relate. Thanks to a jagged line here and a zigzag there, his face no longer seemed as confoundedly boyish.

Leyna's injuries were a different story. This had been particularly so in the beginning, when she had left Cameron Memorial Community Hospital in a wheelchair. The situation hadn't been pretty, but Dave's trusting parents, God bless them, hadn't asked a lot of questions. They had instantly recognized the degree of Dave's attachment to Leyna and had welcomed her into their home, setting her up in the guest bedroom off the kitchen so that she could convalesce. It had been good medicine: by early October she had graduated from the wheelchair to crutches.

Leyna was a night owl, Dave had learned, and was usually still asleep when he left for the day. As part of his new routine, he cracked open her bedroom door to peek at her on his way out. This was always an early-afternoon highlight. The lowlight occurred moments later when he walked across the lawn to his "new" car, a Plymouth Valiant he had picked up for three hundred bucks. Dave longed for his Galaxie whenever he drove the temperamental pile of rust, but he had no choice but to make do.

Of course, the Weiss home sprang to life each day long before Dave's walk of torment to the Valiant. Dave's dad—William Weiss, he of the hastily arranged comb-over and the pasty complexion that came from spending too much time under fluorescent lights—rummaged out the door at 7:30 each morning to open his business, Weiss Drugstore, located blocks away in the downtown. William had owned the place since 1953, and it had given his family a comfortable middle-class life.

He liked to boast that Weiss Drugstore was more than a mere pharmacy. If the neighborhood kids wanted a wiffle ball, they'd find plenty next to the school supplies on the old brown shelves. If Mom needed a gallon of milk, she'd find one in the cooler that was crammed into a corner next to the magazine rack. And if Dad desired a box of condoms, a clerk would discreetly fish one out of a drawer behind the back counter. William aimed to please, and so did his wife, Helen, who did the books and various other tasks around the store while he busily filled prescriptions, often with a nerve-steadying cigarette dangling from his mouth.

Helen also saw to it that she and William started each morning with a hearty helping of food. Breakfast was, after all, the most important meal of the day. The smell of sausage and pancakes, French toast and bacon, or whatever else was cooking sometimes woke Dave, but not Leyna. When she finally did rise, she luxuriated in the solitude of the empty house. It was such a peaceful, wonderful departure from her childhood home, where quiet had meant only that her mother was sleeping off a drinking binge, sometimes in the company of the latest asshole she'd picked up.

During Leyna's first month in Glenview, she spent her afternoons reading on the patio next to Helen's meticulously maintained garden. Once the weather turned nippy in October, she migrated to a green boucle couch in the living room that caught the late-afternoon sun. Sometimes when she was feeling up to it, she crutched around the neighborhood. She had plenty of space to think on the yard-lined streets of this bedroom community, and she decided that even though the circumstances that had brought her here weren't ideal, she was exactly where she wanted to be right now.

The best part was when Dave returned from the *Herald* in the midnight hour. He would slowly open her bedroom door and tiptoe to her bed, mindful not to wake his parents, who were just down the hall. On this particular night, he was holding a postcard.

"Check it out," he said. "You'll never guess who finally surfaced…or maybe you will."

Leyna snatched the postcard and read it, her high-pitched giggle echoing through the room.

"Ssshhhh. My parents."

"See, what did I tell you? He's fine. More than fine."

"I know, I know."

"Look at it this way: At least you'll have someone to stay with if you're ever out in California."

"If he's still there. With Jimmy, who knows? As we speak, he's probably on his way down to South America or something."

Dave shook his head with a mixture of relief, envy, and irritation before forgetting about Jimmy again. Following the rhythm of his new routine, he crawled onto the bed and cozied up to Leyna, who wasn't wearing anything underneath her oversized T-shirt.

Leyna got a kick out of Dave's "advances." He wasn't presumptuous, that was for sure. Before going too far, he'd always pause to await permission, as if her lack of panties wasn't enough of an invitation. Still, there was a certain resolve beneath his clumsiness that warmed her. He had been strong enough, after all, to pull her from the burning wreckage of that car.

Due to Leyna's gimpy leg and the thick plaster cast encasing it, their amorous late-night encounters required a bit of creativity and a lot of trial and error. They had tried the missionary position—that had hurt her leg. They had tried it with her on top—that had been a disaster. They had tried scrunching together on their sides like spoons—the bulky cast had gotten in the way. Finally, through sheer perseverance, they had discovered a position that worked. More or less.

With Leyna lying on her stomach, Dave would climb on top ever so gently. This time, however, in a moment of gratuitous improvisation, he slipped his hands between Leyna and the sheets, cupping her breasts. She was unprepared for the sudden shift of his weight and yelped, "Ouch, my leg."

Dave quickly removed his hands from her breasts and rocked slightly to the left.

"Ouch, ouch. Move over a little. To the right."

Dave moved over a little, to the right.

"Ouch. To the left a little. And down."

Dave moved to the left a little, and down. Then he ventured inside her.

"Ah."

There could be no exultations like those from the free-flowing night in the cornfield—the elders were just down the hall—but Dave and Leyna were nothing if not adaptable. Silently though triumphantly, they both climaxed.

They remained quiet for a while afterward, lying side by side on their backs and watching the ceiling fan spin. Its hypnotic whir eventually made Dave yawn.

"Long day again. I'm bushed."

"I bet."

"Ben really gave it to me tonight, told me I was—how exactly did he put it?—'slower than fucking shit.'"

Giggling, Leyna said, "That guy sounds like an absolute lunatic."

"Nah, he's not so bad. I really love the work, and I've learned a lot from him. The other stuff goes with the territory."

"You have surprisingly thick skin, Dave Weiss."

Dave yawned again. "I'd better hit the sack so I can do it all over again tomorrow."

He grabbed the postcard, gave Leyna a soft kiss on the lips, and tiptoed down the hall to his bedroom. Leyna wasn't tired. She read for a couple hours—Steinbeck's *Cannery Row*—and then sketched a bouquet of tulips before nodding off with her notebook on her stomach. And the next morning, as Helen fried eggs for herself and William while humming Sinatra's "Fly Me to the Moon," it was as if nothing had happened.

So it went. Autumn turned to winter and winter to spring inside this little cocoon Dave and Leyna had created. Although Leyna's leg still ached, especially on damp days, the plaster cast and the crutches were now gone. Hope lived. It was growing stronger every day, and sometimes it presented itself in the damnedest ways:

One night Dave showed up in Leyna's room with two cheap bottles of sparkling wine and paper cups. "Ready to celebrate?" he asked.

"Sure. Any particular reason?"

"Ben gave me a raise. He said—his words—'You haven't embarrassed me yet, so I think I'll keep you around a little longer.'"

"I'm telling you, that guy is crazy."

"Maybe so, but I can't complain about the promotion."

"Nor should you. You should be proud. You deserve it."

After popping open a bottle as quietly as he could, Dave filled the cups with bubbly. It wasn't long before they had drained that first bottle and most of the second. Leyna was feeling no pain—in fact, her leg seemed almost normal.

They did it on their sides. They did it with her on top. They did it with him on top.

"Ah…AHhhh…AAAHhhh…AAAHHHH," Leyna exulted.

"Sssshhhh. My parents."

They did it sitting down. They did it standing up. They even did it with Leyna on her stomach, for old times' sake.

But when the lovemaking ended, the predictable occurred: Dave had been so busy at work that there had been no time to fill his stomach with dinner, and the sparkling wine had flooded his system unimpeded. As they lay side by side on their backs, his world began to spin like the ceiling fan above.

"Are you okay?" Leyna asked, the skin on her forehead crinkling. "You look green."

Dave pulled himself to his feet. "Bathroom…be right back…throw up."

"Do you need help?"

"No…I'm okay…bathroom."

Dave wobbled the few yards out of the bedroom to the guest bathroom off the kitchen. *Almost there. Must…get…there.* He made it just in time to stick his head in the toilet bowl and barf. Once his stomach had been emptied, he spent who knows how long in a greenish mound on the tile floor before rising tentatively.

At 6:45 sharp the next morning, Helen walked down the hall to the kitchen at her usual resolute pace. While frying a package of sausage, she noticed that Leyna's door was cracked open.

"Strange," she said to herself.

Helen went to shut it so that the poor girl could have some privacy. With her hand on the doorknob, she glanced inside to make sure Leyna was okay, but her eyes never made it that far: they stopped at Dave, whose naked body was splayed atop the sheets. Helen's first instinct was to spin around and head for the hills while pulling her hair out, but instead she marched to the bed, nearly tripping over an empty bottle of sparkling wine that was on the floor.

Jostling her comatose son, she demanded, "David Harold Weiss—wake up!"

Dave opened his eyes. Slowly, horrifically, the face of his mother came into focus.

"Get up," he heard her say. "Go back to your room this instant before your father comes out for breakfast and sees this. Get up…*now*."

Without saying a word, Dave wrapped a blanket around himself and scuttled out the door. All the commotion had woken Leyna, whose head was throbbing almost as much as her leg. She couldn't bear to open her eyes, so she pretended to be asleep until everyone had cleared out of the house for the day.

When Dave came calling after his shift at the *Herald*—still looking as washed out as he had seventeen hours earlier—Leyna seemed oddly serious. After an awkward stab at conversation followed by an equally awkward kiss, Dave asked, "Is everything okay?"

"You know how your mom came in here this morning?"

"Crap, you noticed. I was hoping you slept through that little episode."

"No such luck. But as embarrassing as it was, it might not have been the worst thing in the world. In fact, it's probably just the nudge we needed. We can't stay here forever…or at least I can't."

Dave froze. He had known this day would eventually come, but he had been in such an uncharacteristic state of bliss that he had managed to avoid thinking too much about it. With all the stoicism he could muster, he sucked in a breath, saying, "It's true. You're well enough to go back to school, and I don't blame you for—"

"School? Who said anything about school? I was thinking we should get a place together."

Dave exhaled. "A place? Together? Where?"

"I don't know. Somewhere around Chicago, I suppose. Why not?"

"No, no, I think that would be great. Better than great. But you're sure you won't miss being at school?"

"I've obviously had a lot of time to think about it, and I don't see the point in going back to school. You go to school to get ready for life, but I feel like my life has already started, and I like where it's going. It feels…solid."

In the dining room that Sunday over a brisket dinner, Dave cleared his throat. "Mom, Dad—Leyna and I have been here for months, as you know, and…well, I may as well just say it: we've decided to get our own place together."

"I don't think I approve of that," Helen responded, her eyes directed at Leyna. "You're not married."

"True," Dave said, "but we think it's the best option. Besides, this is what people do nowadays. It's 1970."

"The boy has a point, Helen," William said between bites of brisket. "It is 1970."

"Please. You don't even know what that means," Helen shot back.

"What about school, Dave?" William asked.

"I can finish my degree here. Plus, things are going well at the *Herald*. Ben has talked about moving me up to a full-time position, and I think I have enough money to pull this off. I've been saving, and—"

"What about your plans, Leyna?" Helen asked sharply. "Do you have any?"

Meeting Helen's gaze head-on, Leyna replied, "I'll find a job, maybe take some classes somewhere. This was my idea. It's like I told Dave, you two have been so kind and generous, taking me into your home and helping me get better. But I can't stay here forever. I've already been an imposition."

"You haven't been," William said, "and you're certainly welcome to stay as long as you need to, but it sounds like your minds are made up. I don't see what's wrong with it, Helen. It seems like the practical thing to do."

"And your parents?" Helen asked Leyna. "I know you had some sort of falling out with them—or at least that's what you said—but what will they think?"

"It's fine. Really."

And it was, except that Dave and Leyna's meager resources limited their options. After a couple weeks of searching, they found a small apartment in Des Plaines, a gray old town characterized by its proximity to O'Hare Airport and the nonstop chugging of freight trains passing through on their way out west. The apartment building was flanked by I-90 and a peeling water tower, but at least it was closer to Arlington

Heights, where the *Herald* was located.

On a sunny April morning, William helped them pack up. He then watched curiously from his stoop as the Valiant, with the mattress from Dave's bedroom tied to the roof, rolled off to the fledgling couple's launching pad eight miles west.

The first thing Dave did was hang the Special smack-dab in the middle of the living room wall. He loved his guitar. He loved that it had once belonged to the great Pete Townshend. He loved the animal-horn cutaways. He loved the cherry-red color. He even loved the nicks on the edges of the body and the hairline fracture on the neck, all of which signified resiliency to him, much like the bragging scars on his face.

The Special was the apartment's saving grace. Otherwise, the place was a shithole in every respect, with white paint that had become yellowed from cigarette smoke and stains on the carpeting that just weren't going to come out. But Dave and Leyna didn't care. Shithole though it was, it was theirs.

CHAPTER 12

Across the pond in Twickenham, England—in a room filled with musical instruments and recording equipment—hope didn't live as much as it was being resurrected.

Peace, love, and understanding had been taking it on the chin ever since Woodstock. In December 1969 the Rolling Stones put on a free concert at Altamont Speedway in northern California that quickly turned toxic. As mayhem spread through the crowd, someone was stabbed to death by a biker from Hells Angels, who had been hired to provide security and, even more unfathomably, were paid in beer. Several months later, there was the Kent State Massacre, in which the National Guard opened fire during a Vietnam protest at the Ohio-based university, killing four students and wounding nine others.

But Pete Townshend was oblivious to these grim developments. His motivation was purely personal.

Using his *Tommy* spoils, Pete had bought a Georgian house for himself and his wife Karen in Twickenham, a bucolic suburb southwest of London known mostly for its rugby club and now a certain rock-star resident. The home had twelve rooms and a handsome yard, and though Pete could have afforded something bigger, this was good enough, especially since he spent most of his time inside a five-by-five-meter bedroom on the second floor that he had converted into a recording studio.

The room was equipped with a Wurlitzer EP-200A electric piano, a Lowrey Berkshire Deluxe TBO-1 organ, an EMS VCS3 mk1 analog synthesizer, an ARP 2500 synthesizer, an EMS DK1 monophonic keyboard, a 3M eight-track, an Ampex four-track, a silverface Fender Princeton reverb amplifier, an SEA power amplifier, Tannoy speakers, a Premier drumkit, and a collection of acoustic and electric guitars, including a (but not *the*) Gibson SG Special. It was the musical equivalent of Dr. Frankenstein's laboratory.

Dirty dishes were scattered about, and an ever-present bottle of Rémy

Martin sat on the Wurlitzer piano like a muse. Days had passed—maybe weeks—since Pete had been outside in his handsome yard, or anywhere else. He had conjured an idea after Woodstock that was so grand it would make *Tommy* seem like a trifle. The working title was *Lifehouse*, and the central theme was—yes—hope, represented by a line Pete had written in black marker on a wall in his studio: THE SIMPLE SECRET OF A NOTE IN A SONG.

His concept went something like this: People have been confined to their homes by the government and now communicate via a corporate-provided electronic grid. Eventually a revolution spreads over the grid, and they flee their electronic prisons and find unity and spiritual redemption at the greatest of communal experiences: a giant rock concert.

Huddled amidst his machinery, Pete had already composed bits and pieces of the music for *Lifehouse*. Ironically, these rough demos were driven by synthesizers, not guitars. For the first time ever, Pete had come up empty trying to build his melodies from chords—they seemed like recycled versions of his old music—so he had turned to the amorphous sounds of the synthesizer.

Even after that breakthrough, however, Pete reached a point where he could go no further until he fleshed out his idea with a detailed story outline—a roadmap, so to speak. He sat at the ARP 2500 synthesizer he was now using as a desktop and worked in vain to fill his notebook with words. At one point he grew so frustrated that he reached for a Harmony Sovereign acoustic guitar and smashed it to bits. The next day he obliterated a Coral Hornet electric guitar.

But the day after that the heavens miraculously opened, and the words flowed out of him at a feverish rate. He awoke the following morning with his head on the ARP 2500 synthesizer, a small pool of saliva by his mouth. Lo and behold, his notebook was filled. Pete shook off his grogginess and went downstairs to the den, where his wife was curled up in a wide-bottom papasan chair reading *The Guardian*.

"I've finished my outline," he said. "Fancy giving it a look-through?"

Karen was a raven-haired beauty whom Pete had met in art school. It took a unique brand of woman to be a rock and roll wife, one who wasn't inclined to probe too deeply into her husband's pursuits. The booze and the groupies, the long absences while he toured, the eerie silences upstairs of late that had been punctuated by the sounds of guitars being smashed, the spark of madness right now in his bloodshot eyes—well, denial was a useful tool for Karen. Thus, after reading Pete's outline and not being able to make heads or tails of it, she said, "Why not take it to the boys, see what they think?"

Bright and early the next morning, Pete gathered his notebook and demo tapes, climbed into his shining black Bentley T1, and drove 120 kilometers through the countryside to Roger Daltrey's estate in East Sussex. He parked in the circular drive and looked out upon the damp, rolling tract of land. After a minute or two, Roger galloped into view atop a horse—or as Pete murmured, "A fucking *horse*?"—the singer's blond locks blowing regally in the wind.

Roger rode his steed to a stable, and the two met up inside in a wood-paneled drawing room. Pete, eyes wide, watched as Roger slid on a pair of earphones and listened to the demos while leafing through the notebook. When Roger was finished, he rested the earphones on the arm of his red leather chair.

"Well?" Pete prodded hopefully.

"The truth?"

"Yes, yes, of course."

Roger tapped the notebook with his index finger, saying, "The music is interesting, but I don't understand a word of this story."

Bright and early the next morning, Pete gathered his notebook and demo tapes, climbed into his Bentley, and drove 152 kilometers through the countryside to John Entwistle's estate in Gloucestershire. Pete felt like a miniature version of himself as he entered the cavernous foyer, whose towering white walls were decorated with all manner of guitars.

"Where to?" he asked.

There were fifty-five rooms from which to choose, and the bassist guided Pete to the one that had most of the liquor. After pouring two snifters of Hennessy, John rolled the tapes and sat down next to Pete at the oak bar. Taking deep drags off a Marlboro, he read Pete's notebook as the music played.

"Well?" Pete inquired somewhat more cautiously than he had at Roger's.

John scratched his beard, then shook his head. "I don't get it."

"What about the hopeful note? The spiritual awakening? The fresh air in the countryside? The liberation from a life under tyranny?"

John shook his head.

"What about all the bloody happy people at the end?"

There was more headshaking.

"For Christ's sake, John, the story couldn't be any simpler. A nursery school student…an, an imbecile could follow it. How can you not get it?"

Bright and early the next morning, Pete gathered his notebook and demo tapes, climbed into his Bentley, and drove fifteen kilometers through London streets to Keith Moon's flat in trendy Chelsea. Keith, wearing only a pair of red briefs, gave Pete a bear-hug upon opening the door.

"So, you've finally decided to come out of hiding, have you?" Keith said. "Welcome. Come on in."

Pete zigzagged across a floor littered with empty Courvoisier bottles, drumsticks, women's undergarments, the Beach Boys album *Pet Sounds*, yesterday's ham loaf, and a cricket mallet. He then cleared an ashtray and some *Playboy*s from the couch and made himself at home while Keith listened, read, and fidgeted.

"I like it," the drummer said.

Pete allowed a slight smile.

"Just one detail."

"What's that?" Pete asked.

"Where are the tits? This is rock and roll, you know."

"The…tits. You're joking, right?"

"I'm as serious as a heart attack, mate. It needs—"

"You know what? Go fuck yourself."

"C'mon, Pete. No need to get huffy. It's a fair question."

"I'll give you fucking fair, you git."

Pete lifted an end table over his head and threw it at the wall. He then promptly departed, slamming the door on his way out.

Pete had run out of options, except for one that was admittedly dubious. Bright and early the next morning, he gathered his notebook and demo tapes, climbed into his Bentley, and drove nineteen kilometers through London streets to Clive's hovel in trashy Brixton.

"This is a surprise," Clive said. "What can I do for you?"

"Sorry, I guess I should have rung you up first. I need you to look at something I've written."

"I'd be honored."

With the tapes rolling, Pete sank into an armchair that smelled vaguely like feet. Clive took a seat across the room. His perusal of the notebook yielded a series of empty thought balloons, and after a while he only pretended to be reading. Nevertheless, Clive at least understood where his bread was buttered.

"Great story, mate," he said.

"You're completely full of shit."

"I know."

Pete's grand project had suddenly become steeped in gloom, but there was no turning back now. A while earlier, before his labor had begun in earnest, he had boldly thrown down the gauntlet in his monthly *Melody Maker* column. Sharing the idea behind *Lifehouse*, he had concluded:

> I think everybody hears the same note or noise. It's an amazing thing to think of any common ground between all men that isn't directly a reflection of spiritual awareness. It's a note, it's notes, it's music—the most beautiful there is to hear.

He forged ahead in Twickenham, adding lyrics to the music that had already been composed and writing more songs. The other three convened at Olympic Studios in South West London to start learning the material. John brought forth his rapid-fire bass fingering, Keith his swashbuckling drum fills, and Roger his testosterone-charged vocals. After some trial and error, the riffs started to sound unmistakably like The Who.

One day Pete showed up at the studio from out of the blue. He was considerably thinner—and at 6'0" and only 170 pounds to begin with, he couldn't afford to lose much weight without taking on a sickly appearance. He also had a faraway expression in his eyes that Roger found off-putting.

"Up to giving it a whirl?" the singer asked.

"I've been giving it a 'whirl' for the past month since I saw you, trying to finish this flaming pile of shit you three loathe so much, and I feel like I'm getting nowhere. What have you been doing? Riding your horse?"

"Actually, we've been working up some of your demos. They're sounding pretty good, too."

Pete arched an eyebrow.

"There's time enough to iron out the lyrics," Roger added. "First we—"

"Just say it: You mean the bloody *story*, the fucking plot of the thing."

"Well, yes."

Pete went into a small room in the studio that was soundproofed with acoustical foam padding—*Just like the loony bin*, he thought—where he strummed his guitar listlessly. He needed eight takes to get a part right on a song called "Love Ain't for Keeping," a ridiculously easy G-G-A-D-A chord progression that he normally would have nailed on the first try. He couldn't even summon enough resolve to smash the offending Gretsch 6120 hollow body guitar. Rather, he stood up and left without saying a word to his bandmates.

Pete returned to Olympic Studios periodically, often enough for The Who to complete "Love Ain't for Keeping," "Baba O'Riley," "Won't Get Fooled Again," "Pure and Easy," "Behind Blue Eyes," "Water," "Bargain," and a handful of other songs. Though there was still the nagging matter of the plot, which continued to stump everyone, the machinery of The Who was now churning. Unbeknownst to Pete, The Who's manager, Kit Lambert, had arranged a press conference at the Young Vic Theatre to discuss *Lifehouse*.

"Are you out of your fucking mind?" Pete asked the nattily dressed Lambert after learning about the press conference.

"*I'm* fine," he replied. "It's the band I'm worried about. It's been nearly two years since *Tommy* was released. We need something new. At this point, it doesn't even matter what it is. We need to get back out there before they forget about us."

The Young Vic was an octagonal space in the Shakespearian tradition that was located near London's South Bank. Dutifully, Pete, Roger, John, and Keith filed onto the stage and took their seats at a long table, facing the journalists who filled the first couple rows. Although Pete had lost even more weight, his V-neck sweater and jeans felt uncomfortably tight.

"Can you provide some details on your new project?" asked a journalist.

Roger, John, and Keith all turned warily toward their leader, whose clothes were now suffocating him. He was tempted to take them off, but instead, following a well-placed elbow from Roger, he squinted into the faceless tangle and answered the question:

"We are intending to produce a work of fiction, or a play or an opera, and create a completely different type of performance in rock. Rock's real power as a liberational force is completely untapped, so a new type of theater, a new type of performance, has to be devised to present it." Rubbing his chin reflectively, he added, "The aim is change…like a magnificent sunrise breaking through dark clouds."

That answer would have sufficed, but now that Pete had started, he couldn't stop. He felt like he was watching himself from above as he carried on about "people in spacesuits" and "pulse-modulated frequencies" and "reflective surfaces" and "beta rhythms" while his bandmates looked on with growing anxiousness.

A headline the next day in *New Musical Express* read, "Off His Rocker?" The accompanying article noted Pete's waifish physique, as well as his bloodshot eyes and unkempt hair, and ended with the sentence, "This writer, anyway, could make no sense of The Who's latest project."

The band thought it prudent to leave town for a spell, reasoning that a change of scenery would make all the difference. Team Who—Pete, Roger, John, Keith, Lambert, and Clive—touched down at New York's JFK International Airport on an overcast spring afternoon. After settling into their digs at the Waldorf Astoria and relaxing with a brandy or two, the four principals headed to the Record Plant on West 44th Street to make some music.

Built in 1968 and featuring a groovy assortment of plush couches, the Record Plant was already legendary—Jimi Hendrix had christened it by recording *Electric Ladyland* there. The Who had everything it needed, from the studio's hip vibe to its state-of-the-art equipment, but none of this could breathe life into the band's guitarist, whose attempts to write the remaining material were becoming increasingly futile. Weeks of all-night recording sessions yielded only "I Don't Even Know Myself," "The Song Is Over," "Getting in Tune," "Going Mobile," and assorted meanderings that were, as Pete phrased it, "fit for a fucking dumpster."

One afternoon Lambert called a meeting in his fifteenth-floor suite at the Waldorf to go over the "direction" of the project with two lackeys from The Who's record label.

"When do you expect to finish?" asked one of the lackeys.

"It shouldn't be long," Lambert answered. "Right now they're patching up a few details."

"Yeah, like what the fucking thing means," Roger said under his breath.

"It's a new direction," John said. "Synthesizers and the like."

"No guitars?" asked the lackey.

"Guitars, too," John answered.

"Some of it sounds fantastic," Keith said. "We just need to nudge our old mate Pete across the finish line."

"A month? Two months?" asked the other lackey.

"I don't know," Roger answered. "That seems tight. I think that's pushing—"

"It seems reasonable to me," Lambert said.

"How would you know?" Roger asked with burrowing eyes.

"Because you've already been working on it for months," Lambert responded, "and there's—"

"You haven't been in the studio," Roger countered. "You have no idea what's going on. You—"

"We can do it," Keith interrupted. "Why not? Look at *Tommy*: a bunch of rubbish about a deaf, dumb, and blind pinball player, and it was a smash hit."

"Yeah, but at least *Tommy* was easier to follow," Roger said. "This—"

"What if we cut out the spiritual-awareness bunk," Keith suggested, "and just have a bunch of kids going to a rock show and getting laid?"

"That might work," John said.

"Promising," Clive offered from the corner of the room.

"What do you think, Pete?" asked Kit.

"I need some air," he answered. "I'll be right back."

As soon as Pete exited the suite, he began unbuttoning his shirt. *It's as hot as hell in here. I can't take it.* He noticed a window at the end of the hall. *I'm bloody burning up.* He walked toward the window. *Thank God. It's open.* He moved closer to the whistling air. *That feels fantastic.* He moved closer still. *I think I'll jump.*

A woman who was waiting for the elevator clutched his arm; startled, Pete spun around.

"Sir, are you all right?" she asked, her eyes bulging.

Pete thought intently about the question for several seconds before answering, "I really don't know why I'm here."

So ended the *Lifehouse* project. Several months later, in August 1971, some random scraps from it were released under the generic title *Who's Next*. Appropriately, the album's cover photo depicted the band members after they had urinated on a towering concrete slab that was sticking out of a desolate landscape. *Who's Next* quickly went to number four on the charts, outselling even *Tommy*.

CHAPTER 13

Dave and Leyna were moving up in the world. With *Who's Next* playing on Dave's new stereo—a rocking system consisting of a Reference receiver, Quadraflex speakers, and a Technics turntable—they unpacked a surprisingly large number of boxes. Life's accumulation of *stuff* was underway.

Dave was pleased to no end by how crisply the synthesizers and Roger Daltrey's voice were coming through the Quadraflexes on "Baba O'Riley." Like the song said, the exodus was here. Gone were the sooty highway and peeling water tower flanking their humble apartment in Des Plaines. Dave and Leyna had traveled fourteen miles to their new digs in the northern suburb of Evanston, fourteen miles and a world. Directly to their west was a Unitarian church with a sign out front that read NUCLEAR-FREE ZONE and featured a drawing of an X'd-out bomb; to their east, mere blocks away, were the inspiring waters of Lake Michigan; and to their north was Northwestern University and all its youthful optimism.

Dave had been promoted to the position of full-time copy editor on the *Herald*'s sports desk, and Leyna was also gainfully employed as an administrative assistant at the YWCA, which happened to be around the corner from the NUCLEAR-FREE ZONE sign. They were by no means rich, but they were doing well enough to have secured an element of peace, love, and understanding in Evanston.

Their stretch of Burnham Place had more pedestrian than car traffic, and the apartment building they now called home was a classic brownstone that could only be called charming. With a large bedroom and a living room that had a brick fireplace, their second-floor abode met all their needs. It even had a small balcony that Leyna had already decked out with potted chrysanthemums and African violets.

As *Who's Next* rocked on, Dave undertook his most sacred decorating task: the positioning of the Special. The guitar held the most prominent place in the apartment, of course—above the fireplace mantle in the living room—but due to the accumulation of *stuff*, it was competing with a Native American tapestry, a *Catch-22* movie poster, a massive hanging mirror, a watercolor of a river running through the woods that Leyna had painted, and various knickknacks.

"The Special is up," Dave yelled above the music to Leyna, who was unpacking dishes in the kitchen. "Check it out."

Leyna appeared and tilted her head thoughtfully, like she was studying a Renoir or a Monet. "Wonderful."

"You don't think it's getting lost in the shuffle?"

"No, it's perfect."

After she kissed Dave and returned to the kitchen, he examined the Special for a few more minutes.

"You sure?" he yelled.

"Positive."

Leyna already felt at home in Evanston. It was a bit of a walk from Burnham Place to the YWCA, especially since she was still nagged by a limp, but she enjoyed the breezy lake air and peeking into the mom-and-pop shops she passed along the way. Over the past year, Leyna had worked on the reference desk at the Des Plaines Public Library and at Algonquin Records. Those jobs had done little more than help pay the bills, but this one at the YWCA was different. The organization's motto was "Empowering Women," and although she was starting as a glorified gopher, she felt as if she'd found her calling. Among its platforms of empowerment, the YWCA offered shelter to battered women, a place to mend physically and psychologically. Leyna could do some real good here.

After all, she knew something about the battering of women:

On a steamy summer night a month before her freshman year at the University of Wisconsin, Leyna had been holed up in her bedroom in the ramshackle one-story house she and her mother shared on the outskirts of Racine. She was lying in bed reading with the music turned up, the better not to hear Mom, who was drinking in the living room with a man whose name Leyna didn't even know.

Leyna had become adept at blocking out the ugliness around her, but on this night there was a knock on her bedroom door. It swung open a second later, revealing the stout, balding man from the living room.

"Hey there," he said.

Leyna quickly looked back at her book and said, "Where's my mom?"

"Asleep."

"Passed out is more like it."

"Funny."

"Not particularly."

"Whatcha reading?" he asked, stepping into Leyna's bedroom with a leer.

"What do you care? And what are you doing here?"

"Just thought I'd see what you're up to."

"Well, now you know, and now you can leave."

The man came closer to the bed. He smelled of liquor and sweat.

"I've had my eye on you," he said, "but I bet a lot of boys do. You're real pretty."

Now standing over Leyna, he stroked her hair, leaving her no option but to swat his hand.

"Feisty. I like that," he said.

"Seriously, you need to leave."

He stroked her hair again.

"Stop."

"I thought we were just getting started."

Leyna tried to shove him away, but he wouldn't budge.

"You like it rough," he said between breaths that were growing deeper and more uneven.

"No."

"I think you do." Yanking her up by the tufts of her hair, he snorted, "I like playing that way, too."

"You're hurting me…"

The pain intensified when, after throwing her down onto the bed, he wrapped his left hand around her throat and pinned his right forearm against her chest.

"I…I can't…breathe. Please…"

The man's body, fully aroused by this point, shuddered almost convulsively as he mounted Leyna, which enabled her to squirm free. He reached for her ankle and pulled her toward him, but by then she had an iron in her right hand from the ironing board at the foot of the bed.

It turned out Leyna also knew something about the battering of men: leading with the iron, she threw a roundhouse punch that clanked off his left temple like something out of a Three Stooges sketch—except this wasn't funny, especially for the aggressor, whose eyebrow swelled up instantly.

"Fucking bitch!"

Before he could regain his balance, Leyna struck him again with the iron, and she heard his cheekbone shatter.

"Arrrrrrhhhh! I'll fucking—"

The third and decisive blow, to the side of the mouth, scattered several of his teeth across the room and sent him tumbling from the bed to the floor with a thud. The fury in his eyes had turned to agony, and he crawled to the bedroom door, whereupon he pulled himself up using the doorknob and staggered almost blindly out of the house.

After hearing his car roll down the gravel driveway, Leyna followed the trail of blood into the living room. Her mother was out cold on the couch, an empty vodka bottle nearby. Leyna thought of calling the police, but instead, after reasoning that the man was too beaten up to come back, she settled on an entirely different plan, returning to her bedroom to gather all the money she had saved and pack a suitcase.

Leyna spent the next several hours wiping away a stream of tears that had a regenerative effect, and at first light she left a note under the vodka bottle: "Bye, Mom—have a great life." Then she caught a bus up to her friend Eileen's apartment in Madison, where she stayed until classes started and she could get into her dorm. Other than a smattering of halfhearted phone calls from her mother in the ensuing months— each of which Leyna ended by saying, "I'm eighteen, and you can't make me go back there"—the book was closed on Racine, Wisconsin. She felt liberated at last.

Leyna never told any of her subsequent lovers about the assault, not even Dave. It seemed easier that way. She wasn't about to allow herself to get lost in the past, destroyed by it, particularly when the future held so much promise. She had a new apartment and a new job, and she and Dave had plans. First off, they wanted to do some bumming around in Chicago, which was now convenient to do since the city bordered Evanston.

Call it their Togetherness Tour.

Notable among the early stops was the corner of Clark and Addison streets, the site of Wrigley Field. Surprisingly, Dave hadn't taken Leyna there yet. The 1970 season had been a washout, what with the move to Des Plaines and work and all, and this summer had gotten away from them, too. Not that they had missed much. The Cubs had failed to make the playoffs in 1970, and the 1971 season was ending the same way.

With a week remaining on the Cubs' schedule, they sputtered in Dave's Valiant to the Howard Street L station in Evanston. After the twenty-minute train ride to the Addison stop, they made a beeline to the ballpark's ticket window, where, in keeping with protocol Dave had established long ago, he bought two cheap seats.

"Perfect," he said as he eyed the Terrace Reserved tickets.

At the top of the stairs leading from Wrigley's dark concourse to the grandstands, everything burst into a sublime vision of green—the field, the ivy on the outfield wall, the scoreboard in the centerfield bleachers—and Dave got goose bumps, just as he always did.

"Now," he said, "for the sport within the sport. See the Andy Frains?"

Squinting her eyes, Leyna said, "The what?"

"The ushers."

"Those men in the silly blue suits?"

"Yes. We'll want to pinpoint an old one and sneak past him into the box seats up there."

"They all look pretty old to me."

"See that one?" Dave pointed to an Andy Frain who was hunched over in the aisle dividing the Terrace Reserved section from the box seats. "He's our man."

"Well, that's not much of a challenge. I think he might be dead."

Since Leyna's leg wasn't yet up to the rigors of sprinting, Dave took her hand and pulled her past the Andy Frain, whose back was to them. They claimed seats three rows behind the dugout.

"Not bad, huh?" Dave said with a winning grin. "So close to the field we can almost touch it."

His next order of business was to flag down a beer vendor, who kindly dispensed two Old Styles.

"Now what?" asked Leyna.

"We watch some baseball."

The visiting Philadelphia Phillies were worse than the Cubs, but that wasn't evident on this sun-drenched afternoon. In the Phillies' first at-bats, before Dave and Leyna could even put a dent in their Old Styles, they took a 2-0 lead on a home run by Willie Montañez.

"Does this always happen?" Leyna asked when Montañez crossed home plate.

"Pretty much, yes."

Dave's winning grin was gone. And by the next inning, when Philadelphia went up 3-0, he was borderline sulking.

Leyna gave him a sporty punch on the shoulder and said, "Cheer up, old buddy. It's early, right? They can still win."

Dave summoned the Old Style vendor.

Milt Pappas singled in a run for the Cubs in the bottom of the third, but they left men on base in the fifth, seventh, and eighth innings.

"They really aren't very good," Leyna concluded. "It's kind of pathetic."

It became more pathetic in the ninth, when the Cubs went down quietly to end the game.

"And why exactly do you like the Cubs?" Leyna asked.

"Good question, and I have an answer. I've actually given it a lot of thought."

"I'm sure you have."

"You don't choose your team—it chooses you. I wasn't lucky enough to grow up in New York with the Yankees or in St. Louis with the Cardinals or anywhere else with something resembling a baseball team. I'm stuck with these dopes. You learn to make the best of it."

"Me? I'm just in it for the beer, the sunshine, and the company, so I would have to call this afternoon a winner."

In the following weeks, the Togetherness Tour wound through the Shedd Aquarium on the lakefront, the Art Institute on Michigan Avenue, the Maxwell Street Market by the University of Chicago, and Round Records by Loyola University. The latter stop provided the tour with a gust of momentum. After perusing Round Records' stellar collection of bootlegs and other rarities, Leyna bought *Aqualung* by Jethro Tull, a British band she knew little about but came highly recommended by her friends from work. Jethro Tull's musical wrinkle was the flute playing of Ian Anderson, and Leyna was so enamored of the group's Renaissance-rock sound that she monopolized the stereo for the next several days. As luck would have it, Jethro Tull was coming to the International Amphitheatre on October 26. Leyna couldn't resist—she picked up two cheap seats.

Located on Chicago's South Side, the Amphitheatre had opened in 1934, when Chicago was the "hog butcher for the world" and the nearby Union Stock Yards, fetid as they were, bustled with slaughterhouse splendor. The Amphitheatre's original mission was to be the headquarters for the International Livestock Exhibition, but it went on to host everything from political conventions to the NBA's Chicago Bulls. Now, though, the Union Stock Yards were history, and the Amphitheatre was as worn and frayed as the surrounding neighborhood.

Even though Dave had lived almost his whole life in the Chicago area, this was his first trip to the Amphitheatre. Once they were inside, he looked around the dank concrete concourse and said, "Doesn't seem like I've missed much all these years. This place has all the character of a bunker. At least we'll be safe if the Russians decide to nuke us."

He started walking toward their seats, but Leyna, who had already figured the place out despite it also being her first visit, tugged him the other way.

"Follow me."

She led him out of the bowels of the building and down a crowded aisle, all the way to the border of the front section, where a bearded bouncer was positioned stubbornly.

"Tickets," he said.

"Any way to get through?" Leyna asked. She placed her hand on his shoulder with a tender touch and stood on her tiptoes so that her shining face was directly in his line of vision. "I *love* Jethro Tull."

The gruff man's eyes twinkled, and he motioned her past him. Dave, however, remained blocked from the front section.

Rising to her tiptoes again, Leyna said to the bouncer, "Um, he's with me."

He let Dave through, but not before glaring at him and bellowing, "What a waste."

Leyna led Dave farther down the aisle, until only one row separated them from the edge of the stage. She brushed up against a man in front of her.

"Any way to squeeze in?"

The man smiled and made some room.

"Him, too?" she asked.

Begrudgingly, the man cleared more space.

"Thanks," Dave said.

The man just shook his head.

"Pretty great," Leyna said to Dave.

"It really is. I don't know how you did it. Incredible."

When the music started, Ian Anderson, dressed in a green felt vest and tan tights, pranced to and fro. Soon enough he noticed Leyna leaning against the stage. After laying down a momentous flute solo during "Locomotive Breath," he moved toward her and, gazing straight into her eyes, began to dance like a jester jacked on amphetamines.

The crowd went wild; Leyna just smiled; Dave did neither.

"That flute player...he was just flirting with you," said Dave, his face now crimson-colored.

Leyna burst out laughing. "That's nonsense."

"He was, I'm sure of it. What an asshole."

But alas, Leyna went home with Dave following the show, not the flute player. This was, after all, the Togetherness Tour. And for its finale the following week—on November 3, 1971—the couple ventured to the Cook County Clerk's Office in downtown Chicago.

Dave's parents were there, too, and they were dressed in their Sunday best, even though it was Wednesday. Leyna was wearing a white blouse and a snug pink skirt that accentuated her shapely calves, Dave a suit that he probably should have ironed.

With surprising zeal, considering he had already been through this six times since punching in for the day, the justice of the peace began: "We gather here to celebrate and dedicate the joy and deep union of David and Leyna. The essence…"

Dave whispered into Leyna's ear, "I love you."

"I love you, too, Dave."

"…set the tone for your entire life together. It is the visible symbol of the ongoing wedding process in…"

Dave tightened his grip on Leyna's hand, partly out of his habitual anxiousness but mostly out of excitement. Leyna's grip also tightened, with equal parts excitement and resolve.

"Do you, David, take Leyna as your wedded wife, to have and to hold from this day forward, for better, for worse, for richer, for poorer, in sickness and in health, to love and to cherish, till death do you part?"

"I do."

Dave's dad looked on proudly. Even his mom, who had never quite wiped that image from the guest bedroom out of her mind, let forth a warm smile.

"Do you, Leyna, take David as your wedded husband, to have and to hold from this day forward, for better, for worse, for richer, for poorer, in sickness and in health, to love and to cherish, till death do you part?"

"I do."

"With these rings, you are consenting to be bound together as husband and wife. The rings, please."

Dave and Leyna slipped twenty-dollar bands from J.C. Penney onto each other's fingers.

"By the authority vested in me by the State of Illinois, I now pronounce you husband and wife."

The justice of the peace nodded, and Dave and Leyna sealed the time-honored deal with a kiss.

CHAPTER 14

The ad appeared in the March 2, 1972, issue of *Rolling Stone* and took up all of page forty-three:

WANTED

(by me, Pete Townshend):

My Gibson SG Special guitar from Woodstock all that time ago. As you might remember, I foolishly threw it into the crowd at the end of The Who's performance. I haven't seen it since, and I want it back. If you know of the guitar's whereabouts, please contact Clive Lerwick. A handsome reward awaits the person who reunites me with my guitar.

In addition to Pete's plea, the ad contained a photo of a (but not *the*) Special and Clive's phone number. Clive viewed this latest assignment as a hopeless nuisance. For the life of him, he couldn't understand why Pete was treating this silly guitar like some sort of Holy Grail. Clive's phone rang day and night.

He heard from Russell Davenport, who swore he had seen someone try to barter it for chips at the Circus Circus casino in Vegas.

He heard from Steve Bardo, who remembered a shirtless man—"Big, like Tarzan?" asked Clive—using it as a walking stick at Woodstock.

He heard from Elise Fowl, who claimed to be a psychic who could put him in touch with the long-lost guitar.

He heard from Colin O'Brien, who said he had it but then blew his story when he described its color as black, an understandable gaffe since the ad was in black-and-white.

He heard from Chester Cruthers, who said it was hanging in a Texaco station in Amarillo, Texas.

He heard from Sarah Reid, who had no idea where the guitar was but wanted to leave her phone number in case Roger Daltrey had any interest in getting together with her.

Clive did not hear from Dave and Leyna Weiss, who weren't subscribers to *Rolling Stone* and hadn't picked up that particular issue on the newsstand.

Nor did Clive hear from Jimmy Fitzgerald, though he saw the ad all right. Jimmy was leafing through the issue while chowing down a breakfast of waffles in the basement apartment he shared with his buddy Raffy in Santa Cruz. Page thirty-eight, thirty-nine, forty, forty-one, forty-two, forty-three—*bam*, there it was.

The memories rushed back. He thought about the strange sunrise before Townshend tossed the guitar into the crowd. And the two girls, Darcie and Erin, he met in the Sea of Love who convinced him to check out a hippie outpost called Santa Cruz that was seventy-five miles down the coast from San Francisco. And the six laugh-filled days they spent driving there in Darcie's convertible Cutlass. And the easygoing lifestyle in Santa Cruz that won him over instantly. And the fact that he had never gotten around to leaving.

Then he wound back to the guitar.

"Look at this," he said to Raffy, who was eating waffles next to him. "Remember that Who show I told you about at Woodstock?"

Raffy eyed the ad. "Huge."

"Man, the lucky son of a bitch who has that thing."

As intrigued as he was by Townshend's search for his Woodstock guitar, Jimmy cut short his contemplations. Surf was up, and there were only a few precious hours before he and Raffy had to be at work at Aldo's Harbor House Restaurant, an old-time pasta and seafood joint on the water at Santa Cruz Harbor.

Raffy was a tall and lean Mexican American who had been doing his best impersonation of an Italian chef for the past few years at Aldo's. He was a natural. The recipes might have belonged to his bosses, the Aldobrandos, who hailed from the Italian coastal town of Sestri Levante, but Raffy had taken their fare to the next level with nonchalant pinches of this and offhand dashes of that.

When the Aldobrandos hired Jimmy as a waiter in the spring of '71, he and Raffy became fast friends, smoking pot together after work and, of course, surfing. Their apartment was a six-block walk from a point on Monterey Bay called Steamer Lane, and that was exactly how they had planned it when they had decided to get a place together. The most primo waves in Santa Cruz rolled through Steamer Lane.

Located about a mile north of the manmade hubbub at the Santa Cruz Beach Boardwalk, a kitschy amusement park reminiscent of Coney Island, Steamer Lane wasn't for the faint of heart. The swells sometimes rose as high as fifteen feet, and a shoreline consisting of jagged rock made finishing runs uniquely dicey.

Having grown up in Santa Cruz, Raffy was a much more experienced surfer than his friend from the Midwest, but the "Corn Boy" was a quick learner. He had begun in the forgiving surf at Capitola Beach shortly after arriving in Santa Cruz, riding a wide-bodied longboard, or, as some of the weathered locals called it, "a tricycle stick." By the time he met Raffy, he had moved on to the Hook at the end of 41st Street and was cutting through its sporty waves on a shortboard, which was fast and slick and demanded a high level of agility. Eventually, after observing how Jimmy could transform his cumbersome body into something almost balletic on the foamy crests, Raffy proclaimed: "I think you're ready to ride the big surf at Steamer Lane without getting hell-munched."

Maybe it was the *Rolling Stone* ad Jimmy had seen during breakfast—Christ, he didn't know—but as he and Raffy portaged their boards across coastal West Cliff Drive to the rocky point and then felt the spray from the crashing waves below, he was more inspired than usual.

"Look at it out there," Jimmy said. "And smell that salty sea air. We picked the right day to come down here, that's for sure."

"We come down here *every* day, Corn Boy. And every day, it's the same," said Raffy, his sentences elongated by thoughtful pauses between the words. He put down his board at the edge of the point and gestured toward the surf. "Bombs. Righteous bombs."

"Let's blow off work today," Jimmy said. "Why waste our time? You're the best cook I know—you could make a shit sandwich taste good. You're way too skilled to be working at that place for six bucks an hour. And I… well, I…"

Focused on sliding into his wetsuit, which served as protection from both the cold water and the sharp rocks, Raffy offered no response. After putting on his own wetsuit, Jimmy asked, "Ready to rock and roll?"

"Go ahead. I'm right behind you. *Vamos.*"

With his board secured under his arms, Jimmy jumped off the stone shelf and splashed into the bay.

"Fuck yeah. Steamer Lane."

He pulled himself onto his board, paddled out on his stomach, and waited for some action, bobbing like a piece of bait in the grayish, windswept vastness. Within seconds, an enormous wave, a "rhino" in surfer's parlance, charged toward him.

Jimmy caught it at its roiling apex and stood up. As he cut down into the wave's smooth pocket, he noticed sunlight glinting off the whitecaps ahead. Maybe it was because of the *Rolling Stone* ad he had seen while eating waffles—Christ, he didn't know—but the sight reminded him of the sunrise at Woodstock. He pondered the sense of infinite potential that had come with that moment, ignoring the spiky Steamer Lane shoreline, which he was fast approaching. Over the roar of the sea, he heard Raffy: "Bail, Corn Boy, bail."

But Jimmy, still pondering the infinite, stubbornly remained on his board.

"Corn Boy…"

When Jimmy finally jumped, he was struck—not by a rock but by an idea.

Three thousand miles away, in a three-room apartment in Lower Manhattan's Greenwich Village, Mama saw the *Rolling Stone* ad, too.

"Damn it," she said to Jumbo, who was on his third ham sandwich at the card table that served as a kitchen table. "I told you we should have kept that guitar."

"What guitar?"

"Pete Townshend's guitar from Woodstock…the one you gave to that dweeb for a whopping thirty dollars."

"Oh, that."

"Yeah, that. I knew that guitar would be priceless. I just knew it."

Jumbo kept eating.

As seemed to be the case wherever he went, Jumbo felt out of place in this latest environment. Greenwich Village wasn't the countercultural bastion it had been in the fifties, when Beats like Allen Ginsberg and Jack Kerouac had written there, or in the sixties, when folkies like Bob Dylan and Dave Van Ronk had played music there, but it remained home to a variety of—Jumbo's word—"weirdos." He saw them every day when he stepped out of their apartment building on West Fourth Street. It was an urban version of Woodstock.

Their place in Greenwich Village wasn't far from New York University, where Mama was taking postgraduate classes in film while working full-time as a coffee fetcher at Dingelhoss & Pulle Productions, an outfit best known for shooting the "Hey…leave some shampoo for me" Prell commercial. Jumbo hadn't complained when Mama had lugged him with her from Boston after being accepted at NYU. Beggars couldn't be choosers. Greenwich Village was better than his mother's basement in Corning, and it definitely was a step up from Boston. The cramped, narrow streets in that ancient city had made him claustrophobic and irritable.

Jumbo had found work manning the door at nearby Fat Cats, a cakewalk of a job because the patrons weren't exactly the fighting kind. One glare was pretty much all it took to keep the drunks in line. He filled out the rest of his time by eating, sleeping, and fucking. Jumbo was particularly good at fucking, which was an important reason why Mama kept him around.

Maybe it was the *Rolling Stone* ad she had just seen—Christ, she didn't know—but Mama was inspired.

"I'm going out for a couple hours," she said.

When she returned, she was bearing a 35mm movie camera, a tripod, and two umbrella lights from Dingelhoss & Pulle.

"This time we're going to film it."

Jumbo undressed.

After carefully arranging the equipment by the foot of the bed, Mama rolled the camera and then rolled onto Jumbo. She felt almost petite whenever she was in his powerful arms. With his mind mostly blank, Jumbo set Mama on her back and proceeded. He let his instincts do the work, just as he had done on the offensive line in high school, when he had moved with such fluidity.

"Give it to me!" Mama yowled, her meaty legs flailing in the air. "Give it to me!"

Jumbo answered the call—repeatedly, in fact, until she had been transformed into a damp, quivering mass.

A few days later Mama borrowed a projector from Dingelhoss & Pulle, and she and Jumbo watched the images from their fuckfest flicker on the living room wall.

"This looks hotter than I remember," Mama said. "And believe me, it was hot."

"Definitely," Jumbo offered, chewing indifferently on a ham sandwich. "Hot."

"Look at you go. A regular Adonis," Mama marveled.

"A what?"

"Never mind." Switching off the projector, she said, "Let's try again. I want to film it again."

Mama had an idea.

CHAPTER 15

The anthropologist didn't have any ideas, and he hadn't for a while. Furthermore, he didn't know anything about Pete Townshend's guitar, though he did remember the sunrise from Woodstock.

Alúna hadn't been what he'd imagined. After a band of hellions—wolves in hippie duds—materialized following first light, he began to wonder if it had even been real. They needed money, and the anthropologist seemed like an easy mark. Facing the sun with his arms outstretched, he didn't see them coming, but he sure felt them when they rolled him over and took his wallet.

Fate, oh cruel fate.

Now the anthropologist had no cash and no ID in addition to having no car, and he was forced to rely entirely on the kindness of strangers to get home to Ithaca from Woodstock. The ride was rough, taking three days because it wound through Rhode Island.

When he finally walked through the front door of his tidy two-story home—eyes bloodshot, body rank, turtleneck tattered—his wife was appalled.

"My God," she said, "you look like you've been dipped into the La Brea Tar Pits."

Apparently, she had been appalled for quite some time. Within weeks of his return, she walked out the front door of the tidy two-story home carrying two suitcases.

"Where are you going?" asked the anthropologist.

"To find myself. It sure isn't happening here. Not that you probably noticed."

The anthropologist didn't even know what that meant, which bothered him all the more. In the following months, he spent a good deal of time turning over her words, mostly in Yonder's smoke-filled pad.

"She'll be back, Nat," Yonder reassured one evening, as he had done many previous evenings. "Trust me, sometimes it takes awhile to find yourself. It's only been, what, a year? And if she never shows up? Even better. You're a free man."

"Pass that joint, will you?" responded the anthropologist, who hadn't shaved since Woodstock and was now sporting a tangled beard.

Like many people in the working world, Yonder had fallen into his profession. Characterized by a square jaw, a naturally toned physique, and a winning smile, he looked like he could have been an athlete or even an actor, but he had lacked the focus to parlay his charisma into an element of accomplishment—hence his nickname. His fortunes changed, however, after he dropped out of Ithaca College and moved back home to Corning. One night while propping up the bar at a local tavern, he got to talking with a man who let it be known that he had access to vast quantities of marijuana. With little else in the way of prospects, Yonder began tapping into this newfound resource, and he eventually found himself at the helm of a business.

Now he was a man of means, though he lived simply, the better to fly under the radar. His apartment's only distinguishing feature was an upside-down wooden rowboat that was encircled by a scuffed-up leather couch, a few folding chairs, and a stereo. Yonder liked the way the rowboat brought a bit of the beach to his apartment, and it also made for a comfortable footrest. Primarily, though, it was for work: its long, wide belly afforded him plenty of space to clean the seeds from his shipments of pot and weigh out bags.

The anthropologist appreciated the young man's industriousness, even if it was misguided. At first he stopped by Yonder's only intermittently, but the trips from Ithaca to Corning steadily increased. It was an easy enough drive through the thicket and past the tip of Seneca Lake on Route 414. And it got him away. Away from his no-longer-tidy home. Away from the classroom lectures that had become so very tiresome to deliver. Away from himself. By 1972, more than two years after his accidental trip to Woodstock, Yonder's had become his home away from home.

The anthropologist found refuge in the mindless, unconventional rhythm there. Most Mondays at around 6 p.m., for example, Big Mitch from the Corning Glass Works' windshield plant would stop by to pick up his weekly stash of pot, followed by Buster the orderly, Erica the enchanting barkeep, Dale the whatever, and sometimes Tom the guidance counselor. Tuesdays often belonged to Chip the one-eyed baker, Trey the all-state lacrosse midfielder, Jinnene the single mom, and a rotating cast of other characters. Who knew the consumer market for illicit drugs was so routinized?

Now it was 7:30 p.m. on a Wednesday, so the anthropologist was anticipating the staccato knock of Jason the bespectacled photographer from *The Leader*. When it sounded, Yonder swung his feet off the rowboat, bounced up from the scuffed-up leather couch, and opened the door. He gave Jason a soul shake and sat back down on the couch.

"What's up, Nat?" Jason said.

The anthropologist nodded hello.

"The usual, right?" Yonder asked Jason.

"Yep."

Yonder laid a pot-filled baggy on the scale. "Exactly a half-ounce—right on the money. Speaking of which, do you have yours?"

Jason passed along a crisp twenty, and Yonder presented the bag. "Looks like another tasty treat," Jason said. "See you in a week?"

"We'll be here."

Following classes the next day, the anthropologist rode once more to Yonder's. He had been there for a spell when he looked at his watch. *It's 7:10—Dennis the glassblower should be here momentarily.*

The knock came on cue, but the anthropologist observed that it was more forceful than usual. The subtle difference went unnoticed by Yonder, who swung his feet off the rowboat and bounced up from the scuffed-up leather couch. When he opened the door, he saw not Dennis the glassblower but a Glock that was aimed at his face.

"Police! We have a warrant!"

Yonder's winning smile did a 180 as the officer pushed him up against the wall. Four more cops streamed into the apartment, pistols drawn, and made a quick assessment. They saw a scale on the belly of the rowboat, an empty pizza box on the scuffed-up leather coach, and a horror-stricken bearded man in a folding chair.

"Who the hell are *you*?" one of the cops demanded.

"N-N-N-Nathan Diller. *Dr.*—"

"Put your hands up!"

Seconds later the horror-stricken bearded man was on his stomach being frisked. Everything on his person—sixty-four dollars, his driver's license, and his school ID—was confiscated, culminating with a final indignity: the circulation-stopping sensation of handcuffs clamping shut around his wrists.

Fate, oh cruel fate.

CHAPTER 16

Dave and Leyna were still moving up in the world. He was now deputy sports editor at the *Herald*, and she had carved out a place for herself at the YWCA as a communications associate—promotions that were accompanied by bumps in pay. Thus, the continuing journey into adulthood brought them to the doorstep of 447 Greenwood Street in Evanston, where the prospect of home ownership loomed in the form of a redbrick prairie box.

Gazing up at the imposing square frame, two stories high with a steeply pitched roof that was tiled in black, Dave winced. "I'm starting to feel old, like I'm my dad," he said to Leyna. "It's only a matter of time before I have a combover like his."

"Now that would be a sight."

Renee Birchweather, the overbearing Coldwell Banker agent, had told them this would be "a perfect starter house," but as the old bat gave them a tour, Dave couldn't find anything "starter" about it. Leyna saw sunlight streaming into the cozy family room; Dave saw the darkness of debtor's prison. Leyna saw spaciousness in the master bedroom, highlighted by not one but two closets; Dave saw the possibility of losing the shirt off his back. Leyna saw family dinners in the dining room; Dave saw food stamps. Leyna saw such colorful potential in the flowerbeds out back; Dave saw fallow fields. Leyna saw opportunities for entertaining in the finished basement, which had a bar; Dave saw stress-induced alcoholism.

"I just love it," Leyna said as they walked the four blocks back to their apartment on Burnham Place. "What about you?"

"It seems...overwhelming."

"I know, right? But for what they're asking, it's a steal. Isn't it charming?"

"I suppose it is. It doesn't make you nervous?"

"It makes me feel just the opposite, actually. Growing up, I always imagined a home like this, but it didn't seem possible. Now it does. This will be great…trust me."

It certainly was a long way from the pond where they had met five years earlier. But every time Dave looked at Leyna, his hormones still whirled like they had that day. There was no turning back. At the house closing, he swallowed hard and signed his name over and over as Birchweather shoved stacks of unintelligible papers at him.

Afterward they returned to kindly Burnham Place, and Dave rested up for work that night. It was going to be a rough one. Since the sports editor, Randy Peters, was on vacation, Dave was in charge of the *Herald*'s coverage of the high school football playoffs, a task that would involve coordinating eight reporters who would be producing a total of eight stories and three sidebars, all under a tight deadline. This would be his biggest assignment yet as deputy sports editor.

Dave decided he'd need something extra to help him through this test, and he knew exactly what: the Special, which was hermetically sealed in a moving box. After digging it out with the care of an archaeologist, he detoured to the kitchen to say goodbye to Leyna, who was packing dishes.

"What's with the guitar?" she asked.

"A good-luck charm. I figure everyone can rub it as sort of a stress reliever."

"Whatever works."

"Just trying to loosen things up a bit, maybe build some camaraderie."

"I'm sure everything will go great, with or without the guitar. You'll… you'll knock it out of the park. How's that for some sports terminology?"

"Wrong sport for tonight, but nice try."

Dave gave her a smooch and rushed out the door to a '68 Chevy Nova that he and Leyna had picked up after the Valiant had finally ceased to start. The Nova wasn't much better, and Dave had been hoping to buy something new, but now that homeowner expenses were suddenly bearing down on him, he would have to make do. Among its shortcomings, the Nova's shocks were shot, causing the Special to rattle around in the passenger's seat as he drove the forty-five minutes to work.

The *Herald*, owned by the venerable Paddock family, had been printed since 1871. It paled next to the region's Big Three—the *Chicago Tribune*, *Chicago Sun-Times*, and *Chicago Daily News*—but it was the paper of choice for many residents of the city's northwest suburbs, as evidenced by its robust circulation of 100,000. Those readers craved the type of hyper-local coverage the *Herald* delivered, especially when their high school football teams were playing.

Here, at least, Dave was well-served by his built-in anxiety. Success in the newspaper business was predicated on fear—fear of blowing a deadline—and Dave would sooner crawl naked across shards of glass than be late with an assignment. The Special in his arms, he hurried through the expansive newsroom, weaving around the islands of wooden desks. After clearing some of the clutter from his own workspace, he began jotting notes for the daily budget meeting with Cross and the other editors.

At 5 p.m. sharp, Dave reported to the conference room. Cross, seated at the head of the table, barely lifted his eyes from the scribbles on his notepad to greet him. With newsprint ringing the cuffs of his white shirt from another day spent rifling through newspapers, Cross was literally an ink-stained wretch. He was only forty-two but looked a decade older, the result of too much food and too little sleep.

Cross worked his way around the table from the news editor to the business editor before fixing an impatient eye on Dave. "Okay, onto sports," Cross said. "How many games are we covering tonight?"

"Eight," Dave answered.

"Which one are you leading with?"

"Maine South-Deerfield—that's the biggest one."

"Who's covering it?"

"Withers."

"He's an idiot. Why not Holt?"

"Withers has been covering Maine South all season. He knows the team better than anyone. Holt's doing Hersey-Conant. That's a big one, too."

Holt, Mike Holt, was the best writer on the sports staff—the apple of Cross's eye—and he knew it. One time Dave stopped by Holt's apartment to drop off notes for a story, and he answered the door wearing a red silk robe, like he was the second coming of Hugh Hefner in addition to being the best writer on the sports staff. Some minutes into their small talk in the doorway, a sultry voice from the bedroom called: "Mike, aren't you coming back?"

Holt was also a hothead, especially under deadline. If he had writer's block, he'd sometimes blurt out "Fuck!" as a prelude to disconnecting the telephone on his desk and throwing it as far as he could. The harried late-nighters would look up from their typewriters to watch the phone arc across the newsroom, and after it landed in a corner or against a wall, they'd start tapping again as if nothing had happened.

"And the desk?" Cross continued. "Who's working the desk with you?"

"Lightfoot, and Erickson's doing agate."

"Very good, Weiss. Just don't shit all over this, okay?"

Following the budget meeting, Dave killed some time by copyediting a profile Withers had written on Chicago Bears quarterback Bobby Douglass. Among his teammates, Douglas was notable mainly for reeking like booze in the huddle, but such indiscretions rarely made it into print in the rah-rah world of sports journalism. This piece, scheduled to run a couple days from now as part of the preview of the Bears-Vikings game, extolled the virtues of the QB's "rocket arm."

Dave's train of thought was broken when Lightfoot—or "Lighthead," as Holt liked to call him—popped by his desk. Lightfoot was decent at his job, but he never looked people in the eye, which made Dave feel awkward. Lightfoot grabbed the Special and asked, "What's this?"

"Believe it or not, Pete Townshend's guitar from Woodstock. It's a good-luck charm for tonight. Strange, I know, but like my wife said, whatever—"

"Run that by me again."

"It's Pete Townshend's guitar from Woodstock. Like my—"

"You know he's been looking for this, right?"

"No way."

"Yeah, he took out a full-page ad about it in *Rolling Stone* two or three years ago and then another one this year."

"I don't know how I could have missed it."

"I have the issues back at my apartment. He's offering a reward."

"How much?"

"The ads didn't say, but I assume it's substantial. How did you get it anyway?"

"Dumb luck. I was at Woodstock, and I ran into a guy who had it. He suddenly decided he didn't want it, so he sold it to me for thirty dollars."

Lightfoot shook his head in amazement and returned to his desk. Staring at the Special, Dave mulled over this startling revelation: *Townshend obviously is desperate to have his guitar back—the poor guy—and I could really use the extra money right now. On the other hand, he offered it up to the masses at Woodstock fair and square, and it's priceless to me. Nope, I would never give it up.* With that, he returned to Bobby Douglas's rocket arm.

At 6 p.m. sharp, Dave met with his reporters—Holt, Withers, Goldstein, Sanders, Everett, Siptkowski, Blaney, and Garrison—to brief them on their assignments and on the purpose of the Special before sending them on their way. Four hours later, they started trickling back into the building to write their stories, first Garrison and then Blaney. En route to their desks, the two reporters stopped and rubbed the guitar, as they had been advised to do.

Withers showed up fifteen minutes later, looking as if he had been blown through the door by a tornado. His shirt was rumpled and only partially tucked in, and tufts of his thick brown hair were sticking straight up. Nevertheless, he found his way to Dave's desk. "I've only got thirty minutes to write this story—please don't let me fuck up," Withers intoned before giving the Special a hearty rub.

Sanders, Siptkowski, Everett, and Goldstein followed the same routine upon entering the newsroom, minus the Withers-esque prayer.

Cherie, a young news reporter whose ass everyone admired, came over and rubbed the Special, too. Never mind that she wasn't part of the sports department. As the person assembling the police report, she was under a lot of pressure herself trying to keep up with the surge in criminal activity in the northwest suburbs on this unseasonably warm autumn evening.

True to form, Holt was the last to arrive, the better to make a dramatic entrance. Furthermore, any ritualistic rubbing of the Special was beneath him, as he demonstrated by swaggering straight past Dave's desk. He was wearing a wide-collared polyester disco shirt, and he smelled of fancy cologne. This irked Dave, who couldn't understand why Holt felt compelled to wear a disco shirt and fancy cologne in order to stand on the sideline at a high school football game.

Withers surprised everyone by writing his story in under thirty minutes, but he wasn't in the clear yet, not nearly: his prose still had to run the copyediting gauntlet. Gripping the Special, Withers grimaced each time Dave marked the sheet of paper with a red pencil. When Dave reached the end, Withers asked, "How badly did I mess up?"

"Not badly at all, just a couple misspellings. The story's solid."

Withers breathed a sigh of relief.

At that very moment a desk island away, Holt blurted, "Fuck!" Everyone looked up reflexively to watch the phone fly, but there was nothing to see. Rather than wreak havoc, Holt went and rubbed the Special before quietly returning to his writing. It was that kind of night. Like clockwork, the eight stories and three sidebars were written, copyedited, and typeset.

The tension in the sports department dissipated, and Holt, grinning widely, rolled over to Dave's desk. "My story was solid gold, right?"

Dave wanted to tell him it sucked (even though it didn't) just to remove that smirk from his face, but he restrained himself. "Solid gold, Holt."

Holt picked up the Special, placing it between his legs so that the neck was pointed out in front of him. After waving the neck back and forth by rotating his hips, he started rubbing it in a short and fast motion, like he was jerking off. There were laughs all around, even from Dave and especially from Cherie whose ass everyone admired.

"All right, all right, enough already," Dave finally interrupted. "Party's over."

He took back the Special and whisked it away to the Nova, its purpose for the night having been served. He then returned to his desk, where Lightfoot was waiting.

"You need anything else from me?" Lightfoot asked.

"Nah. Go ahead, get out of here."

"What about you?"

"I'm going to stick around for another hour or so—wait for the presses to roll, catch up on some paperwork."

"Okay. Have a good one."

As Lightfoot neared the door, Dave yelled across the newsroom, "Hey, nice job tonight."

Lightfoot nodded and continued on. Once outside, he scanned the parking lot to make sure the coast was clear. *No one here. Should I do it? I may as well try. The car will never be open anyway.* Lightfoot peered inside the Nova's passenger-side window. *Right there for the taking.* He pressed the knob on the handle…and the door opened. *What a moron.* In actuality, Dave was merely unlucky. The lock had a tendency to jam, and this was one of those times.

Lightfoot snatched the Special by its neck, raced across the blacktop, and dumped his score into the hatchback of his Ford Pinto. Driving the eight blocks to his apartment, he thought about all the things he could buy with the money from this guitar. A La-Z Boy recliner. A color TV—two color TVs, one for the living room and one for the bedroom. A fishing boat to use on the Chain O'Lakes—why not? A vacation to California.

Lightfoot bounded up the two flights of stairs to his apartment. His fingers trembling with excitement, he rummaged through a pile of old magazines. *Jackpot.* Lightfoot dialed the phone number in the ad, and Clive answered, "'Ello."

The deep, clearly annoyed voice knocked Lightfoot off-stride.

"'Ello."

"Yes. My name is…ah…ah…I have Pete Townshend's guitar from Woodstock."

"Bloody Christ, what now?"

"I said I have Pete Townshend's guitar from Woodstock."

"I heard you. I've heard it a million times."

"This is no joke."

"Okay, let's get this over with. How do you know you have the right guitar?"

"Because it's a red Gibson SG…and its edges are nicked, like it was banged…and I got it from someone who was at Woodstock…and…anyway, I'm positive this is it."

"Where is it?"

"In the back of my car."

"And where's your bloody car?"

"I'm in Arlington H—. I'm in Ar—. I'm in…"

The harder Lightfoot tried to force the words out, the more they were flattened by his conscience, which had appeared out of nowhere.

"Arlington what? Virginia? Texas? Bloody Christ."

"Ar—"

This is the stupidest thing I've ever done. If anyone finds out, I'll be fired. It's not my guitar to sell. And I don't even like to fish.

"'Ello…'ello…"

Lightfoot slammed down the receiver. *I have to get to the paper before Dave leaves.* He screeched to the *Herald*, and the Nova was still in the parking lot. "Phew," he said to himself, putting the Special back where it belonged.

Fifteen minutes later Dave was on his way home, none the wiser. It had been a long day, and all he wanted to do was see Leyna.

CHAPTER 17

The world Dave and Leyna had settled into seemed like it was right out of "Our House" by Crosby, Stills & Nash, the band that had sung to them under the stars at Woodstock. The song was about the idyllic happenings at a home adorned with vases filled with flowers, embers glowing in a fireplace, and two cats in the yard. Its vibe fit the prairie box to a T, even if there weren't two cats in the yard.

Their neighbor Darna Schwartz often came over to visit while Leyna was digging in her garden. "So much more color than when the Bartons lived here," Darna told her new friend.

The cozy family room proved to be perfect for reading, especially when sunlight streamed in.

The basement bar served as a centerpiece for entertaining, most recently at a gathering of people from work and around the neighborhood to celebrate the beginning of summer. Withers arrived an hour late after getting lost on the way there, and Holt ended up leaving with earthy Natalie Tross from the YWCA, even though she had summed him up thusly to Dave earlier in the evening: "That guy in the polka-dot shirt looks like a complete jerk." Cherie was there, too, and the men admired her ass when their wives or girlfriends were a safe distance away.

The spacious master bedroom fulfilled its role more than ably. For the heck of it one night after dinner and the Woody Allen movie *Annie Hall*, Dave and Leyna even had adventure sex in the extra closet. (It was a big closet.)

And there were Sunday dinners in the dining room with Dave's parents. His mom seemed quite pleased with how everything had turned out; Dave sensed this because she showed Leyna how to make her famous leg of lamb.

The only fly in the ointment was the placement of the Special, which had been banished from the living room to the basement after Leyna had said in her most tactful voice, "It would look fantastic hanging behind the bar."

All in all, however, he hadn't become old like his dad. He was still Dave. His nerves had quieted, too, now that he had grown accustomed to making the monthly mortgage payment and had realized he and Leyna wouldn't wind up living under a bridge.

Yet there was another step to climb, or at least Leyna thought so. At the dining room table one morning not long after their welcome-to-summer party, as Dave was fortifying himself with a cup of coffee, he asked a question that seemed innocent: "So, what do you have planned today?"

"I think we should have a baby."

Dave didn't spit up his coffee, but he didn't swallow it either. It just kind of pooled in his mouth until he forced it down and thought of something to say: "But I have to work today."

Giggling, Leyna said, "Not today, dummy. In general."

"But, um, we've never really talked seriously about this. A casual reference here and there but never—"

"Exactly. So that's what we're doing now: talking seriously about it."

"Don't you want to try out a couple cats first, see how that goes?"

"I'm trying to be serious, Dave."

"So am I."

"We don't need cats."

"Why not? There's nothing wrong with cats."

"Of course there isn't, but—"

"But what?"

"But we've been together eight years, and we've been married for almost six of those years. We both have secure jobs, and we have this house, which, I might add, has an extra bedroom. I'm ready…*we're* ready. We could give our child such a wonderful life. It will be great…trust me."

Just like that, Dave was anxious again:

- What if he lost his job?
- What if Leyna lost her job?
- What if they lost the house?
- What if they couldn't give their child a wonderful life?
- Good lord, what if the three of them wound up living under a bridge?

"Dave? Are you there?"

"I believe so."

"Well?"

"Give me a little time to let this sink in."

Dave hadn't been around babies much, and that was by design. Frankly, they freaked him out. Any attempts to reason with them were futile—they simply spit up in response. Worse, babies were Petri dishes in diapers. They were sick all the time, which meant that Mom and Dad were sick all the time. How anyone withstood the rigors of parenthood was beyond him.

But there was no turning back. Within a few weeks, he swallowed hard and said, "You may as well go off the pill. Let's do it." And therein was the upside. Dave had been so busy brooding, he hadn't even considered this indisputable truth: doing it meant doing it.

The first month, Dave awoke in the wee hours one night to Leyna shaking his shoulder.

"Dave…Dave…Dave."

His eyes snapped open. *Is the house on fire? Are burglars downstairs? Is a repo man at our front door?*

"Dave, are you awake?"

Leyna slid her hand down to his penis.

"I am now."

"Good, because I should be ovulating."

When they were done doing it, Dave went back to sleep. He awoke again to Leyna shaking his shoulder, and this time the morning light was shining into his eyes.

"Dave, are you awake?"

Dave understood the drill: he would place his trust in Leyna's cue, similar to everything else in life, except this latest endeavor would involve a significant uptick in sex. They continued at a Ruthian pace until Leyna stopped ovulating. When Dr. Graham's office called several weeks later to tell her the results of her pregnancy test were negative, her exquisitely hopeful face flashed with disappointment, but she bucked up quickly.

"Oh well," she said. "We'll just have to try again."

Conveniently, "again" arrived on one of Dave's days off. He was tending to the first bullet point on his list of household chores—a fruitless attempt to replace the Nova's burned-out dome light—when Leyna jiggled up to the car bralessly.

"What are you working on, Dave?"

By early afternoon he had given up on his chores and was in the family room watching the Cubs. As a grounder rolled through the legs of Cubs second baseman Manny Trillo, Leyna plopped down next to him on the couch. She was fresh out of the shower, "covered" by a bath towel that was, Dave thought, so tiny it might have passed for a cocktail napkin.

"Any score, Dave?"

When Dr. Graham's office called several weeks later to say that the test results were negative, Leyna didn't buck up quite as quickly, but she stayed on point.

"I guess I was being too optimistic," she said. "This might take longer than I thought. We'll just have to keep trying."

"It's all we can do."

Indeed, Dave was committed to doing it, and he remained so in the third, fourth, fifth, six, seventh, eighth, and ninth months. In month ten, however, their efforts took a clinical turn.

At the dining room table on a rainy Saturday morning, Leyna announced, "I made an appointment with Dr. Graham for us to find out about fertility testing."

"You did? Why?"

"Isn't it obvious? We've been trying for almost a year. Something must be wrong."

"Nothing's wrong."

"You think this is normal?"

"I guess. I don't know."

"Clearly."

"What's that supposed to mean?"

"That you don't seem emotionally invested in this."

"How much more invested could I be? I've been like a stud horse, not that I'm complaining. On the contrary."

Leyna sighed.

"Okay, okay," Dave said, "we'll go see Dr. Graham."

A series of tests revealed no particular problem, though the doctor did prescribe clomiphene to Leyna in order to stimulate her ovulation.

With a whiff of desperation in her voice, she said to Dave, "Maybe this will work."

In month eleven, he was under the kitchen sink, laboring without success to fix a leaky pipe, when he heard a shrill beckoning from upstairs: "Dave, get up here!"

He reported to the bedroom, and after taking off his clothes and slipping between the sheets, he started to engage in his usual foreplay.

"Don't touch my boobs—they hurt from the clomiphene. Just get straight to it."

In month eighteen, he was peacefully reading Tom Wolfe's *The Painted Word* under an oak tree in the backyard. He saw the bedroom window open and considered jumping the fence.

"Dave!"

Leyna didn't bother to even fake an orgasm; Dave had one only because it was his duty.

At the *Herald* in month twenty-one, Cherie stopped by Dave's desk while he was writing up notes for the budget meeting. Parking her hands on his shoulders, she asked, "What's up, Dave?"

"Oh, hi. Not much. Just gearing up for the daily reckoning with Cross."

Cherie laughed.

"What's up with you?" he asked.

"Same old." Her grip on Dave's shoulders tightened. "Not to get too personal or anything, but you seem like you've been dragging lately. Everything okay?"

"Everything's fine. Just some friction on the home front—no big deal. Thanks for asking, though."

"Sounds like you and Leyna need a fun night out. Why don't you come over for dinner Saturday night with me and Gordon? I'll cook my specialty: lasagna."

"Yum, I love lasagna. I'll mention it to Leyna."

The next morning at the dining room table, Dave said, "Cherie was a nice enough to invite us over Saturday night for dinner with her and her boyfriend. Gordon, I think his name is. We don't have anything else going on, do we?"

"No."

"Want to go?"

"Not really."

"Why not?"

"Cherie is kind of slutty, and I've never even met this latest boyfriend."

"Slutty? You've always gotten along well with Cherie, and since when have you had a problem with meeting new people?"

"I don't know."

"Okay, this isn't about Cherie or her boyfriend. It's about the fact that you never want to do *anything* anymore."

"That's not true."

"Name the last time we went out and did something fun."

She looked down at the table and fidgeted.

"You used to be the life of the party, Leyna. What happened?"

"Nothing has happened. Maybe that's the point."

"There it is." Shaking his head, Dave continued, "Everything was fine until you started wanting to have this baby."

"Yes, I want to have a baby, and what's wrong with that? I can't believe you don't feel the same way."

"I do feel the same way, but I'm trying not to let it ruin my life. You're obsessed with this—it's all you ever think about. I love you, Leyna. Isn't that enough?"

"Honestly? No."

"What do you mean 'no'?"

"I need something more. Can't you see? I want a family."

"We're a family—you and me."

"I know, but I feel like something's missing. I can't help it."

"Well, I have no idea what to do about that."

"Neither do I."

In month twenty-five, Dave dragged his aching carcass into the house after finally putting the sports section to bed. The night had been a disaster. Lightfoot had called in sick, leaving the desk undermanned; Withers had fucked up colossally by filing his story an hour late; and Holt had heaved his telephone across the newsroom.

As Dave reached the top of the stairs, he heard sobbing from the other side of the bedroom door. His head bowed, he placed his hand on the doorknob, but he couldn't gather the will to turn it. Instead he retreated to the basement, stopping first in the kitchen to pull a bottle of Old Style from the refrigerator.

Dave switched on the basement light, sat on a stool, and rested his Old Style on the yellow Formica bartop. Between sips of beer, he peeled off small pieces of the bottle's moist label, wadding them up one by one. *What a hopeless mess this has become. I sure didn't see it coming. Maybe I should have, not that it would have made a difference anyway.*

Dave looked up and studied the Special, but it provided no relief. After a while, he wanted to tear the cursed thing off the wall.

CHAPTER 18

It was business as usual at Mojo Dogs: a lunchtime line stretched out the door. This was the fifteenth restaurant Jimmy and Raffy had opened in northern California in the past eight years, and it was all they could do to keep up with the demand.

Jimmy's idea in the Steamer Lane surf had been so ingeniously obvious he was surprised he hadn't thought of it sooner. He and Raffy would run a hot dog joint in the tradition of those on seemingly every street corner in Chicago, except their place would have a twist: in addition to traditional links, it would offer exotic varieties that would cater to the California appetite for all things "out there." Raffy would do the cooking, and Jimmy would handle everything else.

"So that's why I almost surfed into the rocks," Jimmy had told Raffy after they had returned safely ashore. "The idea just came to me out of nowhere, and I didn't want to let it go. It's a can't-miss deal. Are you in?"

"No shit I'm in, Corn Boy. I've lived my whole life in Santa Cruz, and I'll probably spend the rest of it here, too. This could be the closest I ever come to going somewhere, if you know what I mean. When do we start?"

They returned to their basement apartment, and Jimmy called his oldest brother Mickey, who had made a fortune as a trader at the Chicago Mercantile Exchange. After a few minutes of the usual pleasantries, Jimmy outlined his plan.

"How much do you need?" Mickey asked.

"I don't know, you tell me. Seems like twenty grand would get us rolling."

"Hang on a second. Let me run some numbers."

Jimmy drummed his fingers against the kitchen table.

"Yeah, I can do that," Mickey said. "Twenty thousand works."

Meeting Raffy's anxious gaze across the kitchen, Jimmy raised a fist in the air. "Yes!"

"So does this mean you're not coming home anytime soon?" Mickey asked.

"I'm hoping that's exactly what it means. If I'm still out here, it'll be because I'm kicking ass."

"You kick it, and make me some money along the way, will you?"

"Don't worry, brother. Like I said, you've got a 20 percent stake in the business, and me and my friend Raffy have 40 percent each. You won't regret it."

Jimmy and Raffy promptly quit their jobs at Aldo's and leased a space by the San Lorenzo River over on Laurel Street that had previously housed a Jack in the Box. Jimmy decorated the inside of the restaurant with Cubs memorabilia (a Chicago touch) and surfing pictures (a California touch). He remembered seeing two giant fiberglass wieners on the rooftop of a Chicago restaurant called Superdawg; painted as a man and a woman and sporting arms, legs, and wide smiles, they had looked like they were having a blast up there. The idea was good enough to rip off, and Jimmy commissioned two fiberglass wieners for the rooftop of the converted Jack in the Box, except his were mounted on surfboards and clad in swimsuits. He called them the Surfing Wieners.

"They'll see the wieners on the roof," Jimmy told Raffy, "and that will draw them in. The rest is up to you. It's a can't-miss formula."

Sure enough, people stopped to gaze, then came in to graze on the banquet of bunned delicacies Raffy's imagination had produced. Among his experimentations were elk sausage blended with smoked gouda cheese; pork sausage with jalapeños and a pineapple glaze; smoked chicken sausage slathered with goat butter and sprinkled with roasted garlic cloves; "Fire in the Hole!" pork sausage mixed with Serrano peppers; and vegetarian sausage made with heavily seasoned tofu and covered with partially melted chunks of Wisconsin cheddar cheese.

The menu was subject to Raffy's moods and turned over daily, which added to the intrigue. There was, however, one staple—the traditional Chicago-style hot dog—and it was the biggest seller. Steamed, served on a poppy-seed bun, and topped with mustard (never, ever ketchup), chopped onions, fluorescent-green relish, tomato wedges, a pickle spear, and celery salt, it was a magnificent taste of home for the many transplants from the Midwest.

Soon after Mojo Dogs opened for business, one such transplant—Dixon, Illinois, native and California governor Ronald Reagan—saw the Surfing Wieners when he was passing through Santa Cruz on his way up to Sacramento. He couldn't resist stopping.

Jimmy, working the counter, recognized him instantly when he breezed through the door, not the least bit encumbered by the dark suit and starched shirt he was wearing in the summer heat. A younger, stockier man—probably security, Jimmy thought—walked in with him. Just like in his pictures, Reagan's hair looked as if it had been slicked back with dark brown shoe polish. Jimmy didn't care for Reagan's restrictive social policies, but the way he had it figured, any customer was a good customer.

"Hey, Governor," Jimmy said. "What can I get for you?"

Reagan was distracted by the Cubs memorabilia on the walls. Eyeing it nostalgically, he said, "You know, I used to announce Cubs games on the radio."

"I wasn't aware of that."

"It was long before your time. The 1930s."

"So you've never seen them win a World Series either, huh?"

Reagan chuckled and said, "Well, facts are stubborn little things, aren't they? But stay positive. The Cubs have a new manager…what's his name again?"

"Whitey Lockman."

"That's right. I see good things ahead."

"In the meantime, see anything you'd like to eat?"

"Well, let's have a look," Reagan said, shifting his focus to the brightly colored menu on the wall behind the counter. "Wild boar sausage? That's quite something."

"Your best bet is probably the Chicago-style dog. Nothing too exotic. You'll like it. The fries are really good, too. Fresh cut."

"Okay, then, I'll try the Chicago-style hot dog and your fresh-cut fries."

Jimmy even had his photo taken with Reagan—his first celebrity customer—and sent it to the *Santa Cruz Sentinel*, reasoning that any publicity short of food poisoning would be good publicity, even in these liberal parts. The picture certainly couldn't have hurt because the lines continued to grow. Soon a second Mojo Dogs opened in Santa Cruz, and by 1976 Jimmy and Raffy had expanded beyond their home turf with stores in Gilroy, Los Gatos, San Jose, and Redwood City. Three years later they had conquered Fremont, San Mateo, Pacifica, Stanford, and Daly City to the north and Salinas, Marina, and Monterey to the south. And most recently, Berkeley, across the bay from San Francisco, had been sacked. The Surfing Wieners were popping up everywhere.

There was even a company headquarters a few blocks from the original restaurant, not that Jimmy felt the need to be there day and night anymore. He now had "people" to do much of the legwork: a CFO and the CFO's underlings, a human resources director and the human resources director's underlings, and so on. The Surfing Wieners had taken on lives of their own.

Jimmy had used his newfound spoils to buy a 2,500-square-foot Spanish-style villa that he shared with a Golden Retriever named Sam, a parrot named Fred whose favorite word was "tits," and whichever woman was his love interest du jour. Raffy had a house, too—a 2,500-square-foot Mediterranean-style villa—and he shared his with two brothers and an ever-changing assortment of cousins whose names Jimmy could never remember.

Unlike Jimmy, Raffy was still on the go. In fact, the bigger things got, the faster he moved, zipping up and down the coast on his sleek Suzuki GS750 motorcycle—farther than he ever could have imagined—to visit the various Mojo Dogs. These were *his* sausages, and he wanted to ensure that the thousands being served up each day were just right.

Despite the changes the years had brought, one routine remained the same, though now it started with a ring of a telephone instead of a knock on a bedroom door in the old basement apartment:

"You already?" Jimmy answered groggily, propping the phone receiver between his head and his pillow.

"Wake up, Corn Boy. Surf's up. *Vamos.*"

Jimmy nudged his love interest du jour: a platinum blonde named

Gayle from the marketing department at company headquarters. Jimmy didn't know much about her performance at work—she was new to the job, after all—but he had already learned that she was a titan in the sack.

"I gotta go, hun. There's a bunch of food in the fridge, so make yourself some breakfast if you want. I'll talk to you later on."

Both the Spanish-style villa and the Mediterranean-style villa were within walking distance of Steamer Lane, which was just how Jimmy and Raffy had planned it. They met on the rocky point, and as they were putting on their wetsuits, Jimmy asked, "You were up at Berkeley yesterday, right?"

"Yeah, and it was mind-blowing, like the Vatican or something. The people just kept rolling in. This could be our best store yet."

"Wait till you see San Francisco. We're going to hit that town like a steamroller. Literally, our store will be about as big as the Vatican."

"For real?"

"Well, not that big, obviously, but the drawings Dale put together are beyond belief. The Surfing Wieners alone are going to be, like, thirty feet high. Maybe you can drop by the office after this and give the drawings a look."

"No can do. I have to head down south today. You just build the thing, and I'll keep everyone fed."

Jimmy zipped his wetsuit. "Ready?"

"I'm right behind you, Corn Boy."

Jimmy splashed into the water. "Fuck yeah! Steamer Lane." Soon he was atop a rhino, watching the sunlight glint off the whitecaps and pondering the infinite.

Later that same day, 350 miles down the California coast in Santa Monica, Jumbo was watching the sun set over the Pacific Ocean from a chaise lounge on his marble patio. He was decked out in a Hawaiian shirt (size XXL, like a flowered circus tent) and Bermuda shorts. Mama was inside conferring with an interior decorator.

"The walls were supposed to be beige," he heard Mama say. "This isn't beige. It looks like a dog crapped all over our walls."

At last, Jumbo had room to breathe. His house was bigger than every place he had ever lived combined, and the plate-glass windows all around made it feel even more immense. Jumbo had been here for only a couple weeks—by way of a townhouse in West Hollywood and a ranch in Burbank—but he already had established a routine that involved something more than sleeping, eating, and fucking, though those activities were still prominent in the equation.

Nearly every day Jumbo rode his Harley the short distance to the Venice Beach Weight Pen, which more resembled a prison yard than a gym. A menagerie of goons pumped ungodly amounts of iron under the sun there. They grunted and growled and preened, and Jumbo responded by shaking his head in disgust. Most of them had used steroids to build up their bodies, a sign of weakness as far as Jumbo was concerned. He didn't need any help to shit-kick 350 pounds on the bench press. Jumbo was in his best shape since his playing days—he had to be. The demands of his job dictated nothing less.

Right now, though, he was focused on the sunset. At least he was trying to be.

"Look at these floors," he heard Mama say to the interior decorator. "Is that tile or asphalt?"

Jumbo rose from his chaise lounge and moved toward the ocean, eating up a good yard and a half of real estate with each step. A steep set of stairs led down to the water, but Jumbo preferred cutting through the surrounding brush. It reminded him of fishing back in Steuben County, when he'd traverse the woods to find a spot along the Chemung River where the trout were biting. His bum knee almost gave out when he stepped awkwardly on a fallen branch, but he pressed on down the slope, across the road, and onto the fine white sand.

The ocean folded out as far as the eye could see, and Jumbo was mesmerized by its enormity. Yes, he finally had room to breathe.

CHAPTER 19

It was month fifty-one, and Leyna was squatted over a toilet inside the redbrick prairie box, peeing into a plastic cup. The increasing convenience and reliability of home pregnancy tests meant that she no longer had to shuttle a urine sample to Dr. Graham's office and then wait on pins and needles for up to two weeks. She could do everything herself. With the precision of a chemist, she poured her sample into test tubes and mixed in various solutions that were a mystery to her but delivered an answer within a couple hours.

Leyna was expecting the same old result, but she was growing more adept at blocking out such ugliness, thanks in part to earthy Natalie Tross. Since Natalie's improbably exhilarating one-night stand with Holt following the welcome-to-summer party, she had gone on to marry a graphic designer (though she had kept her maiden name), and they had become the proud parents of a boy, Corlander, whom they planned to raise as a vegetarian. By around month forty-nine, Natalie had felt compelled to offer something to Leyna—an idea—and had settled into a chair in her friend's office at the YWCA.

"I'm starting to get really worried about you," Natalie said, pushing aside a plant on the desk that was obscuring her view of Leyna. "Every month you seem more defeated. Sometimes it's like you're not even there."

"I guess I'm not as good at hiding things as I thought."

"There's nothing to hide. You don't have to try to keep everything to yourself."

Leyna exhaled and said, "I just don't get it. The doctors have found nothing wrong—there's no earthly reason why we shouldn't be able to conceive a baby—yet here we are. Sometimes I feel cursed, like something's wrong with me."

"There's nothing wrong with you. You're not the first woman who's had trouble conceiving a baby, and it isn't the end of the world."

"That's easy for you to say. You and Mark have a wonderful son."

"I mean have you thought about adoption?"

"No. I'm not ready to give up on this."

"Who says you have to give up on it? The two routes aren't mutually exclusive. My friend Rhonda and her husband just adopted a daughter through The Cradle, right here in Evanston. It's something to think about."

"This is very nice of you, Natalie. Thank you."

"Just a little help from someone who cares. Sometimes we get so wrapped up in things, we can't see a way out."

Natalie didn't know how right she was. For that matter, neither did Leyna. She didn't see that this conception ordeal had unleashed all sorts of deep-seated emotions regarding her own ill-begotten start: the father who had skipped out on her; the mother who had never really been there in the first place; the sweaty, vodka-soaked lecher who had tried to rape her. She didn't see that month by excruciating month these feelings had risen up from the depths and made her crazy. But her eyes did brighten as she contemplated Natalie's idea.

At the dining room table the next morning, as Dave was fortifying himself with a swig of coffee, Leyna said to him, "So I was talking to Natalie yesterday, and she brought up the idea of adoption. Frankly, I'm surprised we never thought of it. It's at least worth mulling over, don't you think?"

This time the coffee didn't pool in Dave's mouth—it went straight down. Receptive to anything that might return things to the way they had been before, he quickly responded, "It's definitely worth mulling over."

Leyna grinned, and so did Dave.

With this definitive new idea on the table—a Plan B, so to speak—the future began to seem promising again. Hope at least flickered.

And as Leyna's pregnancy test percolated in the bathroom in month fifty-one, she even lost track of the time out in her yard. Having planted a vegetable garden next to her flowerbeds the previous spring, she was engrossed in pulling now-ripe tomatoes from the vines.

Dave, meanwhile, was attempting to fix the dishwasher, which produced an annoying clank whenever it ran. He had neither the knowledge of dishwashers nor the collection of tools to get the job done, but he soldiered on anyway.

Between his muttered curse words, he heard a familiar yell from the bathroom: "Dave!" In this instance, however, the tone was different, not as shrill. Rising from his knees, he walked to the voice.

"Dave, Dave, look at the test tubes."

"What? I don't see anything."

"I'm pregnant."

Leyna jumped into his arms and wrapped her long legs around him. Dave nearly lost his footing, both from the force of her leap and his utter disbelief. He couldn't remember the last time he had felt so happy, or relieved. For a moment, anyway, everything seemed okay.

CHAPTER 20

It was the damnedest thing: Pete Townshend, lord of rock, was stuck in a bear pit somewhere in Switzerland. My, how he had lost his way since Woodstock. He had long since given up on recovering his Special, not that it even mattered by this point.

Pete had rallied briefly after his *Lifehouse*-induced nervous breakdown. Following months of rejuvenating quiet in Twickenham, he and The Who hit the road again and rocked on. He even recaptured some of his creative spark with a rock opera called *Quadrophenia* about a teen wrestling with his troubled emotions in mid-1960s England. The plot of Pete's story was typically convoluted, but the music, once again built around synthesizers instead of guitars, was masterful, and *Quadrophenia* went all the way to number two on the charts.

From there, The Who grew even bigger. It routinely sold out football stadiums in a matter of minutes, and its staging became increasingly elaborate with laser lights and such. Amid the pyrotechnics, however, Pete felt more and more insignificant, like a prop. And the lack of any promising responses to his *Rolling Stone* ads—to his attempts to reclaim something *real*—only added to this sense.

One night in 1973 during a gig at the Cow Palace near San Francisco, a liquored-up and pilled-up Keith passed out mid-beat. Mindful that the show had to go on, Pete called out to the audience, "Can anyone play the drums? I mean, somebody good." Scot Halpin, a visual artist and an aspiring musician from Muscatine, Iowa, walked up to the stage, and the band finished its set.

Five days later Pete summed up the state of The Who in an interview with a reporter from Texas. Sitting backstage at Dallas Memorial Auditorium, with dark circles under his eyes and his face unshaven, he said: "It's reached the point where we could go onstage and do nothing but fart, and it wouldn't matter. All we have to do is show up to the arena and put on our pancake makeup. It's a fucking clown act, really."

Yet The Who rocked on…until September 7, 1978, anyway. Pete was with his wife Karen on Alderney, a tranquil little island in the English Channel, when Clive tracked him down.

"Pete, Clive's on the telephone," Karen said.

"Bugger," he said, taking the receiver. 'Ello."

"Pete, it's Clive."

"I know who the fuck it is. I'm on holiday. What?"

"I've got bad news. It's Keith."

Pete instinctively knew what Clive was about to tell him, so he cut to the chase: "How did it happen?"

"Pills. An overdose. Accidental, it looks like."

"Oh God, he really went and did it this time."

His eyes red with tears, Pete rushed to Alderney's airport and caught a puddle jumper back to London. The next day he locked himself in his second-floor studio in Twickenham to pen the band's official statement. It didn't take long to find the right words:

We have lost our great comedian, the supreme melodramatist, the man who apart from being the most unpredictable and spontaneous drummer in rock would have set himself alight if he thought it would make the audience laugh or make an audience jump out of its seats. We have lost our drummer but also our alter-ego. He drove us hard many times but his love for every one of us always ultimately came through.

The Who should have quit right there, but it didn't.

"This is what we do," Roger said at a group meeting at his estate in East Sussex following Keith's burial. "What else is there?"

Not to mention John needed an infusion of cash, having blown his proceeds from the last tour on houses, cars, clothes, booze, and drugs.

So The Who, now more of a brand than a band, rocked on, planning a tour that began at the Rainbow Theater in London on May 2, 1979. Its new drummer was Kenney Jones, a friend of Pete's who used to play in the Faces. Only twelve songs into that opening show, Pete realized the situation was hopeless. He carried his guitar solo in "Long Live Rock" as far as it would go, and just like he had done countless times before, he looked over to the drum kit so that Keith could take the baton and explode with a rollicking crescendo. But Keith wasn't there, only Kenney and his workmanlike thumping. To fill the void, Pete did a Chuck Berry-style duckwalk across the stage. No one in the frothing audience seemed to notice the difference, which was all the more deflating.

As the tour went on, Pete filled the void with increasing amounts of Rémy Martin. Paris, Edinburgh, Nuremberg, New York, Detroit, Pittsburgh—each stop was a forgettable blur. Cincinnati, however, on December 3, 1979, was not. Thousands of fans rushed the gates at Riverfront Coliseum in hopes of scoring primo seats for this general-admission show, and not all of them made it home that night. The headline in the next day's *Cincinnati Enquirer* screamed, "Stampede Kills 11 Persons at Coliseum Rock Concert."

Jacqueline Eckerle. Karen Morrison. Bryan Wagner. Peter Bowes. David Heck. Stephen Preston. Phillip Snyder. Connie Burns. Walter Adams. James Warmoth. Teva Ladd.

Once more The Who was associated with doom; once more Pete's eyes burned with tears. The Who definitely should have quit this time, but commitments had already been made.

"Fuck it," Pete said, "I don't even care what happens to me anymore."

Fueled by ever more Rémy Martin, Pete rocked on with his bandmates to Buffalo and Boston and Atlanta and Houston and Dallas and beyond. He traveled aimlessly through the wilderness until July 16, 1980, when the tour mercifully concluded.

And now Pete truly was in the wilderness—that bear pit in Switzerland. His presence there was as dumbfounding as it was inevitable. Consider:

By the end of 1980, Roger had grown antsy and John was running out of money again. They began ringing up Pete, who only wanted to be left alone.

"We should start thinking about another tour," Roger said.

"Bugger off," replied Pete.

"Have you given any thought to getting back out there?" John asked.

"Bugger off," replied Pete.

But the phone calls persisted, and a compromise was reached: they would tour one last time. In validation of this finality, they would call it their "Farewell Tour." Pete locked himself in his second-floor studio to write songs for a new album for the tour, but a couple weeks into it, he determined that he had nothing more to say.

"Fuck it," he murmured, "I'm quitting the music business."

Leaving behind only a note for Karen—"I've gone off to clear my head"—Pete drove his Aston Martin V8 Vantage to Heathrow Airport. The first city he saw on the departures board was Geneva, Switzerland. *Why the fuck not?* Pete purchased a ticket in first class, and upon taking his seat on the plane, he thought of nothing until the emptiness was filled with the usual chatter.

"Excuse me," said the man in the seat next to him. He was an American—a yuppie cliché, Pete rightly observed, with his tailored suit, black suspenders, and scrupulously combed hair. "Are you Pete Townshend?"

"So they tell me."

The American chuckled. "What a thrill. I saw your band in 1976 at Madison Square Garden. I was in the fourth row. Outstanding theatrics."

Pete forced a smile.

"There's something I always wondered, though: Why didn't you smash your guitar? I always thought that was your grand finale."

Fucking Christ. There's that ridiculous question again. I bet he can't name five of our songs. What a wanker. But since Pete was stuck next to him for the next couple hours, his words were more polite than his thoughts, even if they were delivered through gritted teeth: "Yeah, I stopped doing that years ago. It seems kind of pointless, you know? I'll leave that to the kids."

Bewildered, the American said, "Nevertheless, an excellent job. You were outstanding."

Pete closed his eyes and pretended to sleep until the plane touched down in Geneva. After clearing customs, he zipped through the polished white terminal with an air of purpose, despite not having any. He dead-ended at the rental car counter, where he picked up a Renault that had an annoying habit of getting stuck in second gear. "Bloody fuck," Pete repeated as the Renault bounced along the Geneva streets.

On the outskirts of the city, he stopped at a market to buy provisions:

a loaf of zopf bread, a wedge of Appenzeller cheese, and a bottle of Rémy Martin. He then drove in no particular direction, winding up about 150 kilometers northeast of Geneva in wooded, snow-covered hills near the River Aare and the Bernese Alps.

As the sun began to set behind him, he grew cold. He hadn't planned on this frosty destination, after all, and was clad in only a windbreaker. *I know just what I need to warm up.* Pulling onto the shoulder of the sparsely traveled two-lane road, he broke the seal on the Rémy bottle and took a swig. The bottle was a quarter-empty by the time the sun disappeared.

The lord of rock peered into the darkness through the windshield of his Renault. *Where the fuck am I?* A few more gulps of brandy later, he decided to find out. In addition to the Rémy, he gathered the zopf bread and the Appenzeller cheese—*Who knows? I might get hungry*—and ventured out of the car. That first step into the unknown was not promising: he slipped on an icy patch of pavement, falling on his back. "Fuck me!" he yelled, the echo of his voice bouncing from blackened hill to blackened hill.

Except for a bruised elbow, Pete was unscathed, so he hiked into the woods, alternating between drinking from the Rémy bottle and gnawing off chunks of zopf bread. Soon his toes, protected only by a pair of Adidas, became numb. "Mother of fuck." His solution was to take larger drinks of brandy, but this made it increasingly difficult to walk straight, and he veered into a tree. "Fuck it all."

Pete reached the edge of a steep slope, though he wasn't aware of this because of the darkness. When he stepped forward, his numb foot didn't touch snow, only air, and he tumbled face-first down the hill. If not for a tree near the bottom that broke his fall, who knows how far he might have rolled? "Fucking fuck."

The zopf bread and the Appenzeller cheese were history, but miraculously, he was still clutching the Rémy bottle. He took a swig. Rising slowly to his feet, Pete doffed his windbreaker so that he could brush off the snow that had gotten packed against his shirt. He then wadded up the windbreaker and chucked it into the night. "Take that, you fucker."

In the distance he saw shimmering lights. *Fantastic. It's like the cocksucking Emerald City.* In fact, it was the city of Bern, a medieval relic renowned for its sandstone towers and cobbled streets. Entranced, Pete weaved forward.

As he neared the banks of the River Aare, he came upon a large sunken enclosure. Lined with a concrete wall, it contained tall wooden poles with sturdy manmade branches (presumably for climbing) and various stone ledges (presumably for lounging). *The Bärengraben. I'm in Bern.* Indeed, Pete remembered seeing something about the Bärengraben in a BBC documentary. The bear was the symbol of Bern, dating to the twelfth century when Duke Something-or-Other slaughtered one out in the woods. To commemorate this hardy heritage, pits were later built around the city to house bears.

Though the lights up ahead were a tempting sight, Pete wobbled instead to the edge of the bear pit and took a gander inside. *Not too bad.* He climbed—flopped, actually—over the guardrail, then stood unsteadily atop the lip of the concrete wall. *Only a couple meters if I'm suspended, give or bloody take. Who the fuck cares?* Hanging from the concrete lip with one hand and gripping the Rémy bottle with the other, Pete let himself drop. A blanket of snow provided some padding but not enough—he felt a shooting pain in his right foot when he landed. "Motherfucking hell!" At least he was still holding his Rémy bottle, which he now needed more than ever. Three medicinal swallows helped to ease the misery of this latest injury.

The pit smelled rank, like the piss of big game. *They're in here somewhere.* Pete hopped around the habitat on his one working foot, searching each crook and crevice for bears. "Come and get me, you bastards. I'm yours for the taking." Nothing. He did another once-over but saw only a mouse scampering across the snow. After drinking his last precious drops of brandy, he threw the bottle at the wall. "Take that, you fuck-all bear pit!"

What Pete had failed to remember from the BBC documentary was that the bears weren't on display in wintertime. As for the piss he had smelled? It had been left behind by vagrants who periodically took shelter there. The lord of rock was in a bear pit, and he was ready for a mortal fight, but the blasted beasts were nowhere to be found. How very fitting.

CHAPTER 21

Doomsday Garrett's face looked like a fucking map. He had been everywhere. And nowhere. As a soldier in the 2nd Ranger Battalion, most of his missions had been classified.

Upon graduating in the top quarter of the class of '76 at Bloomington High in downstate Illinois, Doomsday could have continued his education at an institution of higher learning. Instead he enlisted in the Army with the goal of becoming a Ranger. It wasn't that he had any patriotic ideals to speak of—he simply wanted to find the action.

At first glance he didn't seem to be Ranger material. The Rangers were among the most lethal commando units on the planet, capable of performing lightning-quick surprise attacks under the most harrowing circumstances. And Doomsday? Standing a wiry 5'9", he looked more bookish than brawny. But he had character. A sports coach would have said he possessed "intangibles"; his sergeant at Fort Lewis called it a "red-ass streak." Either way, Doomsday didn't have to search hard for the action. It had an uncanny way of finding him.

Vietnam had reached an inglorious and inconclusive end in 1975, but there was other fighting to be done. And even though the American public wasn't privy to most of it, the proof was on Doomsday's face.

The diagonal scar on his forehead was from Chile in 1977. As a tangential part of Operation Condor—a shadowy initiative aimed at wiping out communist influences throughout South America—Doomsday and a small unit were deployed to neutralize guerrillas who had been staging hit-and-run attacks against the military dictatorship of Augusto Pinochet. The Rangers swooped into a compound near Nancagua before dawn, but they encountered more resistance than intelligence had indicated they would. In the ensuing struggle, Doomsday took a rifle butt between the eyes before driving a knife through his adversary's heart. Fifteen minutes later, the Rangers were gone.

The scar—or crater, more accurately—on his right cheek was from Zaire in 1978. He and his comrades had been called upon to soften the terrain around Kolwezi in preparation for a French and Belgian rescue operation. During a firefight with Katangese rebels, shrapnel tore a chunk of flesh from his face, but he continued on, scoring an untold number of kills. "You brought the wrath of hell down on those fuckers," a fellow Ranger said to him as they choppered out. "It was like doomsday." From then on, no one ever called him by his birth name, Tim.

The scar on his left cheek was from Afghanistan in 1981. The Soviet military had overrun the country, and Doomsday was among the soldiers who were there to help train Afghan troops. While conducting an exercise in the Kokcha River valley, they were ambushed by Soviet loyalists, one of whom fired off a round that grazed Doomsday's face and knocked him unconscious. When he awoke, he was back at the base camp, having been carried to safety by his Ranger brethren.

Now it was 1982, and Doomsday was a civilian. He no longer looked bookish, that was for sure. Damaged was more like it.

After a general discharge from the military, he had returned to Bloomington, where restlessness had quickly set in. In search of action, he had hopped into his recently purchased '73 red Mustang and sped north to the urban landscape of Chicago to surprise a friend from high school, Larry Gilbert. Three months had passed, and Doomsday was still there. Out of a combination of fear and pity, Larry hadn't gotten around to telling Doomsday to leave. For that matter, he hadn't even asked him to pitch in some rent.

While Larry slept each morning after a long night of slinging booze as a bartender at Sheffield's in Chicago's Lakeview area, Doomsday ate the poor guy's food and lounged on his couch. Usually around mid-afternoon, when the restlessness had set in, Doomsday would rev up his Mustang and explore the neighborhoods in Chicago and the outlying areas. Among the highlights so far were the Robert Taylor Homes on the South Side, a sprawling housing project that had reminded him of some of the war zones into which he was dropped as a Ranger; the Chicago Avenue Water Tower and Pumping Station on the "Magnificent Mile," one of the few buildings to survive the great fire of 1871; and a bar near the Naval Station Great Lakes, about forty miles due north of the city, where he had picked up a prostitute who had performed oral sex on him in the back of his Mustang.

One day, in his never-ending search for new terrain, Doomsday headed for the northwest suburbs out around O'Hare Airport. He weaved through the considerable traffic on I-90, sometimes utilizing the shoulder so that he wouldn't have to slow down. Doomsday nearly swerved into an exit sign for a town called Arlington Heights, and it was there that he made a snap decision to get off the highway.

CHAPTER 22

Ronald Reagan had gone from eating hot dogs at Jimmy's restaurant to running the country. In 1980 he had beaten the Democrat Jimmy Carter by a landslide and had promptly declared, "We must act today in order to preserve tomorrow." By 1982, however, tomorrow appeared decidedly bleak, as did today. A crippling recession had pushed unemployment to 10.8 percent, its highest level since the Great Depression.

While the *Herald*'s business reporters chronicled factory closings and company layoffs, Dave immersed himself in the great diversion: the sports section. He liked it that way—less strife.

Everything changed, however, on November 12 of that year. As he had learned much earlier on that road near Angola, Indiana, there was no hiding from chance. And during a conversation at his desk with Withers about whether they should grab McDonald's or Burger King for dinner, Dave was blindsided by it yet again.

His phone rang, and it was Cross, who said, "Come down to my office."

"Cross?" Withers asked apprehensively after Dave hung up.

"Yep."

"What does he want?"

"The usual, I suppose. I'm sure we made a minuscule mistake that not a single reader noticed except him. It would figure, huh? The curmudgeon."

"I hope I wasn't the one who screwed up."

Dave walked across the newsroom to Cross's lair. "You rang?" he said.

"Sit down."

Dave took the one chair beside Cross's desk that didn't have a stack of newspapers and folders on it.

"Have you looked at the paper lately, Weiss?"

Uh-oh. I don't like the sound of that. We must have messed something up really bad. "Of course. Every day. Why?"

"Have you noticed the ads?"

"Um, no."

"There aren't any, or at least there aren't enough. That's why the sections have been smaller, along with your news holes."

"I guess I didn't think much about it."

"And why would you have? You're editorial; you're not supposed to. But unfortunately, ads are what make the paper go round. And when there aren't any ads, eventually there's hell to pay."

"Um…"

"It's this damn recession. The first thing companies do whenever times get tough is cut back on their advertising. It's starting to hit us hard."

"I can imagine."

"You're not following me, are you?"

"Um…"

"I have to lay you off, Weiss."

The words didn't register with Dave. He was simply relieved that he hadn't messed up anything in the paper.

"You and also Jones, Sayers, and Handleman from news. But I called you in by yourself because you've been here the longest. You deserve at least that much respect."

Now the message computed. "Wait, are you saying I'm fired?"

"Not fired, laid off. This has nothing to do with your work performance. It's a numbers game. It's out of my hands."

"Whose hands is it in then?"

Shaking his head disdainfully, Cross pointed down the hall and said, "The bean counters want to trim some of the higher salaries, and we can't very well shit-can—er, lay off—the top guys. Peters stays because he's the sports editor. You're a deputy, just like Jones, Sayers, and Handleman on the news side. You're middle management, and middle management always gets screwed in times like this. Luck of the draw."

His face now flushed, Dave protested, "But my wife and I have a new baby. She quit her job. What am I going to tell her?"

"The good news is they're giving you four months of severance pay.

That's more than the other three are getting. It'll tide you over."

"Then what?"

Cross looked away. "I wish I knew. Look, if things turn around, I'll try to hire you back."

"I'm stunned. I have no idea what to say."

"There's nothing to say, other than if you need anything—a reference, whatever—don't hesitate to call me. You've come a long way since you started. You're a helluva worker, a grinder. Jesus, I took you under my wing."

Word always spread fast in a newsroom; reporters, after all, were trained to dig up the dirt. And so it was with Dave. As he made the long walk back to his desk, the typewriters stood silent and all eyes were on him. Dave was in such shock that he didn't notice. He didn't even see Jones, Sayers, and Handleman, who passed him while heading for what they knew was certain doom in Cross's office.

Dave began to fill an empty box that was under his desk: a framed picture of him, Leyna, and their hard-won baby Matthew at Gillson Park Beach from a few months earlier; his Rolodex; some random sports sections; a baseball signed by Dave Kingman; two cans of Campbell's tomato soup that had been gathering dust for the past several years; a pair of softball cleats; a cassette of *Tommy*.

No one dared approach him as he hunched over his desk—except Holt, who came up from behind and tapped him on the shoulder. The sudden intrusion made Dave jump.

"Easy there, hoss," Holt said, offering up a smile that was devoid of its usual smugness. "I heard the news. It should have been Peters, not you."

"I appreciate that."

"Where is that piece of shit anyway? On another vacation?"

"Remember his memo? An editorial conference in Vegas."

"Same thing, the hack. Everyone knows you're the one who makes this department go."

Dave's eyes filled with tears that he quickly wiped away. "This is… this is embarrassing."

"Don't worry about it. I'm the one who should be crying since I'm stuck on this *Titanic*."

Holt returned to his desk, and Dave kept packing: the issue of *Rolling Stone* with Pete Townshend's "I want my Special back" ad, courtesy of Lightfoot; a copy of *The World According to Garp*; a stack of paycheck stubs; a golf ball.

Now that the ice had been broken, Withers tapped Dave from behind.

"I can't believe it," Withers said. "I just want you to know you're the best editor I've ever worked with."

"That means a lot. Really."

Withers's ensuing handshake, the firmest he had, barely dented Dave's skin. Turning around, Dave resumed his dour work: a pair of brown socks and a can of RavioliOs from his file cabinet; a copy of *The Great Santini*; a picture of him and Leyna at the Chicago Jazz Festival from their glory days back around '73; a can opener.

Lightfoot tapped his shoulder.

"Best of luck, Dave. My dad got laid off once. He was out of work for three years. Things got really tight, but we survived it."

Lightfoot extended a clammy hand, after which Cherie came tapping. With moist eyes, she said, "This is *such* a bummer."

"For you especially. Now you're the one who has to keep Holt in line."

They both faked a laugh, and Cherie hugged him tightly and kissed him on the cheek.

Blaney and Sanders tapped. And prehistoric Paul from paste-up. And Alex and Janice from news. And Jarod from entertainment. All the while, Dave was being overcome by the same discombobulating sensation he had experienced at Leyna's bedside in Angola, that of the room moving without him. It reached a point where he decided he'd better start moving, too—just to keep up. He waved goodbye and, carrying his box of memories, rushed out the door.

The weather outside reflected Dave's mood. Typical of Chicagoland in late autumn, it was overcast, damp, cold, and windy. Leaves blew across the parking lot, and some of them stuck to his pants. He loaded his belongings into a Volvo 240 wagon that he and Leyna had picked up over the summer. The Volvo had seemed like such a smart purchase at the time—it was fuel-efficient yet roomy enough to accommodate the addition of Matthew to the family—but everything had changed. They still had thirty-two months of payments to make on it, and Dave had no job.

Pulling slowly out of the parking lot, he took a last look at the *Herald* office. *Here's to the future that was.*

CHAPTER 23

Doomsday parked his Mustang next to a tavern called Stumpy's and walked inside, his tour of Arlington Heights having been a dud. He had seen a statue of William Dunton (the founder of Arlington Heights, he had learned), a few parks with kids playing soccer, an inordinate number of hair salons and dry cleaners, and several other things he had already forgotten. Maybe Stumpy's would redeem this sterile suburb. If not, at least he would quench his considerable thirst.

Sidling up to the U-shaped bar, Doomsday ordered a Stroh's and a shot of Jack. He sized up the "Happy Hour" crowd and wasn't impressed. At a nearby table, four men dressed in business casual—work friends, it appeared—were engrossed in a conversation that was undoubtedly asinine. Across the U, a middle-aged loser with a wedding band on his finger stared at the bartender's plenteous boobs as she smoked a cigarette by the cash register. In the corner behind the middle-aged loser, two chubby young women slid quarters into the jukebox. Doomsday hoped they'd put on something better than the Hall & Oates song that was currently playing, something with more energy, like Van Halen. When another Hall & Oates song followed, he cringed, put his head down, and fixed his eyes on his beer.

Someone sat next to Doomsday and asked the bartender for an Old Style. Though Doomsday's face was still pointed toward his beer, he observed the newcomer out of the corner of his eye. He seemed agitated. His pupils were darting to and fro, and he kept spinning his beer bottle, stopping only to tear off pieces of the label. Doomsday would have never been mistaken for the compassionate type, but he almost felt sorry for this human train wreck, whose unusually boyish face belied his world-weary expression. Adding intrigue to the picture was a jagged scar along his cheek.

Without lifting his eyes from his beer, Doomsday asked, "That scar on your cheek—where'd you get it?"

The human train wreck—Dave, of course—spun his head to the

right and then the left, unable to locate the origin of the voice.

"I'm over here," said Doomsday, his face still pointed downward. "The scar?"

Dave's world stopped moving as he homed in on this odd creature, who had some facial scars of his own. "My scar?" he said.

"That's what I asked."

"It's from a car accident awhile ago." Dave placed his index finger on his brow. "So is this one."

"Sweet."

"That's one way of putting it. It wasn't so sweet at the time."

"You're still here, right?"

"More or less."

"Then it's sweet."

Dave almost returned to spinning his beer bottle, but he was spurred on by curiosity: "What about the scars on your face? Where'd they come from?"

"The service. But if I tell you any more than that, I'll have to kill you."

If Doomsday had laughed, Dave might have, too. But he didn't, which Dave found disconcerting. Thus, he went back to spinning his beer bottle.

"You look out of sorts," Doomsday pressed. "Rough day?"

"You could say that."

Dave tried to return to his beer bottle, but Doomsday wouldn't allow it, asking, "What happened?"

"I lost my job."

"That's a real shit break. Sorry, man. Truly."

Touched by the sincerity of the man's tone, Dave allowed, "Even worse, I still have to tell my wife. We just had a kid. She's going to flip."

Doomsday raised his arm and snapped his fingers. "Bartender, a shot of Jack for my friend here. He really needs it—he just lost his job. While you're at it, get one for me."

"No need to announce my firing to the entire bar. It's kind of embarrassing."

"Why? It's happened to everyone at one time or another."

After they did their shots, Doomsday ordered two more.

"What's your name anyway?" Doomsday asked.

"Dave."

"I'm Doomsday."

"Seriously? What kind of name is that?"

"I got it in the service. But again, if I tell you any more than that, I'll have to kill you."

This time Doomsday laughed, and Dave followed his lead.

"Where'd you work?" Doomsday asked.

"The *Daily Herald* here in Arlington Heights. I was there about thirteen years, and then this. Hard to believe."

"Why'd the assholes fire you?"

"The economy, my boss said. He told me he'd try to bring me back again when things turn around, but who knows?"

"I wouldn't count on it. Bloodsuckers like that are all the same. They only care about their bottom line. They'll wind up hiring someone at half your salary."

With those pearls of wisdom, Dave excused himself to go to the bathroom. He splashed cold water on his face in an attempt to steady his world, which was once again moving quicker than he was. A shot was waiting for him when he returned to the U.

They raised their glasses, and Doomsday said, "Here's to swimming with bow-legged women."

Down went another round. Dave was now slumped over the U, and he had stopped spinning his beer bottle.

"You know what?" Dave said. "I went into work today, and everything was basically okay. Not perfect, mind you, but okay. Then two hours later, it wasn't. Right out of the blue. Such a travesty."

"Now you're just feeling sorry for yourself."

"No, I'm not."

"Whatever."

Two more shots came and went.

"Anyway, I'm serious," continued Dave.

"About what?"

"Life."

"Holy shit, we're talking about life now?"

"Why not? You start out with such high hopes, and before you know it, they've all gone to hell. Then it's like, 'Now what?'"

"You just keep on keeping on, that's what."

"Sometimes it's easier said than done."

Doomsday pointed at a shrunken man across the bar who looked to be every bit of ninety years old. He was perched precariously on his barstool, held up, it seemed, by nothing more than want-to. It took great effort for him to raise his beer glass to his mouth, but he was getting it done.

"See him?" Doomsday said. "That man right there is a survivor. People like him, people who live as long as he has—they're the real warriors. Think of everything that could have gotten that man along the way. He could have died in an accident or from a disease or a heart attack—you name it. But he's survived—he's won. Shit, we should go shake his hand. As for your 'high hopes'? That's all a load of crap."

"I don't know. There has to be more meaning to life than just drawing a breath."

"Like what?"

Doomsday and Dave didn't shake the ancient one's hand, but they did drink more beer and Jack. In the fog of the evening, Dave lost track of the time, which was a blessing since he wasn't eager to start plotting out the next phase of his life. But eventually, inevitably, he looked at his watch.

"Wow, it's 11:30," he said. "I should probably get going. Duty calls."

"How 'bout one more shot first?"

"Nah. I'm pretty drunk already. Too drunk to drive, that's for sure. I think I need to call a cab."

"I can give you a lift."

"It's kind of out of the way, in Evanston."

"I've got nothing else to do."

"Aren't you drunk, too?"

"Don't worry about me. I'm a professional."

Doomsday catapulted past car after car as they headed east on Dempster Street, like it was a NASCAR race.

"This Mustang rips it," he exulted. "Three hundred and fifty cubic inches of pure manhood."

"It really moves."

"What do you drive? Wait, let me guess: a station wagon."

"Yep, a Volvo. How'd you know?"

"You look like the station wagon type."

"Pretty boring, huh?"

"Let me ask you something, Dave."

"Go ahead."

"You ever shit in a jungle?"

"Um, no, I can't say that I have. I've never even *been* in a jungle."

"Too bad. That's freedom. No one there to tell you not to do it."

"I suppose."

"You just have to watch out for the snakes," Doomsday added.

"Right, because who wants a snake crawling up his ass?"

"Exactly."

"Not to change the subject or anything, but you'll want to go left at the light and then take the first right."

The Mustang screeched left, then right.

"Go a block up, and it's on the right. The redbrick house. It's not the greatest house in the world, but it's home. We've lived there for…"

Before he could finish his thought, they were at the front curb.

"Hey, thanks for the ride," Dave said, "and great talking to you. It was therapeutic in a weird sort of way."

"Why stop now? You got any beer inside?"

Dave thought briefly, if not blearily, about doing the right thing—duty called, after all—but a beer did sound good. "As a matter of fact, I do. Come on."

Dave led Doomsday to the front door. Closing one eye for better focus, he aimed his key at the keyhole, but he kept missing it. On his fourth try, he dropped the key.

"Crap," he said. "I must be even drunker than I thought."

"Here, give it to me."

Doomsday slid the key right in and opened the door. The first thing they saw was Leyna at the top of the stairs. She was wearing blue sweatpants and a loose-fitting gray flannel top, and she wasn't smiling.

"Dave, what's all that racket?" she said in hushed voice. "You'll wake the baby."

Swaying back and forth, he answered, "Just trying to open the door. I think the lock's broken. Remind me to put it on my to-do list."

"How much have you had to drink?" she asked.

"Just a couple beers with my new friend."

"And who might your new friend be?"

"I'm Doomsday," the one and only responded as he handed the key back to Dave.

"Doomsday," she said, rolling her eyes. "Perfect."

"Yeah, we met at Stumpy's," Dave said. "He gave me a ride home. Wasn't that nice? Now I'm repaying him with a quick beer."

"What about the Volvo?"

"It's still at Stumpy's. Safe and sound."

"What about work?"

"I got off early. I'll tell you about it tomorrow."

"Well, Dave and…Doomsday, I have a sleeping baby up here, and he's going to want to eat in a couple hours. So if you'll excuse me, I'm going back to bed. And please keep the noise down. I don't want the baby woken up."

"We'll hit the basement," Dave said. "You won't hear us down there."

They tiptoed to the kitchen to pull a six-pack from the fridge, Doomsday more quietly than Dave. Then they went underground.

"Your wife—she's kind of a bitch," Doomsday said as they sat on the barstools. "Is she always like that?"

"Just sometimes. You know, a new baby and all."

"She's good-looking, though, I'll give her that."

"What about you? Is there a Mrs. Doomsday?"

"Hell no. I'm not anywhere near ready for that, and I don't know if I'll ever be."

"I hear ya."

"Whatever."

"That's exactly right. Whatever."

"This is sweet down here—your own bar." After a gulp of beer that emptied about a third of the bottle, Doomsday stood up and examined the room. "What's with all the album covers on the walls?"

"That was my wife. She has a knack for decorating."

"What about that guitar up there?"

"I've had that forever. It's Pete Townshend's from Woodstock."

"You were there?"

"Yeah."

"From what I can tell, it was a bunch of do-nothings sitting in a field. Was it as stupid as it sounds?"

"It didn't seem like it at the time."

"You were a hippie?"

Dave tried to focus, tried to think back to exactly what he had been in those days, but the room was moving without him again, and it was all he could do to keep from falling off his barstool.

"I don't care if you were," Doomsday said. "I'm just wondering."

"I don't even know," Dave finally answered. "It was a long time ago."

"How'd you get the guitar?"

"Some guy there sold it to me for thirty bucks, and I've held on to it ever since. Not sure why, come to think of it."

"Not sure why the guy sold it to you or why you hung on to it?"

"Both, I guess."

Doomsday reached up for the Special. "You mind?"

"Be my guest."

He took it off the wall and held it laterally at eye level, like he was looking through the sights of a rifle.

"Sweet," Doomsday said.

"You want it? Go ahead. It's completely fucking meaningless to me."

"I don't know, man. You've had it for a long time."

"Consider it payment for driving me home. Maybe it'll bring you better luck than it brought me."

Dave took a sip of beer, but this one didn't go down quite right. Given the unforeseen events of the day, he had never gotten dinner from McDonald's, Burger King, or anywhere else. And, well...

"You look green," Doomsday observed.

"Something just..." The room was spinning, and Dave was trapped in the vortex. "I think I'm going to..."

Dave ran into the laundry room and barfed unceasingly into the sink. While calmly drinking his beer, Doomsday listened to the retching; it reminded him of the noises his Ranger buddy Stu had made after being shot in the stomach in Argentina. A foul odor crept out of the laundry room, but Doomsday was unfazed. He turned to the Special on the bar top, amusing himself by plucking the brittle strings one by one. Though Doomsday was no musician, he could hear that the Special was hopelessly out of tune. Nevertheless, it sounded better than Dave.

When the retching stopped, Doomsday looked inside the laundry room: Dave was passed out on the cement floor. Shaking his head, Doomsday returned to the bar to crack open another beer. As he plucked the guitar strings some more, the high E broke and snapped against his hand. "Ouch." He yanked the broken string off the tuning peg, coiled it, and dropped it into an ashtray on the bar.

Doomsday ran his index finger from scratch to scratch on the Special's faded body, tracing out a picture that interested him briefly. *I wonder where this thing's been. That's a lot of wear and tear.* He shrugged his shoulders. *Whatever. It's just a stupid guitar.*

Stupid or not, it was now his—Dave had said so. After downing the rest of his beer, he seized the Special and casually let himself out of the house. Seconds later, he vanished in his Mustang.

CHAPTER 24

The Special hardly seemed like a prize in Doomsday's hands. A weapon of minor destruction maybe, but not a prize.

There was the time Larry was at work slinging booze while Doomsday, with nothing better to do, lounged on the poor guy's couch, watching Super Bowl XVII between the Miami Dolphins and Washington Redskins. Doomsday wasn't a fan of either team, but one had to pick a side in an event as momentous as the Super Bowl. He chose the Dolphins, mostly because he liked the way their defense, nicknamed the "Killer Bees," flew all over the field and hurt people.

Problem was, the Killer Bees weren't hurting anyone. And when John Riggins ran forty-three yards into the endzone in the fourth quarter to give the Redskins the lead, Doomsday became enraged. He reached for the nearby Special and rammed its body through the TV screen. Somehow the Special withstood the impact, suffering only two more snapped strings, but the TV was beyond repair. As it buzzed incoherently and coughed up puffs of smoke, Doomsday simply said, "Damn Dolphins."

No, the Special hardly seemed like a prize in Doomsday's hands. A blunt tool maybe, but not a prize.

There was the time Larry was slinging booze while Doomsday sat on the poor guy's balcony, tending to a small metal firepit he had just purchased at Kmart. Equipped with firewood, a fifth of Jack, and the Special, Doomsday wanted to see if he could outlast the February cold. After building his fire, he used the Special's neck as a poker to help keep it going. Each time Doomsday jostled the embers, the guitar hissed as its headstock blackened and its remaining strings melted.

Doomsday eventually ran out of firewood, so he decided to burn the Special. Before he could rise from his lawn chair, however, he passed out. Once again the Special had narrowly averted certain annihilation. When Larry returned an hour later, he found Doomsday asleep in the lawn chair with the Special between his legs, the emptied bottle of Jack in his right hand, and frost forming around the etchings on his face.

Civilian life just wasn't agreeing with Doomsday. In Gen. Douglas MacArthur's farewell speech in 1951 following five decades of military service, he had famously said: "Old soldiers never die; they just fade away." The line would have applied to Doomsday if he had been old. At only twenty-five he should have been on the upswing, yet there he was, still squatting at Larry's. Still lounging on the poor guy's couch. Still doing a whole lot of nothing.

The day after the near-torching of the Special, Larry determined that he had no choice but to act. His friend wasn't the same, well, normal sort he had been in high school—he now called himself Doomsday, for crying out loud—so Larry chose his words carefully. And with an ever-present five o'clock shadow and terminally droopy shoulders, he conveyed no sign of menace, which worked to his benefit.

"Remember Mrs. Blagan, that chemistry teacher we had our junior year?" Larry asked.

"Yeah, she looked like an old boot."

"Remember how she called out Ned Lacy in front of the whole class after he got a D on a test?"

"No."

"Well, after that undressing, Ned went on to get an A in the class. Now he's making big bucks working for Abbott Laboratories, right up the road in the suburbs. I've run into him a few times."

"No shit?"

"It's true. Anyway, pretend for a second that I'm Mrs. Blagan."

"What the hell, Larry?"

"Okay, forget about that. The point is Mrs. Blagan was trying to motivate Ned to work up to his potential. The same kind of goes for you. I really looked up to you in high school. You got better grades than I did, had more friends than I did. You were all-conference in wrestling, and I didn't even make the team. But ever since you got out of the Army, you're, um, not really doing anything. It doesn't make any sense."

"So you're tired of me sponging off you, huh?"

Larry braced for the worst, though his shoulders refused to straighten.

"I get it," Doomsday continued. "It's a legitimate beef. You want me to pull my weight around here. Why didn't you just say so to begin with instead of rolling through all that bullshit about Blagan?"

"I didn't want you to take it the wrong way. You've been kind of touchy lately."

"Relax. I take it as a challenge."

Doomsday promptly bought a *Chicago Tribune* from the corner store and dug into the want ads, starting in the *A*s.

Chicago Loop public accounting firm seeks an Accountant. Ideal candidate is a licensed CPA with three years of public accounting experience.

Doomsday had gotten good grades in math at Bloomington High, but he wasn't a licensed CPA. Furthermore, he didn't want to be. It sounded like slow death to him.

Customer service representative needed for growing medical supplies company. Topnotch phone skills a must.

This one looked to involve diplomacy, which wasn't Doomsday's forte. Another whiff.

Nothing Doomsday saw seemed to mesh with his unique skill set. If only a company required the services of someone who could crawl through the brush undetected or scale a mountain in the dead of night or maybe decapitate the occasional bad guy. Of course, his military superiors had decided he wasn't even fit to do those things anymore after he had taken that bullet to the face in Afghanistan and his behavior had turned, as they had put it, "erratic." *Whatever.* He continued to soldier through the want ads, and when he reached the *S*s, something finally jumped off the page: security professional.

Johnson Security Incorporated is a highly respected contract security service firm providing security programs to world-renowned hospitals, corporation complexes, shopping centers, commercial properties, and educational facilities. Responsibilities include interior and exterior patrols, ability to respond to emergency situations, and maintaining access control to buildings.

"Patrols," "emergency situations," "access control"—this was right in Doomsday's wheelhouse. He called the number listed in the ad, and after running through his military background (minus the copious classified material), he was asked to come in for an interview the following day. Shined up in a sport coat and tie he had borrowed from Larry, he sped off in his Mustang to the company's headquarters in suburban Lombard.

When Doomsday returned, Larry was tidying up the apartment in preparation for a poker game that night with some of the friends he'd made since moving to Chicago.

"Good news," Doomsday said as he undid the tie and ditched the sport coat. "I got the job. I start next Monday. No more sponging off you. In fact, I'll probably be able to get my own place soon. The pay's pretty decent. Benefits, too."

"It'll be good for you to have your own place," Larry said with relief. "I won't be in your way anymore."

Since Doomsday had nothing better to do that night, he crashed Larry's poker game. With a bottle of Jack by his side, he sized up Larry's friends—Joe (dork), Peter (dork), and Trent (dork)—and got down to business. At first it was easy pickings: Doomsday claimed four of the first six pots. As the night wore on, however, the law of averages intervened and Doomsday couldn't win a hand to save his life. It was Trent, he of the annoying thin-lipped smirk, who was having all the luck.

After raking in yet another pile of chips, Trent said, "You guys have run into a buzzsaw tonight. I can't be beat."

If there was one thing Doomsday couldn't stand, it was arrogance, especially from a twerp like Trent. "How 'bout a little less commentary?" Doomsday said. "Just keep playing the damn game, okay?"

They kept playing, and Trent kept winning.

"I'm on fire," Trent said, puffing up his pigeon chest. "Literally burning up the room."

Larry knew Doomsday a lot better than Trent did, so he interjected ever so carefully: "Poker's a funny game. Things can change quickly."

But they didn't. Trent won the next hand too, and Doomsday's fists began to clench. It wasn't the first time something like this had happened. During a makeshift craps game in the barracks at Fort Lewis a year and a half earlier, a newish recruit had gone on an inexplicable run.

After taking Doomsday's last dime, the recruit snickered and jokingly called him a "stiff." Though this was a relatively innocent transgression—perhaps not even a transgression at all—Doomsday snapped, wrestling the recruit to the ground and pummeling him before being pulled off by three Rangers. As they were dragging Doomsday away, he managed to cock his leg and kick the recruit's face, which exploded like a water balloon. "You uppity little fuck," Doomsday howled. Not long after that, he was given his discharge.

Doomsday's fists continued to tighten while Joe dealt a hand of five-card draw, loosening only to check his cards. He had two kings, a jack, and two nines—promising. His outlook brightened even more when he traded in his jack and got back a king—a full house. Larry, Joe, and Peter folded, each muttering something about having "nothing," but not Doomsday. Glowering at Trent, he pushed all his chips into the pot.

Trent matched his bet.

"You fucked up," Doomsday said, and he showed his full house.

"I did?" Trent laid down a six of clubs, seven of clubs, eight of clubs, nine of clubs, and ten of clubs. "A straight flush beats a full house. I win again. I'm on fire to—"

Doomsday overturned the table, launching drinks, chips, and cards across the cheap carpeting. He looked around wildly for something—anything—with which to hit Trent. Unfortunately for the Special, it was within reaching distance. Before Trent even realized what was happening, the Special's body, a blur of red mahogany, was arcing toward his face. He lifted his arm high enough to deflect the blow, but the result was the same as it had been with Abbie Hoffman fourteen years earlier at Woodstock: a knockdown.

Though Larry, Peter, and Joe tried their best to subdue Doomsday, they were no match for him, doing more hanging than restraining. They did, however, at least slow him down. "Trent, get out of here," Larry gasped, his face beneath Doomsday's foot but his hands clutching his ankle.

Trent heeded the frantic advice, but he made a critical mistake at the doorway, turning around and saying, "You're crazy, man. Someone should lock you up."

It took a few seconds for those words to fully register, as Doomsday wasn't thinking clearly, if at all. But when they did, Doomsday shook Peter off his back and tossed Joe into a wall. Using Larry's face as a starting block, he then raced out the door, his weapon—the Special—in hand. By the time he reached the front stoop of the apartment building, the taillights of Trent's car were fading into the distance on Belmont Avenue. *The uppity little twerp is getting away.* In seemingly one motion, he ran to his Mustang, flung himself inside along with the Special, and fired the ignition.

Doomsday zeroed in on Trent's car, running a red light at one intersection and barely missing a pedestrian at another. Fifty miles per hour, sixty, seventy—he was gaining quickly. By now Trent was fully aware that the red maniac behind him was Doomsday. He was terrified, yes, but he kept his wits about him. As the light was switching to yellow at the intersection of Belmont and Southport, he hung a left and continued to haul ass.

Doomsday stayed on him. He turned onto Southport without so much as tapping the brake, but the Mustang, overwhelmed by the sudden change of direction, fishtailed into the lane of oncoming traffic. The headlights of a taxi were directly in front of him, and to avoid a collision, he jerked the steering wheel to the right, which sent him hurtling toward a car that was parked near a telephone pole on the other side of Southport. Not even Doomsday could thread that needle: his Mustang skidded head-on into the telephone pole.

CHAPTER 25

Dave awoke with a start in his laundry room. He had been in this position before: prostrate, with no recollection of what had occurred the previous night but a sick sense that it couldn't have been good.

His head pounding and his mouth as dry as ash, he used the sink to pull himself up, only to see vomit pooled in the drain.

"Oh Christ."

It was coming back to him now, like a Kurtzian nightmare at the end of the river. *The horror…the horror*. He had:

- Lost his job.
- Gone to Stumpy's to mull over his dire predicament.
- Met an ex-soldier named Doomsday who—appropriately enough—liked to shit in the jungle.
- Consumed way too much Jack Daniel's.
- Incurred—quite understandably—the thinly veiled wrath of his bride after bringing Doomsday home with him.
- Given away…

"Oh Christ, the Special."

With the grace of a three-legged dog, he made his way out to the bar and looked up at the paneled wall. The Special was indeed gone. He scanned the surrounding area but saw only beer bottles and part of a guitar string in the ashtray. *All that remains*, he thought, tucking the string into his pocket. Horrible as this was, Dave quickly realized he had more pressing worries. Leyna was upstairs with their baby, and he was going to have to tell her that he was out of a job.

He was overcome by both trepidation and shame. Trepidation because he didn't want to upset the delicate normalcy that had returned to his relationship with Leyna. This new normal was different—adventure sex in the spare closet was a thing of the past, as were most other forms of unbridled embellishment—but Dave had accepted this, attributing it to the long, unavoidable journey into adulthood. And shame because he had failed in his role as a provider, especially now that Leyna wasn't working.

But he hobbled onward, up two flights of stairs and into the master bedroom, where the unknowing eyes of Leyna and Matthew locked in on him from the bed.

"What the heck happened last night?" Leyna asked, half-smiling. There was never anything worse than a half-smile on her face when she was holding Matthew. "You look almost as done-in as the day I found you at Woodstock."

Dave poked Matthew's stomach more nervously than affectionately, and the baby wrapped his hand around his index finger. *Not a care in the world*, Dave thought.

"And who was that man you were with?" she added.

"Just someone I met at Stumpy's. If you can believe it, I gave him the Special."

"You're kidding."

"No, and I don't even know where he lives…or his real name, come to think of it. But it gets worse."

"It does?"

He sat on the edge of the bed, turned partially away from Leyna. As Matthew merrily pounded his back with his balled-up hand, Dave cleared his throat. "I lost my job last night. *Laid off*, Ben said. The bad economy. I just can't believe it."

Dave slowly, cautiously pivoted toward Leyna. To his astonishment, however, she hadn't broken into a thousand pieces—far from it. Her expression was both unwavering and sympathetic as she said, "Oh, Dave, I'm so sorry."

"No, I'm the one who's sorry."

"Why? It's not your fault. You did great work there. Everyone knows it."

"Either way, I feel awful."

"I'm sure you do. You gave thirteen years to that silly newspaper. It's such an unfair blow. What else did they say?"

"Basically that they're losing money because of this recession. Ben said people in middle management—in other words, people like me—always get screwed in times like this. Figures. And in the end, all I have to show for everything is four months of severance pay."

Leyna's face turned downright placid. "Four months?" she said. "No worries then. That gives you plenty of time to find something. We'll be fine. Heck, we may even come out ahead on this one." She kissed him on the forehead and added, "First, though, maybe you should power up with a few hours' sleep. You really do look like you've been through the wringer."

Dave should have been relieved, but he wasn't. If anything, her abiding faith in him made him feel even more depleted. He stayed in bed while good old Natalie Tross drove Leyna and Matthew to Stumpy's to pick up the Volvo. He stayed in bed while Leyna made turkey-and-Swiss sandwiches for lunch, which she was sweet enough to bring up to him. And he stayed in bed while she gave Matthew a bath and put him down for the night.

Dave stayed in bed most of the next day, too, staring at the blinds and sometimes the ceiling. At one point Leyna placed a slumbering Matthew next to him before departing for a lunch date with Natalie.

"This will cheer you up," she said.

With Matthew snuggled up against him, Dave thought back to the boy's birth. He had tried his best to be a pillar of strength and stability for Leyna, standing by her side in the delivery room at Evanston Hospital and chanting "breathe…breathe…breathe" to her, just as he had been taught to do in their Lamaze classes. But terror had enveloped him—a helplessness the likes of which he had never experienced—when he saw the crown of a head sliding down her birth canal. What if the baby:

- Was missing an arm?
- Was missing a leg?
- Was missing both an arm and a leg?
- Wasn't breathing?

Dave continued to chant "breathe…breathe…breathe," like it was a prayer. And when Matthew finally emerged—all life and vigor, with two arms *and* two legs—his terror turned to perfect joy. He even cut the umbilical cord without objection or incident.

Of course, that wasn't the end of the story, only the beginning.

Moments of apprehension followed, such as the first several times he changed Matthew's diaper. Even after Leyna showed him how it was done, he worried that he'd snap off the baby's twig-like legs. There were also the middle-of-the-night excursions to Matthew's room to make sure he hadn't been suffocated by his blanket and the deep dives into *Children: The Challenge* to confirm that he was growing normally. But it turned out the life force was strong—babies were a lot sturdier than Dave had originally thought. In time he allowed himself to focus less on potential doom and more on the fun stuff, like putting a baseball in Matthew's crib or reading Vonnegut to him as he cooed.

Dave longed to return to that place of relative contentment, and on the third day he rose. Leyna was as chipper as she had been the previous two days, greeting him in the dining room with a smile, a cup of coffee, and a copy of the *Tribune*.

"The want ads are in there," she advised.

Dave spread them on the table, and with Leyna peering over his shoulder, he dipped into the *E*s to see who needed an editor.

"Anything good?" Leyna asked.

"I wouldn't necessarily say *good*, unless copyediting for *Packaging Digest* counts."

"Yuck."

Dave turned to the *W*s, home of the writing jobs.

"And?" Leyna asked.

"A PR firm, the aptly named Little Group, needs someone to write press releases for a meager $12,000 per year. A definite step backward."

"I agree. It's not like we're desperate."

Before Dave knew it, two weeks had passed. Though he had mailed blind résumés to seemingly every publication in the Chicago area that seemed interesting, nothing definitive had materialized. He wasn't desperate, but he did feel a dull ache.

Mostly he occupied his days by fixing things around the house, which gave him little solace. His latest project involved patching a hole in the living room wall; this followed a project that had involved nailing a picture hook into the living room wall. As Dave was assessing the damage, the phone rang.

"Hey you," Cherie said on the other end of the line.

Dave was surprised at how happy he was to hear her voice, not that it was evident in his monotone response: "Hey."

"Did I wake you?"

"Oh no, I'm just getting some stuff done around the house."

"That's good. So you're doing okay then, staying busy?"

"I'm hanging in there."

"Any promising leads?"

"Nothing yet. It's rough out there. What about you? How's everything going at the paper?"

"A little tense, as you can probably guess. Everyone's kind of walking on eggshells, hoping there aren't any more layoffs."

"Fun, fun."

"Everyone misses you, especially me. I can't come bug you at your desk anymore."

"Yeah, I miss that, too."

"Do you want to meet up for lunch sometime soon? My treat."

"Your treat? Then yes, definitely. Maybe early next week?"

"Sounds good. Give me a call, and we'll figure something out."

Before Dave knew it, another couple weeks had passed. He hadn't called Cherie, nor had he done much of anything else save for further damaging the prairie box. But all was not lost: his mind was still active enough to at least *think* about the great questions before him. He was wrestling with one such concern—whether or not to shower—when the ringing telephone delivered another voice from his past at the *Herald*.

"Yo," the voice said, as if Dave wouldn't need more of a clue to identify His Greatness. And he didn't, which annoyed him even more.

"What's up, Holt?"

"Not much. Still kicking ass, still trying to carry that lunchmeat sports editor they should have fired instead of you."

"I see you still have a way with words."

"That's what they tell me."

"I'm sure they do."

"I have a hot lead for you. I was covering a game last night, and I ran into a reporter from the *Southtown Economist*. He said they're looking for a sports editor. Their old one got a job at the *Cincinnati Enquirer* or something. It would beat sucking wind in your house, huh?"

"That it would. Thanks for the tip."

"By the way, Cherie says to get off your butt and give her a call."

"Oh, that's right. Tell her I've been, uh, busy and I'll call her soon."

Located in Garfield Ridge on the southwest side of the city, the *Economist* was a good hour's drive from Evanston. But it was an established daily newspaper with a respectable circulation of around 50,000. It certainly was a viable option, especially since Dave had no others. With something resembling a bounce in his step, he tracked down Leyna, who was hanging Christmas decorations in the living room. Matthew was beside her on the floor. He was itching to start crawling, but his motor skills hadn't quite caught up with his want-to, so he settled for chewing on an empty cardboard box.

"What do you think?" Leyna said, proudly pointing to a garland she had hung over the oak mantle.

Dave thought for a second about his dearly departed Special and how great it would have looked there. "Nice," he said. "Very nice."

"I know, right?"

"I have some potentially good news. Holt just called, and he told me the *Southtown Economist* has an opening for a sports editor. The old sports editor moved to Cincinnati or something."

"Wonderful. That sounds perfect for you, Dave."

"I hope so. I'm going to call the managing editor from the family room, so can you make sure this bruiser doesn't break down the door while I'm on the phone?"

Leyna giggled and said, "We'll go fold some laundry in the basement. And we'll keep our fingers crossed. Right, Matthew?"

Dave's conversation with the managing editor turned out to be shockingly brief: the position had just been filled. "Tough piece of luck," the editor said in the hacking tone of a chain-smoker.

The newfound bounce in Dave's step turned back into a shuffle as he went down to the basement to report the bad news to Leyna. Peeking inside the laundry room, he saw Matthew on the floor by her feet.

"Position's already been filled," he murmured.

"What?" Leyna said, looking up from the pile of clothes she was folding.

"They filled the position already."

Leyna's expression remained unwavering, and the conversation followed a course that was becoming depressingly familiar:

"Oh, I'm so sorry, Dave," she said.

"No, I'm sorry," he answered.

Right on cue, she gave him the requisite kiss on the forehead. "Keep at it. Things will work out. They always do."

She then returned to the laundry, the very essence of domestic delight with Matthew grabbing at her ankles, trying desperately to pull himself somewhere, anywhere. Dave, meanwhile, went back to bed.

Another week passed uneventfully for Dave but not Leyna. She had wanted this to be a Rockwellian Christmas, what with it being Matthew's first, and nothing was going to steamroll her plans. She bought the boy a Tonka fire truck, a Tonka police car, and a set of wooden blocks. She bought a giant activity cube that was well beyond his cognitive abilities. She bought enough storybooks to fill a bookcase and a Teddy bear that was bigger than he was. She bought a new camera so that she could snap pictures of him playing with all these presents. Basically, she bought like Dave had a job (or would have one soon).

When Christmas morn arrived, complete with a fresh, Rockwellian blanket of snow on the ground, they brought Matthew down to the tree by the mantle and opened the gifts one by one. He didn't pay much attention to any of them, but he did think the wrapping paper was a hoot, chortling each time he tore a scrap.

"We should have just gotten him a few rolls of gift wrap and called it a day," Dave said.

Giggling, Leyna punched Dave playfully on the shoulder.

"Would've saved a lot of money," he added, but his words were muffled by the sounds of giggling and chortling.

After taking out her new camera, Leyna set her mind to capturing Matthew's first Christmas for posterity. Stretched out on her stomach, a nimble mix of concentration and mirth, she wriggled across the hardwood floor in search of the perfect picture-taking angles. She was wearing jeans that fit her like it was still 1969, except they were Guess instead of bell-bottoms. Dave marveled at her remarkable comeback from the dicey days of trying to conceive Matthew. She seemed utterly untouched by time, and Dave's hormones began to whirl.

It was the biggest jolt of energy he had felt since being laid off. He wanted to jump up from the couch and roll around the living room floor with his beautiful wife, preferably without any clothes on. At the very least, he wanted to whisk her off to the bedroom or even its spare closet. But then the phone rang (Dave's parents wishing them Merry Christmas) and Matthew's diaper suddenly needed changing and, well, he hadn't showered for three days. After talking to his parents while Leyna tended to the dirty diaper, he sank back into the couch and back into oblivion.

Another couple weeks passed, maybe more, with Dave making no headway on the job front. And Leyna? Ever chipper, ever hopeful that Dave would come through, she still didn't seem desperate. But maybe she should have been. After all, the clock was continuing to tick down to the end of their four-month grace period. Sometimes Dave would materialize from his stupor and imagine month five and beyond. What if:

- He never found a job?
- They lost their house?
- They wound up living under a bridge?

He'd imagine these apocalyptic scenarios, but then he'd disappear again, powerless and depleted, unable to rise up and pull the proverbial body from the burning car.

CHAPTER 26

Speaking of cars, the red Mustang hadn't burned. But it had been crushed, along with Doomsday's face, which had been launched into the dashboard upon the vehicle's impact with the telephone pole.

Doomsday, however, was not dead. It would take more than that to kill Doomsday Garrett. He even got out of the car under his own power, carrying the still-intact Special with him as if he was about to use it to beat someone, presumably Trent. After staggering several feet, he collapsed onto the sidewalk in front of an astounded rabbi. He then slipped into unconsciousness, at which point the rabbi rushed into a nearby 7-Eleven and called 911.

That had been a couple days earlier. Now Doomsday was fully conscious and resting rather uncomfortably at Northwestern Memorial Hospital in downtown Chicago. There was no doubt that the intersection of Belmont and Southport would be a prominent addition to the map of scars on his face. His broken left jaw was wired shut, his eyes were black and blue, and the rest of his swollen mug resembled a ripe tomato. Doomsday couldn't believe it. He had spent years neutralizing thugs trained to kill with their bare hands and renegades firing bullets at him, yet he had been outmaneuvered by…by *Trent*. Doomsday swore he'd get him just as soon as he was able.

He had tried to leave the hospital the first night, pulling the IV out of his arm and lurching out into the hallway. Clad in nothing but a hospital gown, his butt crack exposed, he headed toward an exit sign. Doomsday nearly made it there, too, before collapsing again. An orderly eventually found him and returned him to his bed, where he had remained.

Since Doomsday hadn't made any friends in Chicago and his parents back in Bloomington didn't even know he was hospitalized, he received no visitors. Not even Larry appeared. (Larry, in fact, had gone a step further than that, changing his apartment locks.) Doomsday passed the mornings by watching *The Phil Donahue Show* and *The People's Court* on a TV that was mounted to the wall; he passed the nights by watching *The*

Fall Guy, *Dynasty*, and the other prime-time trash. Only the afternoons were somewhat tolerable. That was when a certain nurse made her rounds.

"I heard you tried to make a great escape last night," she said upon seeing him for the first time.

"Yeah," Doomsday said through the clenched teeth of his wired jaw.

"Not too smart." She briefly studied his face and then the clipboard in her hand. "Looks like you really messed yourself up, Tim."

"It's Doomsday."

"It says Tim here," she said with a tap of her clipboard against the tray table by his bed. "I'm Jenny Esposito...er, Smith, Jenny Smith. Dang. I got married recently, and I still can't get my new name right. Anyway, you're stuck with me until we can get you out of here."

Though a small woman, she was formidable, as evidenced by the strength of her grip on Doomsday's wrist when she checked his IV. She had straight black hair, brown eyes, and an easy smile that was enhanced by perfectly aligned teeth. Jenny's new husband, James, was an anesthesiologist at Northwestern Memorial. Following a romance of about two years, mostly on the sly to avoid the indignities of the hospital rumor mill, they had tied the knot in a small ceremony in Hawaii. Jenny no longer had to work, but she thrived on the unpredictable bustle of the hospital. She met a lot of curious people here, such as this latest patient.

"Are you feeling any better, Tim?"

"Doomsday. And I'm fine."

"You don't look fine," she said, wrapping a blood pressure cuff around his arm. "From what I understand, you're a very lucky man."

Doomsday shrugged his aching shoulders gingerly.

"Your blood pressure is high."

"So?"

"So you need some rest. In other words, don't try sneaking out of here again."

After scrutinizing his other vitals, she fluffed his pillow, which caught him by surprise since the other nurses hadn't engaged in such pampering, or any pampering at all. "You know," she said, "you're not as invincible as you think."

When she returned the next day, she was toting, fatefully enough, the Special. Doomsday had completely forgotten about it.

"It seems the paramedics brought this into the hospital with you," Jenny said. "I found it in the nurses' station. Obviously, no one gave it to you, and I thought you might want it."

Unbeknownst to Doomsday, Jenny, or anyone else, this was the Special's second appearance in a hospital. A lot had gone down in the interim, and the Special looked about as battered as Doomsday. Jenny rested it against the bed.

"You're a guitar player?" she asked.

"No, I guess you could say it's a souvenir. The Who's Pete Townshend played it at Woodstock."

"Dang, that's amazing, Tim."

"It's Doomsday."

"How did you get it?"

"Some guy gave it to me in return for driving him home."

"Right before your accident?"

"No, I got into the accident chasing some other guy."

She shook her head like a schoolteacher who was about to scold one of her students. "What did I tell you about trying to act like you're invincible?"

"It happened before you told me that."

"You got me there," she said, her face now registering a toothy smile.

Jenny's checking-of-the-vitals routine culminated again with some pillow fluffing, much to Doomsday's delight.

"Everything looks better than yesterday," she said. "You're a lucky man."

Doomsday didn't feel particularly lucky, but maybe Jenny had a point. Just like that old man propped against the bar at Stumpy's, Doomsday had won the survivor lottery—again. He had, however, cut it awfully close this time, and he couldn't help but ask himself, *How long can my winning streak last if I keep going at this rate?*

The next afternoon Jenny entered Doomsday's room so abruptly that it startled him. "Good news," she said.

"What's that?"

"It looks like they're letting you go tomorrow. If all goes well, you'll be out of here first thing in the morning. You're a quick healer."

Doomsday tried to smile, but his wired jaw prevented it from stretching far enough to be discernible.

"By the way," Jenny continued, "I mentioned your guitar to my husband last night, and he was quite impressed. He said it's a piece of history."

"He's a hippie type?"

"God no," she said, bursting out laughing. "But he does like artifacts."

"Then go ahead and take it."

"That's silly. I couldn't."

Grimacing, Doomsday reached for the guitar, which was propped against the wall behind him, and transferred it to Jenny. "There. It's yours."

"Really?"

"Look, you've been nicer than anyone else in this hellhole, and the guitar means nothing to me. I couldn't care less about Woodstock, and I couldn't care less about artifacts. Whatever."

"If you insist."

"I do."

"Thanks, Tim."

"It's…oh, screw it. You're welcome."

The next stop for the Special was the tony North Shore suburb of Winnetka, where Jenny and James lived in an oversized and overstuffed Frank Lloyd Wright knockoff. The house was a bit much for Jenny, a product of a working-class family on Chicago's northwest side, but who in her right mind would complain about such opulent digs? That night as they were finishing dinner, Jenny brought out the guitar and said, "Ta-da."

James's face was expressionless.

"Remember?"

"Um…"

"It's the Woodstock guitar of Pete Townshend's that you were 'oohing' and 'aahing' about when I mentioned it last night."

There was still only blankness on James's face.

"Remember? That patient I was telling you about gave it to me, and—"

"Yes, yes, I remember now. Of course. You caught me off-guard."

The truth was, James barely remembered the conversation, and he had no recollection whatsoever of the "oohing" and "aahing" part. Any interest he had displayed would have been strictly feigned in order to humor his wife. While she had been telling him about her patient's guitar, his mind had probably been straying to Indian Hill Country Club's upcoming platform tennis match against hated Exmoor Country Club. A win over Exmoor would put his club in first place in the forty-five-and-under men's division of the North Shore Platform Tennis League.

Platform tennis was James's passion. Played outside in the winter on a court enclosed with chicken wire, it was more rugged than regular tennis. Nothing surpassed the exhilaration of gathering with his friends and withstanding the bitter elements in the name of competition. As for Pete Townshend? James wouldn't have been able to pick him out of a police lineup.

"It will fit in nicely with the other things in your entertainment room," Jenny said. "Like you said last night, it's a piece of history."

Taking his first good look at the Special, James was unconvinced. It was chipped, scratched, and burned—more like trash than treasure. But his wife had meant well. She always did.

"Yes, it's quite a piece. Thank you," he said.

Dutifully, James took it to his entertainment room. But he placed it against a wall near his antique billiards table, behind a large Tanzanian wood carving of an elephant, just tucked away enough to be out of view. There it sat until the end of March, when James's platform tennis teammates and their wives came to the house for a season-ending party. Jenny did her best to play her new role of a North Shore wife, serving a catered dinner of herb-encrusted baked Norwegian salmon before leading the women into the living room for some chitchat. The men adjourned to the entertainment room, where Henry Stanton—the second Stanton in Jeffers, Stanton & Stanton LLP—found the Special after a ball flew off the billiards table on his badly botched break and rolled behind the Tanzanian wood carving.

"What's this?" Henry asked, lifting the Special.

"That?" James said somewhat sheepishly. "Supposedly, Pete Townshend played it at, ah, Woodstock. I'm dubious. What can I say? One of Jenny's patients gave it to her. You know Jenny. Everyone loves her."

Henry passed the Special to Dean McCarthy (he said, "Hmmm"), who passed it to Brendon Sommers (he said, "Oh"), who passed it to Michael Pendleton (he said, "Huh"), who passed it to Kip Black (he said nothing). Ultimately, it wound up behind an eighteenth-century Venetian end table.

There the Special sat until late summer, when the Smiths' cleaning lady, a Polish battle-ax with a mind of her own, decided she was tired of dusting it. She carried it out to the garage, depositing it behind a stack of old lawn chairs.

No one seemed to notice, so there the Special sat and sat and sat, dirty and forgotten.

CHAPTER 27

It occurred to Dave that he might be in the grip of a midlife crisis. His theory seemed plausible enough: He had reached an existential fork in the road and had no idea which way to go. On the other hand, he wasn't dreaming of busty young blondes or little red sports cars. And since he was only thirty-three, the numbers didn't add up either.

Whatever the reason, Dave had lost his mojo. Eight months had now passed since he had been laid off from the *Herald*, and the world definitely wasn't charging forward as he hung on for dear life. It was at a complete standstill, even if he was at least going through the motions:

- In month four *Packaging Digest* had posted another opening for a copy editor, and this time he had put on a brave face and sent off his résumé. After being called in for an interview, he was sure he sounded gung-ho about the prospect of editing stories about cardboard boxes, but the executive editor, a quietly cordial woman with probing eyes and a faint mustache, formed a different impression. A ding letter arrived a week later stating that she had "decided on another candidate whose skills more closely match the specific requirements of the job."

- In month five he should have landed an interview for a job as a communications associate at the Illinois State Bar Association that would have called for him to manage the workflow of its publication, *Illinois Bar Journal*. Dave wasn't an expert in legalese, but he knew the ins and outs of the publishing process. His mind began to wander, however, when he was writing his cover letter to the executive director, and he typed "Dear Mr. Jines" instead of "Dear Mr. Jones." Worse, and as uncharacteristically, Dave didn't catch the typo. Suffice it to say, Mr. Jones never read beyond the greeting, tossing the letter into his trashcan after muttering, "Moron."

- In month seven he seemed on the verge of a long-awaited breakthrough. *Chicago*, a glossy monthly magazine with plenty of cachet, needed an associate editor, and Dave was actually fired up about it. He was all business in his interview with the managing editor, making a case for himself with both conviction and clarity. Although the managing editor was rightly impressed with Dave's credentials, he was a fastidious man who just couldn't get past the booger that was hanging from his nostril.

People were starting to worry, including William Weiss, who invented excuses to stop by the prairie box and check on his son. For this visit, he was bearing clamps and epoxy.

"What's with all that stuff?" Dave asked upon answering the door.

"It's for that Tiffany lamp you said you dropped. I thought you might be able to glue the shade back together." William walked into the living room and had a look around. "It sure is quiet here," he said. "Where's the little slugger?"

"He and Leyna are out running errands. The grocery store, I think. They should be home soon if you want to wait."

"I'll do that."

"You want some coffee? I just brewed a pot."

"Sure."

En route to the kitchen, they stepped over a Hot Wheels track, a Big Bird puzzle, and a rubber ball.

"Matthew's assembling quite an arsenal of toys," William said. "Pretty soon you'll have to build an addition just to hold them all."

"I know, Leyna really dotes on him," Dave answered as he poured two cups of coffee. "There you go—black, just how you like it."

"How's the job hunt? Any progress?"

"It's still pretty slow, but hopefully things will start picking up. It's only a matter of time, right?"

"Are you and Leyna still doing okay moneywise?"

"Money's a little tight right now," Dave lied. Money was more than tight.

"I'd be happy to float you a loan if you need one."

"Thanks, Dad, but we'll be okay."

Trying hard to conceal the concern that never truly fades from a parent's face, no matter how old the child, William said, "I have an idea. Why don't you come work at the store, just until you find something permanent? Your mother and I don't get around like we used to, and we could really use the help."

"That's hilarious," Dave said with an expression that matched his words. "I didn't even work there when I was a kid. I always wanted to make my own way, remember?"

In the master bedroom that night, as Leyna changed into shapeless gray sweats and Dave a ratty Cubs T-shirt, the couple exchanged notes on the day.

"Your dad looks good," Leyna offered.

"Timeless, right? He looked sixty when he was forty, and now that he really is sixty, he still looks exactly the same. The combover's taken a bit of a beating, but that's about it."

Leyna obliged Dave's quip with her standard giggle before crawling onto her side of the bed and resting her head on the pillow.

"A funny thing happened," Dave added. "He asked me to come work with him at the store, said something about needing extra help."

"And you accepted?" Leyna asked hopefully.

"Nah. I mean, can you see me behind the counter at Weiss Drugstore?"

"Kind of, yes."

"Seriously?"

Now Leyna was sitting straight up, and no giggles were forthcoming.

"It's not exactly what I had in mind for my future," Dave continued.

"What did you have in mind then? Have you looked at our savings account lately? There's about three thousand dollars left in it, and nothing is coming in now that your severance pay has dried up. Something has to give, and soon. I know you loved your job at the *Herald*, and I know you spent ages there—"

"My whole adult life."

"Right, but there's still a big chunk of life left to live. You need to find a way to get past this, don't you think?"

"Of course that's what I think. But…"

"It would be perfect, Dave. You'd earn some money *and* get out of the house. I really think you should do it. It's a win-win."

That was highly debatable, but this wasn't: it was time for Dave to get serious about getting desperate. The next morning, after swallowing hard, he dialed the phone. "Hi, Dad," he said. "Do you still need a hand at the store?"

Meanwhile, Leyna loaded Matthew into the Volvo and drove to Natalie's for a play date. Depending on one's perspective, Natalie's house was either a nest of neuroses or a sanctuary of safety. Even though her boy Corlander was four years old and more than sure on his feet, the baseboards were lined with pillows in case of a fall, and every doorway was equipped with a gate. Since Matthew was new to walking, Leyna preferred to view it as a sanctuary of safety.

As was often the case at these get-togethers, Matthew and Corlander played under lockdown in the basement while Leyna and Natalie sat nearby with cups of herbal tea.

"So what's the latest scuttlebutt at the office?" Leyna inquired.

"You don't even want to know. Remember that economic empowerment program I'm heading up?"

"Yep."

"Corlander, give that truck back to Matthew…please. Remember our talk about sharing your toys?" Natalie soothed herself with a sip of tea. "Boys will be boys. I'm sorry, where was I?"

"The economic empowerment program."

"Yes, well, last week we lost some of our funding. I bet you don't miss those headaches."

"I've traded them for new headaches, and I might be back at work sooner than you think."

"Uh-oh. What's going on?"

"The usual. We're running out of money."

"Didn't Dave just have an interview with *Chicago* magazine?"

"He didn't get the job. Then yesterday his dad asked him to come work with him at his pharmacy."

"That's good, right?"

"You'd think so, but he didn't want to do it. He only agreed after I cajoled him. And even that won't be a financial cure-all, which is why I'll probably have to end the stay-at-home-mom thing and start working again." Leyna studied Matthew anxiously and then soothed herself with a sip of tea. "I wasn't ready for that yet."

"Join the club. But we're lucky there's a daycare center onsite at work. It's very convenient. Mark and I have been pleased."

"I know. I just don't understand what's going on with Dave. I wasn't concerned at first—I was sure he'd have a new job by now—but the more this has dragged on, the more he mopes around. It's like he's lost his survival instinct. I've really, really tried to be patient and understanding, but sometimes it's difficult."

Natalie gently tapped Leyna on the knee.

The goings-on across the room weren't nearly as affable: Corlander whacked Matthew on the arm with the disputed truck. Erring on the side of caution, Natalie suggested they wrap up this latest play date. As Leyna gathered Matthew and his gear, Natalie said, "Did I mention that my brother Scott is coming over for dinner tomorrow night?"

"Not that I remember. I thought he lives in Denver or something."

"He does, but he says he wants to move back here now that his divorce has been finalized. He's looking at houses. Why don't you and Dave join us? The more the merrier. It always gets a little awkward between Scott and Mark. Mark likes art; Scott likes money. The conversation dries up pretty quickly."

"Ah, nothing like a little familial dysfunction. Could be entertaining. Count us in." Leyna gave Natalie a hug and added with a laugh, "Plus, maybe your brother can give Dave and me a loan."

That night, while Dave read Vonnegut's latest, *Deadeye Dick*, on his side of the bed and Leyna leafed through *Architectural Digest* on hers, the day's notes were exchanged. Without looking up from her magazine, Leyna said, "Natalie invited us over for dinner tomorrow evening. I guess her brother's in town. I hope you don't mind, but I accepted."

"What about a babysitter for the little guy?"

"Done. Your parents are available."

"And will Natalie make us wear Hazmat suits so as not to pass any germs on to Corlander?" Dave asked with a sarcastic chuckle.

"Like you're one to talk."

"And will she be serving her infamous tofu casserole, the one that not even the neighborhood raccoons will eat?"

"Dave."

"What? I'm just joking."

"You need new material."

Dave was pretty sure he'd find some over dinner, starting with Natalie's dining room table, which was fashioned out of lightweight bamboo and seemed better suited for a Taiwanese mud hut than a suburban Chicago home. Natalie meshed perfectly with the surroundings: wearing a full-length brown dress, she vaguely resembled a root. The same couldn't be said of her brother Scott, who was clad in a pressed white Oxford shirt, a light-blue seersucker sport coat, dark-blue slacks, and brown hard-leather loafers. It seemed impossible that he and Natalie were related.

Within minutes of everyone starting a first course of garden salad, Natalie excused herself. "I'll be back in two seconds," she said. "I just want to make sure Corlander is asleep."

"Let him be," Scott said. "He's six years old. I'm sure he's fine."

"He's four, and he gets grouchy when he doesn't have enough sleep," Natalie responded.

No sooner did she return to the table than she stood up again.

"What now?" Scott asked.

"The casserole should be done."

"Casserole? Yum," Dave said, and Leyna punched his knee under the table.

"Do you need some help?" Mark offered.

"Sure, dear." For Scott's benefit, she added, "It's so nice of someone to ask."

They returned with five servings of dark-brown goo, and Scott was the first to dig in. Though incredulous about Scott's clothes, Dave decided this dandy might not be so bad after all when he said, "What exactly is this, sis? Did you cook up some of the bamboo from the table?"

"Thanks, Scott," Natalie answered. "As you all can see, I've always been able to count on my big brother for encouragement."

"I think it's quite good," Mark interjected.

"It is good," Leyna added. "Nicely done, Natalie."

"Dave, what do you think?" Scott asked.

Leyna punched his knee, and he said, "I'm a fan."

"It looks like I'm the odd man out," Scott said. "I guess I better eat up."

Save for the stoic noshing of casserole, an edgy silence ensued that Leyna felt obliged to break up: "So, Scott, Natalie tells me you might be moving to the area."

"That's true. I've decided a change of scenery will do me good." Scott stopped eating and began making a pyramid out of the casserole with his fork. "I assume Natalie told you I'm recently divorced."

"She mentioned it."

"Nasty business, as these things usually are. I want to wipe the slate clean, and since I grew up here, this seems like a comfortable place to do it."

"Do you have a new job lined up?" Leyna inquired.

"Basically, yes. I'm in commercial real estate—I own some office buildings in the Denver area. I'll keep a condo in Denver for when I need to travel back there, but for the most part, I can manage my business from here."

"You're lucky," Leyna said.

"Lucky in some things, not quite as lucky in others," Scott said, tapping his casserole pyramid with his fork. "But no, I can't complain. I've done very well. Enough about me, though. Natalie and Mark hate it when I talk about my business affairs—it seems to bore them to death. What about you two?"

"We have a son, Matthew, who's a toddler," Leyna said, her face suddenly alight. "That keeps me plenty busy."

"It must," Scott said. "And you, Dave? What do you do?"

"Oh, I just started working with my father."

"That sounds promising. What type of business?"

"A drugstore."

"A…drugstore," Scott said with a smile—and a condescending one at that, Dave noted. "You own it with him?"

"No."

"You're a pharmacist?"

"No."

"Well…"

"I'm, ah, actually an editor," Dave said. "This is just temporary until I find something suitable in my field."

"I'm sure it is," said Scott, still smiling.

Dave cut into Scott's smirk with contemptuous eyes, and another edgy silence followed.

"More casserole, anyone?" Natalie finally said.

After returning home, Dave and Leyna exchanged their notes from their respective sides of the bed.

"Natalie's brother is a real jerk, huh?" Dave said. "I can see why she doesn't get along with him. He's arrogant."

"A little, yeah, but he seemed relatively harmless."

"What about his snarky drugstore comments?"

"He was just trying to make conversation. I wouldn't dwell on it."

"And what was he trying to prove by dressing up like we were at a five-star restaurant? And did you notice his feet? They looked like a pig's hooves in those brown loafers he was wearing."

"I didn't notice, Dave."

Leyna turned out the light on her nightstand, and they went to sleep.

CHAPTER 28

Maybe—just maybe—redemption wasn't a mirage after all. It was difficult to know for certain, as this spark of hope was cloaked in the usual frustration.

Pete Townshend didn't perish in the bear pit in Switzerland—that would have been too easy. Upon sobering up, he extricated himself from it and followed through with his commitments: he wrote an album for The Who, fittingly titled *It's Hard*, and embarked on the Farewell Tour. After that, however, The Who really did cease to exist, and Pete, in a mad dash to escape his past, went off in a thousand different directions, busying himself with solo music projects, an editorship with the book publisher Faber and Faber, and the prodigious consumption of drugs and alcohol.

But in the early part of 1985, the past came calling again. The culprits weren't Roger and John, who had all but given up on bringing Pete back into the fold; Bob Geldof, an Irishman who looked as if he hadn't stepped outdoors since childhood, was the person on the other end of the line. Until recently Geldof had been the singer in the Boomtown Rats, but now he was trying his hand at saving the world, and he needed Pete's help. Geldof was planning what he hoped would be a transformative rock festival: Live Aid, whose purpose was to raise money to combat Ethiopia's wrenching famine. Scheduled for July 13 of that year, the two-pronged event, featuring one stage at Wembley Stadium in London and another at John F. Kennedy Stadium in Philadelphia, would be broadcast around the globe.

"Yeah, I'll play," Pete said to Geldof. "Why not? Wembley's just a stone's throw from my house."

"I don't think you understand. I don't want you—I want The Who."

"You're joking, right?"

"No."

"Bugger off, Bob. It's not bloody happening."

The phone rang again the next day.

"Pete," Bob said.

"What now?"

"The same thing as yesterday."

"Bugger off."

Pete was foolish enough to answer the phone the next day, too.

"I don't think you understand," Geldof said. "U2 is playing. Dire Straits is playing. Queen is playing. Led Zeppelin is playing for the first time since John Bonham died. Eric Clapton, Neil Young, Madonna, Elton John, Paul McCartney, Bob Dylan, Elvis Costello, Tom Petty, the Beach Boys, David Bowie, Crosby, Stills & Nash, Santana. Shall I go on?"

"Go fuck yourself, Bob."

"The biggest names in the music business are playing, all for a noble cause. How do you think it will look if The Who doesn't play? You'll look like real wankers."

"Is this blackmail?"

"Call it whatever you want, but just know this: the planet will be watching."

That was no exaggeration. When July 13 crept up on the calendar and The Who braced to take its turn on the Wembley stage, the 72,000 people in the crowd were but a drop in the bucket. Another 1.5 billion souls were watching on TV. Little did they know that John was frantically rummaging around backstage for a backup bass guitar, his main instrument having fallen prey to last-minute technical issues.

The actor Jack Nicholson didn't know it either as he delivered his introduction: "Got a big surprise coming up for you from Wembley. Greatness is often overused in rock and roll, but here's a truly legendary rock and roll band. Peter Townshend, Roger Daltrey, John Entwistle, and Kenney Jones. Please welcome The Who."

The legends trotted onstage, at which point a roadie gave John a backup bass that had just been located near some deli trays. Never mind that it wasn't tuned—at least John didn't have to greet the world empty-handed.

Shortly thereafter, the satellite feed short-circuited, and the 1.5 billion souls watching on TV were suddenly in the dark, though no more so than the legends, particularly Pete. He jumped around the stage as he always had, but it was strictly reflexive, like the twitching of a snake's body after its head had been lopped off. The only heartfelt emotions he exhibited were scowls when John, wrestling mightily with his substitute bass, shanked notes. The satellite feed was restored by the finale of the four-song set, "Won't Get Fooled Again," just in time for the 1.5 billion souls to hear Roger flub the lyrics and see Pete fall flat on his ass while trying to swing his leg over a mike stand.

"Never again," Pete said backstage. "That was a fucking disaster."

Indeed, from England to Ecuador, from America to Australia, The Who was skewered in the press. Yet Pete, Roger, John, and even Kenney had been part of something much bigger than themselves. Live Aid had delivered on the promise of that romp in the mud in 1969. Whereas Woodstock, for all its political bluster, accomplished nothing tangible, Live Aid raised more than $140 million and heightened awareness of world hunger.

Somewhere deep inside, beneath his calloused veneer, Pete had grasped the event's possibilities. Why else would he have gone to the trouble of writing a song, "After the Fire," for The Who to play that day? The tune wound up being pulled from the set list, which was probably for the better given how everything unfolded, but it nevertheless gave Pete away, if only subconsciously. The fire hadn't yet been extinguished—hope still smoldered.

CHAPTER 29

The anthropologist started his Volkswagen Jetta, its trunk and backseat filled with luggage, and he backed out of the driveway.

"Off on a new adventure," he said with a goateed smile to the woman sitting in the passenger's seat. "Are you excited?"

This was the anthropologist's first adventure since being hauled into the Corning police station in 1972—and frankly, that had been more of a nightmare than an adventure. Once the dust had settled, he had avoided jail time; Yonder had taken the fall, as well he should have since it was his operation, and had been sentenced to three years in prison. Nevertheless, the anthropologist was a free man in name only. Corning was a small town, and people talked. Word quickly spread to Ithaca, another small town where people talked. The last shred of his reputation smeared, he resigned his professorship, which turned out to be surprisingly easy to do.

The anthropologist set out to start anew, selling his once-tidy two-story home and leaving Ithaca. But he made it only ninety miles up the road to Rochester, for he still had no ideas. He rented an efficiency apartment with some of the money from his home sale, shaved his scraggly beard, and looked for a job, preferably one that wouldn't be too demanding.

He found what he wanted at Wegmans, a chain of grocery stores in the region. Wegmans had elevated grocery shopping to a grand level in the years since John Wegman opened the Rochester Fruit & Vegetable Company in 1916. Each sprawling store featured restaurants in addition to ornate seafood, cheese, pharmacy, catering, cosmetics, butcher, floral, beer, wine, bakery, and gift departments. The anthropologist was assigned to cheese.

Though this was far removed from the learned setting at Ithaca College, he couldn't hide altogether from his nature. Thus, he studied up on cheese, going to the library and reading about the Combalou caves in the Roquefort-sur-Soulzon region of France, the nomadic Turkic tribesmen who first made cheese as long ago as 8000 BC, and anything else he could uncover on the subject.

And by the time he donned his store-issued blue smock, he was a font of knowledge. His very first customer was a middle-aged woman in a Buffalo Bills sweatshirt who, with her hair pushed up into a ramshackle bun and her face lacking a trace of makeup, hadn't yet gotten herself together.

"Good day, ma'am," he began. "Can I help you locate something in particular?"

"Oh, hi," she responded. "We're having friends over for the game today, and I'm just looking for some snacks."

"Cheddar is always a good place to start for a football game. It's a sturdy cheese."

"Okay."

He guided her over to the cheddar display and said, "Many people view cheddar as a distinctly American cheese, but you'll be interested to know that it was most likely first made by the Romans."

"Um," responded the woman in the Bills sweatshirt, scratching her unwashed head.

"That said, the best cheddar today comes from the great state of Wisconsin, and justifiably so: cheesemakers there have spent the past century perfecting it. And, of course, Wisconsin's dairy products are superior. The sharp variety is particularly good, which is why I'm recommending it."

The anthropologist dropped three wedges of sharp cheddar into her cart and guided her to the brie.

"I think you'll find this to be an ideal contrast to the cheddar," he said. "Whereas cheddar is hard, brie has a creamy texture. May I recommend this variety, the Brie de Meaux, which comes from northern France?"

"Um…"

The anthropologist dropped four wheels of Brie de Meaux into her cart and guided her to the gouda.

"Now," he continued, "it may seem as if we've gone only ten feet down the aisle, but we have, in fact, traveled all the way to the Netherlands.

Why? Because that's where this cheese—gouda—comes from. Like cheddar, it has a hard consistency. Go ahead, tap it."

With some hesitation, she tapped it. "Yep, you're right. Hard."

"Part of that is due to the aging process. Some varieties of gouda are aged up to seven years, if you can believe it. May I?"

The anthropologist dropped five hunks of gouda into her cart, and she departed with a perplexed expression on her craggy face, as well as enough cheese to feed not only her friends but also the friends of their friends.

It was a successful first day for the anthropologist, who quickly settled into a comfortable groove at Wegmans. One year passed. Then two. Then three. Then six. Then ten. Then thirteen. In seemingly the blink of an eye, the anthropologist was fifty—gray-haired and wrinkled. And he had… well, sold a lot of cheese.

But he couldn't have called it a waste of a life. For just after his fiftieth birthday, he came up with an idea—a good idea, one that made unquestionable sense. It involved pairing cheese and wine. He ran it past Sue Planck, a veteran of the wine department whose tired yet compassionate eyes widened considerably as she listened.

"We'll create displays that will be fascinatingly intricate and appealing," he said, stopping only to catch his breath. "For example, there will be a display featuring Muenster cheese and gewürztraminer wine. And with it, we'll have a placard describing how the spicy richness of both the Muenster and the gewürztraminer play off of one another. Do you doubt for a moment that both the cheese and the wine will fly off the shelves?"

"I don't doubt it at all."

That night Sue procured a bottle of chardonnay from the wine department and the anthropologist a wedge of gruyère from the cheese department, and the two went to his efficiency apartment to further discuss his idea. After an hour, however, the conversation turned to personal matters. Sipping on the chardonnay and nibbling on the gruyère, Sue told the anthropologist about her ex-husband, who had cheated on her repeatedly before finally running off with a receptionist, leaving her to raise their young daughter by herself. Her eyes grew wearier than usual when she spoke of the travails of being a single mom—the long hours of work just to keep the bills paid, the loneliness—but they roared to life when she informed the anthropologist that her daughter had turned out great: she was living in Toledo, Ohio, happily married to a hotel marketing associate.

Sue had something of a weight problem, but the anthropologist saw beyond her waistline. Her openness put him at ease, so much so that he told her about his own history, including the regrettable string of incidents that had led him to Wegmans. With the compassionate shades in her eyes now dominant, she wrapped her arm around his shoulder. And at dawn they made love on his pullout sofa.

Fate, it seemed, was no longer playing cruel tricks on the anthropologist. He regrew his old goatee, and with the approval of store management, he and Sue enacted their wine-and-cheese plan. Then, as if in validation of his shifting fortunes, a letter arrived from a former classmate at the University of Pennsylvania. He had recently become the dean of a community college, and he had a proposition for the anthropologist: "I'm in something of a bind," the letter read. "Classes begin in six weeks, and the professor who was to teach Introduction to Cultural Anthropology has fallen gravely ill. I immediately thought of you to replace him. From what I recall, there would be no one better, and I've learned that you're available. I think this would be a worthwhile opportunity for you, especially given your current circumstances, so please give it serious consideration. It's the least you could do. After all, I had a devil of a time locating you."

The anthropologist set the letter on his kitchen table and ran his fingers through his goatee. "Interesting," he said to himself.

At Wegmans that day, he was distracted—his thoughts had turned from cheese to teaching. He also thought of Sue Planck, and he found her by the merlot, where she was stocking a shelf. Although he hadn't known her for long—at least not intimately—he had a hunch everything would be okay.

"Yes, I'm excited," Sue said as the anthropologist backed the

Volkswagen Jetta out of the driveway. "I haven't been this excited in a long time. I guess it's never too late to start over."

The Jetta rolled out of Rochester, toward Oakton Community College in suburban Chicago.

CHAPTER 30

At 447 Greenwood Street, the outlook remained hazy, and Dave was wearing his circumstances like a broken-in pair of Levis.

He began his day like most of his others for the past eighteen months: with the fifteen-minute drive in his Volvo to Weiss Drugstore. Since the store wouldn't open until 8:30, the lights were still off when he arrived, except at the back counter, where William was filling prescriptions.

"Where's Mom?" Dave asked upon joining his dad in back.

"She'll be in after lunch," he answered, a smoke burning in the ashtray next to his pill-counting tray. "She has a doctor's appointment. That hip of hers is really acting up."

"I thought it was doing better."

"She just acts like it is. Anyway, it's Friday, and you know what that means."

"Only too well."

Friday brought forth the task Dave dreaded most: cleaning the Slush Puppie machine, which involved taking apart the pieces that dispensed the icy drink and washing them. The first time he had ever done it, the hardware had sat before him like a Rubik's Cube, and upon disassembling and then reassembling everything, he had been met not with an icy drink but a grinding noise, necessitating a call to a repairman.

Shortly before nine o'clock, Marie appeared for her eight-hour shift at the front counter. She was past retirement age—Dave guessed she was 103—but liked to stay busy. Working, she said, kept her strong. As she assumed her position behind the cash register, she nearly bumped Dave, who was carefully fastening the last of the Slush Puppie parts.

"Aren't you done with that yet?" she grumbled.

"Just want to make sure everything operates as it should."

"That'd be a first."

"Hey, it only didn't work once, and that was a long time ago."

"I don't know why you're even bothering. No one drinks Slush Puppies in the winter."

Dave's next duty—inventory—proved to be more engaging than usual. Thanks to cold and flu season (William's most joyous time of year), there had been a run on Kleenex, aspirin and ibuprofen, vaporizers, vapor rub, thermometers, nasal spray, cough medicine, decongestant, throat lozenges, vitamin C, hand soap, electric blankets, bedroom slippers, and magazines.

After phoning in his inventory order to the distributor, Dave hunkered down at a cash register near his dad at the back counter. This, too, proved to be busy, as an influx of the infirmed picked up the prescriptions that William had been filling. With lunchtime approaching, in came Denny Cranston, who owned a real estate office a few doors down and had coached Dave in Little League way back when. Denny wasn't suffering from a cold, the flu, or any other malady.

"A box of Trojans, son," he said.

Blushing, Dave bent down to sift through the condom drawer. "Um, lubricated?" he asked from beneath the counter.

"Yeah, and ribbed."

When Dave reappeared with the Trojans, his face was still red. "Do you need a bag?"

"I'll just slide them right into my pocket."

"Okay then," Dave said. He pushed the condoms across the counter and quickly punched some keys on the cash register. "With tax, it'll be $2.27."

Dave hoped that would be that, but Denny lingered after paying the bill.

"How 'bout those Cubs?" Denny said, casually tossing the box of condoms from hand to hand. "I like the team they've put together this offseason. I think they'll be a contender, especially if the pitching holds up again. They came so damn close last year, didn't they?"

"They really did, Mr. Cran—, er, Denny."

"If that ball hadn't rolled through Durham's legs, they would have gone to the World Series, and we might be having a different conversation right now. These '85 Cubs will just have to toughen up, like we did when we won the Glenview championship. Remember that? There was a lesson in that season we had."

"There was indeed," though Dave had no idea what it was.

Mercifully, Denny pocketed the Trojans and bid adieu, at which point William strolled over to the cash register.

"Why do you think Denny Cranston was buying condoms?" William asked with an all-knowing grin.

"It's pretty obvious."

"I can tell you this much: He won't be using them on his wife. She had a hysterectomy last year."

Cupping his ears with his hands, Dave said, "Geez, Dad. Too much information."

Leyna began her day like most of her others for the past twelve months: with Dave dropping her and Matthew off at the YWCA on his way to Weiss Drugstore.

Her first task was to take Matthew to the onsite daycare center. Miss Stanley, who barely seemed old enough to be a "Miss," was waiting at the door.

"Good morning, Matthew," she said cheerfully. "We're going to have lots and lots of fun today."

"Bye-bye, Mama," Matthew said in a confident tone that came from knowing he was safe and sound.

"Not so fast," Leyna said. "Hugs first."

She kneeled down, and Matthew wrapped his arms around her. "Love you, Mama."

"That's my big boy. I love you, too. You be good, okay?"

"I will."

With that, he spun around and joined Naomi and Tommy over by the dominoes.

"So what's in store for today?" Leyna asked Miss Stanley.

"It's counting day. Then I think we'll do an art project…painting. The kids always love that."

"Wonderful. I wish I could paint with you, but work beckons. You know where to find me if you need me."

The wintry wind pricked Leyna's face as she hurried across the courtyard to her office. It was as if she had never left. Her plants were all back on her desk, along with neatly stacked papers. The one notable addition was a framed picture of Matthew playing with wrapping paper on that very first Christmas.

She opened a folder relating to her latest project: a violence-prevention initiative aimed at helping kids forge healthy relationships in school. But her mind drifted, as it had so often lately. When she looked at her watch, it was already eleven o'clock, and she had barely put a dent in her paperwork. A few minutes later, Natalie appeared in the doorway.

"Are they ever going to fix the heating in here?" asked Natalie, who was wearing a brown turtleneck sweater to combat the chill.

"Ah, the lovely world of nonprofits, where heat is viewed as a frivolous expense."

Natalie laughed and said, "What do you say we go to Gigio's for lunch? Their heating works. Plus, I have a craving for pasta."

"That sounds delicious—both the heating and the pasta—but I was planning to run some errands."

"Again?"

"I know, right? It's the only time I have to do it. There just aren't enough hours in the day. I'm lucky *anything* gets done."

"Join the club. Between work and everything going on around the house, I barely know up from down."

"We definitely need to catch up, though. It's been too long. Maybe Matthew and I can drop by this weekend for a play date."

"That would be great."

When noon arrived, Leyna peeked in at Matthew through the little square window in the daycare center's door before walking two blocks to the corner of Wesley and Lyons. Shivering, she waited for her ride.

"It's noon," Dave said to his dad, "and you know what that means."

"Time to go to your career group meeting?"

"You guessed it. Argh."

"Am I going to be losing you soon to untold riches?"

"You ask that every time, and the answer never changes: if you do, it won't be because of these guys."

They convened at lunchtime every Friday around a back table at The Sandwich Shop in Skokie, a suburb next to Glenview, and their goals were to provide support to each other and come up with ideas for reviving their careers. There was Barry "Boom Boom" Bloom, who weighed in at about 300 pounds and lived with his sister; Dan "The Hairball" Jorgenson, who had boozed his way out of his latest job, which had involved selling upholstery; "Wayward" Lenny Jones, who was trying to get his footing after moving here from Topeka to care for his sick mother; and Derrick "The Bladder" Nesbitt, who excused himself every fifteen minutes to go to the bathroom. The group was connected to the Unitarian church with the NUCLEAR-FREE ZONE sign, and Leyna had heard about it from a work friend who belonged there.

"You should join it," she had said to Dave. "Networking definitely can't hurt. Don't you agree?"

Dave appeased her by following through with her "suggestion," but he couldn't help but think this was par for the course for Leyna, who seemed more concerned these days with what he wasn't than what he was. If she had been looking closely, she might have seen that he was already making a comeback of sorts. Then again, she couldn't be blamed for missing it. Though the arrow was pointing up, it was misshapen, like a street sign that had been clipped by a car.

At any rate, working at Weiss Drugstore hadn't turned out to be the exercise in defeat he had envisioned, even if he was still an editor at heart. The pay wasn't all that great, but the hours were much better than at the *Herald*, as was the stress level. Dave had been around when Matthew had scribbled his first letter (an "i" that looked more like an "l"). He had been around when Matthew had brushed his teeth by himself for the first time (followed by drawing a smiley face on the mirror with the toothpaste). He had been there for all that stuff.

But now it was 12:10 on a Friday—the band of idiots had assembled at The Sandwich Shop—and there was no turning back. Or was there? At the very least, he could take a detour. Dave ignored the open spot in front of the restaurant and kept driving. *I'll just tell Leyna I went to the damn meeting*, he reasoned. *She'll never know the difference, and neither will I. I don't even like the subs at The Sandwich Shop anyway.* He had a hankering for eggs and bacon, and Walker Bros., a block north of Evanston on Green Bay Road in Wilmette, would more than fit the bill.

"How was your meeting?" Leyna asked.
"Oh, that? It was fine. Business as usual."
"What came of it?"
"Forget the meeting."
"I'm curious."
"I'm not interested in my meeting right now. More importantly, are you going to do it?"
"Not this again," Leyna said, sighing.
"I can't help it."
"Clearly, and it doesn't make anything easier."

Leyna pulled the bedsheet over her breasts. Natalie's brother reached underneath, and she giggled. It was the same high-pitched giggle that had once been reserved for Dave.

"That's exactly why I said it," Scott said with a devilish smile.

Dave sipped a cup of coffee while waiting for his eggs and bacon. Looking at his watch, he thought, *It's 12:40, which can only mean that Barry is talking about Dungeons & Dragons and Derrick has run off to the bathroom. Thank God I'm not there.* The waitress arrived with his feast, and it looked scrumptious—just what the doctor ordered.

"Can I get you anything else?" the waitress asked.
"More coffee, please. It really hits the spot on a cold day."
"Sure thing, sweetie."

"I know that's why you said it," Leyna said, "but sometimes it makes me anxious."
"Don't you think it's a little late for that?"

Scott had a point. Seven months earlier she had walked over to the Davis Street Garden Center during her lunch break to see if anything might strike her fancy. She was perusing an assortment of wildflower seeds when she heard someone say, "Leyna?"

Turning around, she said, "Yes?"

"Hi. It's Scott Tross, Natalie's brother."

"Of course. How are you?"

"I'm good."

"What brings you here? You don't strike me as the gardening type."

"I'm not, but I'm trying to get up to speed. Remember Natalie's dinner, when I said I was thinking of moving back here?"

"Yep."

"I finally pulled the trigger. I bought a house about a month ago."

"Natalie mentioned something about that."

"Anyway, there's a large garden in the backyard, and I have no idea what to do with it. I'll probably just call a landscaper. I don't have the time."

"No need to call a landscaper. I'm a whiz when it comes to gardening. What do you want to know?"

"You name it."

Leyna led Scott from aisle to aisle. She noticed that he always leaned within inches of her, always maintained direct eye contact with her, always let her words trail into silence as he contemplated her gardening wisdom. It was both unnerving and flattering.

"When do you have to be back at work?" he asked.

"Not for a little while, actually. Slow day."

"Can you take a quick look at my garden? I have so many other things to take care of, and I really want to get this out of the way."

"Sure. Far be it from me to stand in the way of progress."

Leyna slid into the soft-leather interior of Scott's Mercedes, and they raced off to his house, a large green-painted Victorian that was only a mile and a half north of the prairie box. Leyna paced the garden intently, pausing every few steps to tell Scott what should go where.

"You truly are amazing," he said, and Leyna giggled.

A month later—after a series of phone calls, first about gardening and then about anything and everything—they found themselves back at Scott's house, this time in his bedroom. Soon it became a semi-regular lunchtime routine. Leyna knew better than to keep coming back, but she couldn't help herself—it felt really good.

As for Dave? He remained oblivious, and Leyna alternated between being relieved and angered by this. It was, she thought, par for the course, as Dave was off in his own world these days, attuned to little if anything. He once had been reassuringly on point, from nursing her back to health after their accident to his diligence at the *Herald* to fretting about, frankly, *everything*. All of this contributed to his quirky charm. Now, though, he seemed almost weak.

With Scott, she saw a future. It wasn't about money; if it had been, she would have already left Dave. It was more about clarity. Everything Scott did, whether he was talking to her or holding her, had an air of purpose.

This wasn't to say that her mind was made up. She experienced moments of wrenching guilt, especially when she got into bed with Dave after being with Scott earlier in the day. And in some ways, she still truly loved Dave. He was, after all, Matthew's father. The three of them were a family, just as she had always wanted. So she kept waiting for a spark that would reignite their relationship, a spark she feared might never come.

"Seriously, I can't go on like this forever," Scott continued, running his hand along Leyna's body, the bedsheet rising and falling like waves. "You need to do it soon. You need to tell Dave you're leaving him. It's that simple."

"It's not that simple, and you know it. Do we have to talk about this right now? I have to get back to the office. I'm already late."

His stomach blissfully full, Dave started the Volvo and turned on the radio. "Holiday" by Madonna was playing. Dave didn't care for the song, but he certainly was glad to still have the Volvo. In one of the apocalyptic scenarios he had imagined, a tow truck pulled up to the bridge under which he, Leyna, and Matthew were living and hauled it away.

But alas, they weren't living under a bridge. They were ensconced in the prairie box, which was made of solid brick. When Leyna had first gone back to work to help ease their financial burden, she had complained about the difficulty of sending Matthew off to daycare, even if it was only a courtyard away. But Dave hadn't heard a peep out of her for at least six months; she no doubt had seen that Matthew was doing just fine. If he could convince her that he was doing fine, too—or at least not horribly—everything would go back to normal.

"Undercover of the Night" by the Rolling Stones came on the radio. Dave liked this one, and he sang along to it as he returned to Weiss Drugstore.

With the heat blasting in his Mercedes, Scott drove Leyna toward the corner of Wesley and Lyons.

"I have a pile of work to finish this afternoon," she said. "I feel like I didn't get a single thing done this morning."

"Which reminds me, you asked me about my meeting this morning."

"That's right. How was it?"

"Excellent. I'm closing the deal next week, so I'll be flying to Denver. Want to join me?"

Leyna giggled while shaking her head.

"I didn't think so. But I'll be back Wednesday night. Lunch on Thursday?"

"Now that's something I can arrange."

Stopped at a red light on Green Bay Road, Dave continued to sing along to "Undercover of the Night." His crooning was interrupted, however, by a belch that tasted of eggs and bacon. "Oops," he said, looking around as if someone might have heard him.

When he craned his neck to the left, he saw a Mercedes idling in the lane next to his. *Nice car. Puts my Volvo to shame.* He nearly directed his attention to the song again, but the Mercedes wouldn't let go. There was a woman in the passenger's seat who was facing the driver and appeared to be engrossed in a conversation. Dave pressed his nose against the cold window for a closer look.

The woman leaned back in her seat, providing Dave with a clear view of both riders. *Huh?* She turned toward the Volvo seemingly in slow motion, her face bright with a smile until her eyes met Dave's. He knew instantly, and he wanted to die.

CHAPTER 31

James Smith wanted to make Jenny feel like Cinderella at the ball, and he had planned everything down to the tiniest detail. When she returned to their Frank Lloyd Wright knockoff after her shift at the hospital, his car was already in the driveway.

"This is a surprise," she said. "You never beat me home."

James took her by the hand into the dining room, where she saw a white envelope on the table that had a message written on it: "To my one and only for our five-year wedding anniversary."

"See what's inside," he prodded.

Jenny opened the envelope carefully so as not to tear into the message. "A trip to Hawaii?" she asked.

"Where everything began for us. This is our itinerary. Go ahead, read it."

"The Kapalua Resort?"

"Yes."

"Volcanoes National Park?"

"Yes."

"Whale watching? A snorkeling tour? Surfing? But we've never surfed."

"Time to learn. On this trip to Hawaii, we're actually going to leave our hotel room."

"This is so sweet," she said, putting the itinerary back on the table so that she could give James a full-out hug. "It's incredible. I'm such a lucky woman."

"And I'm a lucky man."

Indeed, neither James nor Jenny could have felt any luckier when, three weeks later, a Town Car pulled into the driveway to whisk them off to O'Hare Airport for their anniversary trip.

"I'm so excited," Jenny said.

"I'm glad."

Enter, quite literally, Deke Ross and Lonnie Knowles. Deke was the brains behind the duo, and he looked the part with wire-rimmed glasses that gave his face a cerebral bent. Lonnie was the muscle, and he looked his part, too, with fingers like sausages and forearms like hams.

As it happened, Deke was every bit as scrupulous as James. He had spent the past week casing the neighborhood, trying to determine which house in this garden of affluence would be best for the picking. The Usonian-style home—a not-so-successful homage to Frank Lloyd Wright, Deke decided—seemed to be a real possibility: (1) it was large, which meant more treasure, (2) it was secluded thanks to an abundance of foliage on the property, and (3) it had an attached garage in which they could hide their van. And when a Town Car arrived one morning to pick up a couple bearing much luggage, Deke considered it to be an act of providence.

Under the cover of darkness, they eased their black Ford van into the driveway and put on surgical gloves. Deke then entered a master code into the keypad on the garage. It was a trick he had learned during his college job at Naismith Garages a few years earlier, and the door creaked open. After sealing the van inside, they proceeded to a doorway that led from the garage into the home.

"Wipe your feet first," Deke instructed.

"Are you serious?"

"Why don't you ever wipe your feet? There's no need to be a pig about it and track dirt into their house."

Following a few halfhearted brushes of his work boots against the doormat, Lonnie said, "There, are you fucking happy now?"

Methodically and quietly, flashlights in their hands, they took stock of each room before sweeping back through to claim their prizes. They took jewelry from the bedroom, artwork off the living room walls, fine china, silver and antique chairs from the dining room, and a wad of cash from a desk drawer in the study.

The entertainment room was a particular bonanza. Carrying the Tanzanian wood carving out to the garage, Lonnie said, "This thing's gotta be worth a ton of money."

Lonnie returned for the Venetian end table, a Harman Kardon stereo system, a Civil War-era bayonet, a small bronze statue of Napoleon, and then a television. He strained to lift the TV, nicking the wall with its edge.

"Careful," chided Deke. "You just chipped the paint."

"Who gives a shit?"

"The people who live here, for one."

"I'm pretty sure they'll have other things to worry about."

After they had procured everything they wanted, Lonnie loaded the van while Deke sat at the kitchen table and wrote a note to James and Jenny:

I want to thank you, as well as apologize for any inconvenience we've caused. We're just trying to make a living. I'm sure you understand. You'll notice that we took great care not to dirty your beautiful house. Thanks again.

Out in the garage, Lonnie had room to spare in the van. Thus, he called an audible and began randomly shoving items into it: a snowblower, a rusty lawnmower, a weathered patio umbrella, a scratched-up coffee table, a hoe, a ten-speed bicycle without a chain, two old lawn chairs, and a cherry-red guitar that looked like it had seen better days.

"There," said Lonnie, and he closed the van doors.

When Deke finished composing his note, they made their getaway to the house they shared outside McHenry, a town in the sticks about ninety minutes west. Once they were safely inside their garage, Lonnie began unloading the van. Deke stood nearby with a pencil and notepad to record the inventory, and the first items to come out were those Lonnie had audibled.

"What's all this?" Deke asked indignantly.

"There was extra room."

"A patio umbrella? A lawnmower that couldn't possibly have been started for three years? A guitar that looks like it was in a house fire? A *hoe*? What are we supposed to do with these things?"

"Sell them with everything else."

"It's junk, and we can't have it lying around here. In a worst-case scenario, it will trace the crime right to us. You need to get rid of it."

"Where?"

"I don't know. Drive out ten or twenty miles and dump it in the river."

"Are you fucking serious?"

"Better safe than sorry. Just make sure to find a remote place. And please, don't let anyone see you."

"You're not coming?"

"I'm staying here to price everything. We need to fence this as soon as possible."

After the van had been emptied, Lonnie put the junk back in and headed farther out into the sticks. Even in the dead of night, he knew exactly where he was, a familiarity that had come from growing up in the area. He decided on a spot about ten miles over the Wisconsin border, before Burlington. It was near a little-known dirt road that abutted the Fox River. Lonnie parked the van in a small clearing and carried the pieces through a dense cluster of trees to the river's edge, punctuating each trip with, "This is a fucking joke."

Positioned on a stone ledge several yards above the water, he proceeded to purge the evidence, starting with the snowblower. Lonnie could see nothing, but he heard the bulky machine splash into the current. Next he released the lawnmower, then the hoe, ten-speed, lawn chairs, patio umbrella, and coffee table. Finally, he grabbed ahold of the Special, giving it an extra-hard heave.

"There," Lonnie said. "I hope he's happy now."

CHAPTER 32

Dave hadn't been prepared for this; adultery hadn't been on his list of apocalyptic scenarios. Leyna had always been part of the picture, no matter how far into the wilderness his imagination had wandered.

Not knowing what else to do, he had raced away down Green Bay Road as soon as the light had turned green. He had no recollection of where he had driven. When he returned to 447 Greenwood Street that night, Leyna was waiting on the couch in the family room. Her eyes were puffy, and she had a box of Kleenex on her lap.

"I called the store," she said. "Your dad said you never came back after lunch. Where were you?"

"What do you care?"

"I was worried."

"I bet you were. Where's Matthew?"

"Asleep."

For the next five minutes, the only sound was the twisting of the car keys in Dave's hand. Dave wanted to yell at the top of his lungs that he hated her. He wanted to call her a whore and a lying bitch and a cunt. But words seemed gratuitous. His eyes—blazing with betrayal—said everything.

Finally, there was this: "Why?"

Leyna, immobilized by Dave's gouging eyes, stared silently at the Kleenex box.

"Why?" he asked again.

"I don't know why."

"That's not an answer."

"I just know that I'm so sorry."

"You didn't look sorry eight hours ago. You looked like you were having the time of your life."

"It seems impossible to explain."

"That's it? I don't even warrant an explanation?"

Her face still directed toward the Kleenex box, she half-mumbled,

"You've been like a ghost, and he happened to come along, and we just clicked like you and I once did, and—"

"So it's my fault? I can't believe this."

"It's nobody's fault."

"That's a convenient way of justifying it."

"I'm not justifying anything. It just—"

"I trusted you."

"I know, but it's not just about trust."

"It is to me. It's everything."

"You haven't felt like a connection's been missing between us?"

"What's been missing, Leyna? I went through a down time. So what? It happens to all of us, even you. But I'm not a…a ghost. I've been here the whole time, flesh and blood. Maybe you would have noticed if you hadn't been so busy—"

"Don't say it."

He didn't. Instead he spun around and stomped out of the family room. There was no turning back now, not for him and not for Leyna. She hated that it had come to this; all these months, she had thought she was being so very careful. Then again, it had been ludicrous to believe she and Scott could have kept this a secret. Maybe she had wanted to get caught—just not at a stoplight on Green Bay Road, before she had devised a gentler way to reach a resolution.

As she discovered at work the following Monday when her best friend Natalie knocked on her office door, the damage extended beyond the prairie box.

"Hi," Leyna said hesitantly, her eyes still puffy. "Come on in."

Natalie remained in the doorway, scrutinizing Leyna before saying, "Scott stopped by this weekend."

"Oh yeah?" Leyna said, and she glanced away.

"He told me what happened, or what's been happening, I should say. I'm shocked."

"I don't know what—"

"I never would have thought it in a million years. Of all people, Scott? My *brother*? My God, you two aren't even remotely alike."

Leyna shrugged.

"I feel incredibly awkward," Natalie said. "I feel like I somehow played a part in ruining your marriage."

"That's ridiculous. You had nothing to do with it."

"If I hadn't introduced you two, this would have never happened."

"That's not why this happened, and you know it. Scott…Scott was a symptom."

"I wouldn't phrase it quite like that, but what do I know? Nothing, as it turns out. I'm sick about this. I have no idea how I'll ever be able to look Dave in the eye again."

After that Leyna didn't see Natalie outside of work. There were no more play dates with the kids, no more heart-to-hearts.

As for Dave, everything around him was moving so fast that he had no hope of keeping up, especially once the wheels of "justice" started turning. James Brown had sung, "This is a man's, a man's, a man's world," but in matters of divorce, the legal system begged to differ, steadfastly upholding the notion that children needed their mothers, even if one such mother had been shacking up with a pig-hooved homewrecker. It was a foregone conclusion that Leyna would be granted primary custody of Matthew. Dave, on the other hand, was rendered an afterthought: his custody of the boy was limited to every other weekend.

When the divorce was finalized in 1986, there was nothing left for Dave to do but pick up the pieces, starting with what remained of his belongings. Here, too, it wasn't a man's, a man's, a man's world. Except for the couch from the family room, a dresser, some chairs, and a coffee table, the court had decreed that everything belonged to Leyna since she had primary custody of Matthew. Not that Dave needed much anyway. Now that child support payments were kicking in, he could only afford a one-bedroom apartment in Skokie whose bathroom had mold on the ceiling. He felt like he was back between the peeling water tower and the sooty highway of yesteryear, the difference being that he was living alone.

With his dad riding shotgun, Dave pulled up to the prairie box in a U-Haul, having picked a time to come when he knew Leyna wouldn't be there. A "For Sale" sign was pounded into the front lawn, and Dave stopped to examine it as he made his way up the walkway.

Placing his hand on Dave's shoulder, William said, "Ready, son?"

"Yep, let's get it over with."

The whole thing took less than an hour.

Leyna and Scott waited until after the prairie box had been sold to officially consummate their relationship. Under the circumstances, Leyna didn't want anything too ostentatious, so they exchanged their wedding vows in the backyard of the Victorian they now shared, next to the fateful flower garden, which was in full bloom. Scott's parents were there, and Matthew sat between them during the ceremony. Natalie was a no-show.

In the blur of it all—the blur of a life that had flown off the rails—the only constant for Dave was Weiss Drugstore, for which he was thankful. He was even thankful for the Slush Puppie machine and crotchety Marie and goofballs from the neighborhood like Denny Cranston. Mostly, he was thankful for his mom and dad, who loved him unconditionally. Parents didn't bail when the going got rough.

Following the divorce, however, Helen was hampered by problems of her own, namely the degenerative condition of her hip, which prevented her from working on a regular basis. Dave picked up the slack, and at least it distracted him. One day, after Helen had been forced at the last minute to bow out of coming to the store, he even took his first stab at accounting, a truly foreign undertaking for someone who had once made his living with words. Sitting at the rolltop desk in Weiss Drugstore's tiny office, he spent an entire morning punching the keys of a calculator, trying to balance the books. When he finished, he rushed over to his dad at the back counter.

"A smile?" said William, who was leaning over the pill tray. "I haven't seen one of those on you for a while. What gives?"

"I never realized this place is such a little goldmine. I always thought you were just kind of getting by. Way to go, Dad."

"Well, I was never going to get rich doing this, but, yes, business has been good," William said with a grin of his own. "If you provide honest service, your customers will stay loyal. That's really all there is to it."

Dave remained in an improbably good mood for the rest of that day, right up until he drove to the Victorian to pick up Matthew for their weekend together. Dave particularly disliked this part of his post-marriage routine. One, it irritated him that his entire Skokie apartment would fit into Scott and Leyna's kitchen and family room. And two, the oak front door was abnormally thick, all but saying, "Don't come in." He knocked on it, and Leyna answered.

"Hi, Dave," she said in a cheerful voice that further tanked his spirits. *Why does she have to act so happy? Why can't she be pissed off like me?*

Leyna had been gardening in the backyard and wasn't wearing makeup. Even at nearly forty, she didn't need any. Her skin was still soft and smooth, and this, too, tormented Dave, for his whirling hormones still hadn't gotten the message that he was out of the picture as her lover.

"Is Matthew ready?" he asked.

"Almost. He'll be down in a sec."

"So when I talked to him on the phone a couple nights ago, he told me you've quit your job."

"Well, you know, I was down to only one day a week anyway, and it's better for Matthew if I'm at home."

"But he's in school now. He's gone all day."

"Just the same…"

"That certainly worked out well for you," Dave said, the words spilling from his mouth like droplets of acid. "I guess you have it all figured out, just like always. Lucky you."

"Oh, Dave. Do we have to do this again?"

Matthew appeared in the doorway with a small backpack slung over his shoulder.

"Ready, pal?" Dave said, glaring at Leyna all the while.

"Uh-huh."

"Good, because I've got big plans for the weekend."

"What, what?" Matthew asked.

"You'll just have to find out."

"Ooo, sounds exciting," Leyna said in that maddeningly cheerful voice.

Before they could make their getaway, Scott showed up in the doorway, whereupon he rested his manicured hands on Matthew's shoulders.

"We need a favor," he said.

"What now?" Dave answered, shifting his glare from Leyna to the pig-hooved one.

"I know you're supposed to have Matthew all weekend, but we wanted to spend Sunday up at the lake house. It's our only chance for the next several weekends. Can you have him back in the morning Sunday instead of the evening?"

Dave felt every muscle in his body tense up. *Is this guy completely clueless? It's like nothing grievous ever happened, just business as usual.* Dave wanted to go off on him—and he swore he would have if little Matthew hadn't been present.

"Is that okay with you?" Dave said to the child.

Following a moment of self-conscious hesitation, Matthew nodded.

"Fine," Dave griped, now alternating his glare between Scott and Leyna. "I'll have him back by eight."

Under the specter of the lake house, Dave's big plans for the weekend were suddenly diminished. A dinner of burgers at the Chuck Wagon seemed woefully inadequate, even if it was Matthew's favorite restaurant. So did going back to his shitty apartment to watch *The Great Mouse Detective* on the VCR. After preparing popcorn, they dimmed the lights and sank into the old couch from the family room to watch the movie. Matthew fell asleep midway through, and Dave carried him into the bedroom. He then returned to the couch, where he spent most of the night tossing and turning.

The next morning Dave poured Matthew an overflowing bowl of his favorite cereal, Trix. As Matthew ate and looked at the comics in the *Tribune*, Dave stole away to his bedroom closet, returning with a baseball glove.

"Look what I bought you," he said. "Brand new. A Rawlings."

With a mouthful of Trix, Matthew said, "Thanks, Dad."

"When you're done with your cereal, we'll play some catch. It's been a while since we've done that."

Dave rounded up his own glove—a Wilson A2000 his parents had bought him in the seventh grade—and they walked to the park. Since the lad was only six years old, this activity called for a gentle touch. Dave lined up a short distance from Matthew, holding up the baseball to let him know it was coming.

"Ready?" he asked.

"Yep. Throw it."

He lobbed the ball to Matthew, who nabbed it effortlessly and fired it right back. The ball snapped into Dave's A2000.

"Holy cow," Dave said, "where did that come from? I can't believe how much you've been improving."

"Scott's been teaching me."

"Of course. I should have known."

Dave felt his muscles tense up again, which translated into a tighter grip on the ball. His knuckles were white when he let it go, this time with more zip than he had intended. Matthew, however, gamely hauled it in.

"Back up, Dad."

Dave moved back five paces, and Matthew delivered another perfect strike.

"How much have you been playing?" Dave asked.

"Every day in the backyard when Scott gets home from work."

His knuckles white once more, Dave zipped the ball over Matthew's head.

"Sorry about the bad throw," Dave said as Matthew ran to retrieve the baseball.

"Hey, Dad," yelled Matthew, who was now a good thirty-five feet away. "I bet I can get it to you on the fly."

Sure enough, he did.

"I just can't believe how strong your arm is getting," Dave said.

"Scott said he'd coach my Little League team when I'm old enough."

"Of course, why not?" Dave said to himself with a clenched jaw. "Never mind me. He already stole my wife. Why not my kid, too? Christ, they're like those buildings he buys."

Dave accidentally whipped the ball as hard as he could, for his

The Amazing Journey of Pete Townshend's Woodstock Special   241 focus was on Scott when it should have been on his follow-through, and Matthew did not gamely haul this one in. It ricocheted off the tip of his glove, hitting his face with a splat.

"Crap," Dave said. He sprinted over to his son, who was laid out and crying, his hands covering his face. "Let me see, buddy. Let me see, let me see."

Matthew moved his hands away, revealing a large welt under his left eye. Dave's mind started to race:

- *What if he goes blind?*
- *What if he suffered brain damage?*
- *What if he expires on my watch?*

"How many fingers am I holding up?" Dave asked.

"Two," Matthew answered between sobs.

"Good. What's the capital of Illinois?"

"Um, I don't know."

"Crap. What's the name of the town you live in?"

"Evanston."

"Good. Let's go home and put some ice on it."

Though his eye continued to swell, the boy pulled through. In fact, he rallied enough to eat dinner at the Chuck Wagon again. They then watched the rest of *The Great Mouse Detective*, after which Dave tucked Matthew in and spent another night tossing and turning on the couch.

By the following morning Matthew had a full-blown shiner. Leyna was waiting at the front door when they returned, and her jaw dropped as father and son walked up the driveway.

"Good God!" she exclaimed. "What happened?"

"Just a little accident playing catch," Dave answered.

Bending over to examine the damage, she said, "It looks a lot worse than little. Did you take him to the doctor?"

"I didn't need to. We put plenty of ice on it. Once the swelling goes down a little, he'll be as good as new."

Leyna shook her head scornfully.

"It's not Dad's fault," Matthew said, and his mouth curled into a frown. "I should have caught it."

"That's sweet of you, Matthew, but your father is supposed to be the adult here, and he needs to be more responsible. Unbelievable."

"That's truly rich," Dave said.

"What is?" Leyna shot back. "You bringing my son home with a swollen face?"

"You lecturing me about acting like an adult. It's almost comical."

"Mom, Dad," Matthew peeped. No one heard him.

"I just hope it doesn't ruin our day," Leyna continued. "Matthew will be so disappointed if we miss out on the lake house. And Scott won't be happy either."

"Whatever," Dave said.

"Whatever?"

"That's right, Leyna, whatever." Dave turned to Matthew: "Sorry about your eye, but we had a great weekend anyway, right?"

"Yep."

"I love you, and we'll talk this week."

Without acknowledging Leyna, Dave returned to his car, which, incidentally, was a used Oldsmobile Omega he had been forced to buy after losing the Volvo in the divorce settlement. His frowning son and flabbergasted ex-wife looked on as he slammed the door and, after two tries, started the junker.

"Bye, Dad," Matthew yelled at the top of his lungs, but Dave was already gone.

CHAPTER 33

The snowblower, lawnmower, patio umbrella, coffee table, ten-speed, hoe, and lawn chairs all sank to the bottom of the Fox River. The Special, in contrast, was amazingly buoyant, floating six miles southward until it washed ashore somewhere near New Munster, Wisconsin. If not for its fortuitous placement under an elm, it probably would have succumbed to the battering of the seasons, but the tree's puissant, expansive branches provided protection for the wayward guitar, as did the leaves that had gathered over it.

Time and again the Special had gone undetected by Norb Gartmann, who had spent most mornings fishing the Fox River for smallmouth bass since his retirement as an insurance agent several months earlier. Being a creature of habit, Norb always took the same path from his Chevy Suburban to the water, right past the Special. On this day, however, he noticed its headstock protruding from the leafy blanket, courtesy of a storm the night before that had stirred up the landscape.

He uncovered the rest of the guitar, placing it next to his tackle box and a small cooler before working the river. It turned out to be a banner morning for Norb: he reeled in eleven smallmouths, four of which were keepers that he jubilantly placed in his cooler. Without giving the matter much thought, he tucked the Special under his arm and brought it home along with his keepers.

Norb never gave these matters much thought, which was why his garage was overflowing with junk. For as long as he could remember, he had enjoyed collecting things: signs, hubcaps, furniture, appliances—whatever. He rested the Special between a propane tank and a stack of magazines, and there it sat, joined periodically by new pieces of junk.

Norb's wife, Shirley, was tolerant of his idiosyncrasies. How else would they have stayed married for forty-three years? But they were downsizing to a condominium in their retirement, and there would be no room for all the souvenirs Norb had accumulated—or any of them, actually.

"I'm planning to have a yard sale," Shirley announced matter-of-factly, and Norb knew exactly what she meant. But he didn't argue with her. He rarely did, not even about things as near and dear to him as this. How else would they have stayed married for forty-three years?

Working her way through the rummage, Shirley placed a six-dollar tag on a rocking chair, a twelve-dollar tag on an Apollo 11 commemorative plate, a three-dollar tag on a set of croquet mallets, and a twenty-cent tag on the propane tank. When she got to the Special, she moaned "Geez Louise" before slapping a one-dollar tag on its body.

On the big day, Shirley laid everything out along the driveway as appealingly as possible. Norb stayed inside as the shoppers trickled through—he couldn't bear to watch them pick apart his collection of curiosities.

"What are you going to do with the things nobody buys?" Norb had asked Shirley prior to the yard sale, his tone hopeful.

"The Salvation Army truck in the Aldi parking lot," she had answered, prompting a barely discernible groan from her husband.

The Special seemed Salvation Army-bound until Todd Hapner arrived on the scene late in the afternoon. Hapner had been the kid in gym class to always finish last in the mile run, and he had grown more rotund as an adult. But he had hit his stride as a regular on the yard sale circuit, where he searched assiduously for diamonds in the rough. Although he was quite sure he hadn't found one in the Special, he nonetheless asked Shirley, "What's this?"

"It appears to be a guitar of some sort."

"Right, but where did it come from?"

"Who knows? My husband just brings these things home."

Todd picked up the stringless instrument, inspected its nicks and burns and water stains. "This really looks like it's been through the wringer."

Shirley lived by a simple rule: if you can't say anything nice, don't say anything at all. She didn't say anything at all.

"But it might have some vintage appeal," Hapner continued. "Maybe I can fix it up. For a buck, it's worth the investment."

He handed Shirley a crumpled dollar bill and walked off with the Special.

CHAPTER 34

Three years had elapsed since the divorce, and Dave still hadn't gotten laid. It was gnawing at him both physically and philosophically—especially considering Leyna's sex life had rolled on without a hitch, or so he assumed. More disheartening, he had never been with a woman other than Leyna, with the exception of unwieldy Mary Jo Womack, who only technically counted.

- Was there something wrong with him?
- Was he doomed to a life of celibacy?
- Was jacking off in perpetuity his last best hope?

It couldn't be. It just couldn't be. The clock was ticking, and he was besieged by a rising, primal sense of desperation. When his loins could stand it no more, he chose the obvious place to start making up for lost time: he phoned his old reporter Holt, who, much to Dave's annoyance, was now a sports columnist for the *Chicago Tribune*.

They brought each other up to date on their lives, a one-sided conversation centered on Holt's professional and personal conquests. When a rare opening presented itself, Dave asked, "Do you ever hear from Cherie anymore? I haven't talked to her in years."

"I ran into her a few months ago, as a matter of fact. And I'm happy to report her ass is as great as ever."

"Good to hear, I guess."

"It's better to see. But even you know that, right?"

"What's she up to these days?"

"She left the newspaper business and took a job as an account executive with some bullshit PR firm downtown. She said she likes it. Go figure."

"Do you know how to get hold of her? I want to do some, ah, networking with her."

"I'm sure you do. But yeah, she gave me her card." Dave heard a rustling and then, "Where the hell is it? Fuck me. Oh, Dave?"

"I'm still here."

"I found it."

Dave wasted no time dialing her phone number.

"Cherie?" he asked.

"Dave," she responded excitedly. "I'd recognize that voice anywhere. Wow. How are you?"

After easing into an answer with some superficialities, Dave spilled the bloody details of his life—his post-divorce (and pre-divorce) depression, his new "career" at Weiss Drugstore—and she didn't hang up the phone. On the contrary, she was, as had always been the case, friendly and curious about his routine. She was single, too, which was the key to the whole deal. There was no turning back.

"Anyway," he said, "I'm calling for a rain check on our lunch date from, oh, 1982 or '83 or whenever that was."

"That's right. You totally blew me off."

"I did, but I had a lot of other stuff on my mind."

"I can imagine."

"So, should we meet up?"

"For sure. I'd love that."

"Any great ideas?"

"Let's see…I still make a mean lasagna."

"And I still love lasagna."

"It's meant to be then. I'm free this Saturday. How about my place at eight?"

Cherie told him where she lived, an address in Chicago's upscale Lincoln Park neighborhood. Dave noted to himself that PR obviously paid a lot better than newspapers…and Weiss Drugstore. But that was neither here nor there. Over the next few days he found himself in a curious position: he was excited about something.

At eight o'clock sharp on Saturday night, Dave knocked on Cherie's door, wearing his nicest button-down shirt and holding a bottle of pinot noir. She greeted him not with a "Hi" but a hug. It was promising.

"I see you're still Mr. Punctuality," Cherie said.

"It's from our newspaper days. I guess I'm still paranoid that Cross will pop out of the woodwork and yell at me for being late."

Talking 'Bout My Generation

Framing Dave with her hazel eyes, she said, "You look great."

"Thanks. You, too."

Her straight blond locks were now poofed and moussed in accordance with the latest style, and she was dressed more elegantly than he ever remembered, in a white silk blouse, black slacks, and black pumps. She had really grown up since her days working the police blotter at the *Herald*. Nevertheless, Holt was right: as Dave followed her into the living room, he saw that her ass hadn't changed a bit. It was as flawlessly round as ever.

"I'm running a little behind today," Cherie said. "I just put the lasagna in the oven, so it will be a bit. In the meantime, why don't we crack open your bottle of wine and catch up?"

"Sounds good to me."

"Let me just get a corkscrew," Cherie said, and she went to the kitchen.

Dave regarded the living room, which was quite chic with its white sofa, white carpeting, and two white armchairs. It was also a disaster waiting to happen, given the bottle of red wine in his hand. *That would not be good*, he thought, a bundle of nerves as he imagined vino splattered all over the immaculate confines.

But Dave sure-handedly surmounted the evening's first obstacle, opening the bottle and pouring two glasses without spilling a single drop. He sat on the sofa, and Cherie made herself at home next to him.

"It looks like you've done quite well for yourself," Dave said.

"No complaints here."

"My apartment looks nothing like this."

"A bachelor pad?"

"Tenement house is more like it," he joked.

Laughing, Cherie said, "I'm sure it's not that bad. And either way, I have no doubt you'll get back on your feet soon. You were, like, the most conscientious person I've ever worked with. If you want, I can put in a word for you at my company."

"Thanks, but I don't know if I'm cut out for PR."

"I bet you'd be good at it. You come off as sincere, and that does the trick every time. Clients love it." She inched closer to him and said, "You really do look good. You're still exactly the same."

They kept talking, but the topics—music, movies, gossip about people from the *Herald*—seemed incidental, mostly because he was fixated on the scent of her perfume. Dave was getting tipsy from the wine, and he surmised she was, too, because before he knew what was what, she was sitting on his lap with her arms draped over his shoulders. It was more than promising.

"I'm glad you called," Cherie said. "You probably didn't even notice, but I had a thing for you. You know, it was my first job out of college, and I was scared to death. You were always so nice. Why do you think I came by your desk all the time?"

"Oh, I noticed, but I was married. That's obviously not an issue anymore."

They started making out, and before Dave knew what was what, he was shirtless and she was slackless.

"Why don't we take this to the bedroom?" she whispered into his ear. "The bed's comfier than the couch."

Trailing Cherie down the hallway, Dave had a perfect view of her ass again, except now it was bare. *Holt would die to see this*, he thought smugly. They entered another white room, whereupon she removed her blouse and bra and jumped onto the bed.

"Whatcha waiting for?" she asked, her boobs still springing from her leap.

Dave hopped around on his left foot as he took off his right shoe and sock, then he repeated the manic dance on his other foot. Before he could get to his pants, however, he heard a sound like that of a large, wounded animal from the front door of the apartment: "Cherie, can we talk? I miss you."

"Oh, great," she said, more annoyed than anything else. "I thought I took back my key. And he sounds drunk again."

"Who's *he*? And what's this about a key?"

Cherie shrugged, and her boobs moved up and down with her shoulders.

"Your boyfriend?"

She shrugged again.

"I thought you didn't have a boyfriend."

"I don't. Not since last weekend anyway, when I broke up with him."

"Then what's he doing here?"

"Precisely—that's why I broke up with him. He gets so clingy and possessive, and I was tired of it. It's like, grow up."

"Possessive? In what way?"

There was another sound, from the kitchen: "You're cooking lasagna?"

"Damn, that's right," Cherie said. "With everything going on between you and me, I forgot about the lasagna. It's going to be burnt to a crisp."

"It looks like it's starting to burn. Where are you, baby? I want to talk."

"Fuck," Dave half-whispered, flattening himself against the bedroom door like a barricade.

"*Baby*," Cherie said indignantly. "What am I, a five-year-old?"

Now the sound was in the living room: "What are your pants and underwear doing on the floor? And whose shirt is that? What's going on, Cherie?"

"Holy fuck," Dave said almost inaudibly.

"Did I mention that he's not very smart either?" Cherie said.

The sound entered the bathroom: "Baby, where are you?"

"See?" she added. "What would I possibly be doing in a dark bathroom?"

The sound turned to footsteps that grew progressively louder.

"Maybe you should go," Cherie said with a sigh of disappointment.

"How?"

She pointed to an open window across the room.

Shirtless, shoeless, and sockless, Dave ran to the window and, without really taking stock of what was below, dove out. Upon leaving his feet, he heard Cherie say, "Call me." Then he heard only whistling air as he dropped five feet before bouncing off a garage roof and falling another ten feet into a juniper bush in the courtyard.

After untangling himself from the prickly foliage, Dave frantically sought an exit. Fortunately, his adrenaline was such that he could barely feel the throbbing of his freshly broken wrist. Two teenage girls, walking around the neighborhood in search of a laugh or two on a Saturday night, found what they were looking for when they saw Dave climb the courtyard fence and tear off to his Oldsmobile Omega.

A month later, with his wrist in a cast, his ego still bruised, and his libido unquenched, Dave steeled himself for more discomfort: his twice-yearly teeth cleaning. Positioning himself in the plastic-covered dental chair, he looked up warily at the hygienist—a new one named Tamara—who asked, "What happened to your wrist?"

"Um, I slipped."

"Ouch."

"That's the word for it."

"Well, I can't do anything about your wrist, but I'll try to go easy on your mouth."

The hygienist's face was plain, but her boobs were firm. Dave knew this because they kept brushing against him when she leaned in to get at his molars. It felt good. And when those boobs continued to sweep across his shoulder even when she wasn't picking at his teeth, he sensed that the contact wasn't inadvertent.

Nevertheless, Dave wasn't taking any chances, not after the debacle with Cherie. He scanned the room to see if she, like the other hygienists, was displaying pictures of a smiling significant other. Nope. He asked her if she had big plans for the weekend. Nope. Nothing, Dave asked, with, say, a husband or a boyfriend? Nope. She said she was unattached. When his teeth were clean, she handed him a baggy containing a toothbrush, a tube of toothpaste, dental floss, and her phone number.

"Give me a jingle," she said.

Dave put the toothbrush, toothpaste, and dental floss in his bathroom and the phone number on his kitchen table, where it fermented for several days. It seemed too good to be true. Such things—the boob sweeps, the phone number in his dental supplies baggy, the "Give me a jingle"—never happened to him.

- What if she really did have a boyfriend or a husband?

- What if she moonlighted as a prostitute?
- What if she was a hermaphrodite?

Disconcerting as those scenarios were, he wound up dialing the phone anyway.

"I knew you'd call," Tamara said.

"You did? How?"

"You seemed edgy, like it's been a while. I have a knack for reading these things."

"Apparently so. Do you still want to do something sometime?"

"How about tonight?"

"Tonight?" Dave paused to assess the situation and to consider if he had anything going on, which, of course, he didn't. "Tonight is good. Sure. Sounds fun."

She suggested they meet at her apartment in Niles, a town just west of Skokie. Dave had been thinking of a neutral venue like a bar or a restaurant, mostly because disturbing visions from Cherie's apartment were still rattling around his head, but he agreed that her place would be good.

"Anything I can bring?" Dave asked.

"Just yourself."

That seemed easy enough. In a world that had ceased to make sense, he was reassured and emboldened by Tamara's straightforward way. After helping his dad close up Weiss Drugstore for the night, he raced toward Niles in his Oldsmobile Omega.

"Right on time," Tamara said as she let him in. "I like that."

Dave dug deep for something to say, but since he knew nothing about her other than she did a nice job cleaning teeth, he came up empty.

Tamara broke the silence by asking, "Should we watch a movie?"

"I love movies. Great idea. Yeah, let's watch a movie."

She guided Dave into her living room, which was the antithesis of chic. It had thick brown carpeting, and one of the walls was lined with wood crates that she was passing off as shelves.

"Nice place," Dave lied.

"It's home. It's about the best you can do on a dental hygienist's salary."

They sat on her afghan-covered couch, and Dave asked, "So, what movie should we watch? Looks like you have a bunch on your, um, shelves."

Tamara went over to the wooden crates and returned with a VHS cassette. Handing it to Dave, she said, "This one really gets me in the mood."

The title on the box—*When Harry Boned Sally*—wasn't exactly how Dave remembered it. Nor did the bare-chested man in the accompanying picture resemble Billy Crystal. Dave homed in on his broad shoulders and vacuous eyes. *Sweet Jesus, that's the guy who gave me the Special.*

Indeed, Jumbo's was a classic American success story. Giddy about the potential of the "test" movie she had made with Jumbo in their Greenwich Village apartment on that afternoon in 1972, Mama had drawn on her meager savings and formed a company, Magic Wand Entertainment. The timing was optimal, Mama reasoned, due to new legislation in New York that allowed for a proliferation of adult theaters and sex shops. She rounded up friends from NYU and anyone else she could find, as well as props and more equipment from Dingelhoss & Pulle, and began shooting adult films in their apartment that she distributed in the city. The public clamored for more Jumbo, and Mama delivered with such offerings as *Midnight Horn-Boy, Fellatio on the Roof, Dildos Are Forever,* and *Screw Me Again, Jumbo*.

And after the introduction of the "home theater" in the mid-1970s thanks to videocassette recorder technology, business really boomed, prompting Mama and Jumbo's move to the heart of the porn industry in Southern California. Mama quickly developed a stable of stars and began producing dozens of titles per month. But through it all, from the early years up to the present, Jumbo's movies remained the most popular—he was still the engine that made Magic Wand Entertainment go. This very moment he was seated on his chaise lounge, enjoying the fruits of his considerable labor by watching the big ball of fire slowly drop into the Pacific Ocean, as he did almost every evening.

Obviously, Dave wasn't aware of Jumbo's career arc or his chaise lounge. What he did know was that he was in a virtual stranger's apartment, and things were getting weird.

"He truly is jumbo, if you catch my drift," Tamara said. "Mind if I pop it in?"

There was no turning back; Dave silently handed her *When Harry Boned Sally*.

His dexterity was limited because of the cast on his wrist, but it didn't turn out to be an issue. After doffing her own clothes, she was kind enough to take off his. Her selflessness continued when she climbed on top of him as he sat there. With Jumbo (Harry) grunting and his costar (Sally) moaning in the background, Tamara drove her body ever harder into Dave's pelvis. It should have hurt, but it didn't. By the closing credits, Dave was drenched with sweat and, more important, purged of his sexual demons.

"I knew you'd be good," Tamara said.

"Why's that?"

"The same reason I knew you'd call me: you hadn't done it in God knows how long. You were like a live wire."

After putting on his clothes, Dave headed for the door.

"Call me if you get edgy again," she said. "No strings attached."

"Thanks, I will."

And he would have, too, had he not noticed strange, raised markings on the tip of his penis a couple weeks later. An embarrassing visit to his physician brought forth an even more embarrassing diagnosis: genital warts. The doctor warned him of the dangers of unprotected sex before writing out a prescription for a podophyllotoxin cream that Dave didn't fill at Weiss Drugstore.

Though Tamara would have been a logical target for his angst, Dave thought of someone else, namely the hulking star of *When Harry Boned Sally*. In better times, Jumbo had bequeathed the Special to him; now, at least indirectly, he had passed on genital warts. Sitting on his bed while applying the podophyllotoxin cream to his ailing penis with his one good hand, Dave realized that nothing had gone quite right for him since the night he discarded the Special in a drunken stupor. He reached into his nightstand drawer, pulling out the guitar string he had found in the ashtray in his old basement bar. It seemed like a relic from a different lifetime.

CHAPTER 35

Yet hope smoldered. It was unmistakable, undeniable. What else would have accounted for the wild applause in San Diego's Mandell Weiss Theatre on July 9, 1992? Pete Townshend was among the audience of five hundred, and even he managed a smile. He was no longer a nostalgia act, someone to be viewed wistfully, with a tinge of pity. Thanks to the resurrection of the deaf, dumb, and blind kid, he was newly vital.

The idea hadn't been Pete's—rather it had come from a ruddy-faced theater director named Des McAnuff—but that was a mere technicality. When they met in earnest for the first time at the Portobello Hotel in London, Pete was still nursing his wounds from a reunion tour with The Who that he had sworn would be his last and had been derisively titled "The Who on Ice" by the press. He also was sporting a cast, the result of a broken wrist he had suffered falling off a bicycle. Des barely noticed—he was simply happy that his proposal to bring *Tommy* to the stage hadn't been rejected outright by Pete.

"It's 1991," Pete said, the broadening bald spot on his head reflecting light from the ceiling. "Does anyone care anymore?"

"I wouldn't be wasting your time if I didn't think so. It has great potential as a theatrical production," Des answered.

"Maybe so, but I wrote it in 1969 when everyone was on acid and looking to go on an amazing journey, as it were. I intentionally left it open-ended to encourage exploration. At least I think I did. Anyway, I don't know how the fucking thing will translate to the stage, especially nowadays."

"It will translate fine. The story just needs to be tightened up a bit."

"The story?" Pete said, and he blinked his eyes in a tic-like manner as memories from his wayward *Lifehouse* project streamed to the fore.

"Yes, the story." Pete was about to end the meeting right there when Des added, "It should be easy enough."

Settling back into his chair but still looking as if he was ready to bolt, Pete asked, "How so?"

"If there's one thing I know, it's theater, specifically musicals. Need I remind you that I won a Tony for *Big River*?"

"I know. What's your point?"

"I've been studying *Tommy* at some length, and all the vital plot elements are already in place. At its heart, it's about the troubles of a post–World War II family in London. It's as simple as that. I want to make it less of a trippy fantasy, turn it into something more grounded and direct. But it's your baby, and I can't do it without you."

Pete grimaced and said, "Fucking Thomas. The little wanker just won't die off, will he?"

Des took that as a yes.

Over the next several months, Pete and Des met regularly at the Royalton Hotel in New York to hash out the particulars. Perched on three-legged chairs that were in keeping with the hotel's Bauhaus motif, they decided the best way to bring cohesion to the production would be to have three Tommy characters—one at age four, one at age ten, and one as an adult—who would interact with each other.

"That's where the real discord is in this story," Des said. "Tommy's at war with himself, and this gives us a tangible way to depict it."

"Bloody right it does," Pete said.

Pleased as all get-out, Pete leaned back in his chair, forgetting that it had only three legs until it flipped over.

"Pete, are you okay?"

"Fuck yes I am," he answered from the floor.

Pete dusted himself off, and they kept working. Among their other epiphanies was to have Tommy reconcile with his fractured family at the end.

"It provides closure that wasn't there when I first wrote it," Pete said. "I'm sure the critics, cynical bastards that they are, will cry foul, but fuck the lot of them. It works."

"I agree, fuck them," Des said before leaning back too far in his own three-legged chair and suffering the consequences.

But the critics didn't cry foul. When *The Who's Tommy* premiered at the St. James Theatre on Broadway on April 22, 1993, following its run in San Diego, most of them were smitten, including the *New York Times*' Frank Rich, who called the ending cathartic.

The catharsis spread unabated to New York's Gershwin Theatre, where, on June 6, 1993, Pete strode to the podium to collect the Tony Award for Best Original Score. After the ceremony, he displayed rare patience in posing for picture after picture with the cast members, some of whom hadn't even been born when he first conceived *Tommy*. He and his young flock then adjourned to a private victory party at the swank Plaza Hotel, and a movement materialized amid the laughs and the libations.

"Looks like you're up, Pete," said Michael Cerveris, the actor who portrayed the adult Tommy on Broadway.

Pete glanced skyward at a chandelier that was hanging from the ceiling of the ballroom.

"No, over there," Michael said, and he pointed to the small stage. "The house band—which, I might add, isn't very good—is on break. And it just so happens that they left their instruments onstage. See?"

Pete nodded.

"Show us how it's really done."

"I couldn't. It's your night, not mine."

"C'mon, Pete," chimed in Cheryl Freeman, the gypsy in *The Who's Tommy*. "It's your night. You're the reason we're all here right now."

"No, really," he answered.

The cast, the crew, and their friends and family began to bang the cocktail tables, chanting, "Pete, Pete, Pete, Pete."

"There's only one way to shut them up," prodded Des, who was seated next to Pete.

The truth was, his objections were merely for show. He was itching to go up there and strum a guitar. Bouncing to his feet, he said, "Oh, bloody hell—one song. Michael, why don't you join me?"

Pete tore into the opening chords of "Pinball Wizard," and the two men—Tommy and his creator—sang the lyrics with everything they had. Looking out at his happy flock, Pete felt more alive than he had in years. It was exhilarating—cathartic, in fact—to embrace rather than run from his past.

Thus, the next morning he resumed his search for the Special. He placed another ad in *Rolling Stone*.

CHAPTER 36

Todd Hapner never saw the *Rolling Stone* ad, which was probably a blessing. If he had come across it and somehow put two and two together, he would have kicked himself for unloading the Special after deeming it worthless.

Dave never saw the ad either, for he had been distracted by the usual soul-crushing matters. Right now, in fact, he was fielding a phone call from his ex-wife.

"And to what do I owe this pleasantry?" he asked. "It's a sunny Saturday morning. Shouldn't you be gallivanting around at your lake house?"

"Please, Dave. Not now. I'm really not up for it," Leyna answered.

"When then?"

She sighed and said, "Can we meet for a cup of coffee or something? It's about Matthew."

"Why, what's going on?" Dave said, his tone turning from acerbic to concerned.

"Just a few things we need to discuss. Can you do the Starbucks in Evanston in an hour?"

"I'll see you there."

Dave arrived early; Leyna, lost in thought, was late. Rolling down Sherman Avenue in her Lexus LS 400, she once again dissected the riddle that had been vexing her: *Matthew lives in a beautiful home. I'm there to tend to his every want and need. He has not one but two dads who love him.* She conveniently skipped over that last point and wound up here: *Everything should be wonderful.* But the root of the problem was pretty obvious, even if she was loath to face it: clarity for her (swapping Dave for Scott) had resulted in mounting confusion for Matthew (a family divided).

Leyna drove a mile past the Starbucks before realizing where she was. When she finally walked in, Dave shook his head incredulously. "Jesus, did you get lost?"

"Very funny, Dave."

"Here, I got you a coffee. It's getting cold."

"Thanks," she said, sitting down.

"What is it we need to discuss?"

"At this point, the best thing for Matthew would be a change of scenery."

Dave knew precisely where this conversation was headed: the pig-hooved one was planning to move back to Denver and take Leyna and Matthew with him. He turned pale. "Over my dead body."

"Huh? I'm talking about a new school for him."

"Oh," Dave said, and the color returned to his face.

"You saw his last report card. He's obviously lost his way at Haven. He's only a year away from starting high school, and we can't afford to let things continue to slip."

"I agree, but don't you think it's a little late in the game to start thinking about such a drastic move? It's August—school starts in two weeks. I can't imagine there are a lot of options by now."

"Scott knows the principal at North Shore Country Day School."

"There it is. Of course he does."

"Please don't make this about Scott. It's actually a very good school."

"Isn't North Shore Country Day private? What's wrong with the public schools?"

"From what I've gathered, North Shore Country Day will offer him a much more nurturing environment than Haven. This could be just what he needs."

"But all his friends are at Haven."

"He doesn't have any friends, Dave. He's spent the whole summer glued to those video games."

"True. I can't believe he didn't even play baseball this summer. We should have never let that happen."

"I don't know how we could have made him play. He was adamant that he didn't want to play anymore."

"And you think we'll have better luck making him go to a new school?"

"Scott arranged a meeting for Matthew with the principal a few days ago. They talked and looked at the school, and Matthew seems receptive to it."

"Why does Scott get to make this decision?"

"He's not. I'm on board with it. And I'm hoping you'll be, too."

"Do I have a choice?"

Leyna fingered her coffee cup silently.

"Fine," Dave said. "I suppose we can give it a try."

The weekends when Dave didn't have Matthew always seemed to drag. To help fill the void following his meeting with Leyna, he ate lunch at their old haunt, the Chuck Wagon. He even ordered Matthew's favorite: the Nikki, a cheeseburger with hunks of gyro meat on top. But that only served to upset his stomach, and he retreated to his apartment in Skokie to take a couple Tums.

Dave thought briefly about calling Rick Blutch to meet for a beer that night. Blutch was a friend from high school who was also divorced and was usually available, but Dave decided he just wasn't up for it. Instead he stayed up until 2 a.m. finishing *The Prince of Tides*, a page-turner by Patrick Conroy about a southern man whose life is fucked beyond recognition but who is ultimately redeemed with the help of a comely Jewish psychiatrist. After switching off the light on his nightstand, Dave lay in bed wondering why he couldn't find a comely Jewish psychiatrist of his own.

Several weeks later, his thoughts were focused on an initiative that was more achievable: balancing the books in the tiny office at Weiss Drugstore. Though Dave's back was to the doorway, he knew from the smell of cigarette smoke that his dad had just entered the office.

"You ever going to give those things up, Dad?" Dave asked without turning around. "Everyone else is."

"If they haven't gotten me yet, they're not going to." William leaned against the desk. "How's the boy doing? How does he like his new school?"

"He seems to be doing okay, but it's too soon to know for sure."

"Keep the faith. It's all you can do as a parent."

"I suppose."

"Anyway, I have a proposition for you."

"Uh-oh, I don't like the sound of that. You're not thinking of buying a new Slush Puppie machine and having me install it, are you?"

"No," William said with a chuckle, "this is much easier. As you know, Mom is retired. And eventually I plan to call it quits, too—smell the roses or whatever it is I'm supposed to do in retirement. But I'd feel better about doing it if I knew the store was in good hands. I've been running this place for as long as I can remember—it's part of me. And that brings me to you. I'm wondering if you have any interest in taking over the store when I retire."

Dave was silent for several seconds before saying, "Boy, I don't know, Dad. I'm not sure I want to get locked into this."

"You've been here for, what, a dozen years? It seems to me that ship has already sailed."

His dad's observation was valid, but Dave remained doubtful. He had been doing the books at Weiss Drugstore for long enough to note that the profits, while still respectable, were beginning to sag. Part of that was due to the insurance companies, which were squeezing pharmaceutical retailers more greedily than ever. But Dave saw the primary reason whenever he drove to work: at seemingly every busy intersection, a Walgreens or a CVS was being built. These growing chains had power in numbers. Since theirs was a volume game, they could sell prescriptions at cheaper prices than independents like Weiss Drugstore and still make money. Sooner rather than later, mom-and-pop pharmacies would be pushed to the margins of history. Dave's instincts told him that taking over Weiss Drugstore would be a losing proposition, and surely his dad knew as much.

There was also this: "But I'm not even a pharmacist," Dave said.

"So what?" William answered, shrugging his shoulders. "You hire a couple. Think about it for as long as you need to. I'm not ready to cash in my chips quite yet."

Dave didn't figure there was much to think about, and he went about the rest of his day as usual. But while doing inventory, he locked in on the brown wooden shelves that held Weiss Drugstore's products. They were faded, the result of four decades of service, but also still sturdy. He ran his index finger along one, cutting a line through the dust. *Yes*, Dave thought. *Yes.*

He had an idea.

CHAPTER 37

Jimmy Fitzgerald looked in the mirror, and for once he didn't like what he saw. In fact, he was terrified by it.

Everything should have been fine, more than fine. Mojo Dogs had become ubiquitous, with stores stretching up the coast to Aberdeen, Washington, and down it to San Diego. Jimmy had lost track of them all, but that was okay thanks to even more "people" who kept the operation running. At only forty-eight years old, he was a man of leisure.

Raffy, on the other hand, was busier than ever. The farthest points of the Mojo empire were now beyond the reach of his motorcycle, so sometimes he boarded an airplane to do his wiener inspections. But he almost always made it home to Santa Cruz the same day to catch up with his wife and three sons. He also still carved out at least an hour early each morning to hit Steamer Lane with Jimmy. That time was sacred—or it had been until recently.

While shaving one day, Jimmy had noticed a spot on his chin. He hadn't thought twice about it. A few weeks later out on the rocks at Steamer Lane, however, Raffy had said, "Dude, what's that on your face?"

"I don't know. A zit or a freckle or something."

"Looks gnarly. You might want to get it checked out."

"Or just pop it."

Jimmy wasn't big on doctors, which made sense since he hadn't been sick a day in his life. But there was something weird about the way Raffy had said, "Looks gnarly." Begrudgingly, he got around to going to a dermatologist, who scrutinized the growth with his index finger before shining a penlight on it.

"It's just a zit, right?" Jimmy asked.

"No, it's definitely not a pimple," the doctor answered. "It looks suspicious. I want to take a biopsy."

Now Jimmy was thinking twice about it. And when the biopsy results came in, he could think about nothing else. It seemed the California sun had taken a toll on his fair Irish skin: the growth was melanoma. But that wasn't all. While removing the cancer, the doctor decided a biopsy of Jimmy's lymph nodes was warranted.

Jimmy didn't surf the next few mornings. For that matter, he didn't leave his house, a beachfront behemoth he had purchased four years earlier. When the verdict was rendered, he was under a blanket on a couch, trying in vain to follow *SportsCenter*.

"Unfortunately, it's late-stage melanoma," the doctor said in the measured cadence of someone who was accustomed to delivering bad news.

"What does that even mean?"

"That it's serious. It's spread into your lymph nodes."

Jimmy gagged as bile rushed up his throat, but he forced it back down.

"Mr. Fitzgerald?" the doctor asked.

"Yeah."

"The first step is to perform a lymph node dissection."

"A what?"

"We'll need to remove the cancerous lymph nodes. After that, the best course of action will likely be radiation. But you'll want to come in as soon as possible to discuss your options in detail."

"I'm going to be okay, right?"

The doctor didn't say "Yes" or even "Maybe." He offered only this nebulous prognosis: "We'll know more once you start your treatment."

Now Jimmy was in one of his four bathrooms, contemplating the hideousness that lurked beneath the incision on his chin. His new golden retriever Jake was by his side, and his parrot Fred was in the sunroom squawking "Tits," but he felt completely alone. Jimmy staggered away from the mirror and through a room stuffed with arcade games and then a kitchen edged with gleaming granite counters. He wound up at his study's rarely used desk, where he pulled out a pen and a piece of paper and started writing:

Weiss,

I'm sending this to your parents' house because it's the only address I know for you. I hope you get it. It's been, what, almost 30 years since I sent you that postcard? A lot's happened since then. I'm sure with you too. Time just goes.

Awhile back, me and my friend Raffy started a restaurant, Mojo Dogs. It really caught on, and now there are a ton of them. You can find them pretty much anywhere on the west coast. They're awesome, if I do say so myself. Sausage made almost every way you can imagine.

But that's not why I'm writing. I just found out I have cancer. The BIG C. Me. Hard to believe, huh? They said its spread into my lymph nodes. Until a few days ago, I didn't even know I had lymph nodes! They said it's serious, and the whole thing is still sinking in. I have to admit, I'm scared. Freaking out, actually.

I have no idea why, but it made me think of you and our trip to Woodstock. (By the way, sorry I bailed on you, bro. You would have done the same thing if you had seen the girls I was with). Any way, like I said, I've been thinking about it, and I wish I was back there right now. Those were great days, huh? Real happy days, like nothing could ever go wrong. The world was rolled out for us like a red carpet. Remember cruising thru those cornfields in your car? I thought you were going to have a heart attack. It was hilarious.

This isn't easy to write about, but it feels good to put my thoughts down on paper. It feels permanent. Write me back if you get a chance. It'd be great to find out how the years have treated you. My address is 520 West Cliff Drive, Santa Cruz, CA 95060.

Jimmy

P.S. What's up with the Cubs? Looks like they're on their way to another last-place finish. I'm starting to wonder if I'll live long enough to see them win a World Series, and that's no joke.

After sealing the letter, Jimmy went outside for the first time in three days to mail it.

Back in Illinois, Dave's renovations were underway—and luckily, he wasn't trying to do them himself. This first job was best left to professionals, primarily because it required sledgehammers. The objective was to tear down Weiss Drugstore's west wall so that Dave could expand his operations into the empty storefront next door.

As ideas went, this one had a fighting chance. Weiss Drugstore didn't have to be pushed to the margins of history—the passing of time could be the very thing that kept it going. For Dave had something to market that mega-chains like Walgreens and CVS didn't: nostalgia. And he had something else: a base of loyal customers his dad had spent generations cultivating. These, Dave reasoned, were worthy assets, and the loan officer at Glenview Bank & Trust hadn't disagreed.

Amid the seemingly wanton destruction, amid the pounding and the mounting debris, Dave could see the finished product in his mind's eye. Leyna would have called it clarity. The space next door would be turned into an old-time soda fountain that would also offer burgers and sandwiches, all served by workers clad in white button-down shirts and black bow ties.

But that was just part of the picture. There would be grand glass cases for the pharmaceuticals behind the back counter and for fine cigars by the magazines. Up front, the kids would be able to grab penny candy out of vintage jars, although, in a nod to inflation, it would cost a dime apiece. He planned to replace the acoustical ceiling tiles with pressed tin, the white paint on the walls with polished mahogany woodwork, the chafed carpeting with checkerboard ceramic flooring, and the old sign out front with a new one that looked even older. To create the illusion, no detail would be overlooked.

"Think of it as Medieval Times meets Weiss Drugstore, except we won't have jousting," Dave had told his dad prior to the construction. "But you get the idea."

"I do?"

"Okay, bad analogy—wrong era, too cheesy. Think of it as a vestige of Main Street, USA. It will still be the same Weiss Drugstore but with a bit of a theme, a theme that plays on a simpler time. For however long people are in here—and hopefully it will be long enough for them to spend some money—they'll forget themselves. And let's face it: we all need to forget ourselves sometimes, especially if we're picking up prescriptions because we're sick. I like to think of it as retail escapism. Who wouldn't rather come here than some faceless Walgreens at a busy intersection, even if it costs a couple extra dollars? We're providing a different kind of value."

His dad had shaken his head and harrumphed out of principle, but he hadn't disagreed. And when Dave had told him about some of his other intentions—such as customer service flourishes like home delivery and merchandise additions like packaged beer and wine (the better to forget yourself)—he had seemed almost proud.

Out of habit, William still stopped by the store from time to time. On this day, however, he was drawn in by curiosity. Watching a sledgehammer-bearing man take a bite out of the west wall, William said, "Wait until your mother sees this. She won't believe it. There's not going to be anything left of the place."

"I prefer to view it as a facelift, an investment in the future."

William didn't disagree.

As for the whereabouts of Jimmy's SOS? In his rattled state, he had scribbled "IN" on the envelope instead of "IL" and had also neglected to provide it with a return address. Needless to say, the letter was hopelessly lost in the postal pipeline.

CHAPTER 38

Doomsday Garrett heard something, a rustling above the ceiling tiles perhaps. Instinctively, he moved toward the noise. He moved toward the action.

In his thirteen years with Johnson Security, most of his assignments hadn't required anything more intense than moving toward a vending machine for a snack, and this one had been no different. He was serving as a night watchman at Continental Diamond Cutters on Chicago's historic Jewelers Row along Wabash Avenue. Located on the first floor of an Adler & Sullivan-designed building that was more inviting than imposing, it looked like an easy mark for would-be thieves, but an intricate web of alarms turned it into a virtual fortress at night. No cat burglar in his right mind would attempt to get anywhere near Continental's cache of diamonds. As he had learned in his three months there, Doomsday was little more than an insurance policy.

Yet he was certain he had heard something. With great stealth, he advanced out of his office in the bowels of the premises, past the Coke machine at the end of the hallway, and into the diamond-cutting workshop. Resting his hand on a cabochon grinder, he stopped to listen. There it was again, a noise from the ceiling up front in the retail gallery.

Doomsday's heart hadn't raced like this since Johnson Security had assigned him to the University of Chicago's Hyde Park campus in the fall of '89. As part of his late-night rounds, he was sweeping through Regenstein Library, a massive concrete slab that housed more than four million books. The first two floors revealed the usual nothing, but on the third floor he spotted what appeared to be the shadow of a prone body emanating from behind a bookshelf. He sprang down the aisle, and it was indeed a body, that of a young male. Next to him was a young female. They weren't dead, however, just sound asleep. Nor were they clothed. Doomsday quickly concluded that the culprit was an empty bottle of Smirnoff at their feet. The only threat here was to public decency, and Doomsday didn't care about that. Tapping them with his foot, he said,

"Happy hour's over. Time to get back to your dorms." He handed them their clothes and sent them on their besotted way.

Doomsday was sure two young lovers wouldn't be at the other end of this noise at Continental Diamond Cutters. Although the workshop was dark, he didn't dare switch on his flashlight. The element of surprise was everything. Way back when during his time in the service, he would have been wearing night vision goggles, and he really could have used a pair now because he walked straight into a workbench. Amid the unwelcome metallic clanging of instruments, he felt something pierce his thigh: a diamond-headed drill bit. The pain was excruciating. Although he desperately wanted to howl, he knew better than to make another sound. He silently pulled the drill bit out of his leg and continued toward the retail gallery.

Doomsday was rusty, and he had no one to blame but himself. Since being released from the care of that pillow-fluffing nurse at Northwestern Memorial Hospital, he had worked at Johnson Security for more than twice as long as he was a Ranger; he had bought a small house in the 'burbs where he had been a quiet, if not solitary, neighbor; and he had developed a paunch. All the while, he had never even gotten around to settling the score with Trent. Maybe this was simply what happened to old soldiers when they faded away. It was an easy life—the years had clicked by, each one a small victory—but sometimes he craved the challenges of yore.

So Doomsday closed in on the noise. His gun drawn, he slowly opened the steel door that led to the retail gallery and its rows of display cases, edging in with due caution. Every step further inflamed his gashed thigh, but he shed the pain, as he had been trained to do at Fort Lewis, and followed his instincts. They led his eyes to the ceiling, where he saw two legs dangling from an opening that should have been filled with an acoustical tile. Doomsday admired the sheer balls it took to circumvent the alarm system by coming in through the ceiling, but only for a split second. The thief had to go down.

CHAPTER 39

Dave was moving back up in the world: the construction at Weiss Drugstore had been completed, and he was still in business; he had settled into a new apartment in Skokie whose bathroom ceiling was mold-free; and he had done a bit of casual dating without breaking a bone or contracting an STD.

Nevertheless, life was far from perfect. There was a new obstacle in his path: adolescence. This one was a real head-scratcher. At some point in the previous year, Matthew—or Matt, as he now wanted to be called—had decided that Dave was a rube at best and Satan at worst.

Books such as *Transitions through Adolescence* reassured Dave that this was all part of growing up, that adolescents marginalized their parents as a way of asserting their independence, but he longed for harmony. He had an idea of where to find it, too: Wrigley Field. It had always worked for him in the past, and this year there was something to see besides a beautiful ballpark. Led by "Slammin'" Sammy Sosa, who was on the verge of breaking the single-season home run record, these 1998 Cubs were going places, maybe even to the World Series.

Dave picked up two tickets for the second game of a September series against the Milwaukee Brewers, and father and son rode the L to the corner of Clark and Addison. As the train jerked down the tracks, Matt stared sullenly at the passengers dressed in Cubbies blue, a collection that included Dave.

"What a freak show," he grumbled.

Matt was tall for his age, already taller than Dave at 5'11", though he had yet to pack much meat onto his bones. No one knew where the height had come from—it was among life's genetic mysteries. He did, however, have his father's light complexion and his mother's smoky eyes. The jury was still out on whether it was a winning combination, especially since his cheeks were pocked with acne.

"You know, Wrigley Field has barely changed since I was a kid back in the dark ages," Dave said.

"You've told me that at least a hundred times."

"And it's always true. That's the beauty of it. Everything else in life changes, but Wrigley Field stays the same."

"Sure, Dad."

Upon disembarking at the Addison stop, father and son made the beeline to the ballpark. Its dark concourse was wall-to-wall people, this being a season of such surprisingly great expectations.

"Brace yourself," Dave said as they climbed the stairs leading to the grandstands.

"For what? Getting run over by that fat lady in the floppy hat?"

"The scoreboard and the ivy, of course."

"Is it time to go home yet?"

"C'mon, Matt, you used to love it here."

"That was forever ago."

One aspect of Wrigley Field that had changed over the years was Dave's ritual of sneaking past the Andy Frains, (a) because they had been replaced by younger ushers with better eyesight and (b) because such shenanigans didn't become a man in middle age. Now Dave paid for good seats, and these—Field Box, about thirty rows behind the Cubs' dugout—had set him back twenty-five dollars apiece. But he wasn't complaining. The sun was shining, and the wind was blowing out.

The grandstands were filled with people who seemed as if they had smiles surgically attached to their faces. Then there was Matt: "It's too bright, and I forgot my sunglasses."

"Take mine," Dave said, handing Matt his Ray-Bans.

"I need to go to the bathroom."

"Okay, but hurry back. The game's about to start."

Matt went down into the dark concourse, skillfully dodging the blue-clad fans rushing toward the sunshine before first pitch. *A total freak show, but this'll get me through this boring day.* Ducking into a bathroom, he slinked past the urinal troughs and into the privacy of a stall. Matt was well-practiced, and he knew how to be quick and inconspicuous. There was no point in even pulling down his pants. He simply took six hits off his joint before stubbing it out on the stall's wall. As he bebopped back through the concourse, his long hair swinging like mop strings, he heard a clamor from the grandstands.

"You missed it," Dave said when Matt returned to his seat. "Sosa just scored on a Morandini single to center."

"No worries, Dad." Matt was happy to have the Ray-Bans, which hid his bloodshot eyes. Now he needed a cure for the munchies. "I'm starved. Can I get a hot dog?"

"Sure thing."

Matt downed the dog in three bites, punctuating it with a belch and a "Tasty." He turned his attention to the ballgame just in time to see Chicago's Jose Hernandez launch a home run. Standing up, Matt pointed to the left field bleachers and quipped, "Whoa, did you check out that fan? He fell flat on his face trying to catch the homer. Classic."

"I told you this would be fun."

"Can I get another dog?"

"Wow, you really are hungry."

That one also vanished quickly, and Cubs slugger Glenallen Hill followed with a drive that was a streak of white against the blue sky. Matt tracked its supersonic flight onto Waveland Avenue before intoning, "Awesome visual."

"Yep, Hill really got hold of that one," Dave said. "Thirty more feet and it would have hit the building across the street."

Moments later Sosa homered. It was his sixtieth of the season, and the crowd gave him a prolonged standing ovation.

"This, son, is history. Sixty home runs, a truly rare feat. It's something you're going to remember for the rest of your life."

"Another hot dog? And maybe a Coke and some cotton candy, too?"

"Seriously?"

A lightbulb went off in Dave's head, though he couldn't be sure of what it was illuminating. Then Leyna called a week and a half later.

"Can you come over to the house?" she asked. "It's important."

"It can't wait? I've got a million things going on at work."

"It's about Matthew."

"Is he okay?"

"He's not hurt or anything, but we need to talk."

"I'll be there in a few."

Dave knocked on the thick oak door with his customary disdain, and Leyna promptly opened it. For the first time, she looked her age. There were circles under her eyes and creases along her forehead, and her ponytail was pulled back so tightly that it seemed to be tugging her skin.

"We're in the living room," she said.

Dave sat in a plush wingback chair and tried to acclimate himself to the scene. Eyeballing Matt and then Leyna and then Scott, he felt like he was at a cross between a military tribunal and a wake.

"Is someone going to tell me what's going on?" he asked.

"Matthew, why don't you tell him?" Leyna said.

"You tell him. You're the one who's all bent out of shape about it."

"Okay then. No reason to beat around the bush: Matthew was caught with pot at school this morning. He's been expelled."

"You're kidding."

"I wish I were," Leyna answered.

"Why am I just finding out about this now?" Dave asked.

"We took care of it," Scott said.

"How so?" Dave responded. "He's been expelled."

"And you think you would have fared any better? At least I saw to it that the police didn't become involved. I doubt you—"

"Can you two stop arguing?" Leyna interrupted. "The issue here is that Matthew has created a real mess for himself. I'm so disappointed."

"Sure you are, Mom. Like always, it's all about you."

"What the heck happened?" Dave asked Matt.

"Mom pretty much nailed it. What do you want me to say?"

"For starters, that you're sorry," Leyna said with a sniffle.

"Okay, I'm sorry. Can I go now?"

"I don't think you have any idea how serious this is," Scott said. "There are consequences."

Leyna looked at Dave anxiously and said, "Scott suggested that boarding school might be a good idea at this point."

"What, you want to just ship him off?" Dave countered. "You're not really going along with that, are you, Leyna?"

"It might be good for—"

"You would never go along with that. I mean, it's insane."

"It's not insane," Scott said. "There are schools equipped to deal with this kind of thing. You have to look at the big picture."

"I'm looking at the big picture, and this seems way over the top."

"What do you suggest then?" Leyna asked, almost pleadingly.

Rising to his feet, Matt said, "When you three geniuses figure out my life, let me know. I'll be up in my room."

"Take a seat," Dave said, and Matt slouched back onto the couch. "What I suggest is that we send him to Evanston High…right here, where we can keep an eye on him. He wasn't arrested, and it's a public school, so they pretty much have to take him, right?"

"He'll find all sorts of trouble there," Scott said.

"It seems he already found plenty of trouble at your school," Dave shot back.

"First of all, it's not *my* school. And second—"

"Please," Leyna interrupted. "Can we please just focus on the future here? What are we going to do?"

"I'm outta here," Matt said, standing up again. "I hate you all."

"Sit," Dave said, and Matt dropped back down. "I'm not too thrilled with you right now either."

"Why are you looking at me like that?" Matt asked.

"Why do you think?" Dave answered.

Leyna started crying.

"See what you've done to your mother?" Scott said.

"Oh, please. She'll be fine, especially after you've punted me off to boarding school."

"You're lucky it's not jail," Scott said.

"It wouldn't be any worse than here."

"Enough," Scott said with sufficient force to spread complete quiet over the room. "Enough." He calmly crossed his legs, like he was in perfect control in his Ralph Lauren khakis and hard-leather loafers, like he was ready to tie the events of the day into a tidy bow. Pivoting toward

Dave, he said, "I've had my secretary start pulling a list of schools that would be appropriate under the circumstances. He needs guidance that we clearly can't give him right now, as well as a fresh start away from the bad influences around here."

"I understand he needs help, but—"

"Look," Scott continued evenly, "this is a lot for you to digest right now. It is for everyone. It's definitely not how I wanted to spend today. But we need to act decisively, show him exactly who's in charge here."

"I don't know. It still seems—"

"Why not sleep on it? When my secretary finishes pulling the list, we'll talk again, and I think you'll see that this really is the best option."

"Fine," Dave said. "I'll at least think about it."

"Excellent," Scott said, followed by the type of self-congratulatory smile that indicated he was accustomed to getting his own way. "That should about do it then. We'll talk again later."

Dave said goodbye and walked toward the thick oak door, but after five steps his legs would carry him no farther. He turned back. "No," he said under his breath. "You know what? No."

"What's that?" Scott asked.

"No."

"I'm not following you," Scott said, and he wasn't smiling anymore.

"This isn't going to happen. You've been a pain in my ass for years, starting with when you fucked my wife."

"Don't do this, Dave," Leyna sobbed, contrasted by this from Matt: "Some fireworks. Cool. This day doesn't totally suck after all."

Dave heard neither voice, only his own: "You've steamrolled me time and again, and obviously you've steamrolled Leyna, too. But it ends here. You're not sending my son away just to make things easier for you. It's not going to happen. This is the life you chose—deal with it. Are you following me now?"

"Take a pill, Dave," Scott said.

"I will, just as soon as you go fuck yourself." Dave proceeded again to the thick oak door, but he couldn't resist turning back one more time. "By the way," he said, "your feet look like a pig's hooves."

Scott gazed down at his loafers in bewilderment. And a week later, Matt set off for his first day at Evanston High.

CHAPTER 40

The anthropologist proofread his syllabus one last time, though he wasn't sure why. It had been virtually the same for the past fourteen years. He took a certain amount of comfort in that. For a man who had once wanted nothing more than to be in the "field," he was happy to be so settled.

Sue Planck, now Sue Diller, appeared in his wood-paneled study, which was stocked with his arcane texts. "You always get so serious the night before your first day of classes," she said. "It's cute."

"'Cute' wouldn't be quite the word I'd choose," he sniffed. "How about 'academic'? It's more germane."

"Always the teacher. Anyway, I have a craving for Mexican. What do you say we get some dinner and a margarita at La Cantina?"

He glanced at his watch. "It's about that time, isn't it?"

The anthropologist was even more puckered now, and most of his hair was gone. But he still had his goatee, as well as a musty closet's worth of turtlenecks that Sue kept threatening to donate to rummage. He had become a familiar face at Oakton Community College. At first he had stayed there as a favor to his friend the dean and then because he liked it. Teaching at a community college had turned out to be interesting, more so than trying to enlighten the well-primed, self-entitled students who enrolled at four-year institutions like Ithaca College. These minds at Oakton were of a rawer variety. The anthropologist saw them as vessels that needed to be filled with knowledge, knowledge he could provide.

By his estimation, 1,500 students had come through his classroom at Oakton—1,500 vessels had been filled. No, his life hadn't been a waste. And sometime soon, when the time felt right, it would enter its final phase: retirement. He and Sue had already started to prepare for it, buying a cottage in the North Woods of Wisconsin. They would cook and take long walks and spend quiet nights by the fire. And he would write. About what, he didn't yet know, but he would write.

First, though, he had to finish what he had started. On the opening morning of classes he looked out at the rows of desks, and thirty mostly blank faces looked back. "Welcome to the 2000 edition of Introduction to Cultural Anthropology," he said. "My name is Nathan Diller. *Dr. Nathan Diller.* Now…let's find out a little bit about you." He pinpointed the blankest face in the classroom. "You, good sir. What do you expect to learn in this class?"

"I don't really know yet. It's the first day."

"May I ask your name?"

"Matt Weiss."

"Well, Matt Weiss, the words 'I don't really know' aren't going to work here. Perhaps if this were a philosophy class, but not in Introduction to Cultural Anthropology. We're here to seek answers, answers about what shapes human cultures. Your job for the next semester, then, will be to know as much as possible."

Matt's face turned red—he felt like everyone was watching him. *What a dick. Maybe I'll just drop this class. I don't even know why I'm here in the first place.*

Actually, that was something he did know. Although he had made it through Evanston High without being kicked out of there, too, his grades had been far from stellar. So he was working at Blockbuster and taking a couple classes at nearby Oakton, the other being English 101, with the hope of eventually attending a four-year college. That was the plan anyway, which wasn't to say it was his. Since he didn't have any ideas of his own, he was just going along with it.

His mom called it a fresh start, and to kick it off following his graduation from Evanston High, she had planned a month-long summer trip for the family to the south of France. It had been brutal. Scott had spent most of the time on his cellphone taking care of work stuff, and she had insisted that every single sight was "wonderful," even the homeless people in Marseilles. The only upside had been that he could drink legally; when he had ordered a beer at dinner their first night, the expression on Scott's face had been classic. Later in the summer, he had spent some obligatory time with his dad, whose latest bonding attempt had been a weekend fishing trip to Michigan where they had caught nothing.

And now, as if it could be possible, things had gotten worse: an old man with a goatee was lecturing him on the importance of anthropology. *I'm outta here*, Matt proclaimed to himself when that first class ended. But before he could leave, the old man intercepted him.

"Matt, may I have a word with you?" he asked.

"Didn't you already in front of the whole class?"

"Yes, well, I apologize for embarrassing you in front of everyone. I simply wanted to set a tone for the class, and I used you to do it because you looked strong enough to handle it. It's a teaching tool. I hope you didn't take it the wrong way."

Aside from his B.O., the old man seemed pretty harmless after all, and Matt said, "Don't sweat it. I'm used to it."

"Good. I'm quite sure you'll find this class interesting. I can't wait to hear your thoughts on our first reading."

It was just Matt and his mom at dinner that night, as Scott was in Denver on business. Leyna had been taking cooking classes, and she decided to test out chicken and artichoke fricassée with morel mushrooms. Matt eyed the jumble of food on his plate with suspicion, asking, "What's wrong with McDonald's?"

"I thought I'd make something special to commemorate your first day of college. It's a big occasion. Tell me about it."

"There's not much to say. It was school."

"That's it?"

"Okay, English was boring, but the anthropology class didn't completely suck."

"That seems promising, at least the anthropology class does. What did you like about it?"

"That I didn't fall asleep. How's that?"

"It could be worse."

His chicken and artichoke fricassée with morel mushrooms virtually untouched, Matt rose from the table and said, "I'll be up in my room. I have some reading to do for anthropology."

"Reading?"

"Don't look so shocked, Mom."

On the second day of class, the anthropologist stood again before the thirty faces: "Our first reading, of course, was 'Shakespeare in the Bush,' Laura Bohannan's fascinating portrait of the Tiv in Africa. I always enjoy starting with 'Shakespeare in the Bush' because it addresses a fundamental point about human cultures. Does anyone know what that is?"

Matt wasn't in the habit of raising his hand in class, but he had actually done this assignment, so what the hell?

"Yes, Matt."

"Yeah, the point is that every culture looks at things differently. Laura Bohannan thinks there's only one way to look at *Hamlet*, but when she shows it to the Tiv, they have their own way of looking at it."

"Indeed. It stands to reason that no values are truly universal. Each culture has its own interpretation of ultimate truth. Well done, Matt."

A week later Matt was buying a bag of Doritos at the student union when he saw the anthropologist at a nearby table. Stroking his goatee between sips of coffee, he seemed deep in thought, and Matt found the scene mildly amusing. *He's probably thinking about the Tiv or the Kayapo or some other crazed group of people no one's ever heard of. Strange dude. Off in his own little world.* The anthropologist was, however, present enough in this one to notice Matt and wave him over to the table.

"Sit down," he said.

Matt hesitated, as socializing with teachers wasn't his style. Then again, this situation was unique: the teacher seemed to like him. "Uh, I guess I have a little time before my English class."

"English. Interesting choice."

"Not really. My dad forced that one on me. He used to be a newspaper editor, so he's really into all that stuff."

"He must be well-read then."

"Yeah, he reads a lot, but he's still kind of clueless."

The anthropologist smiled and said, "At your age, all parents are clueless."

"You don't know my dad."

They continued to chitchat, and the minutes flew by until Matt stood up abruptly. "Oops. I better get going or I'll be late for English. You guys don't like that."

"No," the anthropologist said with a laugh, "we don't like that at all."

Another week had passed when Matt saw the anthropologist again at the student union. This time chitchat had to be avoided at all costs. Matt was supposed to have turned in his paper on David W. McCurdy's "Family and Kinship in Village India" at the end of class that morning, but it wasn't finished—or even started. He spun around and headed toward the exit. Luckily, the anthropologist was staring out the window at an empty field, but to play it safe, Matt camouflaged himself among a cluster of students who were also leaving.

"Matt," he heard the anthropologist say.

Are you kidding me? I'll just pretend I didn't hear him.

"Matt, over here."

Crap. He waved hi to the anthropologist.

"Sit," he said.

Resigned to his fate, Matt trudged over to the anthropologist's table.

"Are you off to English?" the anthropologist asked.

"Yep, don't want to be late."

"Well, the class doesn't start for another twenty-five minutes, so you'll be quite early, particularly given the way you were moving. I wish I could say the same about your paper. What happened?"

"The dog ate it?" Instead of scowling at that one, the anthropologist smiled, which had the odd effect of compelling Matt to come clean: "Actually, I just haven't gotten around to it yet. Story of my life."

"Ah, a procrastinator."

"That's me. It drives my parents crazy."

"Your dad the former newspaper editor?"

"Yeah."

"I can imagine. Journalism isn't a profession for the faint of heart. It's deadline-oriented, so there's no procrastinating allowed among the ink-stained wretches."

"Yeah, he's definitely anal about pretty much everything. My stepdad's even more of a hassle."

"How so?"

"It's his way or the highway. He can be kind of a rod."

"A *rod*," the anthropologist said, chuckling. "That's a funny way of putting it."

"It's true. I don't know why my mom married the guy. For real laughs, you should check her out."

"Her way or the highway, too?"

"Head in the sand is more like it. Everything has to be 100 percent perfect all the time. If it's not, she freaks. I can't figure her out."

"I understand how you feel. My first wife? I never figured her out either."

"Bummer."

"It certainly was. But we're drifting away from the issue at hand, which I have an unfortunate habit of doing. What are we going to do about your paper?"

Shrugging, Matt looked away.

"I have a proposal: if you turn it in by the end of the week, I won't subtract points for it being late. I'll do this because I have utter faith that you can uphold your end of the bargain."

"I guess I can't argue with that deal."

"I should think not. There's one more thing, Matt."

"What?"

"This is just between you and me. I don't want to give the impression to the rest of the class that I'm lenient about such transgressions."

"That's totally fair. Thanks, Dr. Diller."

"You can call me Nathan."

"Will do. And I won't let you down."

Matt didn't let the anthropologist down either. Although he procrastinated some more, he excused himself from his mother's braised Chilean sea bass the night before the due date and locked himself in his bedroom. And with the hip hop stylings of Mos Def, Eminem, the Pharcyde, and then Mobb Deep blaring through his earphones, he spent the next five hours pounding out his paper on the iMac his dad had given him for college.

In the ensuing weeks Matt popped into the student union every day, hoping to see the anthropologist in his signature state of meditation. Most times he was there. They debated music (Gregorian chant vs. hip hop), movies (*Bonnie and Clyde* vs. *Beavis and Butt-Head Do America*), role models (Jane Goodall vs. Chris Farley), food (Thai vs. Taco Bell), beautiful women (Jane Goodall vs. Liz Phair), and sports (Jackie Robinson vs. Tony Hawk). They ran the gamut.

One day they even delved into ancient history. Matt was wearing a T-shirt his mom had bought him that was emblazoned with a peace symbol. He had it on for no other reason than his good T-shirts were in a stinking pile on his bedroom floor, but it prompted the anthropologist to say, "Finally, we've found common ground."

"How's that?" Matt answered. "You took my advice and rented *Beavis and Butt-Head Do America*?"

"Your T-shirt."

Matt discreetly smelled his shirt; nope, it didn't reek.

"It's from my time, so to speak," the anthropologist said. "When I was at Woodstock, I saw that symbol everywhere. It was the hippies' version of the ichthus."

"You went to Woodstock?"

"I did indeed."

"Funny. My parents met at Woodstock."

"It's a small world."

Smaller than either of them could have known.

"Yeah," Matt said, "I never understood that one. My parents act like the furthest thing from hippies. But you I can kind of see at Woodstock."

"Well, I ended up there by accident, and it was most unfortunate."

"Sex, drugs, rock and roll. How could that not have been killer?"

"To start with, my car and money were stolen, and it took me days to find my way home. I felt like a modern-day Odysseus, except there was no happy ending in my Ithaca. My wife left me to 'find herself'— which is to say she didn't love me anymore, if she ever did at all—and I spent months upon months brooding in a cloud of marijuana smoke in a former student's apartment."

"Cool."

"I wouldn't say so," the anthropologist continued, his expression turning decidedly forlorn. "The police raided his apartment one night, and I nearly went to jail."

"Ouch." This, Matt thought, was far and away the most interesting story the old man had ever told, a big step up from his recounting of the time he saw *The Taming of the Shrew* in Central Park. "Then what?"

"Not knowing what else to do, I resigned my position at Ithaca College and moved to Rochester, New York. I call those my lost years."

"More weed smoking?"

"No, I sold cheese in a grocery store."

Matt burst out laughing. "That's something I would have paid big money to see."

"I'm glad you're so amused," the anthropologist said, and he was now smiling, too. "It didn't seem particularly funny at the time, but I was ultimately found. I met my current wife in Rochester, and then I was offered the opportunity to come to Oakton. Now here I am, talking to you. Frankly, I couldn't think of anywhere else I would rather be."

"I feel like one of your 'teaching moments' is coming up."

"Life is filled with teaching moments, my young friend. And the lesson here is that you should never lose hope the way I did. Eventually, fate smiles on all of us. It merely takes longer for some than others."

At semester's end, fate smiled on Matt at least a little bit: he scored a B in Introduction to Cultural Anthropology. He couldn't remember the last time he had scored a B in anything.

CHAPTER 41

"You think what would be a good idea?" Matt asked when Dave called to tell him of his plan.

"Marching with Jan Schakowsky in Glenview's Fourth of July parade, showing our support."

"And who is she?"

"Your U.S. representative."

"Got it."

"Everyone's assembling in the parking lot at Our Lady of Perpetual Help, on Glenview Road just a few blocks west of my store. Let's meet there at about eight o'clock."

"Wait. You're serious?"

Dave was in the parking lot at 8 a.m. sharp, and Matt wandered up about a half-hour later, carrying a Slurpee that was his breakfast. His eyes were red and glassy, though only from sleep deprivation.

"Sorry I'm late, Dad. I had to close last night at Blockbuster. Work's a grind. Not exactly what I had in mind for summer vacation."

"Welcome to the real world. You can't go to the south of France every summer."

"Where is everyone anyway?"

"Seems I got the times crossed. The parade starts at ten o'clock, not nine. I would have called you, but I figured you were already on your way."

"Great. This day just keeps getting better."

Matt's flagging spirits weren't helped by the heat: the parking lot already smelled of melting blacktop. As they waited, he took a seat on the curb and lit a cigarette.

"Those will kill you," Dave reminded him.

"I've got plenty of time before that happens. Look at Grandpa. He still smokes, and he's, like, ninety."

"Seventy-seven, but close enough."

At around nine a woman with short gray hair, bifocals, and an unfaltering smile showed up. She was wearing a faded Al Gore T-shirt from the previous year's presidential campaign, and since she also had a stack of hand signs, Dave presumed she was the top Democrat.

"Are you marching with us?" she asked.

"Yep. I'm Dave, and this is my son Matt."

"I'm Pat. Nice to meet both of you. We need all the reinforcements we can get after the way Bush stole that election. We certainly don't want a repeat of 2000 ever again."

"That's why we're here," Dave said. "Just trying to do what we can to help the cause."

She handed Dave a sign that read "Election Reform—Now!" and Matt one that said "Equal Pay for Women." Then she went off to greet the other Dems who were arriving.

"Am I really supposed to carry this thing?" Matt asked Dave.

"Sure, why not?"

"I don't know, maybe because I'm a guy."

"All the better. It shows empathy."

"And to think, I could be at home in bed right now."

"Well, I'm glad you're here with me."

By 9:45 the parking lot was jammed with parade participants, from the Jesse White Tumblers to the usual assortment of vintage automobiles and military veterans. The Dems were well-represented, about thirty-five strong in all shapes and sizes. There was one Dem in particular whom Dave couldn't take his eyes off, and this somewhat disturbed him since she didn't seem much older than Matt. *Full* was the word that kept coming to Dave's mind. She had full lips, full sand-colored curls that were cropped at her shoulders, full thighs, a full rear end, and a full chest. She was by no means overweight, just solid in every conceivable way. Dressed in a white tank top, blue-jean cutoffs, and black high-top Chuck Taylors, she was also kind of sexy without working too hard at it. Dave worried, however, about the Chucks. *Not the wisest choice for walking in a parade. Not enough support.*

"Dad," Matt said, tapping Dave's shoulder. "The parade's starting."

"Huh?"

With Jan Schakowsky in front waving two small American flags, they veered out of the parking lot onto Glenview Road. The parkways were lined with sticky spectators, and Dave watched the girl throw pieces of candy to the kids. She seemed to take great delight in the way they scrambled to scoop up her offerings. Obviously her Chucks weren't an issue, because by the time the Dems turned onto Harlem Avenue, she was at least fifteen feet in front of Dave and Matt. Dave tried to keep up, but Matt, withering under the sun and from his lack of sleep, was seemingly moving in reverse.

"You mind picking up the pace a little?" Dave prodded.

They had narrowed the gap to five feet when the girl accidentally dropped her water bottle while letting some candy fly. It rolled straight to Dave's feet. Trotting up to her with the bottle, he said, "Here, you don't want to lose this on a day like today."

"Definitely not. It's turning into a scorcher."

"It's supposed to get up to ninety-five. Nothing like summertime in Chicago."

"Except wintertime in Chicago," she said, and Dave laughed.

Now they were walking side by side, with Matt limping onward several feet behind them.

"Too bad about the election, huh?" Dave said.

"Tell me about it. That's why I'm here. Every vote counts, that's for sure."

"That's exactly what I was thinking," Dave said, mostly to himself.

"Plus, I love parades."

"It's my first time marching in a Fourth of July parade."

"Yeah? I haven't been in one since Girl Scouts."

Dave feared that wasn't long ago.

"It's just as fun as I remember," she continued. "I love the way everyone is out and about on Fourth of July. It's my favorite holiday."

"Me, too," Dave said, even though he didn't have a favorite holiday.

Matt fell farther behind them, not that Dave noticed. He was mesmerized by the girl's curls, which sprang like pogo sticks despite the rapidly building humidity. The sign she was carrying read "PETA," and to keep the conversation going, he said, "I like your sign."

"Oh thanks, I made it myself. I'm in the postgrad veterinary program at Northwestern, so it's an issue that's near and dear to me."

"Veterinary school, huh? So that means you're, what, twenty-five, twenty-six?"

"Not quite. Twenty-four."

Phew. That's respectable…sort of. I could live with that.

"And you?" she asked. "Wait, don't tell me. Thirty-nine or forty."

"Not even close, unfortunately. Fifty-one. But I'll take that as a compliment."

"You should."

At long last, Dave's confoundedly boyish face was playing to his favor. His bragging scars seemed to be working for him, too. She asked Dave how he had gotten them, and he explained that they were from a car accident.

"They add character," she said. "They're like little tattoos, which is sooo cool. I love tattoos."

"I see that. I like the one there on your calf. What is that, a butterfly?"

"Exactly. Here, I'll show you my favorite, a tiny little heart I got on my shoulder blade a couple months ago."

She handed him her "PETA" sign and reached for the right strap of her tank top. Dave's eyes grew wide, but just as she was about to reveal the tattoo, Matt poked him from behind.

"Did you see that person in the crowd give me the finger?" Matt asked.

"No." Dave hurriedly turned to the girl again. "The tattoo?" he implored.

"And who's this?" she asked.

"Oh, him? He's my son. Matt."

"Hi, Matt. I'm Betsy."

"What up?" Matt offered before saying to his dad, "Do you mind if I bail? Like I said, the crowd is starting to get hostile, and I didn't get any sleep last night, and I'm frying in the heat, and…"

Dave was still thinking about the tiny little heart tattoo beneath the girl's tank top, and his hormones were whirling with surprising vigor, even doing a few celebratory somersaults, like they were overjoyed to finally be released upon an entirely different kind of scene.

"Dad, do you mind if I leave?" Matt repeated. "I'm really tired from work."

"Sure, sure. Whatever."

"Um, okay. Cool. I'm not working tonight, so maybe we can grab some dinner or something after I catch up on my sleep."

"Sounds good. I'll call you."

Matt handed Dave his sign and promptly departed, and the Dems hung a left onto Central Avenue.

"I never did get your name," the girl asked.

"It's Dave, Dave Weiss. You're Betsy, right?"

"That's me."

"It's a pleasure."

"Same here." She squinted at him through the sunlight and said, "Your face has gotten awfully red. Must be dehydration. You can have some of my water if you want."

"Thanks. I didn't think to bring my own. Rookie mistake."

Dave swapped the "PETA" sign for the water, and although he was pretty sure dehydration wasn't the cause of his red face, he took a swig.

"So you live in Glenview?" she asked.

"No, but I own a store just up the street. Weiss Drugstore."

"Really? I've been there. I love your little soda fountain. It's such a cool retro touch."

"That's exactly the idea. I'm surprised I've never seen you there. You're hard to miss."

"I guess I'll take that as a compliment."

"You should."

"Thanks then." After tossing another handful of candy, she said, "It must be a lot of work owning a store."

"It is, but it beats working for someone else. This way I feel like I have some control over my destiny."

"I really admire that. Someday I'd like to have my own vet practice."

"Well, hopefully you'll get there quicker than I did."

"At least you got there, right? Better late than never."

"You know what?" Dave said, and his grin expanded. "I'll take that as a compliment."

"Be my guest."

To Dave's disappointment, the parade wound to an end in Johns Park, which was outfitted with carnival rides for the holiday and smelled of cotton candy. He could have walked all day. The same seemed true for the top Dem, even though her Al Gore T-shirt was soaked with sweat when she approached Dave and Betsy.

"That was energizing, wasn't it?" she said.

"It really was," Dave answered.

As he handed over his two signs, the top Dem asked, "What happened to your son?"

"He made it about two-thirds of the way through, but then the heat got the better of him, and he left."

"That's okay," she said. "We had a great turnout anyway. If there was one positive that came out of the election, it fired up our base. This is where it all begins, with good old-fashioned grassroots activism."

The Dems, along with the other parade participants, began to disperse, but Dave and Betsy lingered.

"So where's Mrs. Weiss?" Betsy probed. "She didn't want to battle the hot sun? Or is she a Republican?"

"Neither, actually. There is no Mrs. Weiss. Divorced."

A faint smile escaped from her that seemed incongruous with her following words: "Oh, I'm sorry."

"Thanks, but I'm used to it. It's been years."

"At least you got a good son out of it, right?"

"Some days," Dave said with a snicker. "Other days he drives me up a wall."

Betsy laughed.

"But I can't complain, not too much anyway. It's all part of the deal."

"I'm sure. Now, if we could just do something about your face. It keeps getting redder and redder."

"Yeah?"

"My apartment's only a block from here, and it's air-conditioned. You're welcome to stop by to cool off and have an iced tea. You really look like you could use a cold drink."

"That sounds perfect," Dave answered, his hormones somersaulting but his voice remaining steady. "Like you said, this day's turning into a scorcher."

Betsy unveiled a smile that was fantastically full, and as they walked to her abode, two thoughts crossed Dave's mind: *God bless grassroots activism. And God bless the United States of America.*

CHAPTER 42

Sitting on a futon couch in Betsy's living room with a glass of iced tea in his hand, Dave wondered if becoming a vet was the best career path for her. Though he was no expert, even he could see that her cat Oscar wasn't exactly the picture of fitness as he tromped across the floor toward the windowsill like a black bowling ball on chopsticks. Oscar surveyed the great precipice momentarily, but instead of trying to leap up there, he rolled onto his side and closed his eyes. *Smart choice*, Dave thought.

"You still look a little red," Betsy said. "Maybe I should blast the air conditioning some more."

"I'm good, but thanks."

Full also applied to Betsy's apartment, which was stuffed with souvenirs and kitschy trinkets. The haphazard arrangement was overwhelming, but in a good way. There seemed to be a welcoming place for anything and everything here, even Dave on the futon couch with his iced tea.

His eyes circled the room inquisitively, and she asked, "See anything you like?"

"Boy, I don't even know where to start."

"Tell me about it. It's really gotten out of hand, hasn't it? Here, I'll give you the grand tour."

Dave stepped over Oscar and followed her to a bookcase in the hallway next to the bathroom.

"I kind of have a baseball theme going on this shelf," she said. "The bobbleheads are my favorite. It doesn't get much kitschier than that, right?"

"You're a baseball fan?" he asked, his heart thumping hopefully.

Her answer was nothing short of beautiful: "A long-suffering Cubs fan."

"Is there any other kind?"

"Nope."

"I really thought 1998 might be the year, but they were no match for the Braves in the playoffs. And after that, the bottom just fell out…again."

"Tell me about it."

Dave plucked a baseball from the shelf and reflexively cocked his arm like he was going to throw it. "Where'd this come from?"

"Cubs versus Reds, 1995 at Wrigley. A foul ball off the bat of Mark Grace that I caught. He's such a cutie, isn't he?"

"I suppose."

"From here, it turns into a free-for-all." Leading Dave a few steps back toward the living room, she pointed to the wall. "My *Casablanca* poster."

"What a great movie," Dave said.

"I know. I still get teary at the end of it."

Betsy moved on to a V.I.P. lanyard that was hanging from a nail in the wall. "This is from a Tupac concert I saw with my friend Jennie. July 1996 at the House of Blues, right before he died."

"*Casablanca* meets hip hop. This really is a free-for-all."

"What'd I tell you?"

"You and my son would have a lot to talk about—he loves hip hop. At the risk of sounding like an old fart, I don't get it. I'm more of a classic rock kind of guy."

"Then you'll like this Grateful Dead decal," Betsy answered, gesturing toward a rendering of the doodah man.

"Nice."

She continued to guide Dave through her treasury, and he stopped at a pipe-smoking garden gnome.

"You need a garden for your garden gnome," he said.

"Someday…once I get through school and pay off some bills. In the meantime, here it sits with all my other clutter in this tiny little apartment."

"My ex-wife is an avid gardener, but gnomes aren't her thing. They aren't *beautiful*. She doesn't see the humor in them."

"That's no fun," Betsy said with enough edge for Dave to notice.

"Anyway, I like it," he said quickly. "Where'd you pick it up?"

"The Kane County Flea Market, the same place I've picked up a lot of this stuff."

"I've never been there, but I've heard it's pretty neat."

"It is. There are hundreds of people selling everything you could possibly imagine. I'm addicted."

"I can see that," Dave said, and Betsy knocked him with her hip in mock protest.

"I was actually thinking of heading out there Saturday. You're welcome to join me if you want. You never know what you might find." Her smile turned mischievous as she added, "They have lots of garden gnomes. Maybe you can buy one for your ex-wife. I'm sure she'd appreciate it."

Dave let out a belly laugh, imagining Leyna's horror upon finding pipe-smoking garden gnomes littering her flawless tulip patch. "That truly is tempting," he said, "but I think I'll leave her out of this. Sure, I'll go. It sounds like a great way to spend a Saturday."

That evening, after meeting a rejuvenated Matt for deep-dish pizza, Dave sat in his Skokie apartment and played out the possibilities. He racked his brain for an apocalyptic outcome, but this was all he came up with:

- *She's pretty.*
- *She's nice.*
- *She doesn't think I'm a dinosaur.*

At the very least, maybe he'd find something at the flea market for his apartment. Although he had been there for four years, it remained barren, a dirt road to Betsy's Vegas strip. His true home had become Weiss Drugstore, where he was still succeeding in keeping the books in the black. And his family, for lack of a better word, consisted of his employees. Absent among them was Marie, who had met her eternal reward a few years earlier, dying in her sleep at the age of eighty-seven. His workforce nowadays was centered on a cadre of part-time teenagers, mostly from nearby Glenbrook South High School. They helped themselves generously to burgers from the soda fountain, candy, and cigarettes, but since Dave was paying them veritable peanuts, he looked the other way.

Out of necessity he had splurged on a full-time pharmacist, a

Romanian immigrant who spoke English with an almost unintelligibly thick accent but was a whiz at the pill tray. On the weekends Dave utilized a chemist from Searle, Jack Wieland, who wanted to stay abreast of industry trends by doing some retail pharmaceutical work. A former Navy enlistee, he had a crew cut and an authoritative voice that kept the teenagers on their toes. Wieland ran his shifts with such military precision that Dave didn't have to worry about leaving the store in his care and could do things on the weekends like…go to the Kane County Flea Market.

Indeed, Dave was a man on the move. He had brand-new wheels—a 2001 Toyota Camry—and this was no small development: it was the first car since the Volvo he hadn't bought used. And now he was cruising in that Camry to pick up the enticingly uncomplicated Betsy for their flea market expedition. As he turned onto her street, he racked his brain one last time, but this was as far as he got:

- She's smart.
- She's fun.
- She likes me.

The heat had broken since the Fourth of July, and it was seventy-five degrees with a comfortable breeze. If Dave's new car had been a convertible, he would have put the top down. He did have a sunroof, so he settled for opening that.

"Good?" he asked Betsy of the open sunroof.

"Definitely," she answered.

The flea market was located at the Kane County Fairgrounds in the quaint town of St. Charles, which was about forty-five miles southwest of Glenview and sat along the Fox River, the same body of water the Special had ridden before washing ashore. Betsy had been right: it was a happening, anchored by several barn-like exposition buildings that were surrounded by row upon endless row of small canopy tents, vans, RVs, and pickup trucks from which vendors hawked their goods. Since the weather was so inviting, they decided to stay outside.

"Where to?" Dave asked.

"There's no rhyme or reason to it," Betsy said. "We can just head off in any old direction."

That was easier said than done, given the density of the crowd. After zigzagging around a slow-moving cluster of aged women and a morbidly obese man munching on a corndog, they stopped at a tent showcasing hundreds of books.

"Here's a keeper," Dave said, pulling a paperback from the depths of a crate. "*One Flew Over the Cuckoo's Nest.*"

"I've never read it, but I loved the movie."

"You'll have to put it on your list. As good as the movie is, the book's much better."

"It's always like that."

"Isn't it, though?"

Betsy's face swelled with glee as she unearthed a paperback of her own. "Sooo cool. *Black Beauty.*"

"Never read that one. Isn't it a kids' book?"

"It's great at any age. This is the book that made me want to become a vet."

"Really?"

"Yep."

Dave handed *One Flew Over the Cuckoo's Nest* to the thin man behind the crates. "I'll take this one," he said. "And *Black Beauty* for the gir—, er, lady."

"Thanks for the book," Betsy said.

"My pleasure. Something that means so much to you definitely belongs in your living room. Maybe Oscar can use it as a pillow."

Betsy laughed, and they proceeded farther down the endless row. She made a special point of stopping at a table next to a pickup truck.

"Well, what do we have here?" she said with the same puckish smile she had flashed at her apartment on the Fourth of July.

"Garden gnomes," Dave answered, and he grinned, too.

She zeroed in on a particularly garish wheelbarrow-pushing figurine and said to the heavyset man in the white undershirt, "I'll take that one." When the transaction was completed, she gave the garden gnome to Dave.

"It's for your ex," she said. "I couldn't resist."

"She'll love it," he responded playfully.

Continuing along the row, they made fun of the proliferation of stroller-pushing parents, whom Dave compared to the wheelbarrow-pushing garden gnome. Amid their larking, he clasped Betsy's hand, and she pressed his affirmatively. The union felt so natural—so spontaneously, casually right—that Dave didn't think twice about it. There was only the warmth of her skin...and something else.

"I smell funnel cakes," he said.

"I don't smell anything. You have the nose of a bloodhound."

"They smell delicious. Let's go get one."

"You lead the way."

Hand in hand, the vet student with the colorful tattoos and the editor-turned-storeowner with the bragging scars followed the scent, and soon a food truck materialized in the distance. As they closed in on the funnel cakes, however, she wanted to check out a tent with a hodgepodge of collectibles, her favorite kind.

The tent was being minded by an old man with long white hair that drifted anywhere it pleased. He struck Dave as the type who never realized the sixties ended and had kept on living hard through the seventies, eighties, and nineties. Pushing himself up from his lawn chair, he said to Betsy in a gravelly voice, "You look like you've been to a few of these."

"Yeah?" she answered. "How can you tell?"

"I've been at this awhile."

He and Betsy continued to talk, and Dave, growing hungrier by the second, started to fidget. He looked toward the food truck and then at Betsy again, saying, "You almost ready? Those funnel cakes smell really..."

Out of the corner of his eye, Dave spotted something tucked away in the back of the tent, something next to a cheaply framed picture depicting the Battle of Gettysburg. His mouth agape, he pointed his finger.

"Anything I can help you with?" asked the man.

"That...next to the Gettysburg picture," Dave said.

"What about it?"

"Can I see it?"

"No sweat." While retrieving it, he added, "I'm glad someone wants to see it. I don't know why I even bother to keep bringing it to these things. Habit, I guess."

He passed the object to Dave, who carefully ran his fingers along the surface. He examined the scratches, notches, gouges, and other markings. Though he couldn't account for them all, especially the burns and the water stains, there was no doubt about it. This was the Special. The long-gone Special.

The man carried on: "Yeah, I've been trying to sell this for almost ten years. Same with the Gettysburg picture. If you want it—the guitar, that is—I'll give you a deal."

Dave said nothing. He kept looking at the Special, and it was as if the near-entirety of his adult life was reflecting off the weathered mahogany. He thought of Jimmy racing through the upstate New York cornfields so that they could start their adventure without delay. And Leyna rising to the surface of Filippini Pond like a dream. And Jumbo's bone-bruising handshake. And the Angola cop who miraculously fetched the guitar from a field. And the apartment between the sooty highway and the peeling water tower where it hung so hopefully on the wall. And kindly Burnham Place.

"Some guy who was real big—overweight and pasty, if you know what I mean—sold it to me for next to nothing over in Galena, said it was worthless," the man continued, as much to counter Dave's silence as anything else. "Well, I'm not one to think anything's worthless, not in this business, but I have to admit I was beginning to think he was right about this guitar. It's just been sitting here and sitting—. Maybe I should just shut up. This isn't very good salesmanship, is it?"

Dave thought about the night he brought the guitar to the *Herald* as a good-luck charm. And Pete Townshend's *Rolling Stone* ad. And his basement bar in the prairie box. And Matt's much-awaited entrance into the world. And his ugly encounter with Doomsday. And the emptiness, the nothingness, that followed his divorce. He thought of all he had gained and all he had lost, and his eyes welled with tears.

"What's the matter?" Betsy asked.

There was no point in trying to explain, not right now anyway. "Must be allergies," Dave answered, and he wiped his eyes.

"If you don't want that guitar, I have another I can show you, a Strat I got a few months ago," the man said.

"No, no, no," Dave answered hurriedly. "I'll take this one. How much?"

"Ten bucks?" the man said, fully expecting to be talked down to pocket change.

"It's a deal."

Call it divine intervention or fate or maybe just dumb luck, but for the second time Dave Weiss had taken possession of the Special.

"You sure you're all right?" Betsy asked.

"Trust me, I'm great. Fantastic."

"Okay, then lead me to the funnel cakes."

"Believe it or not, I think I'm done. You mind if we head home?"

"Already? Maybe you can find some cool old vinyl albums to go with that vintage guitar, get a theme going in your apartment."

"Nah. I found everything I wanted."

Back at Betsy's place, they ate a dinner of grilled cheese sandwiches and tater tots.

"Cooking's not one of my strong suits," she explained apologetically. "This is about as gourmet as I get. I hope it tastes okay."

"It's perfect," Dave said as he popped a tater tot into his mouth. "A perfect ending to a perfect day."

But alas, the day wasn't quite over. After dinner she showed him her bedroom. Though it wasn't much bigger than a closet and lacked the decorative flourishes of the living room, such details weren't important. Dave and Betsy were really just there to use the bed. Not wanting to let the Special out of his sight, Dave had brought it with him into the bedroom. Betsy thought this to be peculiar, but she wasn't one to question quirkiness, especially when it came to flea market acquisitions.

Without hesitation, Dave removed her shirt and began kissing her neck and shoulders. "There it is," he said.

"There what is?"

"Your heart tattoo. You were going to show it to me at the parade, remember?"

"That's right. What do you think?"

"A tattoo never looked so good."

"You crack me up."

She kissed Dave's lips, and he unfastened her bra, whereupon he discovered that she had a pierced nipple, which he caressed with his index finger. Moving down her midriff, he noticed that her navel was pierced, too. And when he took off her shorts and panties, he located a ladybug tattoo on the right side of her rear end.

"There sure is a lot to find here," he said. "It's like a treasure chest."

"Glad you're enjoying yourself."

"I am. I think I'll just keep on exploring, see what else I can discover."

"Be my guest."

Dave's explorations culminated with ten minutes of spirited lovemaking, after which he had difficulty catching his breath. He couldn't decide if he was in a suspended state of rapture or was having a heart attack.

"You okay?" Betsy asked.

"I think so," he answered between wheezes. "I haven't felt like that for a long, long, long time. Guess I'm showing my age, huh?"

"You were fine."

"Provided you don't have to call the paramedics."

Betsy smiled and said, "Honestly, you were great, Dave. Who cares about all the other stuff, like the fact that you're a billion years older than I am? When it works, it works, right? And I would definitely say this works."

CHAPTER 43

This time Pete Townshend, and by extension The Who, got it right. There were no acts of buffoonery à la Live Aid—no lost instruments, no flubbed lyrics, no ill-executed leg kicks. This performance exuded raw power.

It goes without saying that Pete's latest attempt to find the Special following his Broadway triumph had resulted only in crank calls to Clive, but he carried on anyway. He went back on the road with his bandmates, and the critics didn't even make fun of them. Part of that was because of their new drummer, Zak Starkey. Both young and cocky, he was much more of a thrasher than Kenney Jones had been, giving The Who a reasonable facsimile of Keith Moon.

Mostly, though, it came down to Pete, who no longer approached the shows as if he were being led to the guillotine. Sometimes he went so far as to call the experiences "pleasant." To everyone's surprise, including his own, he also began chasing his white whale again, revisiting *Lifehouse* as a solo project. He assembled all his works from the previous three decades that had been inspired by *Lifehouse* and released them on his website. This wasn't the story as he had imagined it—rather it was a collection of disparate parts—but he nevertheless felt as if he was moving in the right direction.

Everything stopped, however, on September 11, 2001. When the airplanes crashed into New York's World Trade Center that bright-blue morning, Pete wasn't a lord of rock. He was like everyone else: a horrified citizen of the world. Tears rolled down his cheeks as he watched his telly and saw the two skyscrapers collapse, killing nearly 3,000 innocent souls.

In the aftermath the U.S. military sent troops to Afghanistan to hunt for the terrorists who were responsible for this unfathomable assault on humanity. The musical community put its boots down in New York. Paul McCartney—the former Beatle, the ultimate lord of rock—organized The Concert for New York City for October 20 at Madison Square Garden. Paul called Pete, and his reaction was quite different than it had been sixteen years earlier when Bob Geldof had tried to enlist The Who's services in helping the starving in Ethiopia: "We'll do whatever you need, Paul. It's an honor."

When The Who touched down at JFK International Airport, Roger asked a legitimate question: "What the Christ should we play? It's a bit of a somber occasion, you know? Maybe we should play our mellow stuff."

"We don't have any mellow stuff," Pete said. "We're the fucking 'Oo. So we're just going to go out there and be the fucking 'Oo."

Madison Square Garden was filled with 9/11 first responders and the relatives of those who had died, all of whom had been admitted for free, their uniforms or the caps of their lost loved ones serving as tickets. While Pete and company stood offstage, the actor John Cusack and a group of first responders provided the introduction: "Here's a band who loves New York and is loved by New York."

And then the geezers from Shepherd's Bush transformed into the fucking 'Oo, barreling into "Who Are You" with a fury they hadn't known they still possessed. Spurred on by the first responders and their kin, whose fists were raised and who were singing along with every lyric as if their lives depended on it, Pete pushed his fifty-six-year-old body into the danger zone. He punished his guitar—now a Fender Eric Clapton Signature Stratocaster—by bending its strings into notes that couldn't ordinarily be reached, and he whirled around the stage as if he was under a spell.

By the finale of the four-song set, the seminal *Lifehouse* scrap "Won't Get Fooled Again," many in the audience were shouting the words with voices that had grown hoarse. Others were crying, coerced by memories of their youths, when they'd listen to the song on vinyl at parties or on boomboxes while hanging out at the park in the summer sun, and by the hope of recapturing snippets of that innocence in the years ahead. It was—in a word—cathartic.

Much later, *Rolling Stone* would include The Who's performance on its list of "50 Moments That Changed Rock and Roll." But as Pete exited the stage that night with a pungent film of perspiration on his body, he wasn't contemplating his place in history. For the first time since the sunrise at Woodstock, his faith in the potential of rock and roll had been fully affirmed, and all he wanted to do now was take that feeling out on the road with The Who, share it with his fellow citizens of the world.

CHAPTER 44

Dave never made it official. He didn't say to Betsy, "Let's move in together," nor did he ever give up his apartment in Skokie. It happened organically, starting with when he left a couple shirts at her abode, then a pair of running shoes, then his favorite pair of blue jeans, and then most of the rest of his clothes. Finally, on a snowy February afternoon in 2002, he showed up with the Special.

"I've been looking at that spot above your futon couch for a while," he announced. "It's the only patch of wall in this entire living room that isn't covered with something. I thought the Special might look good there."

Dave had filled Betsy in on the story behind the Special, from Jumbo to Doomsday. He had tried to explain what it meant to him—its existential value—and she had understood. Thus, she viewed it not as another decoration in her apartment but as a commitment.

"I love it," she said after Dave had gone about the arduous business of wiring it to the wall, standing on the other side of the living room so that she could devour the totality of the sight.

He consummated the moment by kissing her lips and squeezing her rear, and then they ate a lunch of RavioliOs and lemonade.

"I better get back to work," Dave said. "You have class this afternoon, right?"

"Yep."

"How 'bout if I pick you up afterward? Maybe we can go to the mall or something, walk around, stretch our legs a bit."

"Why not? There's not much else to do in this snow."

Dave wasn't big on malls, but almost anything seemed fun if he was doing it with Betsy, especially public outings. When they were hand-in-hand—the fifty-two-year-old Dave and the twenty-five-year-old Betsy—the more prudish among them looked on reproachfully. These judgments added a quality of grandeur to their affair, making them feel deliciously rebellious, like Bonnie and Clyde, even if they were merely strolling and not robbing banks. Other people, notably aging men who had been sufficiently beaten down by life, stared with envy. Whenever Dave felt the eyes of these hunched-over gawkers upon him, the spring in his step became more pronounced.

So it was on that snowy evening at Golf Mill, the mall near Betsy's apartment. They walked hand-in-hand through the concourse, passing Banana Republic, the Gap, Yankee Candle, and the other staples of seemingly every mall in North America. Despite the cookie-cutter environs, the exercise was invigorating following their respective days of sedentary labor, until they reached the food court and gave in to pepperoni pizza from Sbarro.

On the drive home Dave's cellphone rang, and it was Leyna. Betsy rolled her eyes, as she often did in matters concerning his ex.

"What's up?" he asked.

"It's about Matthew," Leyna said.

"Is something wrong?"

"No, why?"

"You have that tone."

"What tone?"

"I don't know—*that* tone, like you're agitated, ready to come apart at the seams."

"I never have that tone."

"You always do."

"I don't. I'm fine, really."

"Okay, you're fine. What's going on with Matt?"

"Remember the anthropology professor Matthew likes so much, that odd little man?"

"Sure, Dr. Diller."

"Apparently, he leads a month-long cultural studies trip to Europe each summer, and Matthew's expressed interest in going. There won't be another chance to do it after this year, because I guess he's retiring. I just want to see what you think."

"I think it's a great idea," Dave said, winking at Betsy to appease her. "He'd actually learn something, which won't happen if he spends the whole summer working at Blockbuster and hanging out."

"I agree. He'll even get credits for it."

"Good."

"It's expensive, but we'd cover the costs, so you wouldn't have to worry about that."

"Even better."

"Do you want to come by the house tomorrow and look at the literature?"

"Sure, I'll stop by after work."

"It will just be you and me. Matthew has to work."

"What about Scott?"

"Oh, he's in Denver on business again."

"Better still."

"Very funny, Dave. Anyway, he's on board with it."

"I figured as much. I'll see you tomorrow."

Dave clicked off the phone, and Betsy said, "What was that all about?"

"That? It was just Leyna wondering if I wanted to remarry her," he said with a smirk.

Smiling that fantastically full smile, Betsy said, "You're such an asshole."

"The big day's tomorrow. Leyna said you can be a bridesmaid if you want."

"Jerk."

Dave took a hand off the steering wheel to stroke her curls. "Actually, Matt has a chance to study in Europe this summer with a professor from school."

"He's going to do it, right?"

"I think so."

"Awesome. What a blast."

"I know. When I was his age, I was mowing lawns and serving up Chinese food."

At the Victorian the next night, Dave went through the painstakingly constructed itinerary. The group would travel through Germany, Italy, France, and Spain, comparing and contrasting the cultures of each nation under the anthropologist's guiding eye. He had been leading this trip every summer since 1991. It lacked the cutting-edge daring of the expeditions of his youth—sitting with adolescents in a Parisian café wasn't the same as observing the Yanomami in the Amazon—but he no longer desired more than a small taste of the field.

"I have to say I'm surprised by how good I'm feeling about this," Leyna said to Dave.

"Me, too," he responded with an air of purpose. "It will be great."

"It's been a long time coming, huh? It feels right."

"Yep, let's do it."

They did it indeed—they signed Matt up for the anthropologist's educational trip.

The following Saturday, with the Europe matter having been settled with such relative ease, Dave's thoughts were centered on something more mundane, namely how he and Betsy would while away their afternoon. The plan so far was for him to pick her up at work, Terry Animal Hospital right next to Evanston in downtown Wilmette, where she logged about twenty-five hours per week between her studies. Her parents both drew humble salaries as schoolteachers in Glenview, so it fell upon Betsy to finance most of vet school herself and pay her own living expenses.

Dave had met her mom and dad a few times, and it had been awkward since they were roughly his age. In those encounters, meals around Betsy's kitchen table consisting of takeout food and forced conversation about anything except the elephant in the room, Dave had felt more like a male version of Mrs. Robinson from *The Graduate* than freewheeling Clyde Barrow. But he was willing to live with that.

He waited for Betsy by the curb at the animal hospital, and she traipsed to his Camry through the slushy snow. As was always the case when she finished work, she smelled of dogs and cats.

"Any great ideas for beating the winter blahs?" Dave asked.

"As a matter of fact, yes. I feel like getting a tattoo."

"Another?"

"What do you mean another? I haven't gotten one in the eight months I've known you."

"True, and I can't think of anything better to do anyway. You lead the way since I'm not up on the tattoo parlors around town. Just don't be surprised if I pass out while you get it. I have something of a needle phobia."

"Wimp."

"Only about some things. Like needles."

Betsy directed Dave to Red Dragon Tattoos in the Uptown neighborhood on Chicago's north side. Uptown was an urban grab bag, a mix of halfway houses and funky shops, of meth heads and hipsters. At the center of it all was the Aragon Ballroom—or the Brawlroom, as it was affectionately known—which had hosted rockers through the years ranging from the Jefferson Airplane and Iggy Pop & the Stooges to Motörhead and Green Day. Red Dragon Tattoos was a couple blocks from the Brawlroom on West Lawrence.

"Gee, looks inviting," Dave scoffed as they gazed upon a neon sign of a dragon that was bolted to a scruffy old building.

"It'll be fun."

Fun wasn't the first word that popped into his mind when they entered the shop and saw the proprietor, whose pallid complexion and skin-and-bones physique made him a dead ringer for one of the neighborhood meth heads. Dave was, however, heartened by the space itself. He had been expecting a den of debauchery, but it was as clean and aseptic as a doctor's office. And judging from the intricate examples of his tattoos hanging from the drywall, the guy seemed to know his craft.

"Yo, Bets," he said, like they were well-acquainted. "Long time, no see."

"I've been busy. You know, school, work—the usual."

"I hear that. Who's your friend?"

"This is Dave. He's actually kind of my *boyfriend*," she said with a bit of a blush.

"Right on—you always did march to the beat of your own drummer. How goes it, Dave? I'm Claude. You getting some artwork today, too, or is it just Bets?"

"Just, ah, Bets. I'm here to watch."

Dave sat in a red vinyl chair, and Claude asked Betsy, "So what are you thinking?"

"I'm leaning toward a hummingbird on my left ankle to go with the butterfly on my right calf. What do you think?"

"I do kickass hummingbirds."

As she positioned herself in what could best be described as a dentist's chair, Dave wriggled around anxiously in his own seat. Evidently, however, getting a tattoo wasn't a big deal after all, because Betsy's happy-go-lucky expression never wavered when Claude pricked her with what he called his iron. The procedure turned out to be so devoid of drama that Dave grew bored and went over to peruse Claude's walls.

Casually working his way through the gallery, he looked at a fluorescent Giza pyramid, an X with flames shooting out of it, an eyeball, and a Tasmanian devil before spotting a certain rendering that demanded he stop and examine it further. It was unaffectedly simple, childlike even, so much so that he had almost missed it in the bustle of inky flamboyance. Dave studied each line and space, and he realized it perfectly depicted his brave new view of the world.

After the final touches had been put on the hummingbird—which was, as Claude had promised, kickass—Dave said, "My turn."

"You're not serious, are you?" Betsy asked.

"Actually, I think I am." Dave took Claude over to the wall. "This one. This is the one I want."

"Killer selection," Claude said. "And easy to do."

"Wow, you really aren't joking," Betsy said. "I'm impressed."

Dave was strangely at ease as he reclined in the dental-type chair, a sensation that lasted until Claude's iron touched down in the area just above the joint on the middle of his right pinky.

"Ouch," Dave yelped. "Maybe this wasn't such a good idea."

"Try to relax, brocifer," Claude instructed. "This isn't a heart transplant. Just think calming thoughts—think of sheep jumping over a fence."

The iron moved swiftly and relatively painlessly to the same spots on Dave's ring, middle, and index fingers, but his imagination nevertheless began to run amok, and pictures of frolicking sheep morphed into the stench of his flesh burning. Now his face was ghostly white.

"Almost there," Claude reassured.

Claude made his last prick, and as the color slowly returned to Dave's face, he admired his new tattoo. It was comprised of four black letters, one on each finger.

L-O-V-E

CHAPTER 45

Despite missing The Who's performance at Woodstock—or at least the most important part—Dave had always figured there would be plenty of other opportunities to see his favorite band. Life didn't work out that way:

- Only two months after Woodstock, The Who played at the trippy Kinetic Playground in Uptown, a short walk from where Red Dragon Tattoos now stood. With the glory of the upstate New York mud still so fresh in their minds, Dave and Leyna dearly wished they could go. But the wounds from their car accident were nearly as fresh, and her leg wouldn't allow it.

- In July 1970 The Who was at the acoustically perfect Auditorium Theatre in Chicago's downtown Loop. Dave, however, was stationed in the *Herald* newsroom, where he instead listened to the incessant tapping of typewriters.

- Dave was also a no-show for The Who's November 1973 performance at the International Amphitheatre, the site of the pre-wedding Tull pilgrimage, but he wasn't particularly upset about missing this one. Elsewhere, his hormones were happily whirling. Now that he and Leyna had finally started banking some money, they could afford their first full-fledged vacation, and they were on secluded Captiva Island in Florida. Leyna's lissome body, bronzed by the sun, looked magnificent in a bikini as they lounged poolside each day. And it looked even better sans bikini in their hotel room each night.

- Dave had two shots to catch The Who in 1975. On December 4 and 5, the band held court at the Chicago Stadium, which was normally home to the NBA's Bulls and NHL's Blackhawks. But money now was too tight for such an extravagance. Dave and Leyna had recently taken out their mortgage on the prairie box, and he was worried about winding up under a bridge.

- On the road for the first time without the departed Keith Moon, The Who turned up at the International Amphitheatre in December 1979 and May 1980. Dave desperately wanted to pay his respects, but duty called: he was trying to hold his marriage together. As their seemingly futile attempts to conceive a child plodded on, Leyna needed him, or at least his penis.

- In October 1982 The Who rolled out to the northwest suburbs to play two dates at the Rosemont Horizon, not far from his old apartment between the sooty highway and the peeling water tower. This was the group's Farewell Tour, its last hurrah. Even though Dave was stuck on the desk at the *Herald* for both those shows, he wasn't despondent. The Who was scheduled to return to the Horizon one more time in December before hanging it up for good, and he had already secured two tickets and the night off from work.

- A month before that historic encore performance, Dave was laid off from the *Herald*. Shell-shocked, as well as worried about winding up under a bridge, he sold his tickets to Natalie and her husband. On the night of the concert, Dave wasn't even afforded the pleasure of stewing in his bedroom in peace. Leyna had generously offered to babysit little Corlander, who spent the whole time crying for his mother at the top of his lungs.

- What would a Farewell Tour be without an ensuing Reunion Tour? In 1989 The Who cobbled itself together for a set of dates that included three nights at Alpine Valley Music Theatre, an outdoor venue about ninety minutes from Chicago in southern Wisconsin. The comeback was hardly triumphant, with rotten reviews at virtually every stop, but that wasn't what kept Dave away from Alpine Valley. Felled by genital warts, he lacked the desire to go *anywhere*.

- What would a Reunion Tour be without another Reunion Tour? At least this one, commencing in July 1996, wasn't roundly mocked, as Pete Townshend and company did an acceptable job of pretending to care. In November of that year, the tour wound to Chicago's newly built United Center, but Dave was otherwise committed. The responsibilities of moving back up in the world had tethered him to Weiss Drugstore, which was in the midst of a complete renovation.

- The Reunion Tour concept was starting to take on some permanence, though this altered nothing where Dave was concerned. When The Who took the stage at the open-air New World Music Theatre in south-suburban Tinley Park in June 2000, Dave was at Glenbrook Hospital with his mom, who had undergone a hip replacement that afternoon. It was, he figured, just his luck.

But maybe his luck was changing. The Who, amped up from The Concert for New York City, had planned a new tour that would bring it back to the New World Music Theatre on August 24, 2002. That happened to be a Saturday, meaning Wieland would be minding Weiss Drugstore with military precision. It also happened to be two days after Matt would return from his study trip to Europe, meaning father and son could reunite—bond, as it were—by seeing The Who together. And here was the absolute kicker: August 24 happened to be Betsy's birthday. Was there a better way to celebrate? Dave thought not. The stars were finally aligned.

He became convinced of this when, minutes after tickets for the concert went on sale, he logged on to Ticketmaster.com from his office at Weiss Drugstore. Entering "3" in the "Quantity" box and "Best Available" in the "Price & Section" box, he was simply hoping anything would appear on the screen in this virtual crapshoot. *Anything* wound up being three tickets in the very center of the fifth row. Even though the price tag was upwards of $500, Dave bought them without hesitation. He didn't care—this was bigger than money.

He called Betsy, who said, "Sure, I'll go. It's not the first thing I would have thought to do on my birthday, but you know me. I'm game for anything, especially retro stuff."

He then called Matt, who had just awoken for the day and responded with, as far as Dave could ascertain, a yawn.

The following morning Dave stopped by his parents' house, something that had become a semi-regular routine. His dad's memory was starting to go haywire, and his mom had been relegated to a walker. He knew the time was approaching when he'd have to convince them to leave their home of fifty years and move into an assisted-living facility, but he didn't have the heart to do it quite yet.

There was more to this particular visit, however, than making sure his parents were okay. Inspired by the upcoming Who concert, Dave wanted to find the lava lamp he had bought to shine on the Special during the period after Woodstock when he and Leyna had been staying at his parents' house. He thought it would be a nice addition to Betsy's apartment, and he was pretty sure it was in the crawlspace.

Dave let himself in and walked into the living room. "Anyone home?" he hollered.

His dad meandered in from the den, where he had been watching CNN. His comb-over was more askew than usual, but given his age, it was remarkable he had any hair at all. "Good to see you, son. What brings you by?"

"I just wanted to rummage through the crawlspace for some of my old things."

"Have at it."

"Thanks."

"That reminds me, a letter came here for you a little while back. I don't remember exactly where I put it, but it'll turn up. I can't believe I'm still getting your mail."

The letter to which William was referring was the one Jimmy had penned after being diagnosed with cancer, and it had actually arrived a year earlier by way of a mail recovery center in St. Paul, Minnesota. Additionally, there was no chance that it would ever turn up. William had inadvertently placed it in the recycling bin with some junk mail, so it had been transformed into a new sheet of paper.

"Oh well," Dave said. "I'm sure it was nothing important."

Dave's mom appeared, hunched over her walker. As had been her habit the past few months, she started right in on Dave's tattoo: "I still don't know what you were thinking. It's fine for a sailor, maybe, but my Dave? It's so out of character."

The tattoo was also a source of bewilderment for Leyna, though she did nearly giggle upon seeing it for the first time. Among both his son and his teenage employees, it brought him some street cred. And as for Dave himself, he had no regrets.

"Give it a little more time, Mom," he reassured. "You'll get used to it. Everyone has tattoos these days. Even Dad will have one soon."

The crawlspace smelled, Dave guessed, as a freshly dug grave would, but the lava lamp was indeed there, in a box that also contained baseball cards and his journals from high school and college. After kissing his parents goodbye, he called Betsy at Terry Animal Hospital from his car.

"Feel like meeting up for lunch at Convito Italiano?" he asked. "It's a perfect spring day, and they have that nice patio area."

"I'm game. Noonish?"

"I'll see you then."

Convito Italiano was situated in Plaza Del Lago, an upscale shopping center next to Lake Michigan in Wilmette. Dave liked to think he was on vacation whenever he sat on the restaurant's patio. A row of high-rise condominium buildings blocked his view of the lake, but this left more to the imagination. He could still feel the crisp breeze from the water, and it swept his mind off to some exotic tropical locale that was far, far away from the landlocked Midwest.

True to form, Dave arrived first, toting the lava lamp with him to the patio so that he could show it to Betsy. She pulled up minutes later in her 1992 Ford Escort, which was reminiscent of Dave's former Valiant in that it was well beyond its last leg. The first words out of her mouth were, "Awesome. Where'd you find that lava lamp?"

"I knew you'd like it," Dave responded with a satisfied smile. "I dug it up when I was at my parents' house this morning. I was thinking we could shine it on the Special. It's a neat effect."

"Psychedelic, like a Pink Floyd concert?"

"Something like that."

They ordered lunch—spaghetti with tomato basil sauce for Betsy, fried calamari for Dave—and engaged in their usual banter: a little of this and a little of that.

"Not to take away our appetites or anything," Betsy said, "but aren't those condos across the street like death row?"

"What do you mean? They're handsome buildings."

"I don't think I've ever seen anyone under the age of, like, seventy-five hobbling out of them."

"I never thought about it that way, but I guess you're right. They do seem to be havens for retirees, and wealthy ones at that."

"I wonder why that is," she said.

As Dave further pondered Betsy's observation, he took note of an aged couple walking past an empty storefront next to Convito. And just like that, with the crisp lake breeze whistling through his hair, he had another idea.

"I'm not sure why that is," he said, "but you might be onto something."

"Onto what?"

"Think about it. What do old people need more than anything?"

"Hope for an afterlife?"

"Prescriptions."

"That, too, I guess."

"And what is it that I do for a living?"

"Run a soda fountain?" she said, her smile widening fully.

"See that empty storefront over there?"

She nodded.

"Well, you just might be looking at the future site of Weiss Drugstore at Plaza Del Lago. I don't know—I'll work out the name later. At any rate, it would be a pharmacy right at their doorsteps, and one that would deliver, too, for much-needed convenience. The potential is there."

Betsy struck a contemplative pose, saying, "You might be right. And I'm not just saying that."

Could there be any doubt? The stars were aligned.

CHAPTER 46

It was June 27, 2002, one day before The Who's tour was scheduled to begin in Las Vegas, and Pete Townshend wanted to ensure he'd be at his best. Thus, he was sleeping in, with a "Do Not Disturb" sign dangling from his suite's door handle at the Hard Rock Hotel & Casino.

Clive didn't even notice the warning when he banged on Pete's door with his balled-up hand. Though Clive's fist was large and the noise was prodigious, it took at least a dozen knocks before Pete answered.

Squinting groggily, Pete demanded, "What do you want?" He removed the sign from the handle and waved it in Clive's face. "See this? It says DO…NOT…DISTURB. In other words, I'm trying to bloody sleep."

"It's John," Clive said. "He's dead."

"He's…what?"

When The Who had arrived in Vegas for its latest run through North America, John had figured it would be just like the olden days. Only these weren't the olden days. It wasn't 1969, or even 1979; it was 2002. John wasn't twenty-four, or even thirty-four; he was fifty-seven. His hard-driven heart was fifty-seven. And it couldn't withstand the cocaine and the stripper named Alycen he had brought up to his suite at the Hard Rock. It could take no more.

Upon absorbing the news, Pete wondered if his could either. He waved Clive away without saying a word and fell onto the bed, his eyes burning with tears yet again. After spending what felt like hours with his face buried in a pillow, he rang up Roger, who was in the same position on his own bed.

"The fucking bugger," Pete said.

"What the Christ was he thinking?" Roger asked.

"That he was immortal, a rock and roll god…or some such shit. The fucking bugger."

"He's really gone, isn't he?"

"I can't believe he went and did it."

"I'm in complete shock," Roger said. "What are we going to do?"

"That's what we need to figure out."

The two convened in Pete's suite. Pete was still in his underwear and Roger was dressed in sweats, and they did what any good Englishmen would in a time of crisis: they poured themselves cups of tea. Before sipping any, however, they turned off their cells and took the landlines in the suite off the hook.

"Much better," Pete said. "I can't focus with the phones ringing nonstop."

Cutting to the chase, Roger said, "Pete, this is totally up to you. At this point, I couldn't give a flying leap if we just fold up the tent and call it a day."

"And do what?"

"Grow old, I guess."

"I was thinking the same thing, but then it hit me: we already are old."

"Well, we'd have to be off our trolley to keep doing this."

"Remember when Keith died?" Pete asked.

"Every day."

"I wanted to end it all right there, and maybe we should have. It would have saved a lot of heartache. But you wouldn't let us. You said, 'This is what we do. What else is there?' I thought you were a callous git at the time, but now I realize you were right. What else is there? For better or bloody worse, this is what we do. We're the fucking 'Oo, or at least what's left of it."

They agreed that they wouldn't cancel the tour but merely put it on hold until they could find a new bassist. The first person Pete thought of was a well-traveled Welshman named Pino Palladino, with whom he had worked on some solo projects. Pino immediately accepted the gig, though he second-guessed his decision after Pete said, "Roger and I have talked it through, and we don't see the sense in wasting any precious time. We'll play on July 1 at the Hollywood Bowl, just as we had originally planned, so you have three days to learn the material."

And after a couple scattershot rehearsals, the stage lights did indeed go up at the Hollywood Bowl. Pete and Roger, dressed in black, came out first, followed by the stand-ins, Pino and Zak Starkey. The cheers were louder than usual, and Pete strode to the mike and said, "For fans that have followed us for many years, this is going to be very difficult. We understand. We're not pretending that nothing's happened."

That would have been impossible anyway. During each song, from "I Can't Explain" to "See Me, Feel Me," Pete looked over to where John would have been standing, and he wanted to disappear. But there was nowhere to go—nowhere to hide—so he kept on playing. The next concert, on July 3 at the Shoreline Amphitheatre in Mountain View, California, brought more of the same, but amid the pain, a sense of acceptance solidified. Taking his cue from Pete, Roger announced to the crowd, "Rock and roll was never meant to be easy. Nor was life. You just get on with it."

There was no turning back. The fucking 'Oo got on with it.

CHAPTER 47

Since Dave had only just signed the lease, the space was completely empty. Nevertheless, he could see the finished product in his mind's eye as he paced from wall to wall. Weiss Pharmacy-Plaza Del Lago wouldn't have a soda fountain, polished mahogany woodwork, or grand glass cases—such overhead seemed needless. This store would be more utilitarian, geared toward a single purpose: supplying the honey hole of senior citizens across the street with pharmaceuticals and handy old-age accessories like laundry trolleys, magnifiers, and portable oxygen machines.

Dave stopped pacing briefly to digest the irony of it all. He had set out to be nothing more than a wordsmith, and now he was knee-deep in his second venture as a business owner. None of it made much sense to him, but Weiss Pharmacy-Plaza Del Lago was, he had to admit, a good idea. Smiling wryly, he resumed his pacing, only this time his mind refused to follow. Instead it stubbornly returned to a different idea, one that had been percolating since late June, one that both saddened and enlivened him. He had avoided committing to it for as long as he could, but inertia was no longer an option. If he didn't act soon, the moment would pass.

Unfortunately, the first order of business would involve calling Holt, a difficult undertaking in itself. Having recently won a national Associated Press award for his column writing for the *Tribune*, he would undoubtedly be more full of himself than ever. But Dave also knew the SOB would deliver. Swallowing hard, he came to a standstill again and dialed Holt's number on his cellphone.

"Dave Weiss, how the hell are you?" Holt asked in a voice that suggested he'd only marginally care about the answer.

"Pretty good, Holt. And you?"

"Sensational. Did you hear about the AP award I won? It created quite the buzz over here."

"I did hear something about that."

"Yep, another notch on the belt, but you're only as good as your last column, right? And today I'm really up against the proverbial wall of shit. I'm trying to finish a column on the Cubs, and it's not flowing at all. They'd be much more interesting to write about if they ever won something for a change. *That* would be a story. How am I supposed to keep coming up with a new spin on the fact that they eternally blow?"

"I'm sure you'll find a way."

"True."

"Just don't throw any telephones across the newsroom in the process."

Chuckling, Holt said, "Speaking of which, why the call out of the blue?"

"I, ah, need a favor. The Who's playing here tomorrow night, and I read in your paper that they're getting into town today. I figured there might be someone in your newsroom who knows where they're staying."

"Those guys are still around? Didn't their bassist seize up or something?"

"He did, but the rest of the band is still alive."

"And what, you want to go to their hotel and throw rose petals at them like a sixteen-year-old schoolgirl?"

"Something like that."

"You're a strange bird, Dave, but I'll ask around and get back to you in a few minutes. At least it will distract me from this column my lunchmeat editor is making me write."

While waiting on Holt, Dave paced some more, but he didn't travel far before his cell rang.

"Holt?" Dave asked.

"Yeah."

"That was quick. Any luck?"

"Of course. I talked to one of our entertainment editors. The guy's kind of a doucher, but he's plugged in. He said your boys are staying at the Hilton on Balbo and Michigan. He even knows their room numbers since one of his writers is going over there tonight to interview them. The singer…what's his name?"

"Roger Daltrey."

"He's in 437."

"And the guitarist, Pete Townshend?" Dave asked.

"443."

In Dave's excitement, the following words slipped from his mouth: "You're the best, Holt."

"What can I say?"

"Anyway, many thanks. And good luck with your column. Remember, for Cubs fans it's all a matter of faith that their beloved team will win next year, even if next year always seems to be another four or five years away."

"Hey, that's not a bad line. Mind if I use it?"

"It's all yours."

His plan in motion, Dave locked up the future site of Weiss Pharmacy-Plaza Del Lago and drove to Betsy's. She was at Northwestern for a class, so when he arrived, her apartment was as still as a museum after closing time. Not even Oscar, in the midst of an afternoon nap that was a prelude to his evening nap, stirred. It was better this way—Dave could go about his work without any distractions. Nevertheless, the job took longer than he had anticipated, partially because he was delayed by second thoughts and partially because he knocked over a vase that shattered into dozens of pieces on the floor and woke Oscar with a hiss. After calming Oscar by feeding him a can of Friskies and sweeping up the broken glass, he headed downtown.

Dave had decided to take Lake Shore Drive due to its scenic proximity to the waterfront, but he turned onto the thoroughfare as the rush-hour snarl was forming. Lurching toward his destination, he thought, *Just my luck. All I want to do is get this over with, and I'm at a virtual standstill.* Someone directly behind Dave in a Corvette honked his horn, as if that would magically accelerate the flow of traffic. Dave was tempted to give him the finger, but (a) that wasn't his style and (b) his cellphone rang.

It was Leyna, and she had *that* tone, though with good reason in this instance.

"Is something up with Matt?" Dave asked worriedly. "He seemed great when we picked him up at the airport yesterday."

"Matthew's fine. Just a little jetlagged, that's all."

"Okay, then…"

"My mother died."

"Leyna, I'm so sorry."

"Don't be. I haven't talked to her in thirty-five years."

"How'd you find out?"

"I ran into someone from my college days who's from Racine, too. He gave me the news. Actually, he thought I already knew. She died a year ago. A heart attack, apparently."

"Are you alright?"

"I guess I'd rather not even have found out. I left that part of my life behind long ago, and I wanted to keep it that way."

"What did Scott say?"

"I haven't told him yet. He's been tied up in meetings all day."

"Oh…I see."

"I'll tell him when he gets home."

"You sure you're alright?"

"I'm fine, really," she said, but the cracks in her voice belied that sentiment.

"Well, I'll see you tomorrow. In the meantime, let me know if there's anything I can do."

Dave recognized that those were only words—there was, in reality, nothing he could do—but he was glad he had spoken them just the same. As recently as a year ago, any type of goodwill gesture toward Leyna would have hardly seemed possible.

"Thanks, Dave," she said. "Take care."

No sooner did the call end than the jackass in the Corvette began honking again. Turning onto Michigan Avenue, Dave shed the Corvette but not the congestion. By then, however, his journey was basically complete, and the valet at the Hilton welcomed him with a polite smile and a "Hello, sir."

Inside, the lobby was stiffly arrayed with people from a podiatry convention. As Dave passed through, some of the conventioneers observed him curiously, their eyes fixed on the guitar he was carrying. Was he a musician? Was he part of some other convention, one centered on collectibles? Dave was neither, of course. If forced to come up with a label, he would have called himself a concerned citizen.

When Dave had first read about Entwistle's death in late June, he had reacted with shock and then a bleak realization that the stars weren't aligned after all and, it seemed, never would be. The next day he had gone to The Who's official website expecting to read about the band's decision to call it quits, but he had encountered a distinctly different vibe: a note from Pete stating that he felt a duty to keep going, even if there might not be any joy in doing so. Dave's idea had materialized right then and there.

He stepped into the Hilton elevator, and his blood pressure rose with it. Thinking back to an article he had once read about a Led Zeppelin tour in which the band members had ridden motorcycles up and down hotel corridors, Dave envisioned the elevator doors opening to mayhem. But save for a few stiff souls—podiatrists, no doubt—the hallway was eerily silent, almost monastic. Under the circumstances, this seemed appropriate.

Dave treaded along the red commercial carpeting past rooms 435, 436, 437, 438, 439, 440, 441, and 442. He stopped at 443, and there was no turning back. The Special had proved to be unexplainably durable, surviving Woodstock and a car crash and Doomsday and lord knew what else. But it was, Dave kept telling himself, merely a block of mahogany. And even if it was something more than wood—something as abstract as an ideal—it didn't belong to him. The guitar was rightfully Pete Townshend's, and he needed it now more than ever. He certainly needed it more than Dave did.

So Dave let the Special go, this time, unlike the last, with a clear head. He gently leaned it against the door, tucking a note between the strings that read, "Make it sing."

CHAPTER 48

Clive was the first to see the Special, when he walked a few doors down the hallway to room 443 to solidify the evening's dinner plans, but he didn't recognize it. Considering all the phone calls he had fielded about it over the previous three decades, this lapse was somewhat surprising. Then again, the guitar barely resembled its old self. Clive figured it was another undesired gift from a whacked-out groupie. Ratty as the thing was, he even considered pitching it into a garbage can at the far end of the hallway. But the effort seemed too great, especially since he was famished and wanted to get dinner rolling ASAP, so he simply knocked on the door.

The fifty-seven-year-old man who answered—Pete Townshend—appeared weary, with a slight stoop. This changed, however, before Clive could say as much as "Hi, mate." Pete's frame straightened in one fluid motion, and he exclaimed, "Holy mother of fuck!"

Clive assumed he had done something particularly offensive, though he hadn't a clue what. In such instances, he usually erred on the side of caution and kept his trap shut.

"Where did it come from?" Pete demanded.

"What?"

"The guitar, you nitwit."

Oh, he's steamed about the guitar. "Sorry, mate," Clive said. "It was leaning against the door. I should have just pitched it before—"

"Let me see."

As Clive handed over the Special, the note slipped from the strings and fluttered to the ground, and Pete snatched it out of midair with the reflexes of a twenty-year-old. His face became feverishly red when he read the contents, which filled Clive with more trepidation.

"Well, I'll be the dog's bollocks," Pete said. "Do you have any idea what this is?"

"Didn't we agree it's a guitar?"

"It's not *a* fucking guitar. It's *the* fucking guitar."

"Your guitar from Woodstock? How can you tell?"

"I don't bloody know. I just can."

"Blimey."

Pete drew the Special close to his body.

"It's a shame it's so beat up," Clive said, "but after all this time, I guess—"

"In the early days, before we could afford the likes of you and the rest of the circus, we had to scrape by. We traveled from gig to gig in a piss-poor van. We even slept in it, froze our willies off some nights."

Clive nodded nonchalantly, like this was merely another of Pete's many stories. But in truth, he was alarmed by the maniacal flare in Pete's eyes. He had seen it before, back around the *Lifehouse* period.

"When I'd smash up a guitar, I didn't always have one waiting in the wings for the next gig," Pete continued. "If there was anything left of the thing, I'd have to figure out a way to put it back to together. I became quite good at it, repaired a lot of lost causes. Sometimes I was able to get two or three gigs out of them. But this one really looks like it's been through the wringer."

"The—"

"Look at it," Pete said, holding the guitar up for Clive. "See the burns? The water marks? The scratches on the pick guard? The gouges all over the bloody thing?"

"Gouges everywhere," Clive agreed.

"Christ, the neck is even a bit warped."

"I can see that," Clive said, even though he couldn't.

"And whoever restrung it did a horseshit job."

Clive was starting to become less concerned with the fire in Pete's eyes than the growling in his own stomach. He wished the old windbag would get to the point. "After a spot of dinner, it won't seem so—"

"Maybe this one really is a lost cause," Pete said, "but you know what? I'd like to have a go at fixing it. I think I can do it."

Pete instructed Clive to pull out his notebook—and not, the trusted heavy sensed with sagging spirits, so that he could write down a dinner order.

"Ready?" Pete said. "I need a soldering kit, a half-dozen clamps, a set of hex wrenches, a set of screwdrivers, a file, Gorilla Glue, a Gibson TPBR bridge, two P-90 single-coil pickups…"

"P-80?" Clive asked.

"No, P-90. Christ."

"Got it, mate. P-90."

"Six Schaller machine heads, a three-way Switchcraft toggle switch, and four volume/tone controls."

"Anything else?" Clive inquired, his pencil still dutifully pressed against the notebook.

"I'm sure there is, but it's been years since I've done this, and I really won't know until I get into it. I'll pilfer whatever else I need from the guitars I have lying around here. It'll be close enough, like an organ transplant. Oh, and get some more Ernie Ball .052 nickel strings. We can never have too many strings."

Before placing his notebook in his back pocket, Clive asked, "And what should I bring back for dinner?"

"Dinner? Piss on dinner. We have too much work to do."

After Clive went off into the Chicago gloaming, Pete sat on his bed cradling the Special. He had questions, many questions. *Where has it been? Why is it so banged up? Who brought it here? What took so long? Why now? Why not after those desperate ads I placed in* Rolling Stone? *Why at all? What's the bloody method to this madness?* It irked Pete that he'd probably never know the answers, but in the end all that really mattered was the issue at hand: making the guitar playable. He had spent years wondering how it would sound.

The moment, however, still wasn't quite within reach. Two hours passed, and Clive hadn't yet returned. *Maybe the poor bastard finally upped and quit this time. I couldn't blame him, and wouldn't it figure if he did it now?* But Clive came back—just like he always did—and his hands were full.

"Bloody hell," Clive groused. "Some of this was hard to find, and I got lost and wound up in a dodgy neighborhood."

"But you have it all?"

"I think so."

Pete neatly spread everything out on the floor and began the reconstructive surgery. Clive, meanwhile, ordered room service for himself: a roasted chicken, a steakhouse burger, whipped potatoes, and a bottle of Christian Brothers brandy. He then watched as Pete directed the soldering iron into the innards of the guitar's body.

"Is smoke supposed to be billowing out of it?" Clive asked.

"Yes, it's fine. I know what I'm doing."

"Of course."

Squinting his aging eyes, Pete said, "The wiring is completely shot."

"I'm not surprised," Clive opined.

"Mind fetching the Epiphone from the closet? I need to do some pilfering."

Clive gave him the guitar, which Pete quickly tore apart for his transplant pieces.

"Anything else right now?" Clive asked.

"No, take a load off."

As Clive sank into a chair for his well-deserved rest, the phone rang, and he trudged across the suite to answer it.

"Roger's on the blower," he said.

"What does he want?" Pete asked.

"He has some questions about the set list. He wants to pull 'Love Reign O'er Me,' says he's been having trouble with that one."

"Tell him I'll ring him back later."

Clive sat down again, but before he could get comfortable, there was a knocking at the door. He moved more quickly this time, thinking it was room service. It was, instead, the reporter from the *Tribune*, and Clive's stomach growled mournfully.

"The bloke from the newspaper is here to do his interview," Clive yelled into the suite.

"Tell him to bugger off," Pete yelled back. "This is delicate business. I need to concentrate."

Around the time Clive's dinner finally arrived, Pete began work on the Special's neck; a few hours later, the new machine heads were in place on the headstock and the mangled frets on the fingerboard were as restored as possible.

"Getting there," Pete said, his eyes more aflame than ever. "Getting there."

Clive was now quite plastered, having washed down the roasted chicken, the steakburger, and the whipped potatoes with most of the brandy. "Sure you don't want a nip?" he asked.

"No, let me be," Pete answered, clutching a screwdriver. "This bridge is giving me fucking fits, and I still have more to do on the wiring."

Sometime after 2 a.m., Pete stood up. His legs ached from kneeling on the floor for so long, but his work was done. Or so he hoped.

"What do you think?" he asked.

Nearly incoherent though he was from the brandy, Clive still knew where his bread was buttered. "Looks mint, mate."

"As usual, you're completely full of shit. It looks like a baboon's arse, but that's not important. The question is, will it work?"

Clive brought over a Vox amp from the closet, and Pete plugged in. It was the first time the Special had been plugged in anywhere since the early hours of August 17, 1969. Taking a deep, contemplative breath, Pete said, "Oh, what the fuck?" He struck an E chord, and his face exploded into happiness as a thick sound reverberated through the suite and beyond.

"Did you hear that?" Pete said. "Brilliant. Different from what I remember—probably because of all the retooling I've done—but fucking brilliant."

"Uh-huh," Clive answered.

"Okay, listen to this."

Pete played a single note, a D on the third fret, prolonging it by wiggling his hips and bending the string as far up the fingerboard as the muscles in his hand would allow.

"Fantastic sustain," Pete said when the note had finished ringing. "My hours of labor tonight paid off, don't you think, old friend?"

Clive nodded approvingly.

"Listen again," Pete said.

He unfurled another D, and with the same result: it endured resoundingly.

"Brilliant," Pete repeated. "I'll be fucked if I know what perfect beauty is—I have no idea what the simple secret of a note is supposed to sound like—but this has to be bloody close."

CHAPTER 49

Jimmy Fitzgerald, cancer-free for five years, looked upon the ocean from Steamer Lane's rocky point. He had long since pushed his desperate, unanswered letter to Dave out of his mind, as well as almost everything else from that period. One of the few tangible reminders was the SPF 100 sunscreen that was slathered on his face like a coat of white paint.

Holding his surfboard, he turned to Raffy, who gave him the sign: "Go ahead, Corn Boy. I'm right behind you. *Vamos*."

Jimmy jumped into the water, yelling up to Raffy on the rocks, "Fuck yeah. Steamer Lane."

Jimmy had grown soft in the middle, but when a rhino came charging, he wrestled it as nimbly as ever and slid down into its glassy pocket with his usual ease. Riding toward the saw-toothed shoreline, he saw that this was a particularly special morning: lustrous colors were bursting from the whitecaps in the distance. The conditions were perfect for pondering the infinite—and that was exactly what he did.

Jumbo Bauer mounted the young woman like she was a throne. Magic Wand Entertainment was filming the first installment of its epic trilogy *Lord of the Cock Rings*, and this scene called for him to screw a buxom maiden in a mysterious forest.

Jumbo was fifty-three, but being a freak of nature, he was as chiseled and virile as a twenty-five-year-old. He reveled in the fact that, unlike most of the other aging stars in his profession, he didn't have to rely on gimmicky performance-enhancing drugs such as Viagra. Not that Jumbo's longevity could be attributed strictly to genetics. Mama looked after her thoroughbred with great care, keeping him on a lean, high-protein diet and making sure that he exercised religiously.

The director yelled, "Action," and Jumbo shut down his thoughts, a process that required little effort. Operating in a purely primal state, he nailed the buxom maiden (and, in turn, the scene) in just one take. As always, he had carried himself like a consummate pro.

The anthropologist should have been packing, but he was reading. Specifically, *The Third Chimpanzee: The Evolution and Future of the Human Animal*. It was among his favorites.

His wife didn't share his enthusiasm when she checked in on him in the study.

"At the risk of being a nag," Sue said, "the movers will be here bright and early tomorrow morning, and it doesn't look like you're making much progress. Would you like some help?"

"No, but thank you for offering again," he politely responded.

While the anthropologist had been guiding his final student trip to Europe, Sue had packed up their house in preparation for their transition to the North Woods. He had insisted, however, that the study be left to him.

"Three days will be more than enough time," he had told her. "The Europe trip will be behind me, so I'll have no distractions."

The anthropologist carefully placed *The Third Chimpanzee* into the moving box, thanks to Sue's prodding, but he became stuck again at *Cows, Pigs, Wars, and Witches: The Riddles of Culture*. And then at *The Forest People*. And then at *The Teachings of Don Juan: A Yaqui Way of Knowledge*.

"Interesting," he said to himself. "So very interesting."

The anthropologist and his wife would make it up to the North Woods. Eventually.

James and Jenny Smith now lived in a gated community with a guardhouse out front. It only made sense. And their home, an English Tudor seven miles north of Winnetka in Highland Park, was nearly as aesthetically pleasing as the Frank Lloyd Wright knockoff.

They had never recovered their valuables, nor had there been any sign of the robbers who had taken them. But time had a funny way of marching on. The old artifacts had been replaced with new artifacts, and as James and Jenny rode to O'Hare Airport on this late-August day to catch a flight to Hawaii, they could scarcely believe they were about to celebrate their twentieth wedding anniversary.

Doomsday Garrett was resting not so peacefully under a marker in Bloomington, Illinois, that said only this: "Tim Garrett, 1958–1997."

The end had come quickly that night at Continental Diamond Cutters. Though he had astutely detected the pair of legs dangling from the ceiling, he had failed to notice the shadowy figure crouched in the corner of the retail space. Upon hearing the sound of a trigger being pulled, Doomsday had cursed his carelessness, cursed the two-bit thief, and cursed the universe. And then, with a .45-caliber bullet tearing through his brain, there had been only darkness.

It was a stunningly permanent setback for someone whose sole objective had been to be the ninety-year-old man at the end of the bar defiantly drawing another breath.

Dave Weiss opened his Camry's sunroof so that he could welcome in the elements. The weather, after all, was gorgeous, with temperatures in the mid-seventies and nary a cloud in the sky.

"Much better, eh?" he said to Betsy.

"Definitely," she concurred.

Reaching over to squeeze her thigh, he said, "I'd expect nothing less than a beautiful day on your birthday."

"Or on the day you finally get to see The Who, right?"

"There's also that."

"I still can't believe you tried to give that cool guitar to Pete Townshend, even if it was his first," Betsy said. "I'd be shocked if he got it. I bet a hotel employee stole it."

"You're probably right, but it was worth a shot."

"Just don't go taking any more stuff off my walls," she said, now squeezing his thigh.

"It's a deal."

Dave steered his Camry into the Victorian's driveway. He had been to this house so often over the years he could close his eyes, tap the brake, and come to a stop at the exact same place every time. He took no pride in this trick.

"I'll be back in a minute, provided Matt's ready, which is always an iffy proposition," he said.

Dave knocked on the thick oak door, and Leyna answered with a pleasant smile. She had obviously regrouped since hearing the news about her mother. "Matthew's still getting ready," she said.

"There's a shocker."

"He slept in."

"Slept in? It's four o'clock."

"He's still tired from his trip to Europe."

"Did he actually do any studying there, or did he stay up all night every night drinking vino with the natives?"

"A little of both, I'd imagine. Anyway, would you like a cup of coffee while you're waiting?"

"Yes, thanks. The caffeine will do me good. I'm not used to staying up late at concerts anymore."

"You were never really used to it, Dave, but I'm sure you'll be fine."

They sat at the kitchen island, and Leyna poured the coffee into china cups.

"Where's Scott?" Dave asked.

She let out a sigh—the kind that sometimes complemented *that* tone—and said, "He left for Denver this morning."

"Good lord, he must own half the city by now with the amount of time he spends there."

"It gets a little quiet around here. Matthew has his own life now, and, well, you know. Did I tell you I'm taking a pottery class?"

"No, you didn't. That'll keep you busy."

Pointing to a bowl on the island, she said, "My latest creation."

"Nice."

Leyna stood up and walked to the kitchen window with a limp so slight Dave wouldn't have noticed it if he hadn't known better. She cast her eyes on the woman in the Camry; it was the first good look at Betsy she had ever gotten. "Matthew's right—she *is* young. A midlife crisis, Dave?"

"Nah, I already went through that. I've progressed to the lecherous-old-coot stage."

Leyna didn't even try to stifle her giggle.

"You know," Dave said, "there's something I've been meaning to thank you for."

"Me? I can't imagine what."

"Remember how I didn't want to go work with my dad at Weiss Drugstore, but you made me do it?"

"Yep. As I recall, you were none too pleased."

"Well, thank you. Thanks for giving me the push. I needed it."

"That's really nice, Dave. I'm just happy it worked out." She poured him more coffee and said, "So you must be excited about the concert tonight."

"I really am. Who would have thought I'd be bringing my son to see them? Who would have thought they'd still be around after all these years?"

"Not me. It seems like ages ago that we saw them at Woodstock."

"Speaking of which, remember Pete Townshend's guitar?"

"Of course. How could I forget?"

"You'll never believe it, but I found it last summer at the Kane County Flea Market of all places. I bought it for ten bucks."

"Wow, you're kidding!"

"Nope."

"What are the odds?"

"A gazillion to one?"

Giggling again, she said, "I'd love to see it sometime."

"Too late now. I dropped it off at Townshend's hotel yesterday. Who knows if he ever got it, but it seemed like the right thing to do."

Leyna's face was aglow with this talk of the Special. "Remember that guy who sold it to you? Jocko? Dumbo? What was his name again?"

"Jumbo, I, ah, think," Dave said awkwardly.

"That's right. What a character. I wonder whatever happened to him."

"Who knows?"

"Probably pumping gas somewhere, I'd imagine."

They continued to reminisce about Woodstock, and Matt was surprised to hear laughter coming from the kitchen. Curious as he might have been, he wasn't about to let it show. Upon joining his parents at the kitchen island, he dryly said, "Let me guess, you two are reliving the groovy days of the sixties."

"Kind of, yeah," Leyna said.

"What a thrill," he answered with a faux yawn.

"What's with that Rage Against the Machine T-shirt?" Dave asked. "Where's the Who shirt I bought you for the concert?"

"It's too small. This one fits better."

"Nuts, I was sure I had gotten the right size," Dave said. "Anyway, we better hit the road."

"Just don't keep Matthew out until all hours of the night," Leyna said, her voice tightening, registering a trace of *that* tone as she returned to the here and now. "He's still jetlagged, and I don't want him getting sick. He starts classes in a few days."

"Fear not—I'll see to it that he's able to get his usual fourteen hours of sleep."

Matt did his best to glower before father and son hurried out to the Camry. When they got in, Betsy rolled her eyes.

"Sorry about that," Dave said to her. "You'd think my son had been primping for the prom."

"Hilarious," Matt said flatly.

"Strap in, everyone," Dave said. "Tinley Park is every bit of an hour away, maybe closer to an hour and a half depending on traffic."

Betsy killed some time by flipping around the radio stations, Matt by lighting a cigarette.

"Jesus," Dave said as smoke filled the car. "Can you roll down your window or something?"

Turning toward the backseat, Betsy said to Matt, "I like your shirt. Isn't Tom Morello great?"

"My favorite guitarist," he answered. "Too bad we're not seeing Rage tonight."

"Buck up there, Matt," she said. "This will be a lot of fun in a retro kind of way."

"Only if you sneak me some beer."

Betsy hushed her voice for dramatic effect, saying, "I'll see what I can do when your dad's not looking."

As Dave listened, it occurred to him that Betsy was more of a big sister to Matt than a mother figure. He wondered how he had reached this strange juncture in his life, this strange juncture that had followed all the other strange junctures:

- What if Betsy's water bottle hadn't rolled straight to his feet during the Fourth of July parade?
- What if Scott's Mercedes hadn't wound up idling next to his Volvo on Green Bay Road? What if he had never found out about Leyna's affair?
- What if he hadn't drawn the short straw during the recession of 1982 and had kept working at the *Herald*?
- What if his sperm hadn't finally, miraculously coalesced with Leyna's egg after so many misfires? What if there had been no Matt?
- What if that banker hadn't blown through the STOP sign near Angola? What if, as planned, they had made it to Chicago and Leyna had continued on to Madison? Would he have even seen her again?
- What if she had never risen to the surface of Filippini Pond?

Betsy and Matt kept talking—now about their favorite *Simpsons* episodes—and Dave began to wonder about the strange junctures still to come:

- What if Leyna was right? What if he really was in a midlife crisis?
- What if this thing with Betsy was a half-baked attempt to travel back to his twenties and relive his life?
- What if their relationship was fleeting?

Dave didn't know the answers to the last three questions—or any of the others, for that matter—but he did know this: if he was engaged in some kind of a do-over, if he was indeed retracing the dots, he wouldn't worry so much this time around. There was, he concluded, no point. *It is what it is.*

"Look," Betsy said excitedly. "It's right over there."

Rising above the surrounding subdivisions, the New World Music Theatre was a faceless brown monument to suburban sprawl. The roof of the open-air pavilion was propped up by a series of steel poles that, with their swirling seams, resembled giant toilet paper rolls, and from the top of the steeply pitched lawn section, concertgoers could look out upon the strip malls.

Dave parked the Camry in a large lot, a gravel swath of sameness, and mumbled, "It ain't Bethel, New York, that's for sure."

"What'd you say?" Betsy asked.

"Nothing. Just trying to get the lay of the land."

Up close the New World Music Theatre looked more like a Russian gulag than a faceless brown monument to suburban sprawl, but Dave wasn't concerned either way. Once the sun went down and the stage lights went up, the place would be rocking. He took Betsy's hand, and Matt walked beside them to the entrance.

"I'm the youngest one here by thirty years," Matt observed.

Her smile switching into its mischievous mode, Betsy added, "And not including you, I'm the youngest by about twenty-five years."

"Looks like you're both out of luck then," Dave said. "Me? I fit right in."

"How come we never do what I want to do?" Matt asked.

"Because I suck at video games?" Dave answered drolly.

Following a reflective pause, Matt said, "Point taken. I guess this is as good as anything."

"Sometime soon I'll take you to a sweaty little concert at the Metro," Betsy said. "If your dad wants to join us, he's welcome to. Otherwise, it's just you and me."

"That's cool," Matt said.

Inside the chain-link gate, there seemed to be a concessions stand at every turn. They stopped at one, and Dave bought two beers and a soda. He didn't bat an eye at the twenty-seven-dollar cost, not on this night. Dave's mood was such that he even gave Matt a sip of his beer before Betsy could sneak him one.

"What the hell?" Dave said with a shrug. "You'll be twenty-one in less than a year anyway. Same difference."

Since they had arrived early, they milled around the concessions stands and watched the parade of gray. Betsy snuggled up to Dave, whispering into his ear, "You know, Dave, you don't fit in here as much as you think. You might be ancient, but I don't see a single gray hair on your head."

"Grecian Formula," he quipped.

"It's working."

Dave kissed Betsy on the lips, and some of the old-time passersby gawked enviously; Matt, meanwhile, puffed on another cigarette and did his best to appear bored. A half-hour before the start of the concert, the trio proceeded to its seats. This afforded Dave plenty of time to smile proudly.

"You can't get much closer than this," he said.

"No doubt," Matt responded. "We're close enough to see their wrinkles."

Matt's joke would have been funny if it hadn't turned out to be so true. When The Who walked onstage, Dave himself was taken aback. Not even liberally applied makeup could hide the deep lines on Pete Townshend's face. Dave's disappointment intensified when a roadie gave Pete a Fender Eric Clapton Signature Stratocaster, but Betsy intervened with a comforting pat on the back.

Oh well, he thought. *It is what it is.*

Besides, the first sounds from the Strat—the opening riff of "I Can't Explain," the song that had begun everything in earnest for The Who decades earlier—were pretty great.

What followed, however, was not great, or even good. Midway through "Love Reign O'er Me," Roger forgot the lyrics, and his expression took a panic-stricken turn when nothing came out of his open mouth. Roger could have just gotten on with it after the song ended, but he opted for a different route:

"We'll do that again, 'cause we've had a few technical problems up here," he informed the assembled. "And we won't let you down. We'll do the fucking thing again until we get it right."

"Maybe we should just do everything again," Pete chimed in.

"Yeah," Roger said with a laugh, "let's start again. We'll try to improve it this time."

And so with the stand-ins following Roger and Pete's lead in befuddlement, The Who started "Love Reign O'er Me" for a second time.

"Dad," Matt shouted into Dave's ear. "They're playing that song over again."

"I know."

"What kind of a clown act is this?"

"It's rock and roll, the pure kind. No lip-syncing, no Teleprompters. Just go with it, son."

"Until they keel over?"

But The Who did not keel over. On the contrary, it played the next three songs—"Eminence Front," "Behind Blue Eyes," and "You Better You Bet"—with mounting power. Betsy, ever the figure of fun, responded by swinging her hips to the music and singing along with what words she knew. Out of the corner of his eye, Dave was surprised to see that even Matt was at least tapping his foot. And by the last song, "Won't Get Fooled Again," he was nothing short of astonished to see Matt's entire body in motion and his fist raised.

Dave couldn't have asked for a better finale, but there was more: when The Who returned to the stage for an encore, Pete was holding the Special.

Betsy exclaimed, "Oh my God!"

Matt shouted, "Fuck yes!"

Dave was speechless.

And Pete? He started playing "Amazing Journey" from *Tommy*.

He struggled at first to find the right notes, and he couldn't figure out why. This enraged him, to the point where he considered smashing the Special to pieces. But after remembering he didn't do that sort of thing anymore, he played on and ultimately dialed in.

Out in the center of the fifth row, emotions were flowing freely. There was peace: the wide smile Dave observed on Matt's face. There was love:

the warmth of Betsy as Dave danced with her hand-in-hand. And there was understanding: *It is what it is.*

Up onstage, Pete now felt as if the Special was playing itself. He looked to the drum kit, and he saw not Zak Starkey but Keith Moon. He looked to the other end of the stage, and he saw not Pino Palladino but John Entwistle. He looked at Roger Daltrey, and he saw not an aging singer but a survivor just like himself. He looked beyond the lawn section, and he saw not neon light rising from the strip malls but a celestial glow. And for a moment—in that moment—anything seemed possible.

It was all the same to the thousands of people in the audience. They didn't see what Pete saw. But Dave knew—he could read it in Pete's eyes. And damn if it wasn't the best song of the night.

THE END

ACKNOWLEDGMENTS

When I was in high school, I loved The Who. My dad, skeptical and staid parental figure that he was, insisted I'd eventually outgrow the band and embrace the masters—Bach, Beethoven, and the like. Indignant, I wrote the following on a piece of paper and gave it to him: "I will never get sick of The Who!!!!" It was dated May 17, 1980. For my 50th birthday in 2014, he framed that faded scrap and presented it to me. So, thanks, Dad. Thanks for keeping my rebellious flame burning, even if it wasn't your intention.

Writing a book of any kind is a daunting undertaking. But this is particularly so with fiction. A novel is the ultimate crapshoot—one never knows if it will see the light of day. I want to give a special tip of the hat, then, to the publishers of this novel, Rick Kaempfer and David Stern, for believing in and getting behind my quirky idea.

I also want to thank the usual suspects, namely my family. My wife Cassie for getting behind *all* my quirky ideas. And my kids Cole and Olivia, who are usually graceful about putting up with their old man.

And I want to give a shout-out to my roguish comrades on the Party Line. A longtime email/text group made up of colleagues-turned-friends, the Party Line is where ideas big and small get their first airing.

Finally, for those who read this thing: thank you, thank you, thank you.